# Train to Glory

# Acclaim for *Train to Glory*

**2016:**

First-Place Winner, Arizona Authors' Association Literary Award for Children's Literature

Finalist, in Young Adult Fiction: Arizona Book of the Year

Dante Rossetti Award, Chanticleer Book Reviews & Media

**2017:**

Finalist in Young Adult Fiction, Desert Rose (Romance Writers of America) Golden Quill Award

"*Train to Glory* is a fascinating novel that has adventure, romance, action, and intrigue and a cast of interesting, well-defined characters ... is a well-written story that readers will find thought provoking and informative."
—*Michelle Stanley, Readers' Favorite Book Reviewer*

"The prose is impeccable and the powerful descriptions paint a sizzling setting for readers to revel in. Fast paced and very entertaining, this book will come across as a great source of entertainment for many young and adult readers."
—*Divine Zape, Readers' Favorite Book Reviewer*

# Also by Lisa Y. Potocar

*Sweet Glory*

*Train to Glory*

# Train to Glory

*a novel*

*Award-Winning Author*

## LISA Y. POTOCAR

*Train to Glory*

This novel is a work of fiction. However, several names, descriptions, entities, and incidents included in the story are based on the lives of real people.

Published by Lisa Y. Potocar, September 2017
www.lisapotocarauthor.com

*Cover design by Paper and Sage*
www.paperandsage.com

*Interior design for print format by By Your Side Self-Publishing*
www.byyoursideselfpub.com

*Interior design for digital format by LK Ebook Formatting Service*
design.lkcampbell.com

*Photography by Charles Lambert*

Published in the United States of America

Print ISBN: 978-0-9990488-2-5
eISBN: 978-0-9990488-3-2

1. YA Fiction/Historical/United States/19th Century/Civil War/Women's Equal Rights
2. YA Fiction/Historical/Romance
3. YA Fiction/Historical/Mystery

# Dedication

To all of the beautiful women in my life who have boldly gone where others have feared to tread—but especially my twin sister, Lita, as she forges a new path in life.

And to my husband, Jed, who firmly believes women ought to be granted equal rights to tackle anything a man can if she has a mind to it.

## Author's Personal Note

Dear Readers,

I'm sure you all know the saying, Actions speak louder than words. Well ... I think I've found two ways to show you that you're incredibly dear to me and that I genuinely cherish your feedback.

Nearly all of you expressed a desire for a sequel to *Sweet Glory*. This caused me great consternation because I'd already started work on another manuscript. And because I just couldn't imagine a plot for young adults, in particular, that could follow my debut story. Still, I couldn't ignore your pleas, so I thought LONG and HARD about it. Then, one day—

*Shazam*!

A morsel of an idea magically appeared in the flying particles as I was dusting the living-room furniture. (Hmmm ... funny how the creative spark for this sequel should come floating to me in the midst of the only chore that I really hate to do). Anyhow, I took off in flight to where my husband was riveted to some suspense/thriller, shouting, "I got it. I got." He didn't even have to look at my face, which felt as if it was glowing brighter than a bonfire at a pep rally, to know what had me flushed—he'd witnessed it too many times before. He kindly muted the TV and listened to my babble. The brown flecks in his hazel eyes began to sparkle, affirming that I was on the right path.

Some of you thought *Sweet Glory's* ending cheated you from relishing in Jana's reunion with her family while others thought I'd written it intentionally this way to set up a sequel for *Sweet Glory*. I'd love to take credit for the latter, but the cat's out of the bag on that one (per two paragraphs above). In either case, I've written the beginning of this story for all who thought *Sweet Glory's* "Epilogue" fell short.

So, without further delay, I give you: *Train to Glory*. I hope that I've done justice to your wishes. I hope that you'll never tire of telling me your wishes. And, most importantly, I promise to always listen to you.

Now, what are you waiting for? Get on with this reading . . . after all, it roots from your wishes.

Warm regards,
Lisa Y. Potocar

# Part I

*Home*

*Without a struggle, there can be no progress.*
—Frederick Douglass, West India Emancipation Speech, 1857

## Elmira, New York

*May 11, 1864*

Jana Brady stepped onto the platform between passenger cars of her homecoming train and eyed the depot for her family. A rapid *crack, crack, crack* made her tense. Her pulse took off in an unbridled gallop while her quaking hand fumbled at her hip for the worn walnut grip of her Colt revolver. She crouched, inching sideways back into the cover of her coach. When someone nearby cursed the boxcar handlers for hurling building planks out of the train and scaring the dickens out of everyone, Jana realized she'd been fooled once again. *Will these grisly aftereffects of war ever go away?* she wondered, willing the hand that held Ma's daisies to stop trembling.

As the cool mid-morning breeze swirled about her, Jana took a deep breath to calm herself, and she choked on the caustic odor of fresh paint. It drew her eyes to the bright red bricks of the station house, forcing her to compare its metamorphosis with her own.

Would her outward feminine deportment help her parents see past her lie to the woman she'd become? She longed for them to understand her childhood impulsiveness had been tamed by her war experiences, including the two most impressionable: First, when she caused injury to herself as she fired her pistol at some burlap Rebels against orders and premature to her mare being used to the sound so close to her ear. Second, when Elizabeth "Miss Lizzie" Van Lew taught her it took time to create deception in spying—even though she'd wanted to storm Castle Thunder Prison the very moment she'd landed in Richmond, Virginia, to help free her soldier-sweetheart, Keeley, and other Yankee soldiers.

1

Her bigger worry in reuniting with her family was the chasm of hurt she feared she'd cause Ma and Pa when they learned she'd been off soldiering and spying instead of nursing the whole time she'd been away. Deceiving her parents nauseated her—the same way she'd felt after forcing down the hard, weevil-infested biscuits on the march with the army.

As if to soothe her distress, the sun poked its head over a cloud and speared the weathervane atop the depot's roof with a shaft of its light. The gauge's gilt arrow aimed northwest in the direction of the wind—and the Brady homestead. Sensing it as a sign all would turn out well with her parents, Jana returned to the platform's doorway. She stretched to her full height of five feet six inches and searched the noisy crowd for her parents. She felt proud of who she'd become and was ready to share her accomplishments with them.

On the platform packed with people greeting arrivals, passengers awaiting the next train out, and workers routing baggage and other stowage, a familiar voice rose above all others. "They ought to be ashamed of themselves, throwing those large boards around with so many soldiers returning from the battlefront and sensitive to gunshots. Are you all right, dear?"

"Oh, Ma," Jana said, praying she hadn't observed her going for her sidearm—hardly the response of a field nurse. With daisies in one hand and her floral-embroidered carpetbag swinging off her other arm, she gathered her skirts and advanced down the iron steps and into Ma's outstretched arms. Her tears of joy dropped through the openings of Ma's crocheted shawl to stain the shoulder of her Sunday dress beneath a deeper plum. By Ma's and Pa's sides, nothing ever felt wrong with Jana—or the world.

"Oh my, Jana, you've grown into such a lovely young woman who carries herself with dignity." Ma hugged her tighter. "I've missed you so."

"I've missed you too, Ma." Using her reception as a barometer, Jana trusted her parents had at least come to terms with her having run off to nurse in the war. Before she'd eloped from home, they'd given her half their blessing, but it had come attached with the impossible restriction she get Dorothea Dix's approval to join her nursing corps.

Ma pushed away, allowing her and Jana to inspect each other.

Wiping away her tears, Jana observed that except for an additional wrinkle or two on her lightly tanned face, Ma hadn't changed a bit. Her walnut eyes were still vibrant, and her sandy hair hadn't lost its curls. She'd even shed the weight gained from the birth of her last daughter, Molly.

"You might be a little too thin, but"—Ma began fluffing Jana's already puffy sleeves as if she could plump up Jana too—"I suppose it's understandable with you following the army. You must've been every bit deprived of nourishment as we witness of the soldiers home on furlough. Unlike them, though, I'm glad to see your eyes are bright and your complexion is a healthy pink."

Ma's words jabbed at Jana, tempting her to spill her beans without the entire family assembled. Thankfully, she heard someone calling out her name.

A trio of her sisters came skipping toward her, sliding across the platform just shy of bowling her and Ma over.

Jana blinked twice. The last time she'd seen her twin sisters they were sprigs; now they were fifteen years old and fully bloomed. They were replica dolls of Ma, only they'd managed to maintain a milkier skin tone armed as they were with bonnets and their parasols opened.

Studying Jana from head to toe, Rachel slapped a hand to her chest. "My goodness, a Garibaldi dress? I'm jealous, Jana."

"Me too," Rebecca said, fascinated with Jana's brimless hat and its ivory plume of ostrich feathers, which Jana felt dipping in the wind and tickling her ear.

For dramatic effect, Jana brushed away imaginary lint from the gold epaulette of her blouse's shoulder. "I dropped into Washington on my way home to have it specially tailored." She'd save telling them she hadn't just *dropped* into the federal capital, but she'd escaped there following her near hanging. And once they discovered she'd been off soldiering, they'd realize she'd chosen this dress for her homecoming as a bit of irony: Besides the blouse's military-style shoulders and collarless neck, it and its matching skirt were dyed navy in keeping with the Union soldier's uniform, and the red tie around her neck mimicked the one sported by Union General George Custer.

"What happened to the tomboy we once knew?" Rachel asked, her chestnut eyes raking Jana over suspiciously.

In a tone rivaling the suspicion in her twin's eyes, Rebecca said, "After all your time away at the battlefront, we can't believe you were nursing the whole time. We'll be sorely disappointed if you have no greater adventures than that to tell us about."

*You must be joking,* Jana thought, pinching her lips together to suppress a smirk. Neither twin had a stitch of tomboy in them, but she was delighted they still lusted for adventure vicariously through her stories. She had a ton to tell.

Swatting the air in exasperation, Ma said, "A woman might not have the same adventures as a man, but hers can be daring too."

*Just you wait, Ma,* Jana mused. *You'll swoon when you hear how I had the same adventures as a man—and disguised as one, to boot.* This time, she caved in to her smirk.

Rachel's and Rebecca's heads whipped toward one another.

"Did you catch that devilish look? We're in for a treat," Rachel exclaimed.

"Oh, do tell us now," Rebecca said.

As she'd always done to tease her sisters, Jana mimed sewing her lips together to show they'd have to wait for the entire family to be gathered before she'd utter another word. This threw them into their usual pouts, which Jana ignored by turning to the tot, no taller than a yardstick and using the folds of the twins' calico skirts to play peek-a-boo with her. Kneeling to Molly's level, Jana recognized in her a perfect blend of Ma's soft features and Pa's green eyes and mellower shade of his more youthful carroty hair. Even though she'd left home when her youngest sister was only a few months old, she could've easily picked her out in a crowd. "Hello, Molly. Why, you're all grown up. How old are you now?"

She counted out three on her fingers and held them up for Jana to see.

"You probably don't remember me rocking you to sleep; I'd love to snuggle with you again, if you'd like—unless you feel you're too old for it."

Molly's lips spread wide with glee, showing two rows of tiny white teeth. Throwing her arms around her big sister, she squeezed so hard Jana felt the crocheted snood that bound up her auburn tresses indenting the nape of her neck. Then she smudged Jana's cheek with a sticky kiss.

"For you, Ma," Jana said, handing the daisies to her so she could scoop up Molly.

Ma's eyes glittered. "You didn't forget." She referred to the tradition Jana had started when she was ten years old: Jana would gift Ma with a seasonal bouquet whenever Ma allowed her out of her chores to play with her slingshot or go hunting with Pa. These daisies were more of a peace offering. How she hoped they'd work their magic.

"They're nothing grand; they were all I could find that would last until I got home."

"They're special to me," Ma said.

Noting a gap in her family circle, Jana said, "Where're Pa and Eliza?"

"When you wrote to say you'd be bringing home a mare, Pa figured it would be wise to see her off the train and comfortable in her new surroundings straightaway," Ma said.

Given the unusual nature of a nurse having her own horse, Jana had addressed vaguely in her letter home that she'd needed one to transfer her between battlefield assignments. She was relieved when Ma was either too caught up in her homecoming or her explanation was adequate enough for her to question it right now.

Ma added, "Pa figured you'd appreciate that more than his being here directly to greet you."

"He reckoned right." Jana cherished Pa's sensitivity to animals; he'd taught her the slow, gentle approach to taming Commodore, and she'd applied it on Maiti back when each man in her regiment was charged with breaking in his own horse. *Won't Pa be proud when I tell him I was promoted to paddock instructor after my superior officer recognized my talent?*

Standing tiptoed to see over Jana's shoulder, Ma pointed and said, "There they are now."

Jana circled around, spying her eight-year-old sister gently nudging Jana's stallion with the heels of her knee-high riding boots toward the stall car, where Pa was leading Jana's dapple gray down the ramp.

Noticing Jana's tapping foot, Rachel relieved her of Molly.

Jana sped off toward the back end of the train, maneuvering through a maze of stevedores assisting travelers in the identification and transport of their baggage.

Upon her presentation, Pa's eyes widened. "Could this refined young lady be our long lost tomboy?"

Mockingly, Jana curtsied and then rushed into his arms, muscled from a lifetime of farm labor. She basked in the familiarity of his aroma clinging to his Sunday suit—a more masculine potpourri of dried juniper berries, cloves, and cinnamon that Ma mixed together each fall, wrapped in a sachet, and set in his wardrobe cabinet.

"It's good to have you home, Jana."

"It's good to be home, Pa."

"What about me, Jana? Aren't you going to say hello?" Eliza said.

Jana twirled around. "Well, hello, E—," she cut herself short when she saw her sister's looks, a mirror image of herself at the time she'd left home. And if Eliza were to trim her auburn tresses, she'd resemble Pa as had Jana when she'd first donned her cropped hairstyle to play the role of a cavalryman. Eliza's wardrobe of coat and riding pants, along with her tanned face and freckled nose, betrayed her rough-and-tumble ways. With her back to Pa, she said, "I see Eliza's given up her fondness for dolls and taken my place hunting by your side." She shifted her stance and crossed her arms, pinning Pa beneath her gold-flecked hazel eyes. "I'm shocked you've let her carry on in this way."

"Why?" he asked, his eyes a mirror of hers with their gold flecks smirking at her.

"Because you and Ma tried awful hard to put an end to my days as a tomboy."

Thrusting his palms outward, he said, "And just look at you now. You turned out all right, didn't you?"

Jana understood his subtler message: He and Ma wouldn't spoon-feed Eliza her womanhood before she was ready and force her into running away from home too. The proof was in her casual wear, which she'd somehow managed to get over on Ma for Jana's homecoming. Her parents' leniency with Eliza just might persuade them to come to terms quicker with her soldiering.

"Speaking of beauties"—Pa rubbed Maiti's dapple gray back—"this here's one fine horse. She seems more likely to saddle a trooper than a nurse. Lots of good horses have been stolen around the county by cavalrymen on furlough searching for substitutes after theirs were shot down beneath them. How'd you manage to hide her at the battlefront?"

Jana turned to greet her nuzzling horses. "I'll tell you about it later, Pa." Pressing her forehead against both of their muzzles, she wallowed in the prickle of their whiskers and the warm snuffles of their grain-scented breaths against her cheeks. She said to Commodore, "I've missed you, boy," and to Maiti, "How was the ride, girl?"

In a coordinated move, Commodore snorted and Maiti tossed her head up and down.

Jana had hated to leave her black beauty behind, but it would've been hard to hide him for the few days between her enlistment and her regiment's transfer out of Elmira to their seventy-two-day layover in Gettysburg, Pennsylvania. She'd had her own difficulty blending in. Commodore would've been as fierce a warrior as Jana's mare, who because of her vigor to form up faster for a fight than any other cavalry horse, Keeley had named Maiti—meaning *strong battle maiden* in his native Gaelic. Now, Jana was glad she could bring Commodore a stablemate. "I knew you two would get along." Rubbing the thinning wintry fur along Commodore's neck, she said, "Thanks, boy, for accepting her." She looked to Pa and Eliza. "And thank you both for making Maiti feel right at home."

Shepherding the rest of her flock along, Ma said, "If we're to have Jana's homecoming supper, I must get home to roast the turkey."

The mention of Ma's cooking got Jana's taste buds watering for her apple and sausage dressing, a permanent pairing with turkey in the Brady household and one of her favorite dishes. *Thank goodness I'm too old for Ma to send me to my room without any supper*, Jana thought, stifling a snicker.

Eliza stabbed her chest with her thumb. "The turkey I got with my rifle, right, Pa?" At his nod, she grinned with the same satisfaction as the porter who'd just nabbed a handsome tip from Jana for transferring her and Maiti's trunks from the baggage car to the Brady wagon.

*Ma and Pa might think twice about letting Eliza carry on with her tomboyish ways when they hear my story.* Jana silently bemoaned that she could be potentially opening Pandora's Box on her sister.

"All aboard," Pa called out.

Patting their bench, the twins gestured Jana between them and behind the one occupied by Ma and Pa with Molly in their middle.

Pa pulled the lever, and the wagon brake released with a squeal. Then he flicked his signal whip over the mules' fuzzy gray ears to start their march homeward. With Maiti hitched to the wagon, and Eliza keeping Commodore apace alongside, the Brady clan set off for their farm.

Staring wide-eyed at the hordes of mule-and-horse-drawn conveyances parked at the depot and competing with them to leave it, Jana said, "I've never seen this much activity here at once. Is there something special going on in Elmira?" It was too early for the agricultural fair, which happened each fall. Maybe there was a Shakespearean performance planned.

"If you consider a population explosion something special, then, yes. Since your absence, Chemung County has grown by at least fifteen hundred residents," Ma said.

"The increase," Pa reminded her, "from the exposure Elmira got with New York making it a rendezvous point for volunteer soldiers from all over its western half. It opened eyes to our city's progressive nature and as a major connection to anywhere in the United States with its two railroads and canal."

The thriving businesses and shops and the new homes, which sprang up all along their route, proved to Jana that Elmirans had profited through the Union army's local purchases in feeding and outfitting the thousands of soldiers who'd been formed into infantry, artillery, and cavalry regiments here. While Northerners' bounties grew, the converse was true for Southerners—starved by Union ships blockading their ports and preventing them from trading for goods. Jana had been subjected to Richmond's poor and paltry fare during her stays in Miss Lizzie's mansion and prison, where she'd been forced to fast a few times.

Rising from her thoughts, Jana heard Ma reciting the names of the men from around their county who'd been lost to war. She recognized one or two in name only from her regiment, over seven hundred strong at the height of its formation. She'd barely become acquainted with all one-hundred-and-thirty men between her Company *D* and those of Company *B*, usually paired as a squadron in training and battle.

Clucking her tongue, Ma said, "Who would've predicted that most of them would die from dysentery or cholera instead of battle wounds? Thank goodness for the United States Sanitary Commission. Perhaps their stringent standards for cleanliness in camps and prisons will lessen the numbers dying from disease." She called over her shoulder. "Did you have any dealings with the Sanitary Commission while you were nursing, Jana?"

Ma had just delivered to Jana the perfect segue into her confession, and she felt especially emboldened as they drew alongside the military camp. Here she'd tasted "sweet glory" in the snowflakes melting on her tongue when she'd gotten the idea to disguise herself as a cavalryman. Peering through the gaps of fallen boards in the high wall, where the guards once watched for deserters, she swore she saw the ghosts of her Porter Guards marching in battle formation across the thirty acres between Foster's Pond and Water Street and heard their sabers rattling, small arms discharging, and officers and buglers alternately calling out orders. What better place for her to bare all than where it had begun for her? "Stop the wagon, Pa." Silently, she prayed to the ghosts to show themselves to Ma and Pa and stir up the same fever for war that had resonated throughout Camp Rathbun back in 1861. How could they dismiss her fervor to fight in uniform, then?

# Elmira, New York

## May 11, 1864

Jana fished the letter out of her carpetbag she'd depend upon for help in telling the story of her adventure while Pa reined in the mules.

Again, Ma called over her shoulder to Jana. "Did you forget something on the train?"

"No, but you might want to put me back on it when you hear what I have to say."

Ma and Pa pivoted on their bench, regarding Jana with the same befuddlement they showed the day she'd declared she wanted to be a nurse at the battlefront.

Eyeing her communication, Eliza said, "Is that another note for Ma from Mr. Walt Whitman? Ever since you sent it to her, she reads it every day. Pa finally bought her a frame for it, so she can't wear out the ink."

Jana would be a hypocrite to laugh at Ma. Her obsession with Keeley's likeness had compelled her to tuck away the daguerreotype with him in it before she marred its delicate surface. Maybe Ma's joy with her gift would provide Jana leverage for receiving her forgiveness. After all, the only way she would've ever crossed paths with the poet was as a soldier assigned to the same hospital, where he was also tending the wounded after the battle at Fredericksburg, Virginia.

"Then, tell us what has you suddenly solemn," Ma said.

"You asked me, Ma, if I'd come in contact with the Sanitary Commission while I was nursing. My answer is no, and it's time you knew why."

To the mysterious edge in Jana's tone, Rachel and Rebecca scooted to the edge of their seat, and Eliza swiveled sideways in her saddle.

"I'd like to read a letter I wrote you but fortunately never had to send. It'll help explain some things you ought to know before I'll truly feel welcome home."

"What could you possibly have to tell us that would ever make you unwanted to us?" Ma said, clutching the daisies high against her chest.

Jana regretted she was about to compound Ma's anxiety; however, she'd defend to her death the path she'd chosen.

Trying to mollify Ma with a little jesting, Pa mimed a judge pounding his gavel and said, "Silence in the courtroom. Everyone's entitled to a trial by jury. Let's wait to sentence Jana after we've heard her case." Then he leaned back and crossed his arms, poised to listen.

Jana's breath caught upon hearing Pa's joke, an eerie foreshadowing of the opening of her letter, which she unfolded and began to read:

May 4, 1864—

"Your nineteenth birthday," Rachel and Rebecca shouted in unison. They quieted under Pa's grimace, which said one more outburst of the kind, and he'd whip the cravat off his neck, tear it in two, and gag them with it.

Jana started over:

May 4, 1864, Camp Lee, Virginia

Dear Ma, Pa, and my darling sisters,

If you're reading this letter, written in my hand but sent to you through a secure underground network by a dear friend, who shall remain anonymous, then I've gone to heaven on this day. I hope you can find solace in my departure from this world when you've heard my remaining words.

I'm proud to have served my country, and I don't regret for one second that my life has come to an end on the gallows for my having been found guilty of spying against the Confederate States of America.

Pausing to the gasps and gaping jaws, Jana respected her family's need to process the direness of her disclosure.

"I don't understand." Ma frowned in bewilderment. "How were you spying if you were nursing?"

"Would you mind if I waited to answer that next in my letter?"

Not giving Ma a chance to reply, Eliza said, "Who's the *friend* who would've sent us your letter?"

Pa didn't seem concerned with Jana's answer; his eyes were panning the forested hills westward for a piece to some puzzle he was obviously trying to solve.

"I'm sorry, Eliza, I can't reveal their name now—maybe ever. It could jeopardize their life even long after the war is over."

Shifting his focus to Jana, Pa said, "The newspapers circulated a story a week back about a woman who hung for spying in Richmond. But ... she's dead."

"No, she's not, Pa. That woman was me."

All eyes clung to Jana in disbelief. Her family's quiet crescendoed above a mingling of noises from a locomotive's blasts, passersby engaged in lively bantering, and horses nickering and neighing.

Jana felt alone. Even Eliza, rendered speechless, had abandoned her. When she could no longer tolerate their silence, Jana injected intrigue into her voice and said, "I faked a heart attack on my gallows." Her ploy stirred them, and their arching eyebrows spurred her on. "Then I got lucky when the doctor missed my pulse through the high, stiff collar of my dress and pronounced me dead."

"That was really you? Weren't you scared?" Eliza said.

"I was frightened out of my skull." The involuntary movement of Jana's hand to her throat and her wince at the memory of the noose around her neck made everyone wince too.

Ma said, "Are you having nightmares, dear?"

"No, Ma, I only have these reactions sometimes when I talk about it."

Pa joined Ma in a visual examination of Jana's body language, followed by Ma saying, "Should you talk to the doctor about it?"

Given her sharp reaction, Jana couldn't blame them for wanting to assure she wasn't downplaying the gravity of her aftershocks. "If it becomes a problem, I promise I will, Ma."

Eliza pretended to yawn and began thwacking her riding gloves against the curved pommel of her saddle.

Although Ma glared at her impatience, she said, "Well, we won't dwell on—"

Eliza cut her off. "How'd you keep your cool to pull it off, then?"

"Lots of training to hold my breath and strengthen my leg muscles and chin so I could swing by both for the few seconds I needed in between collapsing onto my haunches and noose and being rescued from that awkward position. And the black hood the hangman slipped over my head helped too. It calmed my nerves when I couldn't see the crowd and allowed me to concentrate on the performance of my life—pardon the pun." Capitalizing on everyone's attentiveness, Jana flashed back to earlier in her prison stay when her idea to fake a heart attack spawned. "Weeks before my execution, I fainted from hunger. A rumor spread around Richmond that I was suffering from a heart ailment. It dawned on me then if I was to intensify the perception by fainting a few more times, maybe I could pull off my death from a heart attack on my gallows. The hundreds of spectators who turned out to watch me hang rejoiced that the stress of my impending death hadn't exacerbated my condition and sent me to my grave. And that's the card I played to fool them all—except the doctor and the commandant of my prison who I suspect were on my side. The warden wanted no part of hanging a woman, especially me. He said he admired me for cleaning the prison hospital and nursing its inmates, but he couldn't turn a blind eye and let me escape. In the end, I think he did just that when he saw some twitch by me proving I was still alive because he hurried to cover me over with his uniform jacket and to have the guards whisk me away in my coffin."

Clearly still stuck on the part of Jana's letter that declared she'd gone to heaven, Molly asked, "How come I can see you if you're in heaven? Are you an angel?"

Rachel, Rebecca, and Eliza tittered; Pa grunted with partial amusement; and Ma explained to Molly, "Jana is telling us that the plan for her to go to heaven was changed, and she'll remain with us—hopefully for a long time."

"Yay," Molly said, clapping her hands.

Jana could kiss Molly for lightening the mood, and she hoped she'd repeat it after she read her next sentence. *Then, we'll see, Ma, if you still want me around for any length of time.* "May I read on?" Jana asked, trying to suppress her edginess to be done with her confession.

Fiddling with the daisies, Ma deferred to Pa, who nodded his consent.

Jana suspected Ma sensed they were about to be blasted with some unpleasant news; beneath her act of nonchalance she was bracing herself to meet it. Maybe it would've been wiser to apply Pa's horse-training method and dish it out more piecemeal. She'd be devastated, though, if they ever found out about her soldiering when a former comrade called her "Johnnie" on the streets of Elmira—remote but not impossible. There was also the matter of her guilt, which demanded immediate erasure. Why let it grow gangrenous only to require amputation later anyway? Sucking in a deep breath, Jana plunged into her letter:

> I came to this end through the call to duty I felt drawing me to fight for the preservation of the Union and abolishment of slavery in the only way I deemed noble at the time I left home: disguised as a young man who enlisted with the Tenth New York Volunteer Cavalry Regiment.

Again, Jana paused—this time to a mutually guttural gasp, which nearly blew her off her seat.

Dropping the daisies onto her lap, Ma said, "Spying? Soldiering? You weren't off nursing as you maintained in your letters? What were you thinking? You could've been killed."

"I could've been killed nursing at the battlefront, Ma, and you and Pa accepted that—the proof is in your acknowledgment of it before I ran away and in your decision afterward not to track me down and drag me home. What's the difference if I was nursing, soldiering, or spying? The risk was the same."

With a heavy sigh, Pa said, "I'm afraid, Julia, we have ourselves to blame for Jana's change in course from nursing to soldiering. We placed the impossible restriction of her having to get Dorothea Dix's permission to join her nursing corps when we knew full well no exception would be made for her, a far cry younger than thirty years old and a far sight prettier than plain."

"Don't blame yourselves, Pa. If I'd really wanted to nurse, I would've gone to the field on my own as many other women did and as you thought I'd done. The truth is I never wanted to be a nurse; it was my cover for leaving home so I'd be free to volunteer in the army."

"All those lies," Ma said, wilting unto herself.

"It was my only way out, Ma. What daughter in her right mind's going to seek her parents' permission to go off soldiering?"

"We might've discussed it," Ma said.

"It would've been a one-sided discussion. Admit it, nothing I said would've convinced you to let me go."

Ma said, "Yes, but we might've brought you to your senses."

"No, you wouldn't have. My mind was made up to fight for my country in uniform, and the first time you and Pa turned your backs, I would've run off to do it."

"What if you'd been shot down and buried in a trench just like thousands of soldiers have been?" Ma's bottom lip began to quiver. "How would we have known where to find you so that we could bring you home to a more comfortable resting place and send you off with prayers and songs of praise?"

"If I'd been shot down trying to evacuate the wounded from the battlefield, who knows what would've become of my body, especially if the burial party was in a hurry? I could've been thrown in a trench, and you wouldn't have been wise to my final resting place in that case either."

Ma's expression twisted up in horror. "Surely that would never have happened to a woman."

"Want to bet? I've seen war in all of its ugliness, and chivalry is the first thing to go when it comes to survival or the easy way out." To soften her blow to Ma's subscription for a good death—a reflection shared by the general populous as well—Jana said, "The bonds that are forged between men together at war mean no one ever has to die alone."

"This is all pure madness," Ma said.

"I agree, Ma, war is exactly that. But if you're referring to my soldiering, you and Pa instilled in me that a woman ought to be able to tackle anything a man can if she has a mind to it. Are you telling me now there's a limit to your belief? Isn't that hypocritical?" She felt disappointed with her parents' stubborn refusal to understand. With her pitch heating to a boil, Jana said, "If I were your son and I volunteered to fight for my country, you'd throw me a going-away supper and later listen to my war stories with pride."

Recoiling to Jana's rare display of outrage, Ma and Pa locked eyes, seeking each other's counsel. They'd always had an uncanny ability to read one another.

And Jana could usually predict which way her parents' wind was blowing, especially when it came to their mulling her over. This time she was hard-pressed to tell if they were moving toward vindicating or gathering ammunition against her. If the latter, she wondered, *What more is there to say?*

Appearing to conclude the same, Eliza peeked over Jana's shoulder and said, "It looks like there's more to your letter. Can we get on with it?"

"Yes, please," Rachel and Rebecca said.

"I promise, I'm through with my difficult news," Jana said. "There are a few more surprises, but trust me, they're much more pleasing."

Pa said to Ma, "I reckon we owe it to Jana to hear her out."

"Yes, it appears we do," Ma said, intent on brushing from her skirt the tiny yellow florets that had shed from the cores of her daisies.

Taking advantage of their concession, Jana read on:

> My only two regrets are that I didn't get to see you all one last time and that you'll never see the woman I've matured into—all ironically thanks to my soldiering. I came to appreciate my womanhood through my acquaintances with Nurse Clara Barton and Doctor Mary Walker (and even Poet Walt Whitman) who showed me that I didn't have to give up on my gender to enjoy plenty of exciting adventures, especially when it comes to pioneering into roles reserved for men; in my work of caring for others by assisting in surgery, evacuating and nursing the wounded, and playing the role of midwife; but mostly through my daily interactions with my three closest comrades who awakened different sides of me and are special to me. I'd like to introduce them to you now:
>
> First is Leanne "Leander" Perham, whom you'll remember from town. Contrary to what you thought, Ma, she didn't run off to find the woman inside of her. She enlisted in the army purposely to rid herself of her fear for fighting that prevented her from standing up to her pa whenever he got liquored up and harmed her or her ma; after she'd deserted, she secreted her ma away to live with the family of our other cavalry comrade (Charlie Watson) instead of fighting her pa. I'm awfully proud of her. Leanne's bent to be a man more than a woman made me appreciate my feminine side, which I knew I'd one day embrace even though deep down I'll always be a tomboy and adventurer at heart. I

hope I'm allowed these attributes in my afterlife ... snicker, snicker.

Next is Charlie Watson. Left behind as the eldest male in his family after his pa's accidental death, he enlisted for the pay to provide for his ma and younger brother. Four years younger than me, his innocence brought out my mothering instincts, although he proved his mettle many times, especially in our skirmish at Leesburg when he shot down a Rebel about to kill Leanne. Still, he loved how I fussed over him like his ma does. Before I headed to Richmond, I got him promoted to hospital steward so he'd be out of the line of fire.

Last but not least is Keeley Cassidy. By the time of his enlistment at twenty-one years old, he'd persevered through great hardships, including the deaths of his mam, da, and younger siblings in the Great Famine of Ireland; surviving his own death from disease aboard a ship crossing the Atlantic to the United States; starvation and the wrath of gangs while living on the streets of New York City; and prejudice against the Irishman for the better-paying jobs. He's well respected by the men in our regiment, who recognize his charisma for leading men and his being more battle hardened than most of our commanding officers. Like Charlie, he enlisted for the pay on which to build his dream hearth and home—one we'd planned to build together. Yes, you've read that right. I love him with all of my heart. The proof is that I jeopardized my life when I took a bullet in my arm at Brandy Station, Virginia, trying to save him from the Rebels' clutches. Then I sacrificed my life trying to rescue him and other Yankee soldiers from prison—the offense for which the Confederacy deemed me a spy and for which I've been executed. He loves me with all of his heart too. This proof lies in the simple fact that he's always accepted me for me, especially my adventuresome spirit in my wanting to fight for my country as a soldier. You'd love him too, Ma and Pa. He believes as we do that a woman ought to be allowed to tackle anything a man can if she has a mind to it. Like you, Pa, he's very handsome. And, Ma, just as Grandpa Brady used to claim your cooking could lure frightened men into battle by their noses, Keeley's love for me could lead me anywhere. After the war, Keeley had planned to come ask your permission, Pa, for my hand in marriage. That's not to be; however, I made him promise to visit and share with you our stories, missing from this letter and too numerous to pen. Given all he's been through, I just know he'll survive the war and keep his promise to me. So I hope you'll invite him to stay until he lands on his feet. He embraces hard work, and he'll even bake bread if you need him to, Ma. It won't be anywhere near as doughy and tasty as yours, but the patients at Chatham Manor, who we helped nurse in the aftermath of the battle at Fredericksburg, Virginia, really appreciated it. I know you'll all fall in love with him and never want him to leave. I can only hope that's the case because then I could rest in peace knowing he was being well cared for.

I never meant to hurt you with my lie I was off nursing the entire time

I was away. My desire to join the fight for my country no matter the cost to myself, as you always instilled in me, Ma and Pa, overcame me. If it'll comfort you any, Nurse Clara Barton (whom I mentioned earlier in my letter) was nearly killed when she took a bullet in her skirt while crossing the Rappahannock River to get to some wounded holed up in a church in Fredericksburg. That could've been me if I'd been nursing since I too would've raced through a raging battle to evacuate the wounded and give them the best chance to survive.

After I ended up unconscious from my wound in the hospital, and it was discovered I was a woman, my commanding officer, Colonel Hugh Judson Kilpatrick, lamented having to discharge me. He said I was better qualified to be a soldier than the men who paid for a substitute and stayed home. It wasn't hard to convince him to assign me elsewhere—Keeley will fill you in on my spying capers, which ultimately led to my hanging. I accepted the job, knowing full well the dire consequences if I were caught. I hope you'll forgive me for putting my life on the line enough times to guarantee a sorrowful outcome for you but a noble one for me.

Until we meet again,
Your loving daughter and sister, Jana

With her confession anted up, and all of her cards on the table face up, Jana's guilt vanished.

"I suppose we ought to be counting our blessings that Jana's home in one piece," Ma said to Pa.

"And praising her for her courage and perseverance," Pa said.

Facing Jana, Ma said, "We've been fools. Please, forgive our hesitation to honor your sacrifices."

Pa scratched his clean-shaven chin. "I reckon where family is concerned, beliefs don't always wholly stand up to the test."

"Well, it did with her Keeley, even when his belief was challenged by his concern for Jana's safety." Ma smiled at Jana. "I already admire your Keeley."

"Speaking of Jana and Keeley"—Pa slapped his thigh—"how's that for a bit of irony? Dressed as a man, Jana snagged a man."

Jana laughed. "If I were you, Pa, I'd never say that to Keeley. As much as he can take a good ribbing, I doubt he'd appreciate anyone suggesting he fell in love with me when I was a man. Though, Charlie and I can vouch that he knew all along I was a woman and that he respected my reason for not telling him."

"What was your reason?" Eliza asked.

Rachel said, "It was probably the same as she had for not telling Ma and Pa she wanted to soldier."

"Huh?" Eliza said.

"He would've stopped her from soldiering," Rebecca said.

"Yes," Jana said. "I sensed his feelings for me, and I was afraid if I confirmed for him that I was a woman, he'd turn protective and have me booted out of the army and the line of fire. And I wasn't about to leave him, Leanne, and Charlie behind—especially Keeley and Charlie who couldn't turn themselves back into women and desert any time they wanted like Leanne and I could."

"What makes you ready now to keep out of the line of fire with Keeley still in it?" Ma said.

"Keeley and I agreed only one of us can be soldiering; our worries for each other's welfare is a distraction that could get us killed in battle." Jana would let her parents digest all she'd fed them today before she told them of her intention to return to the field and to a nursing assignment as close to Keeley as possible. Although, they'd be glad to hear Keeley had made her promise to stay in the hospitals away from the battlefields.

Ma reached over and stroked the back of Jana's hand. "We're proud of you and your good sense. It's plain to see how you've blossomed under your accomplishments."

"You bet we are," Pa said. Then he gathered Eliza in a sidelong glance. "Is there any hope for Eliza snagging a man dressed in her men's britches?"

"Pa!" Eliza said.

Ma scoffed. "Don't put any notions of going off to war into her head. One daughter's enough."

"Don't worry, Ma. I'm happy at home and my heart's already taken," Eliza said, patting Commodore's neck.

"Oh boy, we've created another holy terror," Pa said.

Everyone shared a laugh.

When the merriment subsided, Rachel asked, "Do you have a likeness of Keeley?"

"Yes"—Jana jolted up in excitement—"I have a daguerreotype of me, Leanne, Charlie, and Keeley in our uniforms." Fetching it from her carpetbag, she held it up for all to see, pointing to Keeley before she passed it around.

Rubbing the silver-plated sheet of copper, Ma said, "I agree, Jana, your Keeley is quite handsome."

Starry-eyed, Rachel and Rebecca bobbed their heads in agreement.

"He's even more handsome in person," Jana said.

"We look forward to meeting your gentleman, and we're glad he had the good sense to send you home," Ma said.

"Keeley's going to love you all," Jana said, silently thanking the ghosts of Camp Rathbun, who she was convinced had helped prod Ma and Pa into feeling proud of her development into adulthood. Returning her gaze to her sweetheart, she felt her and Keeley's love flaming bright in the depth of her soul. It was a force that, if ever extinguished, she'd be lost without.

## Elmira, New York

### June 26, 1864

Perched on a three-legged stool, Jana clamped her thumbs and forefingers around the top of her Holstein's teats to prevent milk from backing up into the udder. Then she let her other fingers fall into place below them and began gently squeezing and pulling the teats. Gloomy notions of Keeley sloshed around her brain in cadence with the milk filling her bucket. She'd had no communication from him since before the battle at Trevilian Station, Virginia, over two weeks ago, and he'd promised to write often. Under the command of General David McMurtrie Gregg, who'd played a prominent role in the Union attack, Keeley and his Porter Guards most assuredly had been in the thick of fire. The newspapers' claims that this cavalry battle was bloodier than the one Jana and her friends had fought in the year before made Jana relive the horror of Brandy Station: the cries of the wounded and the smell of death that hung heavy in the scorching air from soldiers and horses being torn apart by flying shards of exploding cannonballs and from enemies in a dismounted clash slashing each other up with their sabers. The notion of Keeley having to suffer through that all over again made her stomach roil to near-retching.

A balmy liquid smelling of fresh milk splattered the nape of Jana's neck. She jerked, kicking her tin pail; its contents emptied all along the wide plank floors as it rolled with a nerve-wracking clatter rivaling a volley of rifles.

Having grown to loathe loud noises, especially those that mimicked the sounds of battle, Jana plugged her ears until the racket subsided. She swiveled around on her stool to see Pa grinning and aiming a teat at her.

Pa's merriment abated when he noted Jana's scowl. "I didn't mean to create chaos. I just thought you needed some nudging out of your brooding," he said, knowing full well she'd been despairing over Keeley ever since they'd learned there were around seven hundred Union casualties at Trevilian Station.

Invisible to them from the other side of her cow, Ma called out, "Have you lost your confidence that Keeley will survive the war? From what you've told us of his tenacity and good sense, I just know he'll be all right."

"Yes, but—," Jana stopped herself from telling them about the noose around her stomach that was tightening by the minute from her nagging intuition Keeley had run into trouble and was calling out to her for help. They'd just tell her to be patient—there'd be news from him soon. Her delay in returning to the field and failure to be there for him shattered her heart as if it had been hit by flying shards from an exploding shell. She could no longer worry about wrecking Ma and Pa's joy over having her home; the second they finished milking, she'd tell them of her plans to leave straightaway. Too late in the day to make travel arrangements, she reluctantly fetched her bucket and returned to her stool. She'd just started milking when the drumming of a horse's hoofs against the lane to the Brady homestead reached their ears.

Who could it possibly be? They weren't expecting company tonight. The neighboring farmers would be too busy with their own cows right now to visit. And twelve-year-old Eddie Potts whom Pa had hired to help with the morning and evening milking wasn't expected back until after his pa's furlough from his infantry regiment ended next week. Rising from her stool, Jana ticked off the tempo of the horse's hoofs, which beat faster as they neared the barn—but not as fast as the anxiety beating against her temples.

Pa scrambled to the wide-open barn doors to await the arrival of their interloper.

Appearing from around the hindquarter of her Holstein, Ma wiped her hands on her apron and wisps of her hair away from her forehead, which was creased in concern.

The rider slowed his gelding, its summer coat frothy with sweat and its nostrils flared and puffing. He'd barely reined his mount to a stop when he leapt from the saddle, his boot soles kicking up dirt as they smacked the dry earth. After hitching his horse to the post outside, he strode toward Pa.

Something in his swagger struck Jana as familiar, but the heavy shadows of late afternoon loitering just inside the barn's threshold darkened his face, barring his identity.

Their visitor snatched his leather slouch hat from his head and began twirling it in his stumpy fingers. "Mr. Brady, Mrs. Brady," he said, paying his respects to Ma and Pa.

To the unmistakable voice, Jana blurted out, "Leanne Perham, is that you?"

Moving a few paces into the barn, Leanne came into full view. Jana could see civilian life agreed with her—she'd added some weight to her five-foot-three-inch frame to make her slightly stocky since their cavalry days.

Flanking Jana, Ma exhaled in surprise. She'd probably seen plenty of women sporting a bob—the latest hairstyle trimmed up to the jawline—but Jana doubted she would've ever seen a woman, as Leanne presented herself now, with her hair cropped up to the ears like Pa's.

Leanne hiked up her denim pants and said proudly, "Name's Leanne Watson now. My ma and Charlie's ma reckoned we should change our surname in case that no-good pa of mine ever got it in his craw to come huntin' us down."

With her skirt hem swinging about her ankles as she sped toward Leanne, Jana thought, *What is that pressing for Leanne to risk showing herself in these parts while her pa still lives nearby and to draw her away from providing for her new family?* She reached out to shake Leanne's crack-begrimed, calloused hand and contemplated how disappointing it was that Leanne's pa would never know she'd used her excellent training to open her own smithy—far more successful than his.

"Hello, Johnnie … er … I mean, Jana. I'm glad to see you're lookin' fit after yer long imprisonment and run-in with the gallows."

Feeling her skirt hugging her hips, Jana realized she too had gained back some of the weight she'd lost from her wartime famine.

"As I've said before, ya ain't no coward, Jana," Leanne said, staring admiringly up at Jana, three inches taller than her.

Beneath Leanne's twitching right cheek and its bristling mole, Jana knew that she was trying to soften a bad blow by diverting her with kind words, which at one time Leanne had to be weaned into giving and taking. Her delight in being recognized by Jana, Keeley, and Charlie, who praised her every chance they got, inspired her to recognize others. *Too bad her pa will also never see she's overcome his verbal abuse,* Jana thought, but instead said, "Thanks, Leanne. It means a whole lot coming from a brave warrior like you." She looked to Ma and Pa. "You remember Leanne?"

"Yes," Pa said, "and Mrs. Brady and I are mighty grateful to you, Leanne, for watching our Jana's back during your time together at war."

Latching her steel-gray eyes onto Pa, she said, "It's good of ya to say so, sir, but she watched over me, Keeley, and Charlie plenty more. Heck, she's got more courage than an army of brave men."

As Ma swept up even with Jana, she flashed Jana a sidelong glance that read, *I see what you mean; Leanne really does think of herself as a man.* She extended her hand for Leanne to shake. "How nice of you to come, Leanne. Is all well with your ma?"

Leanne's smile soared to the clouds. "I ain't never seen her so happy."

"I'm glad," Ma said. "Did you ride horseback all the way from Buffalo?"

"No, ma'am. I hopped the Erie Railway to Corning and rented my horse at a livery there to avoid Elmira and runnin' into my pa." She addressed Pa. "If I could borrow a towel, sir, I'll wipe my horse down proper."

While Pa fetched one from a nearby wall hook, Ma continued her inquisition. "Did you come all the way here just to visit Jana?"

Leanne's smile dropped flatter than the Johnny cakes they used to fry by the dozens for their messmates during their winter confinement in camp. "No, ma'am." Draping the towel over her left shoulder, she reached into the waist pocket of her light riding coat and extracted a letter, which she showed as proof but refused to relinquish. "It's from Charlie. He figured it'd be better if I told ya his news in person."

"I think I already know it," Jana said.

"Ya do?" Leanne said.

"It's something bad about Keeley, isn't it?" Growing lightheaded, Jana wobbled slightly and flung her arm out to balance herself.

Closest to her, Pa reached out a muscled hand and grabbed her elbow to hold her steady.

"Please, Leanne, don't tell me he's ..." Jana trailed off, unable to say the morbid word.

With her boot tip, Leanne shuffled around a stray stick of straw. "Charlie says Keeley's come up missin' since the battle 'round Trevilian Station, which I'm sure you've heard all 'bout by now."

"Do you mean captured missing?" Jana's hopes rose to the first swell of optimism that came to her: *He escaped from prison once; surely he'll do it again.* However, they capsized to Leanne's grimace.

"Apparently, he was wounded in a dismounted charge over a fence. His head was bleedin', and he was unconscious when two of our men dragged him into the woods out of range of Rebel artillery."

"How does Charlie know all of this?"

"Do ya remember our commissary officer?"

"Noble Preston?"

"That's him. He saw Keeley take a rifle butt to the head right before he took a bullet in his hip during the same charge. Later, Preston was brought to the house where Charlie was tendin' the wounded. Knowin' he and Keeley are friends, he asked Charlie 'bout him. When Charlie didn't find Keeley amongst the wounded, he asked Preston if he remembered anything else. He claims he might've seen Keeley staggerin' off."

"What do you mean *might've* seen Keeley staggering off?" Jana said.

"Preston says he was goin' in and out of consciousness from his own bleedin', and he can't exactly vouch for anything he saw during that time."

"If what your commissary officer says is true," Ma said, "it sounds encouraging that Keeley moved off on his own accord. Don't you agree?"

"He could've stumbled into the arms of the enemy," Pa said.

"That ain't likely if what Noble says is right and Keeley headed north toward where our regiment broke camp the morning of the battle and opposite the Rebels' retreat south."

Jana burst out, "I'm going after him."

"Haven't you tempted fate enough? And what about Keeley? Is that what he'd want?" Ma said.

"There's no danger of me being caught in any crossfire with the fighting concentrated around Petersburg—that's at least eighty miles south of Trevilian Station."

"What about civilian hostility? I doubt Southerners will take kindly to a Northerner—even a woman—traipsing about their countryside," Ma said.

"We've had some very positive encounters with the country folk, right, Leanne?" Jana said.

"Yup. Did ya tell yer ma and pa 'bout our stay with Anna and Marcus? They would've put us up and stocked us with forage even if Jana here hadn't helped 'em with the birth of their baby." Leanne shot Jana a look of pride. "And did ya tell yer ma and pa they named their baby after ya?"

Ma and Pa smiled in acknowledgment.

Drawing up the hem of her apron to mop up the perspiration that had broken out across her forehead during her near fainting spell, Jana began twisting it in her hands. She felt a powerful magnetic draw to be off in search of Keeley. First, she'd have to convince Ma and Pa to let her go. She capitalized on Leanne's proclamation about Anna and Marcus's kindness to show she'd be safe in the South. "Most Virginians are small farmers who don't own slaves; their greater grudge is against neighboring planters and statesmen who got them into war over slavery. They're only aggressive when they're cornered into defending themselves or their homes against murderers or thieves, Yankee or Rebel alike. I'll be perfectly safe."

"What if Keeley's been captured? Will you risk your life again spying to free him?" Pa said.

"That would be foolish of me, Pa. If I go anywhere near Richmond, I run the risk of being caught. The Rebels will make sure they hang me this time. And that'll do Keeley no good. But I have connections near enough there whom I need to contact in person to ask if they could check that Keeley's being well tended if he's back in Castle Thunder Prison. I'm determined to go; I have to know what happened to him."

Pa set his jaw firmly. "I'm going with you. My field hand can shift his duties for a short time to the barn, and Rachel and Rebecca will just have to help Eliza and Ma with the milking."

"No, Pa, it's too dangerous with both armies desperate for able-bodied men. You can't prove you exceed the age for enlistment, and they'll hogtie you into service. Worse yet, you could be captured and imprisoned by the Confederacy." Ever since he learned she'd lied about her age so she could fight for her country, he thought he should've done the same. She'd use the same argument against him now that she had when he'd first expressed his regret. "You're needed here, Pa. Look what you've done for the families in our community. You've volunteered your time and labor and donated food to those barely fending for themselves with their male kin off fighting or dead. Your deeds are worth more salt than any by those Union generals who came before Ulysses Grant; President Lincoln would agree with that."

"And *I* agree with Jana, Thomas, you're needed here," Ma said. "I won't have *three* of you traipsing about Rebel country."

In Ma's words, Jana caught two subtle and heartening references: She already considered Keeley family based solely on Jana's love for him, and she knew that in the end Jana would have her way to leave with or without her blessing. Still, she coveted her parents' blessing. To secure it, she said, "I think I've proven myself pretty good at getting out of sticky situations, and you can bet I'll be extra cautious about getting into any. I don't relish hanging a second time."

Leanne spoke up. "Don't ya worry, Mr. and Mrs. Brady, Jana ain't goin' it alone. I promise to stick to her flank like a fox chasin' a chicken."

"I know you won't take offense to this, Leanne," Jana said, "but your masculine appearance gives me the same concern about you going south as I have for Pa. It'll be embarrassing for you to have to sort out your gender with either army."

Leanne scanned the area, then lowered her voice to a near whisper. "If I think I'm gonna hold us up or cause us danger, I'll put on a dress. So, like it or not, you're stuck with me."

If Jana wasn't so worried about Keeley, she would've flopped into the bountiful hay in the loft and laughed until she snapped a rib in two.

"Well, what's it gonna be, Jana, are we gonna stand 'round talkin' or git goin'?"

Jana looked to Ma and Pa for their approval.

With a sigh, Ma said, "Try to keep us informed of your whereabouts."

"I promise, Ma." She gave Ma's hand a squeeze. "I'll be full of relief when I bring Keeley home."

Leanne fetched a paper from her saddle bag and waved it about. "Charlie got Preston to draw us a map of Trevilian Station; he marked Keeley's movements from the point of his injury to where he staggered off. So we can give ya a general idea where we'll be searchin'."

*Good ol' Charlie—still watching our backs*, Jana thought, reveling in having such loyal friends.

"Well, what are you waiting for, Jana? Go find your Keeley," Pa said.

"Oh, Ma, Pa, you're the best parents anyone could ever wish for." Jana took turns hugging them. In their arms, she felt Keeley had a fighting chance and, within herself, she felt the bittersweet seed of a new adventure beginning to bud.

# Near Trevilian Station, Virginia

## July 5, 1864

Jana clamped her lips around the rim of her mug, washing its tinny taste down with the coffee Leanne had just finished boiling. Not keen on burning her tongue, she blew on the tarry liquid before she took another sip. The steam sifted through her and, for a moment, she imagined it was the fire of Keeley's love coursing through her vessels to feed her soul. She believed this sustenance could keep her alive for a very long time if she were ever stranded without food. It was the same breadth of love he'd pledged to her, made her long for his kiss, and drove her mad to find him.

Darn the logical side of her brain. It constantly challenged Keeley was still alive; it had good reason to be skeptical. Before she and Leanne had left for Virginia, they'd confirmed through their many contacts Keeley wasn't imprisoned in Richmond, back with his regiment, or amongst the wounded Porter Guards transferred to the Washington hospitals. And after six days of combing the area around where he'd gone missing, they'd yet to find any trace of him. Could it be his spirit was crying out to her for help in giving him a good death, with friends around to properly see him off into the next world? She wasn't ready to surrender to that notion just yet. Not when her intuition told her he was still alive. It would be a cruel twist of fate if she were to stumble upon him lying motionless in the woods—his sparkling emerald eyes, dazzling dimples, and heart dead to her. Would her grief-stricken heart induce her to mortally wound herself as Juliet had when she found Romeo dead? She shook her head to dispel these nightmarish ponderings.

"Are ya all right, Jana?" Leanne asked.

"Yes, thank you." Jana shifted on the knotty log she'd fashioned into a seat and peered at Leanne skittishly when she asked, "Do you believe two people separated by distance or a person and a spirit can transfer thoughts to one another?"

"Whoa!" Leanne nearly toppled off her log. "Ya caught me off guard on that one."

"Well?" Jana said.

"Days before I deserted from the army, I felt my ma cryin' out for help. When I got home, I found out my pa was gittin' more violent with her every day, and she'd been prayin' for my return. And ..." she trailed off. With her short arms fully extended, she began pushing around some burning logs with a long stick to even out the flame beneath the grate for ideal cooking.

"And what, Leanne?"

"Well," she said with a grimace, "I ain't never told nobody this, not even my ma. But it sure would be good to tell somebody."

"I promise not to laugh at you and to keep whatever you tell me a secret, even from Keeley."

"I trust ya on both accounts, not to mention with my life." Jana touched her hand to her heart. "I'm flattered you trust me that much, Leanne. The feeling is mutual."

Continuing to poke at the fire, she said, "It's just plain weird, and I have a hard time understandin' it myself."

To the mysterious edge in her voice, Jana elevated her rump to avoid splinters before moving an inch forward on her log. "Maybe I can help you make sense out of it."

"Well ... when we were in Fredericksburg, and I was assistin' Dr. Walker with amputations, one soldier got it in his head he wasn't gonna live through his surgery. Before he'd let us knock him out with chloroform, he made me promise I'd write his wife 'bout his fate. As he'd reckoned, he died right on the operating table. And I swear"—she gulped—"I saw his spirit rise from his body. It pinned me under a stare before it disappeared. I know that dead soldier was holdin' me to my promise."

"And did you keep it?"

"Dr. Walker promised to do it for me 'cause we got sent back to our regiment before I could. For a few days after that soldier died, I felt him hangin' 'round me, badgerin' me to send his letter. Then, one day, he up and disappeared, and I ain't felt him since. I'm guessin' it's 'cause Dr. Walker finally sent the letter, allowin' his spirit to pass on to eternity."

"Too bad I didn't know about your experience sooner, I could've asked Dr. Walker while we were together at Castle Thunder Prison if she remembered sending the letter and when, so we could pinpoint if the spirit disappeared around the same time," Jana said.

"Anyway, is that what ya meant by yer question?"

"Yes. I feel Keeley hovering about me, badgering me to take some kind of action on his behalf, and it seems he's sticking around too until I do." She slumped under the weight of her gloom, which was trying to crack her like Leanne had just done to the eggs she dropped into the iron pan alongside some frying bacon.

"Now, don't go thinkin' he's dead 'cause of my experience. Ya yerself said the communicatin' could be between the livin'. I just know we're gonna find him, and he's gonna be all right."

"How do you know that?"

Over the spit of bacon and sputter of eggs, Leanne said, "Why would he die now after all he's lived through? Don't make a lick of sense to me."

"But don't you think by now all of our inquiries around this area would've drawn him out if he's in hiding or at least encouraged someone who's hiding him to come forward?"

"Nah." She flipped a slice of bread toasting on the grate and eggs and bacon from the fry pan onto a tin plate, then passed it to Jana. "There's lots of space between farms, and folks 'round here are too busy mindin' their work to go 'round gossipin' 'bout our snoopin'. We've got a lot more ground to cover—eat up so we can git to it."

Leanne's confidence sifted through Jana, and she suddenly felt the deep pockets in her stomach that needed filling. With renewed vigor, she gobbled up her breakfast.

"Just like old days 'round the campfire with our messmates, huh, Johnnie?" Leanne said with a grin.

"Not quite, Leander," Jana said, returning a grin. "The food was never this tasty." She licked her fork clean. "Thanks for all of your good cooking."

"Thanks for doin' the dishes." Leanne rose from the campfire and stretched. "I'd rather be cookin' any day."

Despite the stress of their mission, the days spent with Leanne resurrected some of the camaraderie Jana missed between her, Leanne, Keeley, and Charlie during their days in the cavalry guarding posts on the lookout for messengers, deserters, or Rebels; scouting the strength and position of enemy troops; foraging for food; and sitting around the campfire. It was a loneliness that could only be filled with Keeley back in her life full time. Eager to get on with their search, she carted the dishes, herself, and her clothes to Nunn's Creek for washing. She had no qualms about living in nature once again—without the modern conveniences of an artesian well, washboard, and clothesline—as long as the creeks didn't dry up and come between her and clean clothes so she wouldn't be steeped in the aroma of campfire, which left her smelling more cured than a slab of pork in a smokehouse.

Leanne doused the fire with sand and went to bathe while Jana watered and fed the mule its oats. Together, they packed the wagon, then Leanne fetched her knapsack from beneath the wagon bench and from it the crude map around Trevilian Station that Noble Preston had sketched for them. Unfurling and flattening it out against the wagon's sideboards, she and Jana pinned it beneath each of their hands.

With her index finger, Jana outlined the shape of an elf's shoe: Starting at its softly rounded tip at Louisa Court House, she traced north along the Marquis Road, southwest along Nunn's Creek Road, and east along the Gordonsville Road back to Louisa Court House. "We've pretty much exhausted the entire area within our shoe—where the Tenth joined the action on the first day and near where Keeley was wounded and left the scene. Don't you think?"

"Yup, I do," Leanne said with a click of her cheek.

"Since farther up the Marquis Road is where General Custer was battling with Major General Fitzhugh Lee, it would make sense that Keeley would've strayed as far from there as his wound would permit."

"Maybe he went back to Clayton's Store thinkin' our Porter Guards would retreat to where they encamped the night before—only they never did."

"Exactly my thought, so we'll concentrate our efforts along the Marquis Road, north of where it intersects with Nunn's Creek Road."

With their route charted, they broke camp.

Leanne cracked the whip in the air over the mule's tannish-gray hide and set it into a trot. While the wagon wheels churned up a tornado of dust that obscured the Marquis Road behind them, the mule's hoofs kicked up a hail of sand and grit that threatened to plug their pores, cake their nostrils, and leave a clayish aftertaste on their tongues. They armored their faces with handkerchiefs to better weather the storm, but Jana felt sorry for the leafy trees all around them—their only defense was in the upward turn of their veined palms to petition the sky for a drenching rain and hearty drink.

Removing her straw hat and waving it before her sweaty face, Jana fanned the aroma of burning hickory through her handkerchief. "Do you smell that?"

Leanne lifted her handkerchief away from her nose and sniffed. "Yup," she said, pointing to wisps of smoke drifting out of the woods along a well-beaten path, wide enough to accommodate a stagecoach. Steering left into it, she slowed the mule to a cautious advance.

The cooler temperature beneath the dense canopy of leaf-and-needled trees lasted a short duration before they rolled back into the merciless rays of the sun and a clearing that supported a small, tidy farm. A woman about Ma's age, with coal black strands of hair run amuck from the netted bun at the nape of her neck, nearly tripped over the hem of her faded skirt as she sped down the steps of a white frame house to tend to the contents within a cauldron suspended over high flames.

"She seems to be faking being distracted, don't you think?" Jana said.

"Yup. The racket we're makin' should've nabbed her attention by now."

When they stopped the wagon before her, she kept her eyes to her laundry, stirring it around with a wooden paddle. Gilt buttons attached to the wool of an army-issued shell coat peeked over the bubbles of the soapy brew.

It put Jana on guard, and she wondered if this woman might be harboring a soldier. Though, even in its saturated state, the wool seemed awfully dark for it to be the light gray of a Confederate uniform.

Finally, the laundress spoke. "If y'all are here to forage food *too* now, I've given all I have to the last *two* with none left to feed myself."

The tremor in her voice, her words spoken in the present tense, and her emphasis of *too* and *two* were clues she had unwanted company—probably soldiers who'd deserted. "We've come to inquire if you've seen or tended to our friend, a Union cavalryman who's gone missing," Jana said while she discreetly skimmed the property for the perpetrators.

With a pleading in her whiskey-colored eyes and a subtle backward nod of her head toward the house, she said, "I've neither seen nor tended to any such Yankee. And I don't take kindly to trespassers, so I'd be moving along if I were y'all."

The sun glanced off the barrel of a rifle, which had parted the curtains of a second-story window and was aimed their way. Surreptitiously poking her elbow into Leanne's bicep, Jana directed her eyes there.

Leanne must've also detected the movement because she jabbed Jana back, then addressed the woman. "Sorry to bother ya, ma'am, we'll be on our way." Taking up the reins, she coaxed the mule around and headed out the wooded drive. Well beyond earshot, she said, "We're gonna help her, ain't we?"

"You bet," Jana said, conducting Leanne to a spot in the woods perfect for hiding their wagon and mule.

Earnest as a barn cat about to pounce on a mouse and bat it around until she grew bored, Leanne said, "Git yer arms. Something tells me we're gonna need 'em."

*If Leanne doesn't pass out from the heat, her fervor for a fight will get her,* Jana mused as she strapped on her waist belt with the new Colt she'd bought before they left Elmira holstered to it. Then she fetched her rifle from the wagon bed.

They deferred any plan of action until they could get a better grasp of the situation and how the surroundings could work to their favor. In doubling back to the farm, they flopped on their bellies in the scrubs fringing the woods. The matron had abandoned her laundry and was nowhere to be seen, so they settled in to watch.

Leanne broke their silence. "What if we were s'posed to see that gun in the window?"

"What do you mean?"

"We've made it plain we're from the North. Maybe her kin was killed in the war, and she's got a vendetta against all of us Yanks. So she's makin' us think she's in trouble when she's really lurin' us back there to kill us—just what the witch tried to do to Hansel and Gretel with her house made of sweets."

Sniggering at Leanne's amusing analogy, Jana said, "I thought you didn't like to read."

"I don't—doesn't mean I don't read or don't like to be read to. My ma used to read to me. She hated that fairy tale, but my pa made her read it to me 'cause he said it'd teach me not to trust nobody." Leanne grunted. "Guess he never reckoned I'd use his own advice against him."

Jana eyed her squarely. "Did you ever think that when your pa was sober and still being mean, he might've been trying to chase you and your ma away so that when he got drunk he couldn't abuse either of you anymore?"

"Nope. I never gave it a thought, and I don't reckon I ever will," Leanne said, though her hard stare hinted she might be intrigued by Jana's theory.

"Well, your pa's right about one thing: People aren't always trustworthy, and our damsel in distress might've sent us away long enough to gather reinforcements for help in our capture—or worse, as you suggested."

"I ain't gonna be hanged, and I promised yer pa I'd make sure ya never came close to it agin."

Jana shuddered to her vision of a scratchy noose around her neck again, only this time with the other end barbarically tied around the limb of a tree. It prompted her to say, "We'll proceed with caution before we—"

*Crash!* The farmhouse door slinging open against the exterior wall cut her off. Two soldiers, clad in tattered navy blue shell jackets with yellow trim and sky blue trousers with padding in the britches, stomped across the porch. On their heels was the woman farmer wringing her hands and wailing, "Please, don't take my chickens. My cupboards are bare from all I've fed y'all. My husband's dead in this horrible war, and I'm all alone to work this old farm."

Leanne whirled toward Jana, her jaw muscles knotted tight. "The bad guys are Yankee cavalrymen," she growled, then started up off the ground.

Holding her down by the coat sleeve, Jana said, "I'm just as outraged as you are, Leanne, but my pa taught me danger's got to be handled in a calm—not rash—way. We'll do no good for the poor widow if we go racing in there hotheaded and get ourselves hurt or killed."

The thieves continued to cross the yard, unsympathetic to the woman's impoverished state.

Gathering her skirt up to her ankles, the homesteader bolted to the lead and threw herself in front of the henhouse door.

The stubbier of the Yankee plunderers shoved her aside, paving the way for his stick-figured accomplice to enter the building.

"I don't think there's any actin' goin' on here, do ya?" Leanne said.

"I'd wager a gold twenty-dollar double eagle you're—"

Leanne interjected, "Who's that slitherin' through the grass behind the henhouse? And what's he gonna do with a pitchfork?"

"By his garb, I'd say he's a neighboring farmer come to the rescue."

"Let's go show him he's got backup before he gits himself shot."

Twigs snapped underfoot as Leanne and Jana tramped across them, catching the attention of the farmer. They ducked behind a wide white oak just in time to avoid his detection. With his face pointed their way, they gasped in unison. "It's Keeley!" Leanne said.

Jana wanted to leap out of the woods and into his arms and hug and kiss him madly, but Leanne held her back with her outbreak of questions: "What's he doin' here? Why's he dressed that way? Why hasn't he contacted ya?" And for the second time that day, Jana's brain posed another disturbing notion about Keeley that punched her in the gut: *Maybe he's changed his mind about me and he's found a better future for himself here.*

A cacophony of clucking snatched Jana from her speculation. Out of the henhouse tore Stick, carrying a hen upside down by its legs. The domestic bird flailed its wings in a frenzy trying to free itself from its captor's hands. In one swift move, Stick unsheathed the knife hanging from his gun belt and swiped it across the hen's throat. The head bounced off the red-clay earth with a splatter of blood, and more blood poured from the neck. Stick stood mesmerized by his handiwork while Stub chased down a rooster, sneaking off toward the woodshed.

The woman farmer shot ahead of Stub, waving her arms at the cock to shoo him away.

"I've had enough," Leanne said.

"Me too. Let's team up with Keeley to exterminate those louses."

The words were barely out of Jana's mouth when Leanne took off in a sprint.

Following close on her heels, Jana warned herself to put the widow's concerns above any pain that might root from her reunion with Keeley—lest it be a distraction to her that got Leanne, Keeley, or herself hurt or killed.

Keeley jerked around to Jana and Leanne's noisy swoosh through the tall grass. Crouching in a defensive posture, he raised his pitchfork at them.

"He acts like he doesn't know us," Leanne muttered as they came to a halt before him.

Jana stepped around Leanne, her instincts telling her to keep her distance from the sharp tines of his weapon. "Keeley, it's me, Jana"—she pointed her thumb over her shoulder—"and she's Leanne. We're your friends."

"Ye know meself?" he said, the sparkle in his emerald eyes dead to her in a manner that made Jana feel foreign to him.

She opened her mouth to reply, but her voice box froze up. It took her mind a full minute to process the revelation he had amnesia and come to appreciate he was alive and well and hadn't voluntarily given up on their love. The ice began to melt around Jana's voice box; as she attempted a reply, she was halted by the amplified shrieks from the widow, who was pleading with her perpetrators to go away.

Having obviously come to terms with Keeley's predicament faster than Jana, Leanne hastened to say to Keeley, "Ain't no time to explain things. Yer friend's in a real pickle and needs us. For now, you're gonna have to trust we're yer friends, and we're here to help ya rid of those thievin' vermin."

Keeley relaxed his stance and white-knuckled grip on his pitchfork.

While Leanne had been putting Keeley at ease, Jana had devised a plan, and she huddled up with them to outline it. Then she nodded at Keeley's pitchfork and said, "You're going to need something more convincing than that for our assault." Relinquishing her rifle and extra cartridges to him, she drew her revolver, and Leanne discarded her rifle in favor of her six-shooter.

"Thanks, lass," he said with a grin that brought out his seductive power.

*Not now,* Jana thought, looking away to avoid falling under his spell and becoming useless to the widow. She pointed to their positions and took off to set up at the back corner of the henhouse opposite Leanne and Keeley. Holding up her hand high enough for them to see her middling fingers, she counted out three on them. Then they stormed into the barnyard, firing skyward as they went with a *pop, pop* of Jana's and Leanne's pistols and a *crack* from Keeley's rifle.

Stopping dead in their tracks, Stick and Stub crossed their arms over their heads to dodge the rain of bullets.

The widow started to collapse to the ground and, with Jana and Leanne covering him, Keeley darted to her side and caught her in his arms. "Are ye all right?" he asked.

"I am now, my dear friend," she said, reaching her hand up to pinch his cheek.

Keeley made sure she was steady on her feet before he released her.

Taking a few steps toward the crooks, Leanne snarled, "Drop yer knives and pistols and kick 'em to me before I git trigger happy."

They hesitated, and Leanne emptied two bullets—one between Stick's feet, the other before Stub's toes, which poked through his holey sock and knee-shaft boot. The dirt exploded where the projectiles entered and drilled their way into the ground. This time, the scoundrels scrambled to obey Leanne.

When she had their full attention again, Leanne said, "I *really* hate bullies, 'specially those who pick on defenseless women and take advantage of their kindness. Thanks to ya two, I'm ashamed to call myself a Yankee." Unsheathing her knife from the left side of her waist belt, she flashed its sharp blade. "And I'm *really* considerin' slicin' yer throats to even the score for yer murderin' the hen."

The bandits stood stiller than the barn behind them.

"I'm thinkin' ya men are deserters, and now you've just added thievin' and assault to yer lawbreakin'. The way I see it, we've got three things we can do with ya: Deliver ya to the Rebels for 'em to lock ya away in their rat-infested prisons where you'll probably die or deliver ya to the Yankees for 'em to put ya before a firin' squad for yer multiple war crimes."

With his face blanched whiter than a ghost's, Stick stammered, "You ... you said three things."

Stub, whose eyes were large with fright, bobbed his head.

"Oh, yeah. We'll give ya a head start out of here before we offer ya up to the locals, who're salivatin' to hang one Yankee for all the others' sins against 'em." Leanne swept her eyes toward the headless body of the hen and licked her lips. "But ... I'm feelin' charitable since you've done the ugliest part of preparin' our supper tonight, and I'm leanin' toward the third choice. What d'ya think?"

Raising their grubby hands in surrender, Stick and Stub began slinking backward, then they reeled about and skedaddled into the woods.

"You were brilliant, Leanne," Jana said.

"Glad ya approve," she said, blowing on the end of her smoking barrel before she holstered her revolver.

Jana said to the matron, "You can rest assured they'll never come back."

Swiping the back of her hand across her sweaty forehead, the widow said to Keeley, "We sure got lucky when these two happened along, didn't we?"

"Aye, I wasn't sure how I meself was going to take care o' those brutes with only a pitchfork."

The woman farmer swept Jana and Leanne up in her look of relief. "I'm sorry I couldn't tell y'all earlier that I was harboring a Yankee. I tremble to think what those two rogues would've done to my houseguest if they knew he was with me."

"How did he escape their notice?" Jana asked.

"He hid in a secret room off our attic, where my husband and I used to hide escaping slaves."

"When I heard me benefactress's cries"—Keeley's muscled shoulders cringed—"I sneaked out o' the house and through the woods to where ye came upon meself."

Narrowing her puzzled eyes on Keeley's hostess, Leanne said, "Ya helped slaves escape?"

She nodded. "Like me and my husband, most Virginians don't own slaves to help till their land, and they oppose slavery and secession. But ... for the same reason General Lee chose to lead the Confederate army, most Virginians don't want interference from the federal government when deciding upon matters that make our beloved Commonwealth unique to other states. And I must qualify, as my newfound friend here can confirm, we have former slaves living and working on our farm."

"Ain't that ... er ... uh ..."

The Southern abolitionist finished Leanne's query. "Hypocritical?" She chortled. "It does sound that way, doesn't it? After their master was killed in battle, their mistress decided to move back with her family in Philadelphia, so she freed them. Besides their manumission papers, she gave them any records, such as their bill of sale, that might help link them to long lost relatives. Isaiah, Jess, and their two children sought food and a day's rest with us on their journey north, and my husband and I befriended the weary travelers. With our two grown sons off to war and adamant about settling elsewhere afterward, my husband and I agreed that we had more land than we could manage ourselves, so we offered Isaiah and Jess a parcel on which to build their home and a share in the sale of our profits in exchange for their help. They've been with us for over three years now, and they're content with their new lives and grateful for our protection from greedy slave catchers who can still round them up, burn their freedom papers, and resell them into slavery—a lingering threat while the Confederacy disavows that Lincoln's Emancipation Proclamation has freed the slaves in the states and territories hostile to the Union."

"Aren't they afraid of the Commonwealth law that decrees a freed slave has a year to leave Virginia or face re-enslavement?" Jana's knowledge of this came from Miss Lizzie, her mentor in spying who'd protected her slaves from re-enslavement by freeing them only verbally so there would be no file with the state government. When no one was watching, she treated them as equals. It endeared them to her enough that they risked their lives to help her spy on the Confederacy.

"I've hidden their manumission papers and other records where no one will find them; by all appearances, they are my slaves until the law changes."

"Where're Isaiah, Jess, and their young'uns now?" Leanne asked, scanning their perimeter as if she expected them to come popping out of one of the buildings or the woods.

"They escaped with me over the North Anna River to my sister's farm just before the battle around Trevilian Station erupted. After the armies cleared out, I left Isaiah and Jess behind to help my sister close her farm. Then they'll bring her here to live with me until our husbands return from the war. I figured I could get along all by myself for a short duration with my neighbors' help."

"Yer husband? Didn't ya tell those rascals he got killed in the war?" Leanne said.

"I'm not superstitious," Keeley's patron said, "but I dread lying about matters that could come true. It just spewed out of my mouth—a subconscious attempt to get those two villains to have mercy on me. As y'all saw, it fell on deaf ears."

Sensing her discomfort, Jana abruptly changed the subject. "How long has Keeley been here with you?"

She cast her guest an admiring glance. "Ah, so that's our Irishman's name."

"His full name's Keeley Cassidy," Leanne said.

While they watched him mouth his name over and over again in an attempt to jar loose some nugget of recall from his brain, the matron returned to Jana's question. "He's been here since I found him holed up in my hayloft when I returned from my sister's homestead a few days after the battle. I knew he was Union by the color of his uniform, cavalry by the crossed sabers on his kepi, and a casualty—rather than a deserter—by his inability to remember anything."

It dawned on Jana that the uniform she and Leanne had seen her laundering earlier must belong to Keeley. "Besides his amnesia, did he suffer any other injury?"

"Just the bump and bruise in the outline of a rifle butt on the side of his head," the matron said. "May I ask who y'all are and how y'all know Keeley?"

"I'm Jana Brady and she's Leanne Perham; we're both from Elmira, New York," Jana said, hoping the reference to her hometown would joggle Keeley's memory since he loved it there, but he remained unmoved. "We're Keeley's cavalry comrades; we fought alongside him disguised as men." She was elated when Keeley didn't flinch at the news. It was a good sign he might be recalling some of the principles ingrained in him, especially—she hoped—the one subscribing to a woman's being able to tackle anything a man can if she has a mind to it.

The middle-aged woman snapped her fingers. "Two real-life Deborah Sampsons—no wonder y'all made quick work of disarming those rogues."

To Leanne's befuddlement, Jana explained how Deborah Sampson had disguised herself as Robert Shurtliff to fight in the Fourth Massachusetts Regiment during the Revolutionary War, and she later received a pension from the government for her service.

"Well, I'm glad to meet y'all." She protracted her long fingers when she reached out to shake Jana's and Leanne's hands, then she introduced herself as Mrs. Versella Stock Barney. "Please just call me Versella, as Keeley and all of my friends and neighbors do."

Leanne scratched the inside of her ear as if she'd heard wrong and was clearing the wax out of it. "What kind of name's Versella?"

Versella giggled. "I get that reaction all of the time. It's German. My father was of that descent, and he came from good *stock.*" She beamed when Jana and Leanne snickered at her pun. "I get a kick out of saying that," she said.

"Well, we didn't actually introduce ourselves fully," Leanne said. "Jana and Keeley are more than just friends—they're plannin' to git hitched after the war."

With a small upward curve at one corner of his lips, Keeley cocked his head toward Jana. He appeared genuinely intrigued as he gave her a thorough going-over, making Jana blush and her heart flutter.

"Just so you're clear, ya didn't fall in love with Jana thinkin' she was a man," Leanne said. "Ya knew all along Johnnie was a woman, but ya couldn't git the truth out of her. She was afraid if ya knew, you'd tattle on her and git her kicked out of the army, which ya kind of did when she took a bullet in the arm tryin' to save ya from the Rebels at Brandy Station."

"Ye did that for meself, lass?"

"Yes . . . as incredible as it sounds."

"Not after what ye—and o' course Leanne too—did for Versella and meself today," Keeley said.

Jana glued her eyes to the blued steel of her pistol's barrel, afraid to have anyone see her longing to fall into his arms and bask in his tenderness.

Whether intentional or not, Versella intruded upon Jana's yearning. "How about we do as Leanne suggested earlier and roast the hen in a reunion supper?"

"I'll pluck the hen for ya," Leanne offered.

*How can it be a reunion supper when Keeley doesn't know us?* Jana wondered and suddenly realized that Keeley might never come to know them again. What would she do? She felt her mood falling into a chasm of despair, from which she reached up, grabbed the edge, and pulled herself out before she spoiled everyone's celebratory spirit. Keeley was alive and for the most part well. That's all that mattered—at least for now.

## Near Trevilian Station, Virginia

July 5-6, 1864

After a supper of roasted hen, candied carrots, and gravy over biscuits, Versella shooed Jana and Keeley into the sitting room to get reacquainted. Leanne would help her clean the kitchen and prepare dessert.

Seated opposite Keeley, Jana wished the rectangular sofa table was the only thing coming between them. The long, stifling silence bewildered Jana, and she felt a great sadness envelop her; their hearts no longer beat as one, and she wondered if they ever would again. How could she converse with someone who remembered nothing? And who could fault him for withdrawing into himself while he digested what he'd learned at the dinner table? Versella had encouraged Jana and Leanne to tell all about themselves, Keeley, and their time together in uniform in hopes of rousing his memory. Now, his incessant staring at her preyed upon Jana's nerves more than the quiet. Was he wondering how he could've become entangled with a woman who'd want to dress as a man and wield a gun and saber in a war? The temperature in the room rose a degree with each minute that passed under his scrutiny. When she imagined the perspiration streaming down her back overwatering and killing the flowers embroidered into her armchair, she bust out in a nervous giggle.

"What's so funny, lass?"

"Oh, I doubt you'd find it funny," she said but thought, *The old Keeley would; I'm not sure if the new one will.*

"Try meself."

*Why not?* Jana thought. *It'll be a good test to see if he still appreciates my silliness.*

She took the plunge, omitting to tell him that his nerve-wracking inspection of her was compounding her overheated state.

He extracted a handkerchief from the pocket of his flannel shirt and wiped the sheen from his forehead. Gleaming as devilishly as a leprechaun wreaking mischief, he said, "If ye could overwater the flowers, I could flood the room."

Their merriment evaporated the tension between them, along with some of Jana's moisture.

"Seriously, lass, I have a feeling me staring ye down is adding to yar discomfort."

Jana's lips parted in surprise. They'd always been able to read each other, and she wondered if this sensitivity to her was his love beginning to dig its way out.

He followed it up with, "Y'are beautiful, brave, and smart—it's hard to believe *I* snagged yar attention."

With her body temperature rising again to the heat of her flush, Jana welcomed the small breeze that made the lacey curtains pirouette. Her relief and Keeley's words emboldened her to ask, "How exactly do you feel about me having disguised myself as a man to fight in the war? Please ... be honest. It's important." She had to know where he stood—if he disrespected her for it, and he never recaptured his memory, it would be a battle to win back his love. She held her breath, waiting for his reply.

Keeley's answer tumbled out over his pencil-thin lips with conviction. "I admire ye for it, lass." The crow's feet at the corners of his eyes multiplied to his smile. "If I didn't admire ye for it, how could I have fallen in love with ye while ye were in uniform?"

Jana exhaled with relief, and his declaration emboldened her more. "Now that you know of our vow to marry, how do you think you and I should proceed?"

Leaning his sturdy torso slightly toward her, he planted his forearms on his thighs and clasped his muscled hands together. "Well, it seems y'are the strongest link in the chain to bringing back me memory. If I may be so bold to say, it would be advantageous for meself to be around ye for a while ... unless y'are uncomfortable with that."

Jana's heart lifted, and she wanted to spin and swirl about the room. Warbling with excitement she didn't even try to squelch, she said, "I'm very comfortable with that, and I know my ma and pa will be too."

"I don't mean for ye to think I'm inviting meself into yar home—I could find other accommodations near ye."

"My ma and pa are expecting me to bring you home, and I think that's the best place for you while you recuperate." She was thrilled he'd want to go home with her because she couldn't picture him anywhere else but by her side.

He scratched his head. "I don't want to be a burden."

"You won't be a burden." She longed to smooth the coarse strands of his coppery hair that he'd displaced; instead, she tucked a limp strand of her own auburn tresses behind her ear. "It was our plan after the war ended to build our lives together on my ma and pa's farm. We won't be doing that until we sort things out..." Jana trailed off to the depressing notion they might never sort things out. She quickly picked back up, saying, "My pa would love to have another man around the house, and you could pay your way by helping with the chores."

He hooked up an eyebrow. "Why would yar pa love to have another man about the house? Are ye an only child?"

She laughed. "Actually, you might want to reconsider my offer when you learn I'm the eldest of five sisters. If you think you can handle being in constant companionship with six females, including my ma, then we've struck a bargain."

"Aye, we've struck a bargain." He reached out his calloused hand to shake hers and said, "I don't relish meself being homeless on the streets o' New York City again, and I can't see meself hauling oysters upriver the rest o' me life."

She gasped and covered her mouth with her hand.

"Have I said something wrong, lass?"

Her pitch crescendoed. "Yes...er...I mean no. You remembered being homeless in New York City and your livelihood."

"Aye, because ye and Leanne told meself as much."

"No, we said you lived in New York City, but not that you were homeless, and we said your work brought you to Elmira, but not what you did."

"Aye, y'are right," he said, gazing toward the open window as if he expected further revelations to come flying in.

They fell into a more comfortable silence, which was intruded upon only by scattered orchestras of male cicadas competing against each other to be most melodic. Their interminable drudgery plucked Jana's heartstrings—she knew she was about to embark upon a similar journey to bring harmony back to her and Keeley's relationship. The greatest hope was in his willingness to try. Aloud, she thought, "There's hope yet."

"Hope yet for what, dear?" Versella asked, appearing out of nowhere with Leanne lagging behind.

"For Keeley getting his memory back," Jana said, then described Keeley's minor breakthrough.

Placing her tray on the sofa table, Versella settled herself on the couch next to Keeley. "Hallelujah! Let's celebrate with some pie."

The aroma of sugared peaches baked between two flaky crusts further buoyed Jana's spirit, but it tormented her taste buds when she felt compelled to turn down the slice Versella held out for her.

"Take it," she said. "One can never be too full for sweets."

"It's not that," Jana said. "You've been so kind and generous I'd hate to think we're eating you out of house and home, especially with the extra mouths you'll have to feed soon."

Versella laughed merrily. "Don't y'all worry about me. I've got plenty of food."

"But you told those thieves today they'd taken all of your food. And how are you thriving when the rest of the South is starving?" Jana said.

"That was all an act." Versella set the plate on the table and slid it toward Jana. "I'll just bet y'all will gobble your pie down when you hear my story." Reclining back into her sofa of russet and white stripes, she explained, "My Harold used to tease me that I spent too much time thinking ahead until I drilled it into his skull how much I despise being taken by surprise. I imagine the worst scenario and prepare for it." She grimaced. "Though these days, I seem to be putting out fires more. Anyway, after the first shots were exchanged at Fort Sumter, I imagined a long war with all of the land between the Union and Confederate capitals as the battlefield and two armies tramping all over it pillaging our food. I sold my neighbors on my prophecy and, so far, neither army has been smart enough to figure out that we're all using a few of our chickens and livestock and our smaller vegetable gardens as decoys to keep them from discovering our greater stocks nestled in the woods. We also have preserved fruits and vegetables and sacks of flour hidden in secret cellars beneath the floorboards in our barns."

"Aye, I can attest to her bountiful stores," Keeley said.

So preoccupied by his memory loss since they'd found him, Jana just noticed Keeley was the fittest she'd ever seen him—further proof Versella wasn't sacrificing anything. Jana's watering taste buds thanked her when she finally picked up the pastry and sampled a bite. It rivaled Ma's award-winning apple pie.

"How come ya look like you're starvin', then, Versella?" Leanne said, her words garbled by a mouthful of pie.

Versella giggled and patted the hollows of her cheeks. "Oh, that. I've always been thin, and it's exacerbated with the heat and extra tilling I do with my Harold away. Thanks to Keeley's help on the farm, I've rested more and fattened up some." She cast her eyes toward Keeley, and they glazed over with sorrow. "I'm sure going to miss our Irishman. However, I'm glad he's got y'all to watch over him."

Worried about leaving Versella alone, Jana said, "We'll stick around until your family comes."

"Nonsense, they'll be here tomorrow, I'm sure. If not, I'll be all right. What are the chances there are any more stragglers around to hassle me? Now, don't y'all fret. If I feel I'm in any real danger, I'll skedaddle to one of my neighbors. I worry more about the risk y'all are taking being here. I can't imagine my being able to successfully hide three of you from any scouts, so I think it's best if y'all were on your way tomorrow"—she winked—"before y'all eat me out of house and home."

The foursome joined in laughter, which came to a halt when Leanne's merriment abruptly abated.

To the alarm clouding her face and amplifying her voice, Leanne said, "With or without yer family here, Versella, ya need to git a dog that'll warn ya when trouble's brewin' so you've got plenty of time to run away from some vermin figurin' to harm ya or so ya can git into a defensive position with yer rifle ready."

Jana found it incredible how quickly Leanne's small voice and features could explode with big emotion when she feared for another's safety.

Versella alleged to know a neighbor who could probably part with at least one of his many hounds, and she promised to pay him a visit tomorrow. "Now, that's what I call planning ahead," she said with a clap of her hands. "Speaking of which, we need to plot your journey home. It's dangerous enough for two women to be traipsing about the countryside, but a man, seemingly fit and of conscription age, is bound to draw the attention of both armies."

Keeley frowned and straightened on the couch, all mirth disappearing from his face. "I can't go back to Elmira just yet. I need to report in to me regiment so they know me fate."

Addressing Jana and Leanne, Versella said, "Where's his regiment now? Is it fighting with General Grant around Petersburg or in the Shenandoah Valley?"

"Probably with Grant 'cause last we knew our regiment retreated from here back to White House, where our other friend or"—Leanne cleared her throat—"my brother's a hospital steward."

Shifting to the edge of her cushion, Versella said, "Why that's got to be at least fifty miles southeast of here, not far from Richmond. Y'all aren't considering going there, are y'all? Keeley especially will risk being caught by Southern scouts and imprisoned again."

Keeley's jaw set firm. "It's a matter o' me honor; I won't be labeled a deserter."

He'd need someone as a compass back to the regiment, and Jana wasn't letting him out of her sight until they arrived home. "Are you up for a trip to White House, Leanne?"

"Yup. I'd like to see Charlie and make sure he's doin' all right."

The four of them back together again just might joggle Keeley's memory. And Jana figured it would be advantageous for Keeley to be examined by the very competent Dr. Pease, who could render him a discharge and prognosis for his amnesia.

Sighing with resignation, Versella returned to the solace of her cushion back and said, "If it comes to being stopped by either army, y'all will have to do some great acting. Jana can easily fake a Southern belle." Her eyes homed in on Keeley and Leanne. "But we'll need better disguises for y'all."

"I've gotten along this far just as I am," Leanne said, peeling back her men's shirtsleeves and picking pie crumbs off of her denim trousers.

Versella's tone took on an uncharacteristic sternness when she said, "For all of your sakes, Leanne, there are too many dangers in being stopped at all. From afar, it'll appear as though Jana's traveling with two men of conscription age. Keeley can't afford anyone getting a good long look at him." With her eyes blinking in cadence to the tapping of her fingertips against the sofa's armrest, she fell deep in thought. Finally, she lifted her head and fixated on Leanne. "We could dress y'all in some of the suits I kept from my sons' younger years. It might be a stretch, but y'all could act as Jana's son."

"I can do that," Leanne said, her cheeks glowing brighter than the chimney lamps, which Keeley had turned up awhile back at dusk.

To Leanne's favorable reaction, Versella said, "Very well." Then she turned to Keeley. "As for you, y'all can't go parading around the South in a Yankee uniform—or even as a civilian. Amnesia won't be an excuse to keep y'all out of prison." She grimaced. "I'm afraid I only see one possibility for y'all."

Certain they were thinking alike, Jana said, "To dress as a lass."

Versella nodded.

With a clatter, Keeley dropped his cup onto its saucer. Incredibly, not a drop spilled from the wobbling cup, which eventually righted itself. "Y'are suggesting I wear a skirt? Ye can't be serious."

"You won't have to play the role for too long," Jana said. "We should be within Union lines in four days; to save you from any embarrassment, you can change into your uniform right before we reach White House."

Keeley crossed his arms over his chest in defiance.

To prod him along, Jana said, "We'll never ever tell a soul about it, right, Leanne?"

"Ya can count on me."

"If we run into any soldiers, I'll do all of the talking and, if necessary, declare you mute," Jana said.

"Splendid idea, Jana," Versella said and slapped her armrest. "It's all set. I feel better about y'all's leaving."

With them ganging up on him, Keeley slouched into his sofa cushion. "I don't pretend to like it, but I'll do what it takes to keep us all safe."

That was the Keeley Jana knew and loved!

Before dawn flung out its first flares, Jana slipped from the cozy feather mattress in one of Versella's upstairs chambers. She used the sponge, cake of soap, and basin of cool water on the bedside table to bathe. After donning her blouse and skirt, she followed the smell of frying eggs, cured ham, and the good coffee from last night down the hall. She reached the top of the staircase at the same time as Leanne whose transformation as Jana's son was complete in the white dress shirt, loose trousers held up by suspenders, and waist-length jacket with only one button at the top—her entire costume acquired circuitously from Versella's son. Her hair, which she continued to keep cropped up to her ears, rounded out her masculine appearance.

Leanne removed her soft cap by its short visor and waved it toward the stairs. "After ya, Ma," she said, obviously at home in a boy's britches.

Laughing all the way down to the kitchen, Jana and Leanne skidded to a stop at the sight of a strange woman seated at the large farmhouse table.

*That's odd*, Jana thought, *I didn't hear a wagon pull up, and Versella's guest is still wearing her riding gloves and bonnet.*

To their noisy entrance into the kitchen, Versella whirled around from her cookstove. "Good morning, Jana, Leanne. Y'all come meet my sister, Iva."

Iva peeled her face away from her steaming mug of coffee, squinting at them with pitiable emerald eyes that dared them to laugh at her.

Jana's and Leanne's mouths gaped in surprise.

"If ye don't want flies in yar mouths, ye might want to be closing them," Keeley said.

Leanne bit down on her lip to smother her laughter while Jana tried to allay his embarrassment by saying, "It's for the best, Keeley."

"He makes a handsome woman, don't y'all think?" Versella said, proud of her handiwork.

Keeley scowled. "I don't pretend to be enjoying this at all."

Taking her seat at the table across from Keeley, Jana said, "Have you lost your sense of adventure along with your memory?"

"There's a fine line between adventure and the absurd, lass. I'll face a firing squad before I'm ever cowed into this again."

Plopping down in the ladder-back chair beside Keeley, Leanne drew a glower from him when she began gobbling down the food set before her and nearly choked on a bite of ham as she strained to hold back her laughter.

"Well, now that y'all know Keeley isn't really my sister, why don't we come up with a name for his disguise that's better suited for him?" Versella suggested.

"In coming up with cavalry names for us," Jana said, "Leanne felt it was best to use a name that sounded close to ours so we'd answer to it right off."

Leanne snapped her finger. "How 'bout Kelly? Kelly Cassidy?"

"Perfect!" Versella said as she pumped water from her indoor well for brewing more coffee.

Keeley frowned.

After the dishes were cleaned and stowed away in her cupboards, Versella presented them with a small wooden box. She swung open its top and swept them all up in her somber eyes. "I trust y'all are wondering what I'm doing with this remarkable quantity of morphine. Well, I'm an agent in its smuggling between Washington and Richmond. I hope y'all will forgive me for wanting to provide comfort to our wounded."

"I'd do the same for ours," Jana said.

"I meself am glad for yar part in it. How else would ye have eased me headaches in those first few days after ye found meself?"

"Ya can trust us, Versella. We ain't ever gonna rat on ya," Leanne said.

"Well, this is going to get y'all out of a pickle," Versella said. "The South scarcely has any, and the North is probably short on it. Should y'all be stopped by either side, y'all will use it as a front, contending that y'all are bringing it to their respective field hospitals."

The prospect of another clandestine operation between her and Keeley sent nervous tingles up and down Jana's spine. Even though the last caper had been well planned, it still went awry when a simple little hug between them whacked traitorous materials against the Confederacy from her grip and nearly ended with her hanging.

Having heard the details of that fluke last night and, now seeming to read her mind, Keeley leaned toward Jana with a provocative twinkle in his eyes and said, "Don't worry, lass, we won't be botching this quest. There's no prospect o' our hugging with Leanne sitting between us."

It might be hanging by a thread, but Jana was convinced the remnants of the bond they'd shared before his amnesia still lived on inside Keeley and were just waiting to burst out.

In the front yard, they all took turns hugging Versella good-bye. Keeley was the last to board the wagon. Unused to a skirt about his feet, the toe of his boot caught in the hem, and he tripped up the step.

Leanne reached down and, with a playful grin, said, "Let me help ya up, Kelly."

As Keeley's cheeks reddened, Jana frowned at Leanne, warning her it would do no good to ruffle Keeley's feathers any further; they needed him to embrace his disguise to avoid endangering their lives.

Versella clung to the wall of the wagon bed, her eyes welling with tears. "When this war's over and it's safe, I hope y'all will return for a more peaceful visit. I'd be proud to introduce y'all to my family and show them that"—she summoned up a smile and a wink—"not all Yanks are bad."

Taking up the long leather straps, Jana steered the mule and wagon around, turning their backs on their hostess and the searing morning sun. Leave it to

Versella to think of everything—she'd suggested Jana handle the reins because the driver was usually the target of any interrogation and the less attention paid to Keeley the better.

Shortly after crossing the sluggish North Anna River, Jana, Leanne, and Keeley journeyed a little out of their way to Iva's farm to alert her, Isaiah, and Jess that Versella was all alone. They found the farmhouse boarded up with a note tacked to the door, indicating they'd left that morning. Having passed no other travelers, the trio assumed they'd taken a side road, perhaps to inform a neighbor of their departure. Either way, they were relieved to know Versella would be in the company of her family that day. It put them all in good spirits for their trip.

They took the rutted road down the eastern bank of the North Anna River to keep their distance from the parallel tracks of the Virginia Central Railroad on the opposite bank, where there were bound to be either Rebel scouts protecting it or Union scouts tearing it up.

Over the first three days of their four-day trip, Keeley listened intently to Jana and Leanne's reminiscences of the adventures they'd had with him and Charlie. By the third evening's layover, Jana and Leanne were hoarse from their jawing, and Keeley kiddingly complained his eardrums were ringing from it.

Their first night out, Leanne had insisted Jana and Keeley rest around a campfire while by the full moon, starlit sky, and a lantern, she fed and brushed the mule and checked its shoes for wear or loose nails. She'd make sure it was in good shape for when they got to White House and donated it, along with their wagon, to the army. They'd have no further need for either since the best route home from there would be by steamship to Washington and train the rest of the way. Her choice in whistling "Home Sweet Home" suited her forthcoming reunion with Charlie, the first in a little over a year.

Illuminated by the firelight, Keeley glowed brighter than the lightning bugs all around him.

Jana sighed, wishing he was lighting up like a firefly to attract her as his mate. Her exhalation stole him from his introspection and started his staring at her, which she'd grown used to.

As if he'd read her mind about the mating of fireflies, he said, "I appreciate that ye and Leanne have told me all about meself and me past. Though, I'm a wee bit curious as to the kind o' man I am who"—his cheeks flamed as orange as the embers beneath the burning logs—"attracted ye to meself."

Ambushed by his question, Jana choked on her spittle.

"I'm sorry, lass. If it's too personal for ye, please don't feel ye have to answer."

"No, it's fine. I just didn't expect it, that's all." But if he'd had guts enough to ask her, she'd have guts enough to answer. Now, she felt her own cheeks flaming hot as she said, "I fell in love with you by your smile. In it, I saw all of your goodness: honor, loyalty, compassion, and charm."

His emerald eyes sparkled and his dimples flashed—the irresistible virtues that could distract her in battle and get her killed. "Ye saw all that in me smile, ye did, lass?"

"Yes, and your actions supported it too. You saw right through my disguise, yet you respected whatever reason I had for not telling you my secret." She wrapped her arms around herself, wishing it was Keeley hugging her instead. "You accepted me for me."

"Just so ye know, I too see goodness in yar smile, lass, and through yar actions to help meself in me time o' need."

*He admires me for disguising myself as a man to fight for my country and he sees goodness in my smile and actions,* Jana tallied his praises in her mind. Were these signs he could fall in love with her again?

Leanne ambled over to the fire, interrupting any further exploration between them.

Later that evening, long after Jana had cradled herself beneath her blanket, she felt the gentle sway of the wagon bed as Keeley crawled in and pulled up his own blanket. To keep up the pretenses they were sisters by marriage should any army scouts happen upon them while they slept, the three of them had agreed he should sleep on the wagon bed with Jana. And as he'd done each night, he crawled in after he thought she was asleep to prevent any awkwardness in their sharing a bed. How was it possible for her to feel comforted lying next to someone who regarded her as a stranger? She pretended to roll over in her sleep so she could move closer to him—to feel his warmth—and to bask in his familiar scent. In response to a subtle shift of his hips toward her, her heart soared to the sky and swung on a star the entire night. Would it be easier than she'd anticipated for him to fall in love with her again?

On their last day, while the wagon continued its listing over the road gouged by heavy rains and an infinite number of wheels, hoofs, and marching feet from both armies traipsing over it, Keeley nearly tripped on the hem of his skirt when he leaped into the wagon bed and started rummaging through the supplies.

"What are you doing?" Jana asked.

"I'm looking for me uniform. I've had enough o' this costume and, according to yar estimated arrival, we're but a wee bit away. Wouldn't ye agree, lass?"

Jana was about to relent until she spied a squall of dust ahead. Every muscle in her body tensed, and her hands grew clammier beneath her riding gloves.

"Uh ... you better get back to your seat, Keeley. We've got company." As he scrambled back to Leanne's side, Jana's brain nagged at her, *Even the best-laid plans go awry.* Would the bumbled exchange between her and Keeley at Castle Thunder Prison, which had risked both of their lives, haunt her with each sticky situation she encountered for the rest of her life? She prayed they all played their parts to perfection.

## White House Landing, Virginia

### July 11, 1864

Squaring her shoulders, Jana determined to maintain control over the situation. "Remember," she said, "let me do all of the talking. And try not to seem shocked by anything I say. In spying, I learned to create deception, so I might have to embellish the truth or tell an outright lie to keep us safe."

"Ye won't have to worry about meself giving ye away, lass. Unless me memory returns by the time they catch up with us, I won't be knowing yar fact from fiction."

Sitting rigidly in the wagon, Leanne said, "And *I* ain't gonna put ya in no position to be hung agin."

"One last thing: hold your gaze steady on our visitors to give the impression you have nothing to hide," Jana said.

The riders heading their way were uniformed, but distance, the swirling sand, and the closeness in colors of the Confederate gray to the Union blue masked whose side they were on. This was a confusion that had oftentimes drawn friendly fire in battle. Jana had experienced the reverse at Brandy Station. Having mistaken advancing troopers as their own, Jana's unit allowed the column to swoop down upon them, recognizing too late that they were Rebels as identified by their flag and battle cry, the latter made famous at Bull Run and heard everywhere since. Not that it really mattered which army's soldiers swarmed down on them now—their excuse for traipsing about the South would be the same for either side.

Inspired by the billowing earth kicked up by the approaching party, Jana said, "Hurry, let's tie our handkerchiefs around our faces to make it look like we're hiding from the dust rather than their scrutiny." They'd narrowly finished concealing themselves when the soldiers reined in their mounts. They proved to be Yankees by their navy shell coats and cavalry by the yellow trim on their coats and the brass crossed sabers stamped on the crown of their kepis.

The leader raised a staying hand for Jana to bring the mule to a halt. He sported the two-striped chevron of a corporal on his dusty lower coat sleeves and the yellow trim down the outer seams of his sky blue trousers, reserved for noncommissioned and commissioned officers.

A downward tilt of his head sent a sandstorm of fear gusting through Jana, and she felt Leanne's flinch. The number *10* over the crossed sabers on his kepi gave away that he and his troopers were their former comrades.

In a regiment of nearly one thousand men, Jana and her friends had only really gotten to know those from their Company *D* and Company *B* with which they were usually paired as a squadron in battle. Fortunately, these men were unfamiliar to her. Still, she took seriously her vow to protect Keeley from embarrassment; until she could convince the corporal to let them pass, she'd regard him and his men as the enemy. The scouts had their faces wrapped in handkerchiefs too, and this gave Jana another idea. To deflect attention back to the troopers, she began swatting the dust before her and coughing. "You must've seen us coming, Corporal. You might've given us the same courtesy of slowing down well in advance so as not to choke us." She prattled on, "Virginia sure is beautiful, though if this is a typical summer here, I'll take the sulfur smells of Washington's swamps over it any day."

"You're from Washington, ma'am?" He drew the pointed end of his handkerchief away from his mouth so he could spit tobacco.

Jana tolerated tobacco-chewing as long as the chewer was considerate about where they spat. Even so, the corporal had just bestowed upon her another ruse to badger him into wanting to be rid of her. She glared at his puddle of spittle, then at him.

"Sorry, ma'am, I couldn't very well swallow it."

"You're going to rot your teeth," she chided him. "Most people would kill to have a mouthful as straight and pearly as yours."

The corporal lowered his face in shame toward the pommel of his McClellan saddle. "You're right, ma'am, it's a nasty habit. I plan to quit as soon as I get back home to my wife's good cooking. For now, it helps curb my hunger."

"Good. You'll be better off without it, and your wife will be glad of it."

Peering toward the hazy horizon, the corporal said, "Speaking of being better off, it's a bit dangerous, especially for three Northerners, to be roaming around *Rebeldom*."

Jana wanted to laugh. She'd always found her regiment's derogatory nickname for the Confederacy amusing. Either way, now was not the time for anything other than feigned merriment. "We're not roaming around, Corporal," she said.

"Then, may I ask where you're heading and why?" He cringed a little, as if he expected another tongue-lashing from her for prying into her affairs.

"First, tell me, am I correct in my understanding that you're with the Tenth New York Cavalry Regiment?"

"Why, yes, ma'am. How'd you know?"

"My husband enlisted with your regiment, and we're headed to White House, where we were told the Porter Guards' wounded were taken after the battle around Trevilian Station."

"Some wounded remain, but Dr. Pease saw the bulk of them to Washington by steamship."

Jana's shoulders sagged in disappointment upon learning of the surgeon's absence.

Mistaking Jana's drooping demeanor to do with his news about few wounded remaining at the army depot hospital, the corporal said, "Maybe I can help you, ma'am. What's your husband's name?" His eyes skimmed over Leanne and roosted on Keeley.

Jana tensed to his preoccupation with Keeley.

Before she could answer him, he said to Keeley, "Pardon my staring, ma'am. I've seen your color eyes once in my life; they were on one of our troopers, whom I only met once in passing when we were in Maryland guarding bridges and the ferryboat for transporting train cars across the Susquehanna River between Perryville and our station at Havre De Grace."

*Darn Keeley's dangerously beautiful eyes, which can lure me into battle and him into a compromising position,* Jana thought.

Keeley patted his handkerchief over his mouth.

"She's mute, sir," Jana said, then began squealing with delight to draw the corporal's attention back to her. "The trooper with eyes like hers could be my husband and her brother. His name is Keeley Cassidy. Do you know him or his whereabouts?"

Lifting his handkerchief to spit again, he eyed Jana bashfully. "I beg your pardon, ma'am, for being witless on both accounts."

She dismissed his apology with a flick of her wrist. "We've searched the countryside all around Trevilian Station for stragglers, and our last hope is at White House. If you don't mind, Corporal, we're anxious to get there."

"I'm not sure I can let you by without a pass."

"We don't have one, but we have something better." She extracted the wooden box from between her feet on the buckboard floor, opened it to display the medicinal vials within for the corporal to see, and then closed and returned it to its place. "We've heard the field hospitals are short on morphine for the wounded, so we brought an ample supply. We prefer to hand it to the surgeons ourselves. Not that we think you'll abscond with it, but the likelihood of you getting captured over us is greater. We wouldn't want it ending up in Rebel hands, would we?"

"No, ma'am, I reckon not."

"So you're going to let us pass?"

He leaned his palm on his thigh. "Put it this way, if I ever came up missing, I'd want my family to come hunting for me. And if I were injured and in pain, I'd want to know there's plenty of morphine on hand."

His troopers laughed.

The corporal added, "We're on a scouting mission, but we're only about a mile out from New Castle, where you'll cross the Pamunkey River to White House. It wouldn't be too much of a delay for us to escort you back there."

"That's not necessary, Corporal. We've come this far on our own, and I'm confident we'll make our destination without incident, especially now that we're inside Union lines. Besides, I don't want to be responsible for delaying your mission and getting you in trouble with your captain. And quite frankly, we've breathed enough of your dust to last us a lifetime."

This time the corporal joined his men in laughter.

"If you're sure you're comfortable going the rest of the way without an escort, we do have some good ground to cover yet today, so we should get going," the corporal said.

"We'll be fine, thank you."

Tipping his cap at Jana, he said, "I hope you find your husband, ma'am." He peered at Leanne and Keeley. "Good day to you, son, ma'am." He reined his horse aside, signaling for the others to do the same. "We'll let you on by before we move out."

"That's kind of you, Corporal." Jana tapped the mule's hide to guide them past what she hoped was their one and only obstacle to their destination. All of her muscles fell flaccid with relief when the cavalcade spurred their horses on and their resounding stampede disappeared into the distance.

They withdrew their handkerchiefs from around their mouths, and Leanne whistled and said, "Ya sure are slick, Jana."

Peeking around Leanne, Keeley cast Jana a smile that sucked her in like quicksand. "Aye, y'are a master o' deception, lass. It's no wonder ye escaped yar hanging."

Jana wanted to reach out and caress every inch of his triangular face; instead, she contented herself in letting her eyes run down his long dimples and across his uniformly thin lips. She no longer cared if he caught her staring at him. What did she have to lose? Maybe he couldn't feel his love for her, but she'd keep right on reminding him how she felt until he either succumbed to her or told her there was nothing between them.

Leanne cleared her throat to interrupt their mutually silent admiration, which induced a blush across Jana's and Keeley's cheeks.

To deflect his flush, Keeley fanned his face with his gloved hand as a woman about to swoon would and said, "I thought for a wee second the corporal was going to ask meself to go courting."

Leanne said with a smirk, "We could call yer courtship *Kelly and the Corporal*."

"Aye, it's got a nice ring."

The trio keeled over in a grand hoot.

Still chuckling, Keeley again stood, hoisted his skirt to expose his petticoats beneath, vaulted over the bench onto the wagon bed, and began rummaging through the supplies. He shed his dress faster than Jana had her filthy one yesterday. When he reclaimed his seat next to Leanne, he breathed a huge sigh of relief. "It's good to be back in men's clothes." He shook his head. "I don't envy ye women having to struggle into all o' those undergarments every day."

Seeing Keeley in his uniform brought Jana back to the first time she'd seen him wearing it when they were stationed at Havre De Grace—most likely the same "passing incident" the corporal had referenced minutes before. Keeley had persuaded the men to petition Secretary of War Stanton to either mount or disband their regiment as cavalry if they weren't going to receive their horses and carbines, and Jana had been assisting him in getting signatures. He'd turned to her, trading pencil for lap desk to give her a chance to sign, when his triumphant smile abruptly changed to confusion. Leaning in closer to her, his eyes began raking over her face, which she thrust downward toward the parchment to avoid his scrutiny. She could see him shaking his head as if he was trying to expel some ridiculous notion and, when she finally got the courage to look up, he was smiling again. He was pleased to have his petition signed, yet she was convinced he'd found her out. Either way, she was drawn to his smile, which brought out the most charming dimples and brightest emerald eyes she'd ever seen. It had sent butterflies fluttering all through her as nothing had ever done before. The sound of him brushing dust off the sleeves of his uniform peeled her away from her pleasant memory and made her realize he'd permanently seared himself into her soul and she'd always love him—no matter how painful the outcome for their future.

Twenty minutes later, they boarded a ferry and began cruising across the meandering Pamunkey, a very narrow but deep river. Here and there a black bass drifted above the surface to feed on a bug while below its surface sunfish and yellow perch could clearly be seen fleeing from their coal-belching transport. Over the ferry's bow was a breathtaking view: a broad green meadow, dotted with fully blossomed trees and a colorful spray of flowers, stretched far inland from high-and-low bluffs. A handful of Union steam-and-sailing vessels remained moored to the extensive docks and wharves that had probably been built in 1862 when White House served as the main army supply base and depot hospital. Other than this ongoing military presence, who would believe a war raged well within a hundred miles of this picturesque place?

The land toward which their ferry chugged gently sloped away from the river's embankment. About six rods up near a brick spring house, a photographer was setting up his tripod with an attached camera box and aiming it their way.

Jana found it odd for a cameraman to be wearing the army-issued fatigue attire of a hospital steward: forage cap and sack coat with the green half chevron of caduceus and snakes on the upper sleeves over sky blue trousers with the 1 ½ inch crimson stripe of a non-commissioned officer down the outer seams. All of the photographers she'd seen in camp or on the battlefields were civilian.

As fast as the cameraman's head disappeared beneath the black cloth attached to the rear of the camera box, it popped back out. He sidestepped his equipment and came sprinting down the grassy hill, waving and calling out their names.

"Charlie?" Jana and Leanne said in unison to their quizzical looks at each other.

Shy of the landing, the captain cut the steam, lowering the engine's roar to a whir; they glided to a stop where the height of the riverbank was level with their ferry's deck. Their landing spot made it easy to lay a wide plank from deck to shore and evacuate their wagon and mule, which a team of black laborers busied themselves in doing.

Charlie reached their float and said to the leader of the gang, "Hey, Jim, I can take care of the wagon and mule."

"No, sir, we gits paid good by the fed'ral government to do dis here work"— he snickered—"more than we ever got workin' any cotton fields. Don't wants nobody thinkin' we're sleepin' on da job and have it taken away from us."

"All right, but let me help my friends off first."

With a nod, Jim stepped aside.

Charlie's baby blue eyes shone bright behind his spectacles. "I knew you'd find Keeley," he said to Jana and Leanne, his voice squeaking and betraying he was moving into manhood.

Having last seen Charlie a little over a year ago, Jana observed some other major changes in him. He was nearing sixteen, and his Adam's apple and a few sprigs of soft blond hair over his lip had sprouted. He'd also grown into his ears, which, last they saw, were elephant-sized compared to his head and face—both much fuller now. Contrary to his development, he'd regained some of his carefree visage of twelve when he'd first enlisted and was untainted by the horrors of war. She was glad the work of hospital steward agreed with him.

Charlie grabbed Keeley's hand in both of his and gave it a hearty shake, and his new height at six feet enabled him to look Keeley level in the eye when he said, "I'm glad you're all right. Where've you been? I was worried you were captured again. You promised to keep in touch. Why didn't you?" When he finally took a breath, he appeared baffled by Keeley's lackluster return in greeting.

Angling her head back to better see Charlie, Jana squinted into the sunlight beaming at the back of his head. "Keeley's recuperating from a rifle butt to the head that has left him with no memory whatsoever."

"You mean he doesn't know us or who he is?"

"I might've forgotten our time together, lad, but I feel as if I know ye all with what Jana and Leanne have told meself."

Charlie's eyes stuck to Keeley's like leeches trying to bleed some recollection out of him, but Keeley's brain refused to budge. "I'm sorry I scolded you, Keeley." To make up for it, he said, "In tending the wounded, I've noticed that a positive outlook is good for the mind and body. Keep your chin up, and you'll have your memory back in no time."

Keeley grinned. "I'll tuck yar good advice away in me mind for safekeeping, lad, and recall it when I need some cheering up."

Slapping Keeley on the back, Charlie said, "You see, you've got something to remember already." Then he whirled on Jana and Leanne, splaying his arms wide and scooping them up into a great big bear hug.

Jana returned his hug. "We're so happy to see you, Charlie."

"Just like old times." Charlie peered over his shoulder at Keeley. "Well ... almost."

That prompted Jana to say, "We heard Dr. Pease has gone to Washington. Is there another surgeon on duty who could examine Keeley?"

"You're in luck, Dr. Pease is back from escorting the wounded who needed lengthy convalescing to Washington."

"Really?" Jana said, hearing her excitement bubbling like the water running through the spring house.

"Yes, and your timing is perfect. Doc's retiring from field duty, and he's taking me to Baltimore to serve with him at the Newton United States General Hospital."

Leanne pushed away from Charlie. "Does that mean you're gonna be far from the battlefront for the rest of the war?"

"I am."

"Does yer ma know yet?"

"No, I just found out. I'll write a letter for you to take to her explaining it," Charlie said.

"She's gonna be happier than a pig wallowin' in mud like me."

Addressing Jana, Charlie said, "I have you to thank for convincing Colonel Kilpatrick that I'd make a better hospital steward than a soldier. I don't know how you did it, but I couldn't be gladder."

"Your nursing skills did it, Charlie. I only brought it to Kilpatrick's attention." That was only partly true; the rest she, Keeley, and Leanne had agreed never to tell Charlie whose honor and piety might've forbidden Jana to lie about him just to remove him from the line of fire. After the battle at Brandy Station, Leanne had decided to desert home, and Jana had convinced her superiors to send her south to spy and help free Keeley and other soldiers from the prisons in Richmond. It had left no one to watch over Charlie. So Jana had told Kilpatrick that Charlie's poor vision was a danger to his comrades upon whom he'd fired a few times when he mistook them for Rebels—the bullet that had scarred her arm was one of those times.

"Either way, I love my job, especially working with Dr. Pease. I've learned a lot from him about medicine and nursing. I'll take you to him right away, then get you settled in. You'll be staying a day or two, right?"

"If you have room for us," Jana said.

"You'll have to bunk in a tent," Charlie said.

Leanne shrugged. "As ya said, Charlie, just like old times."

Charlie backed up two feet to better inspect Jana. "I hope you don't mind my saying that you're much prettier as a woman." He turned to Leanne. "And I don't think I've ever seen you so happy." His voice squeaked again and then crackled with concern. "Are you?"

"Ya bet I am—all thanks to ya, Charlie."

"I rest easy knowing you're taking care of our family. I can't wait to hear all about home." His tenderness changed to teasing when he spied Leanne's costume. "What in blazes are you wearing, Leanne? Are you trying to outdo Dr. Mary Walker's strange outfit of skirt over men's trousers?"

Jana elbowed Charlie. "And just what's wrong with Dr. Walker's wardrobe? It's no different from bloomers."

"And ... uh ... aren't bloomers extinct?" Charlie said with a lighthearted snort.

"Maybe Leanne's starting a new fashion," Jana said.

"As long as she's comfortable, I don't care how she dresses. Doc and I have seen nurses faint from too many layers of clothing in this heat and from corsets constricting their breathing," Charlie said.

Glancing at her young boy's frocks with a grimace, Leanne said, "I can promise ya I ain't gonna start no new fashion with these clothes. They were just part of an act to git us here."

"Huh?" Charlie said, to which Leanne summarized their escapades at Versella's farm. He puckered his pencil-thin lips into a pout. "Sounds like I missed some fun. Although, it might've been a little scary meeting up with those Yankee renegades."

"No scarier than ya pickin' off that Rebel in our skirmish at Leesburg and savin' my life." Leanne nodded toward the camera. "Anyway, it looks like you're havin' yer own fun."

Charlie nodded excitedly. "I haven't had time to write and tell you, Leanne, but I've discovered an occupation for me when I go home for good." He pointed his thumb back toward the camera. "With our rounds done and all of our patients stable, Dr. Pease gave me some time off this afternoon to practice before the photographer leaves for the battlefield and takes his equipment with him. He's actually one of Matthew Brady's field photographers, and he taught me the tricks of the trade. I promised him I'd never tell Mr. Brady I took some of the images he's forwarded to the studio in New York, and he allows me to practice with his equipment whenever he's not using it. He said I have a real eye for capturing scenes and a knack for profiling people I've never met through their portraitures, which we take in our temporary studio." Fishing a tintype from his breast pocket, he said, "Let me show you what I mean by the first one I ever took and copied as a keepsake."

Jana, Leanne, and Keeley gathered around Charlie who showed his image of two Union soldiers seated beside each other and whose kepis flaunted the small gold bugles of infantry.

Charlie said, "As I watched their faces gradually define in my chemical bath, many similarities in their features made me believe they were kin." He pointed to the deep notches around the older male's eyes. "I could tell something was troubling him."

When Charlie paused for effect, Leanne said, "Well, don't keep us waitin'. What'd ya learn?"

"That they're brothers and the elder one enlisted to get revenge against the Rebels for the death of their father. He didn't know his younger brother had followed him to war until it was too late to stop him. Now, besides worrying about their ma being home alone, he has to worry about keeping himself and his brother alive."

Jana could identify with the older brother's dilemma—she'd always fretted to the point of distraction over the welfare of her three friends before a skirmish or battle.

"Ye read all that through their likenesses, ye did, lad?"

"Yes, and again I have Jana to thank for the lesson in paying attention to details."

"How?" Jana said, feeling her face crimping to her curiosity.

"Back when we were evacuating the wounded from the battlefield during the truce at Fredericksburg, you figured out that a near-dead soldier and a dead soldier lying next to him were husband and wife by a few signs the rest of us missed."

"Don't be modest, Charlie," Jana said. "That was much easier to deduce—the groom practically connected the dots for me when he gave me the portrait of him and his bride in their wedding garb and he kept uttering *wife* while he was trying to roll over to face her."

"Still, they were all very subtle clues that you pieced together faster than I think a trained Pinkerton agent would have and made you perfect for spying." Before Jana could dispute him further, Charlie turned to Leanne. "I did some ciphering, and I think we can put aside some of the money I send home from my pay to buy a camera and supplies, if you think that's all right. Actually, the few extra dollars I get from the difference in rank between private and that above a first sergeant, which I've been collecting since last June, might take care of it. Then, one day, I could set up a studio and take portraits to do my part in contributing to our household."

Aglow with the pride of a sister whose advice was being sought by a younger sibling, Leanne said, "Why don't we ask yer photographer friend if it's possible to git some used equipment? Then we can figure out how much we need to git ya started."

Jana was impressed with Leanne's business savvy, which she'd obviously acquired from operating her own smithy.

"I could even set my shop up next to yours." The trill of excitement in Charlie's voice scaled down a few notes when he said, "Speaking of shops, who's minding yours?"

"Billy."

"Little Billy?"

"Yup. Yer brother—"

Charlie interrupted, "Our brother, Leanne."

"Well, he ain't so little anymore. He's fourteen now, ya know. And he's smart as a whip—just by watchin' me, he learned how to run the shop and keep the business ledgers."

With longing in his tone, Charlie said, "When my three-year enlistment ends around December, I'm going to muster out of the army. I want to go home." He hugged Leanne again as he repeated his appreciation for her taking care of the family in his absence.

Using the heel of her boot to tamp down one of hundreds of grass divots that had been dug up by a hoof, Leanne said, "They take good care of me too, and it ain't nothing to do for those ya love."

Jana and Charlie telegraphed to one another their understanding of how far Leanne had come in opening her heart to loving and being loved.

Sensitive to Leanne's discomfort in lingering too long on anything sappy,

Charlie addressed them all when he said, "Would you like to see my photographs after we've seen Dr. Pease?" To everyone's enthusiastic utterances, Charlie recruited their help to pack his camera onto the wagon bed. And to everyone's suggestion that he lead the way to the hospital, he took control over their wagon.

Immediately after they were underway, Keeley peeked around Jana at Charlie. "Maybe I'll take up photography too"—his bewitching eyes switched to Jana—"as I meself have an eye for beauty."

"For people or landscapes?" Jana said with a coquettish smile.

"People, though I might be a better judge o' the lasses than the lads."

"And would that be of their inner or outer beauty?"

"I confess to both."

"Then, I'd agree with you, Mr. Cassidy—photography is your calling."

Charlie snickered. "Are you sure you don't at least remember Jana, Keeley?"

"Sure sounds that way, don't it?" Leanne mumbled.

Keeley said, "I'm just having fun getting reacquainted with her and, o' course, ye and Leanne too."

Jana's pulse competed to keep up with her galloping heart. While she delighted in these flirtations—the same ones that had kindled her and Keeley's relationship the first time around—the notion he could easily conclude she wasn't the perfect mate for him upended her gaiety. She tried to follow Versella's wisdom to always be prepared, but she could conceive of no guard against the grief she anticipated she'd endure, should they ever reach such a crossroad. Her silence drew an apprehensive stare from Keeley. She forced a smile so as not to infect him with her gloom and mentally kicked herself for her tendency to worry.

As Charlie turned the wagon southward, he brought their attention to the splendor of a plain that sprawled across the low bluff overlooking the river. "Can you imagine waking up to this view every morning?" He frowned as he pointed out two chimneys bookending one another at a modest distance apart, then he explained that Union troops retreating from the spot in 1862 had torched the manor against the orders of General McClellan; he'd promised Mary Custis Lee that he'd preserve this historical landmark where her great-great-grandmother Martha Custis courted and maybe married George Washington. "It might've been left alone," Charlie said, "if she'd owned it instead of her son, William Henry Fitzhugh Lee—as you know, a despised Confederate general like his pa."

"Do ya s'pose *the* White House in Washington got its name from this one?" Leanne said.

"Dr. Pease and I have been wondering about that," Charlie said. "Although the federal White House was being built during George Washington's presidency, and he never got to stay in it, it seems awfully coincidental, don't you think?"

"I do," Jana said, her mood brightening some to Charlie's lesson in history—her favorite subject. "And I also think you have many talents, Charlie: hospital steward, photographer, profiler, and now tour guide. You'll have your pick of occupations after the war."

They all laughed, their merriment subsiding when Charlie turned away from the river and into a field fringed by patches of shade trees and occupied by a dozen or so triangular-roofed tents.

Familiar with the organization of a field hospital, Jana knew that the predominantly larger tents were designated for the sick and wounded and that each could accommodate eight canvas-covered-wood folding cots. She caught a whiff of the boiled-egg stench associated with swampy land and understood the logic in pitching each tent atop a plank floor that was elevated on wooden piers. Lucky for them, a steady breeze blew to chase away the ghastly odor and the bites of the pesky mosquitoes.

"Can you believe there were three hundred tents here at one time? It was a city similar to our winter encampments," Charlie explained. If he hadn't told them this, the proof would've been in the vast web of dirt avenues, which had been stripped of its grass under a trample by the Union Medical Corps. "Most have been forwarded to the new army supply base and depot hospital at City Point, closer to General Grant's battle lines around Petersburg; the rest will be sent there when this post is completely evacuated." He reined in the mule outside a small tent, pulled the brake, and disembarked from the wagon. "I've got to warn you that the medical supply tent is in a shambles with us packing up, though I assure you Doc and I know where to find everything we need." Advancing up the three steps to the tent's entrance, he parted a flap and gestured them inside.

Jana followed first, trading the fresh air for the predominant odor of canvas with a hint of chlorinated water, which they'd probably used to sanitize the floor. The oversight of a clean environment for the patients' welfare more than likely belonged to a hospital steward, so Charlie was obviously observing the teaching of Clara Barton, who'd drilled this notion into the four of them when they'd nursed alongside her in Fredericksburg. The smell of the cleaning solution would probably be suffocating if the tent wall hadn't been heightened for better ventilation, which also contributed to the cooler temperature inside than out. Before her eyes fully adjusted to the dimmer light, she saw only clutter, and her first thought was, *Shambles? More like a twelve-pound Howitzer blew up the inside.* But then everything came into focus. Although medical paraphernalia had been removed from drawers and shelves and littered every inch of space, for the most part it was organized: medical books and patient note cards stacked on the desk; double-bladed surgical knives, amputating saws, forceps, scissors, and scalpels spread out on an examining table; wooden crutches, arms, and legs leaned against one tent wall; and lidded boxes and leather cases containing powdered and liquid medicines lined another wall. Just as she'd observed of the doctor the first time she'd met him, he was engrossed in packing. This time, he moved about in a far less frantic pace than when he'd been participating in the Tenth's transfer out of Elmira with only a few days' warning. Identical to Charlie, he was dressed down to the leisure layers of his uniform while his formal double-breasted frock coat and green medical-department waist sash, both which marked him as a commissioned officer within the Union army, hung on a coatrack next to Charlie's single-breasted waist jacket and crimson dress sash of worsted wool.

"Dr. Pease?" Charlie said.

Bent over one crate trying to stuff it full of books, the doctor straightened and bumped his head on another, which was filled with glass syringes and all sizes of medicinal bottles and began teetering on the edge of a desk.

Charlie scrambled to catch the box with its tinkling contents.

Just in case it dropped, shattering glass and splattering liquid everywhere, Jana covered her mouth with the back of her ungloved hand to thwart the tiniest drop of laudanum from passing her lips. She'd suffer through the pain after another bullet removal before she'd voluntarily submit to its vile taste and woozy effects for several days following a single dose of it. If she were one of the wounded right now, she'd be cursing Charlie for saving that medicine.

"Whew! That was close," Dr. Pease said, eyeing his hospital steward cradling the crate. "How many times have you rescued me from my follies, son?"

"About a million?" Charlie said, chuckling.

The surgeon harrumphed. "How about a billion?" Then his bespectacled eyes detoured from Charlie to the newcomers, landing on Leanne in particular. "If you're from the Sanitary Commission, you're a little late for an inspection. We're evacuating this post."

With his arms still occupied, Charlie wiggled his nose and cheek muscles to push his spectacles up onto the bridge of his nose. "They're not from the Sanitary Commission, Doc, they're my—"

Dr. Pease interrupted Charlie to inquire of Leanne, "Don't I know you from somewhere, young man?" To her pinched lips, he began scratching his head, bald from his prominent forehead back to the peak of his crown where a thin tuft swept across it from ear to ear and met up with a lush mane that circumscribed the rest of his head.

Setting his box down, Charlie tried a second time to make introductions.

Again, Dr. Pease cut in, "Ah, yes, I remember you now." His bushy mustache, draped over his bottom lip, bristled. "You're the volunteer from Elmira who threw a fit about me doing a physical examination because you alleged to have already had one done in Buffalo. Then you duped me into passing another recruit with just a cursory evaluation while I was harried packing up my equipment and supplies for transfer out to Gettysburg. Come to think of it, I don't think I ever again saw that recruit whom you promised to bring to me."

Leanne smirked. "Well, you're seein' her now." She pointed her thumb toward Jana. "That recruit was my friend here. I'm sure ya heard 'bout her. She got kicked out of the army after she took a bullet in the arm at Brandy Station and was discovered to be a woman."

"How could I not have heard of her?" Dr. Pease groaned. "She was a source of my embarrassment."

"Considerin' you've come this far with the army, and now they're askin' ya to run a hospital in Baltimore, I'd say she didn't ruin yer reputation too much," Leanne said.

With a small tilt of his head, Dr. Pease said, "You're right about that, young man." He faced Jana. "Actually, after your escapades in spying, I received a pat on the back by the army as if I'd discovered you myself." He huffed. "Imagine that."

Jana mumbled, "I nearly blew my assignment, though."

Scratching his stubbly chin, Dr. Pease said, "I'd hardly call your fooling the Confederacy into believing that you worked alone in your spying in order to protect others in Richmond from hanging and to preserve the operation there nearly blowing it; I'd call that loyalty to comrades and country, not to mention courageous." His cheeks twitched to a sudden notion. "What could be so important to bring you within twenty-four miles of Richmond and for you to risk the Rebels discovering you're alive?"

Charlie leaped to say, "That's what I've been trying to tell you, Doc. These are my friends from the cavalry. You're now reacquainted with Jana Brady, our soldier-spy, and"—he motioned toward Leanne—"you kind of know Leanne."

"Huh? Leanne you say? The one you call your sister?"

"Yes, sir, the very same," Charlie said, bestowing a look of adoration upon her. "And if you'll remember, she also runs her own smithy and takes care of our family."

Dr. Pease rolled his eyes at himself in frustration. "Are you telling me I passed two women into the cavalry?"

"Yup," Leanne said. "We're sorry we had to take advantage of yer runnin' 'round crazy as a loon to git in, but we were desperate. Jana wanted to fight for our country, and I needed to git the fear of fightin' out of me so I could stand up to my pa the next time he got drunk and came at me or my ma. When I finally got the guts, I deserted home to take her away to live with Charlie's family, and I did it without even havin' to lay a finger on my pa. I've never been happier in my whole life, and I don't care if anyone calls Leander Perham a deserter—he doesn't exist anyway—he's now Leanne Watson."

Dr. Pease's expression turned to mush. In a soft tone, he said, "Your duty to your ma, Miss Watson, is no less admirable than a soldier's to his country. Unfortunately, some of our bigger battles are at home and, as you found out, blood isn't always thicker than water." He turned and slapped Charlie on the back. "Knowing this young man as I do, I'm sure you and your ma will be very happy living with him and his family."

"We already are, sir." With an uncharacteristic sniffle and tearful eyes, Leanne said, "Thank ya for yer wise words. I'll never forget 'em."

Dr. Pease turned to Keeley. "Let me guess, you happened upon these two and escorted them here out of harm's way."

Without allowing Keeley a chance to answer for himself, Charlie said, "It's the other way around, Doc. Jana and Leanne found him and brought him here. This is my friend Keeley Cassidy—the trooper I told you about who went missing around Trevilian Station. Jana and Leanne found him in the care of a local woman there; he's lost his memory from a bash to his head by the butt of a friendly rifle. He doesn't remember any of us, not even Jana, his fiancée."

Jana said, "Keeley wished to report to his regiment and, given your medical fame, we risked our lives in bringing him to you for an examination."

"I appreciate your confidence in me," Dr. Pease said, looking at each person. "Now, let me ask you how you know the bash to his head was from a friendly rifle? Did he remember this and tell you it himself?"

"No, Commissary Officer Noble Preston did," Charlie said. "He claims Keeley was injured in the same scramble over the fence that got him a bullet in the hip, and they were too far from the Rebels at that point to be engaged in close combat."

"Do you remember anything prior to your injury, son?" Dr. Pease asked Keeley.

"Not a wee thing before waking up in a barn."

"Actually," Jana said, "a few nights ago he recalled all on his own having been homeless on the streets of New York City and his job of shipping oysters upriver to Elmira."

Dr. Pease directed Keeley to a chair. Then he went about preparing for his examination in a slow amble, making Jana think he already knew the diagnosis but was going through the motions to delay having to disclose something unpleasant. On a lamp table next to Keeley rested an iron stand with an arm securing a glass-ensconced tallow candle, which he lit with a match that injected a dose of sulfur in the air after he extinguished it. Additionally, as the surgeon crossed the tent to retrieve a brown leather case from his examining table, he circulated the smoke of burning animal fat, which made the luminary and reminded Jana of Ma's oven-roasted brisket of beef.

For a split-second, the aroma transported Jana home around the supper table where she pictured herself, Ma, and her sisters watching Pa carve the meat. An empty chair jolted her back to the present. Had she just seen her future—without Keeley in it? A nervous sweat broke out over her upper lip from her desperation to hear Dr. Pease's diagnosis. She hardly heard Charlie's explanation of the box in the surgeon's hand: "That contains an ophthalmoscope from Dr. Pease's private practice. It refracts the light so he can see into the inner eye, and it gives Doc an edge in diagnosing over his colleagues."

"Very nicely and simply stated, Charlie," Dr. Pease said, making Charlie glow with pride. Then he went to Keeley and stood over him. "Show me where you were clobbered, son, then tilt that area toward the light."

Obeying the surgeon's instructions, Keeley removed his kepi and pointed behind his left ear, where the surgeon began a practiced riffle through his hair.

Charlie scuttled for a blank card, then pushed aside some books and papers to carve out enough space on the desktop for him to take notes. He barely had pen in hand and its quill dipped in an ink well before Dr. Pease began narrating: "No evidence of a fracture or gash that would've required stitching and swelling is absent; there was marked bruising in the beginning as evidenced by continued discoloration in this latter stage of healing." Predicting Dr. Pease's next move, Charlie abandoned his notes to fetch a chair, which he scuffed across the floor and set before Keeley for the surgeon's use. He navigated back to his seat behind the desk. Armed once again with pen, he readied to scratch more notes.

Dr. Pease cupped Keeley's chin in his palm and gently angled his face toward the light. With his naked eyes, he probed Keeley's eyes and reported: "Pupils are equal and react well to light; no sign of concussion." Then he extracted two handled pieces from his leather case, placing the one that resembled a tiny mirror with a hole in its center against his right eye while he placed the other that resembled a magnifying lens against Keeley's left eye. Again, he reported: "No sign of hemorrhage or retinal detachment." Repeating the procedure on Keeley's right eye, he concluded the same, then said to Keeley, "Other than one small recollection, you say you've had no memory for about a month now?"

"If me memory serves meself right," he said with a dimpling grin.

His joke and Leanne's and Charlie's guffaws passed over Dr. Pease, who was staring at the ceiling and either ruminating over his findings or how to delicately relate his adverse report.

*How can Keeley jest now while I stand here waiting with bated breath for the doctor's prognosis?* Jana wondered, then supposed it was because he had nothing to lose compared to her. While his past could be reconstructed and he was free to fall in love all over again—and with someone else—her mind was manacled to her heart, and her heart was manacled to her love for him.

Finally, Dr. Pease returned from his pondering. "The good news: By all appearances, you're physically fit; there's no evidence of hemorrhage or any other trauma to your brain from the blow. It's also encouraging that you had a recollection, albeit miniscule. The bad news: Only one out of a few cases of total amnesia that I've followed ever recovered fully; most have had small brain spurts similar to yours that never strung together into anything substantial."

Dread wrapped its tentacles around Jana's throat in a strangulating squeeze, causing her to choke on her words. "Are you saying Keeley will never regain his memory?"

"Every case is unique. I believe the mending of the brain is dependent upon Keeley's having possessed good physical health and a strong constitution beforehand. Those conditions were preexistent in only the one case that I saw where there was full recovery in both short-and-long-term memories." To the ongoing quiet, Dr. Pease heaved a heavy sigh. "I wish I could tell you something more definitive. Unfortunately, we know so little about the brain under amnesic circumstances."

Dr. Pease's news hacked through Jana like an amputating saw, trying to sever any hope of Keeley's love ever returning to her. With everyone's eyes upon her, she grew faint and reached out for something solid to lean on.

Leanne was there in a flash to grab onto her elbow and hold her up.

Having sprung from his chair, Charlie was already in motion when Dr. Pease suggested he get Jana some water, which he fetched from an end table, poured out of a glass pitcher, and carried to Jana.

Jana swigged the cool spring water and felt herself immediately placated. "I guess I was a little dehydrated from the heat," she said, knowing full well she wasn't fooling anyone.

"Are ye all right, lass?" Keeley said, bringing his chair to her and helping Leanne to lower her into it.

Jana summoned a weak smile. "Thank you, I'm fine." Peering at Dr. Pease, she said, "Forgive my interruption. Please, go on with whatever you were saying."

"No apologies necessary, Miss Brady. Are you sure you're all right?"

"Yes, thank you." She was touched by everyone's concern. They seemed more worried about her than they were Keeley—perhaps they also realized she had more to lose than he did.

When Dr. Pease seemed satisfied with her improvement, he turned back to Keeley. "I'm afraid I'm going to have to recommend your discharge from the army, son. We can't have you becoming disoriented and a menace to yourself and others in the thick of battle."

Tapping his kepi onto his head and tugging the hem of his jacket to straighten it, Keeley said, "I understand, sir," without an ounce of pity for himself.

Jana marveled at his impassiveness to the grim news. His will to venture forward awakened her to the parallels between him and the one case the doctor purported had enjoyed a full recovery—Keeley also had good physical health and an especially strong constitution prior to his memory loss. He'd endured greater tragedy by the age of twenty-three than any person ought to have. On the one hand, Jana wished she could wave a magic wand and erase his greatest sorrow in the deaths of his mam, da, and siblings; on the other, she realized this and his other struggles had built his character, and they were bound to have left a trail of crumbs that could lead him out of the maze of his memory loss. It left her with no other choice than to keep the good and bad memories alive for him. To her sudden optimism, she imagined herself as the biggest, fattest crumb that stood out most in sparking his way back to her. *Now that would be a true testament of our love and worth the earning,* she thought.

The train's iron wheels screeched along the track, and the locomotive blew a mighty huff as it chugged to a stop at the Elmira depot. Opening the forward door, the conductor allowed in some coal-burning smoke while the balance of the billowy mass sailed past their window.

Coughing on the fumes, Jana was roused from her thoughts, which she'd been forced into almost their entire journey with their cramped quarters making it impossible for her and Keeley to speak intimately. What little conversation they had was relegated to his drilling her about her family so he'd know her sisters apart when he met them or explaining to other passengers that his amnesia crippled him from discussing his soldiering.

Jana and Keeley remained seated to avoid those clogging the aisle and clambering to disembark. The platform was unusually crowded, and the pushing and shoving would probably be worse out there. There was no hurry to detrain, but her fidgety legs betrayed she was itching for Keeley to meet her family.

Lost in his own reflections and sitting stiffer than the telegraph pole that they'd just passed, Keeley leaned toward her. "What's got yar petticoats squawking, lass? If y'are worried about bringing meself home to yar parents, should I be too?"

"That's not quite what's worrying me. My family's going to love you." More than that, Jana knew her family was the best medicine for what ailed a person. She was certain he'd fall in love with them too, and this bode well for her. Though, she wouldn't tell him this. Instead, she said, "I know my sisters. They'll be squawking to meet you, and I'm worried they'll turn into vultures and swoop down to pick you over with questions you can't answer or are uncomfortable answering."

"Ye've written to tell them all about me memory loss, aye?"

Jana nodded.

"Then, I can't be bothered by questions that are foreign to meself. And by yar accounts, it seems I've been through worse in me lifetime." He smirked playfully. "I'll take five females swarming around meself any day over the flock o' Rebel buzzards ye tell meself did in a ditch at Brandy Station."

Returning his smirk, Jana said, "We'll see how you feel about it after you meet my sisters." She gathered her skirt and rose from her upholstered seat. "Well then, Mr. Cassidy, shall we soar into the vulture's nest together?"

"Aye"—he rose and gestured her out into the aisle—"lead the way, Miss Brady."

Jana stepped out onto the platform between passenger cars and immediately spied Pa anchored at the base of their iron steps. Curiously, his hat was pulled low over his face and, when she called out his name, he motioned for her brisk disembarkation. She descended to the depot platform, barely hearing Keeley's thud behind her when in one fluid move, Pa grabbed her arm, signaled for Keeley to follow, and began practically dragging her away.

When Jana opened her mouth to protest his brusque behavior, he said loud enough for only her and Keeley to hear, "Let's get out of here fast. And for Pete's sake, Jana, keep your face down."

"Why? What's wrong, Pa?"

"You're famous, that's what's wrong!"

"What?" Jana said.

Before he could answer, someone shouted, "There she is," which was followed by a thunderous vibration in the planks underfoot from a stampede across them.

Jana was ripped away from Pa and Keeley and swallowed whole by a sea of newspaper reporters armed with pencil and paper and demanding to know all about her life as a soldier. Tossed about like a ship on white-capped swells, she broke out in a dizzying sweat from the heat of the sun and invasion of bodies and nearly suffocated from an overpowering potion of shaving cream, cologne, and pomade. Over the shouting, she heard Pa politely pleading for them to give her space, and then she felt a gentle hand gripping hers and guiding her out into the open.

"Are ye all right, lass?" Keeley said, swinging her around behind him and drawing her up tight against his back.

"Yes," she said, swigging the air to revive her senses, which now threatened to swoon under Keeley's natural scent and their caressing bodies. With her hand, she fanned her flushing cheeks, ablaze with her desire to snuggle in his arms.

"Are ye sure y'are all right?"

"Yes ... truly ... I am. Thank you for coming to my rescue."

"I owe ye, lass."

*Oh, Keeley,* Jana thought, *give me something to hope for!* In his words she'd heard no greater regard for her welfare than one repaying a debt. Or was he intentionally keeping his emotions superficial to sidestep leading her on in this early stage of their rediscovery?

This time, Pa took her arm more gently when he ushered her away from the platform, leaving Keeley to guard their rear.

A reporter hollered, "Aw, c'mon, Thomas, all of Chemung County wants to hear her story. I only need a few minutes."

Giving a backhanded wave, Pa said, "She's had a long trip and needs rest. Afterward, it's her decision about any interview."

It was thrilling that anyone besides her family would want to hear about her soldiering, even though she thought of it as a personal accomplishment for which she sought no fame.

Arriving at the wagon, Pa and Keeley nearly tripped over one another trying to give her a hand up. She held her tongue from reminding them that if she could mount a horse with a saber and pistol dangling from a belt, she could certainly climb aboard a wagon with only a skirt to hoist and a carpetbag swinging from the crook of her arm. She wanted to avoid perpetuating a picture of her masculinity to Keeley. Despite his telling her he admired her for fighting in uniform, he might dislike this degree of independence and adventuresome spirit in a woman he'd choose to marry. If his memory could be erased, surely his convictions could've gotten jumbled too. And if that were so, she wondered if she could ever be desperate enough to alter herself to fit him snug as a glove tailored specially for him just to win his love.

Pa stepped aside, conceding her hand to Keeley's.

As Keeley assisted her up into the wagon, Jana gave his hand a brief squeeze. She was disappointed when he didn't react and, to the detached feel of his clasp, she answered the question she'd asked of herself seconds before: She'd rather never love again than alter herself to win Keeley's love just to cling to what they'd once had. She blinked back tears in recognition this could one day be her reality.

Keeley peered up at her. "Shall I go inquire about yar trunk, lass?"

To avoid him from seeing her moist eyes, she pretended to be preoccupied with rummaging around in her carpetbag, and she was grateful when Pa answered for her.

"I'll go." Pa eyed Keeley's gun and saber. "No one's going to hassle Jana with you guarding her."

As he strode off to find her trunk amongst other trunks, furniture, portmanteaus, and packing crates, which porters were piling up outside the baggage car, Jana opened her fan and waved it before her face to dry her eyes, feigning still being overheated from her previous experience.

It prompted Keeley to say, "And ye were worried about vultures swooping down upon meself? Compared to those reporters, yar sisters can't be any more threatening than chicks."

She was glad when her tears of laughter covered over her sorrowful ones, and she and Keeley were still laughing when Pa returned and directed the stevedore to rest Jana's trunk on the wagon bed.

Reaching into the pocket of his jean overalls, Pa jingled some coins as he fished out a tip.

Keeley put up a staying hand. "Allow meself, sir. It's the least I can do for ye taking meself into yar homestead." He tipped the porter, who scuttled away in search of his next client, and then he took his seat next to Jana. Extracting his pistol from his holster, he laid it on his lap and said, "This ought to help keep the rowdies at bay."

Climbing up into the driver's seat, Pa pulled the brake to liberate the mules, and they set off on a slow roll. "May I ask what you two found so funny a few minutes back?" When Jana finished telling him, he grunted. "They aren't quite as devilish as vultures, but they aren't as angelic as chicks either. More like nosy fledglings." He peered around Jana at Keeley with a grin, which stretched from ear to ear. "How about taking on the job of tempering my wild girls?" He shot up to a sudden notion. "Speaking of wild girls, where's Leanne? We didn't leave her at the station, did we?"

"She stayed at White House to visit Charlie a few days longer," Jana said.

With a gentle poke of his elbow in Jana's arm, Pa said, "Any chance they might make a match?"

"Pa!"

"Well, stranger things have happened"—he paused for effect—"including women disguising themselves as soldiers to fight for their country, huh?"

Jana winced inwardly. It was going to be difficult keeping everyone, especially her family, from obsessing over her time in uniform. But then she realized the hypocrisy of that: Why would she stifle their enthusiasm over something she'd once—until war had reared its ugly head—been euphoric over herself? She'd stand proudly by her accomplishments and hope Keeley's new self could embrace them too. Segueing back to the moment, she eyed Pa, then Keeley, and said, "Is an introduction necessary at this point?"

Transferring the reins to one hand, Pa thrust out his other to Keeley who took it in a hearty shake.

"A pleasure to meet ye, Mr. Brady."

"Why don't we drop the Mr. Brady? Makes me feel old. Just call me Thomas. All right if I call you Keeley?"

"Aye, I wouldn't have it any other way."

Pa said, "Sorry you had to deal with the madness back at the station. Eliza was proud of her big sister's triumphs in uniform and she shouted it from the hilltops all around us. By now, I think all twelve thousand Elmirans know about it." He clicked his cheek. "I appreciate your watching Jana's back, and I admire your coolness under fire. Though, I reckon those things are second nature to cavalrymen."

"I can't say whether or not it is, Thomas. I can say that I appreciate yar opening yar home to meself—a total stranger."

"You're no stranger. Jana's told us all we need to know about you to consider you worthy of our hospitality."

Jana was glad Pa had avoided linking his and Ma's charity to her and Keeley's displaced courtship; she wanted him to believe her family was opening their arms to him purely because they wanted to, not because they were conspiring to push them back together.

"I'm eager to pull me weight and ready to do some chores so I'm not a burden."

"That's admirable of you, son. We can come to terms on that after you've settled in." Pa grimaced at his clothes. "Speaking of chores, forgive my appearance. I barely finished milking before I came to fetch you."

Jana bumped him. "You don't have to impress me, Pa. I love you any way you are, even with you smelling like the inside of the barn." Batting her eyelashes at Keeley, Jana hoped to open his eyes to her—the woman with whom he'd once fallen in love.

"Whew! I'm relieved to hear it," Pa said.

It suddenly struck Jana that Pa had come alone. "Where *is* everyone?"

"Home."

"How'd you manage to get away without at least Eliza accompanying you?"

"Oh, she begged to come, but Ma and I anticipated the mob. We thought it best that there be less of us to worry about and that we wean Keeley into us rather than make him feel like he was the Bastille being stormed."

Jana expected a witty reply from Keeley whose face grew foggy. When he began massaging his temples, she feared he was experiencing some unexpected aftermath from his head bash. She touched his lower arm. "Are you all right, Keeley?"

His reply was mumbled but intelligible. "The word *wean* brought about a disturbing picture o' meself on horseback, charging toward some burlap dummies. Simultaneous to a puff o' smoke, me horse veered"—his eyes popped wide with horror—"into yars, and it threw ye from yar horse."

"No, Keeley, it was my fault. I shot my pistol during a drill before our horses were used to the sound of the gun so close to their ears. My unsaddling happened when my horse veered into yours. Fortunately, you stayed astride your horse."

"Were ye hurt badly?"

"Just bruised, more in spirit than body," Jana said, remembering both the lie she'd told him about wearing a corset to shield bullets after he saw it poking through her cavalry coat and the bruise on her rump she'd felt with every bounce in the saddle for a while afterward.

Pa shot Jana a questioning glance. "Haven't heard that story yet."

Shrinking in embarrassment, Jana knew Pa must be wondering how she could've committed such an error after his thorough instruction in training horses. "I wasn't hiding it from you, Pa, the subject just hadn't come up yet."

"I'm sorry to have tattled on ye, lass," Keeley said with a grimace.

Perking up to his sensitivity, she said, "It's all right, Keeley … really. I'm happy you remembered something, and that's cause for celebration." She was happier his recall had everything to do with her—maybe she flamed bright in his soul after all.

"Aye, I'd have to agree it was a pretty good one."

During the momentary lapse in conversation while they all grasped the enormity of Keeley's breakthrough, Pa took a detour to Camp Rathbun. Jana was astonished to find that in her brief absence, the federal government had finished its transformation of a portion of the rendezvous camp into a Confederate prison. Pa declared five thousand Rebels would be crammed into the barracks, which still existed from when Jana and Keeley's regiment had formed here, and thousands more would be accommodated by tents.

Pa meant well in bringing them here to try joggling Keeley's memory; he never would've come if he knew the horrors it dredged up for Jana. Ironically, she now found this same ground she'd once held sacred for the patriotic fervor it had sowed into her revolting. She gazed loathingly upon the high walls that caged men like animals in a traveling zoo. The fetid odor blowing up from Foster's Pond, the camp's southernmost border on the north bank of the Chemung River, evidenced poor sanitation. An omen of countless deaths to come from dysentery—as had afflicted other prisons, such as the one near Andersonville, Georgia, and Camp Douglas in Chicago, Illinois. And the longer it was in existence, the more deaths that could be expected from exposure to extreme weather, besides from starvation. How could the Union adequately feed such a lot?

Pointing out a towering platform to their right, Pa said, "The Means brothers built it for busybodies to watch the prisoners through binoculars. They reap ten cents from each voyeur."

With a huff of disgust, Jana thought, *How appropriate the surname of "Means" for those exploiting the prisoners' sufferings.*

The busybodies waiting their turn hooted it up while they ate cakes and drank lemonade they'd bought from vendors who lined the street.

"I'm sick of wicked profiteers," Jana said, "especially those who mass produce factory shoes that blister our soldiers' feet and after a few wears crumble to nothing."

Pa said, "Here photographers are growing rich selling postcards they make from pictures they mass produce of the prison and its activities."

*Charlie would never stoop to this level even if his family was starving,* Jana thought. And she was convinced that one day the natives of Elmira would be sorry they'd ever allowed it to be memorialized; it would put a permanent stain on their city's history, which up to now was a proud one.

Noting Jana's comportment crumbling like the mass-produced army shoes, Pa said, "I'm sorry I brought you here. I can see it's had a negative effect on you." He wrapped an arm around her and kissed her forehead. "Let's go home."

"However depressing it is, Pa, you can't protect me from the world."

"Want to bet?" He smirked. "We'll give up our subscription to the *Elmira Gazette* and confine you to the farm."

She smiled for his sake while she bleakly pondered, *Those precautions might shield me from the outside world, but another battle to win Keeley's love awaits me at home.* Nestling into Pa's embrace, she sought a respite before the storm and, in her peripheral vision, she noted Keeley's tender smile to their closeness. It saddened her that his time with his mam, da, and siblings had been cut short. She believed everything happened for a reason, though in this case, she had difficulty believing he'd lost his family to Ireland's Great Famine just so their paths could cross. It wasn't a stretch, however, to believe fate was steering them together for another reason—maybe for Jana to gift him with the family that had eluded him for far too long. Shifting her eyes heavenward, Jana silently vowed to his mam and da to make him happy—even if it meant her having to set him free.

## Elmira, New York

### July 22, 1864

Along the country road to home, their rear wheel stumbled into a rut and bucked the wagon, throwing Keeley's pistol to the floor with an earsplitting clang and Jana into his arms.

Jana flushed from the awkwardness of their contact, which chilled when she felt his rigid embrace and quickness to extract her from him.

Turning away to hide his own blush, Keeley retrieved his firearm. As he holstered it, he stammered and stuttered, "It ... it s-s-seems we won't be needing this anymore."

Feeling triumphant, Jana thought, *Good ... our closeness rattled him.*

"Any good with that gun?" Pa said, trying to divert his own smirk.

"Aye, if ye consider one shot to bring down a pheasant with its beak barely above a thicket good. Me caretaker in Virginia called meself a deadeye, given the number o' birds I'd bag in short order."

"Never fired one before. Would you show me how?" Pa said.

"You can use my Colt to practice with, Pa."

"I'll have to take you up on that, Jana."

"Do ye hunt birds at all, Mr. Brady ... er ... I mean, Thomas?"

"I do. Matter of fact, Jana used to hunt with me. Talk about deadeye. Once when we were out hunting deer, she killed a black bear—its forelegs raised and claws primed to take a swipe at me—with a shot straight through the heart."

"How about I teach ye to fire a Colt and ye take meself out hunting?"

"Sounds like a fair trade to me," Pa said.

It gladdened her that Pa and Keeley were planning to become better acquainted through activities other than chores.

"Might we need Jana to come along and help with the instruction?"

Jana grew hopeful that his including her was a sign he wanted to be with her.

"I'm flattered, Keeley, but too many cooks spoil the broth, and I have faith in your training skills."

As Pa was pointing to some of his hunting grounds, a doe and a fawn sauntered out of the woods and disturbed a flock of turkey, slumbering in the roadside scrubs. They rose with a cacophony of clucks, cackles, and yelps and, as they flew overhead, Jana felt the perturbed flap of their wings.

"How come they never come out when we're hunting them?" Pa muttered.

"If I didn't know better, I'd think it was a wee bit contrived on yar part. If ye'd warned meself, I would've kept me gun at the ready and given ye me own demonstration."

Chuckling, Pa said, "Just you wait, son, around the next bend is a wild-pig exhibit."

"Aye, now I see where the lass gets her quick wit."

Pa sat up prouder than a peacock in a traveling zoo showing off its colorful tail feathers while Jana silently recounted, *Another point in my favor on top of Keeley's admiring me for my soldiering and his seeing goodness in my smile and actions.* Feeling Keeley's smiling eyes upon her, Jana gave his forearm a gentle squeeze to show her appreciation for his compliment and held her breath in anticipation of his reaction. She squelched her surprise when he shifted slightly closer to her. Was she making progress in winning him over? She felt an ease she hadn't felt since she'd learned she was a stranger to him.

While Pa maneuvered Keeley back to more jabbering and jesting, Jana breathed deeply to take in the sweet-smelling air, purified by a light rain that had dampened the dusty road. Then she reveled in more of Mother Nature's palette she sometimes took for granted: Water droplets clung to the broad leafy hands of the oaks and appeared as emerald bracelets sparkling in the sun; a rainbow arced high into the sky; and a meadow buzzed with butterflies, bees, and hummingbirds flitting between the red, orange, yellow, and purple petals of the wildflowers. So lost in these splendors, Jana barely felt the remaining twenty minutes to home pass by.

Pa stopped the wagon at the crest of their drive so Keeley could enjoy the sweeping view of the Brady homestead. With pride, he surveyed the land upon which he'd toiled all of his life and had made more profitable than his father and grandfather had; however, his forefathers had never experienced a large army tarrying in Elmira and purchasing up their produce to fatten their coffers. It thrilled Pa to be able to, on special occasions, gift his family nicer seats at an opera or play and a supper of oysters at the Red Tavern.

Their lane slithered downward into the valley about a quarter of a mile where it forked: the right branch leading to the barn, cribs, henhouse, and smokehouse; the left to their farmhouse of four stories, including the root cellar and attic. Fanning out behind the buildings were their fields, where cows lowed as they lazily grazed and silky green stalks of corn and gold-bearded wheat stems swayed in the breeze. Public lands in which Jana had spent much of her childhood abutted their property. She relived those carefree days of wading barefoot in the meadow of hip-high grass to pick Ma some of its orange-bonneted lilies. Or picking and eating wild strawberries at the edge of the forest. Or being perched on a large bough high up in a pine tree pretending to be on the lookout for British soldiers and loyalists marching through the forest on their way to clashing with patriots on nearby grounds in the Revolutionary War's Battle of Newtown. She wished Keeley could've enjoyed a childhood as lighthearted as this. At the very least, she knew her family would help him recoup some of what he'd been missing in a loving home. She linked her arm around Pa's and said, "It's good to be home."

With awestruck eyes, Keeley said, "Might I have been the victim o' a duping? A few cows? Modest growing fields? It's a much grander operation than ye did justice to it."

"What nonsense have you been feeding Keeley while I was lost in the sights and sounds of home, Pa?"

He snickered. "Just as Ma and I reckoned to wean Keeley into us, I reckoned to wean him into our spread."

"Honestly, Pa, I can't leave you alone with him for one second without you wreaking havoc," Jana said, teasingly.

Straining red to keep from laughing, Pa said, "He offered to do chores, and I didn't have the heart to tell him he'd be at them from sunup to sundown."

"Now, Pa, tell him you're kidding before you scare him off."

Digging at a callous on his palm, Keeley said, "Don't worry yarself, lass, something tells meself I'm a wee bit used to hard labor."

Pa busted out with a howl of laughter, which echoed around the valley as he got the wagon descending to the Brady's slice of heaven.

Catching sight of Commodore and Maiti prancing around their private paddock in a frolicsome way, Jana cast aside her propriety and let loose a whistle that could rival a steam locomotive's.

They cantered to the gate and whinnied in reply as Pa gave her a sidelong glance to say she'd never win Keeley's love acting like a heathen.

Jana just laughed, happy to be home. She knew, above all else, she simply had to be herself. Somehow, she believed, love would find her again. Jana's deviation from convention gave her the perfect tactic for prying out of Keeley his preference for his marrying kind. "I'll always be a tomboy at heart, Pa, and there's no point in hiding that. No woman who lives and works on a farm can ever be purely a lady. Don't you agree?"

Comprehending her ploy, Pa again subtly jabbed her with his elbow and said, "I know how I feel about it; I won't bias Keeley with my answer."

"Well, now, I have to agree with Jana who tells meself that before I lost me memory, I aspired to farming. If that's me calling, I'd want a bride who doesn't cry over a wee bit o' dirt under her fingernails."

*Hallelujah!* Jana thought as brilliantly colored fireworks of silver and gold, pink and purple, yellow and green exploded before her. She smiled warmly at Keeley. Then the devil landed on her shoulder to warn her that after Keeley spent some time farming, he just might yearn for a less laborious, more sophisticated trade—and a prude to go with it. The fiend's advice might've been kindly meant, but he'd cut short her celebration and spoiled the moment. Pretending to brush lint from her shoulder, she flicked it away, hoping the wagon wheels had rolled over the rascal.

Circling around in front of the great gaping barn doors, latched to the outer walls to keep them from flapping in the breeze, Pa pulled the brake to still the mules.

They spied Eliza shuffling about the henhouse yard feeding the chickens. Contrary to her bottomless scowl, which she directed at Pa, the chickens clucked gaily as they hopped about pecking at the dried kernels of corn she tossed around by the handfuls. She dumped the rest of her bucket into a small heap, turned it upside down to keep it dry, and came toward them in a listless amble for one who'd begged Pa to accompany him to the train station. When the toe of her brogan caught in her skirt hem, she kicked at it and nearly tripped. This betrayed the source of her grumpiness, which Jana knew had everything to do with Ma and Pa's insistence she don a dress to properly greet Keeley.

Pa opened his mouth to admonish her behavior. He closed it when Keeley climbed down from the wagon, removed his kepi, and bowed before her. "It's a privilege to meet ye, Eliza. I'm Keeley." With a subtle wink back at Jana and Pa, he said, "On the ride here, yar pa was telling me that y'are both pretty and good with a rifle. Those are qualities I admire in a lass."

Aiming a gloating grin at Pa, Eliza said to Keeley, "Is that why you love Jana?"

Pa shook his head while Jana contemplated cutting out Eliza's tongue for putting Keeley on the spot. At the risk of being hypocritical, though, Jana would kiss Eliza if she were to ask this same thing again in the future after she'd given Jana and Keeley some time together.

Keeley seemed unscathed by Eliza's assault. "Aye, I admire both o' those things in yar sister," he said.

*Very diplomatic*, Jana thought. *If farming doesn't work out for him, as the devil had so disturbingly posed, he'll make a great lawyer, statesman, or both.*

The squeals of a small child drew everyone's attention toward the house. Molly was bouncing up and down to see over the side rail of the front porch. "Keewee, Keewee, Keewee's here!"

With an inviting smile, Keeley waved to her, and she came running, making a beeline directly toward him.

Jana scrambled from the wagon and mistimed her lunge, falling short of latching onto the ribbon tied around Molly's waist to hold her back from ambushing Keeley.

Lacking her typical shyness to strangers, Molly surprisingly dove into Keeley's wide-open arms, and he scooped her up.

*Who can resist his charm?* Jana thought.

"Appears there's a new king in our castle," Pa muttered with pretend dejection.

Keeley tapped Molly's nose and said, "I'm glad to meet ye, Molly, and I appreciate yar warm welcome."

"You talk funny," she blurted out in a nasally whisper.

"That's because I'm Irish."

Her mouth opened into a great big *O* that got stuck when it dawned on her this clarified nothing for her.

Keeley explained, "I come from a different land than ye, lass, and that's why I sound different."

"Where's Irishland?"

"It's across a great big ocean, far away from here, I'm afraid."

"Why're you afraid?"

"I'm not afraid in the sense that I'd be o' a ferocious bear; it's more that I'm sad because it's too far away for meself to ever visit there."

"Does that mean you're going to stay here with us forever and ever?" She threw her arms around his neck and smacked his cheek with her lips.

"All right, Molly, that's enough of the Spanish Inquisition," Pa said, relieving Keeley of her and setting her down.

Ogling the dewy spot on Keeley's cheek where Molly's lips had touched it, Jana thought, *You lucky, lucky girl, Molly.*

"Ma's itching to see you, Jana," Pa said. "Why don't you take Eliza and Molly up to the house and let her know we're home. Keeley can help me unhitch the mules and carry up your belongings."

To Commodore's and Maiti's whinnies, Jana said, "Sorry, Pa, I'm being called elsewhere."

"Afraid it's up to you, then, Eliza," Pa said.

"Seriously, Pa," Eliza groused, "you don't think Ma knows you're home with all of Molly's screaming?"

When Molly grabbed Keeley's hand to baulk at going anywhere without him, Pa said, "You see, Keeley, I wasn't kidding when I said my girls needed tempering. It's plain to see I have no control over them."

Jana pleaded Pa with her eyes. "Would you mind unhitching the mules so Keeley can come with me to meet Commodore and Maiti? We'll be done by the time you've finished, and I'll take Eliza and Molly up to the house, then."

Once again, Pa understood her tactic. "When I'm done, I'll fetch Keeley for help with your trunk." His eyes narrowed sternly upon Eliza and Molly. "You two come with me."

They obeyed and Keeley remarked, "It appears ye don't really need me help with the wee ones, Thomas. Ye have it all under control."

"If that's true, I've got Jana to thank for it. She broke me in," Pa said teasingly as he put his back to Jana and walked away before she could object.

Motioning for Keeley to follow her, Jana fetched two carrots from a sack hanging just inside the barn and shoved them into her skirt pocket. Commodore and Maiti had their necks craned over the top fence rail, and Jana nudged between their heads, drawing their whiskered muzzles into her neck.

As she basked in their horsey smells, Keeley said, "They're some beautiful, well-bred horses."

Jana kissed her black stallion's bristly forehead. "Keeley, meet Commodore, a Christmas present to me from Ma and Pa when I was around ten years old." When her dapple gray mare began pressing her muzzle into Keeley's chest, she said, "Do you remember Maiti? She obviously remembers you."

"I can't say I do, lass, but I'm smitten with her already," he said, scratching her head beneath her forelock and gazing into her warm brown eyes.

*Is that all I have to do to gain your affection—turn myself into a snuggly horse?* Jana thought, squelching a giggle so as not to pique his curiosity and then have to make something up.

"And how is it that I should remember her?"

"She was my faithful horse in the cavalry, and it was you who named her Maiti because of the way she formed up faster for a fight than all horses and most men."

He regarded her with pride, as if she'd been his battle maiden.

Snapping a carrot in half, Jana wiped dirt from one piece and popped it into her mouth while she held out the other for Commodore to slobber up from her palm.

Keeley raised his eyebrows with amusement and curiosity.

Swallowing the last of the earthy vegetable, Jana explained, "That's something Charlie thought up. It builds upon my pa's gentle approach to training horses by rewarding them a carrot with each step they obey, which I taught him, Leanne, and you back in Bladensburg when we were charged with breaking in our cavalry horses. Charlie believed he could gain his mare's trust by showing her they stood on equal ground; from what I saw of the easy connection made between him and her at the outset, I'd say it truly works. Remind me to tell Pa that later—he'll be impressed."

Keeley followed suit and bit off half, feeding the other end to Maiti. With a frisky undertone, he said, "Aye, the way it ought to stand between a man and woman ... I mean the woman gets the dirty half o' the carrot, the man the clean one." He broke out a toothy grin followed by a laugh. Before Jana could say something witty, his faced fogged over, and he began to massage his temples as had happened on their way home from the train station.

"Are you having another vision, Keeley?"

Unlike for his earlier revelation, he squeezed his eyelids tight as if he was trying to wring something extra out of his vision. He frowned, then opened his eyes. "I saw us in an immense paddock and, while other troopers were chasing down their horses, ye were showing meself to use carrots to train me horse."

His second vision with her in it made Jana momentarily lose her presence of mind, and she threw her arms around him in a victory hug. In the midst of their hearts beating together in a lively Irish jig, her breath caught when she was sure she felt him reciprocate her hug—it was weak but real. She pushed away from him so as not to overdo the intimacy. Their eyes met. Neither could nor would she conceal from her countenance the depth of her love for him. And she swore she saw in him a spark of something that tempted her to throw her arms around him again—even as he shifted nervously in his boots. "I'm sorry if I got too caught up in the moment; I couldn't help myself because we ..." she trailed off, suddenly feeling foolish.

Uncharacteristically serious for him and, with an intensity that could drain all of her deepest, darkest secrets from her, he said, "Please, lass, say what y'are thinking."

"We ... we shared an affection that was natural and reciprocal, and it's going to take me some time to adjust to this having changed between us. It won't be easy for me to rein in my desire to hug you with every happy or sad occasion." She bit her bottom lip to stop it from quivering and bringing on tears. "But I will because it's wrong of me to suppose you'd want to be hugged as often as I'll want to throw my arms around you." She bowed her head to hide her longing.

Keeley cupped his hand around her chin and lifted it. Full of compassion, he said, "Please, Jana, I want ye to be yarself. We are friends, and friends do hug." He flashed his dimples at her. "And I'm not opposed to a beautiful woman, such as yarself, giving meself a hug whenever the mood strikes ye."

Jana felt herself flushing to both his words and the thought that popped into her mind: *How about me kissing you whenever the mood strikes me?* Instead, she said, "Thank you, Keeley, I appreciate your understanding."

"This can't be easy for ye, lass. And if ye at all feel uncomfortable with having meself here, I'd hope ye'd tell meself."

She'd never send him away, but she felt it only fair to say to him, "And if it gets too uncomfortable for you to be here, I'd hope you could tell me."

"Aye, I promise," he said, glancing toward the nuzzling Maiti and Commodore, then to Jana with a tender smile.

Pa rounded the corner with Eliza and Molly on his heels. "All done with the mules and ready for Keeley to help me with—," he cut himself off when he spied Jana and Keeley staring at one another.

With Keeley's cheeks turning the color of his coppery hair, Jana leaped to dispel his discomfort, addressing Pa in particular when she said, "Keeley's just had another memory to do with us training our horses in Bladensburg. It happened when he was feeding Maiti a carrot."

"Ah," Pa said, clearly understanding Jana's reference to his horse-training method.

"I'll go tell Ma we're here." Jana sprouted wings like the butterfly flitting around her as she flew off to the house and left Eliza and Molly in Pa and Keeley's charge. Her energetic clomps rattled the windows facing the front porch and rumbled the floorboards in the entryway and short hall back to the kitchen.

Rachel and Rebecca dropped the pole beans they were trimming and nearly toppled off their chairs when she raced into the kitchen.

"What on earth?" Ma cried as she spun around, her spatula flinging bits of the sizzling potatoes and onions she'd been stirring on the stovetop.

The exercise and aromas of baking bread and smoked ham brightened Jana's mood more. "I'm sorry, I didn't mean to scare you," she said, skidding to a stop. "I was excited to tell you that Keeley had two recollections since Pa picked us up at the train station—both to do with me."

"That's wonderful," Ma said, setting down her spatula and wiping her hands on her apron before she hugged Jana. "I've been so worried about your mental state ever since you wrote to tell us about Keeley's affliction. I'm glad you're home safe and he's showing progress."

"When do we get to meet your Keeley?" Rachel asked.

"We've been made to wait long enough," Rebecca added, making her lips pouty.

Pushing away from Ma, Jana said, "Other than Ma and Pa, is anybody else happy to see me?"

"We're very happy to see you," Rachel said, "and we can't wait to hear all about your adventures. Right now, though, we're more interested in meeting Keeley."

Still pouting, Rebecca said, "It's so unfair. We're older than Eliza and Molly, and we should've been granted the privilege of meeting him first."

Ma scoffed at them. "You'd think you were meeting the Prince of Wales."

"We *are*," Rachel said.

"Any man who can make Jana lovesick *is* a prince in our book," Rebecca added.

Joining their fun, Jana said, "Prince? I'd rather have a knight." She sobered to say to Ma, "I don't want to look a gift horse in the mouth, but why do you suppose he's had two recollections since we arrived in Elmira?"

"You did tell us that before his enlistment, he found and fell in love with Elmira," Ma said. "Perhaps he feels a comfort here that puts his mind at ease and makes it agreeable to remembering."

"He fell in love with me too, Ma, and I know we felt incredibly comfortable in each other's company. So, if your logic is true, how come I haven't really broken through to him?"

Ma opened her mouth to say something, then stopped herself.

Having reared five girls, she probably understood the workings of the mind better than those who spent a lifetime studying only that. Jana had always cherished her advice, and she said, "Please, Ma, I can take whatever you have to say."

Ma blew away a wisp of her hair that had loosened from the hair net at the nape of her neck. "Well, maybe he feels pressured by you."

"How?"

"You're one to wear your heart on your sleeve, and I'm sure he sees your disappointment with his inability to remember his love for you. For your sake, he's probably pressing himself to remember, and that's stressing him from remembering at all."

Sinking into a chair, Jana said, "Are you telling me that I should alter myself to accommodate him?" She remembered her resolution back at the train station to do just the opposite and be herself around him.

"In a roundabout way … yes," Ma said. "Try acting as if nothing has changed between you. It will allow things to flow more naturally and give him some breathing room."

*Does that include throwing my arms around him in a victory hug?* Jana tittered silently at her own thought.

"Acting, after all, is your forte," Rachel said.

To the sound of Molly pummeling Keeley with questions, Rebecca said, "Here's your chance to start anew."

Three pairs of eyes urging her on inspired Jana to her feet. "Hurry, everyone, go back to what you were doing before I came in." She sped to the root cellar door, flung it open, and hid behind it on the top step. When she heard Pa's voice on the other side, she opened the door, calling out, "I couldn't find the pickled cucumbers, Ma," then pretended to be surprised by the others' arrival. "That was quick, Pa."

Ma and the twins smiled slyly at Jana.

"The work gets done faster with two and when you're hungry," Pa said, sniffing the air and rubbing his stomach. "Besides which, Eliza was champing at the bit to bring Keeley here. She wouldn't let us get any farther than the front hall with your trunk, Jana, so we'll carry it up afterward." He nodded at Jana, deferring to her to make Keeley's introduction.

"Ma, meet Keeley, my"—she stopped herself from saying fiancé—"cavalry comrade."

Keeley removed his kepi, held it to his chest, and bowed. "It's a pleasure to meet ye, Mrs. Brady, and I most humbly thank ye for taking me into yar lovely home and family. I was telling Mr. Brady ... er ... Thomas that I hope I won't be a burden. I'm ready to do me share o' chores."

"Please call me Julia. And there's plenty of time for chores. You'll rest today, and we'll discuss business tomorrow."

"Thank ye, Julia," he said with a grin, which enhanced his amiable features and hypnotized Ma and the twins.

Snapping out of her trance, Ma said, "Well, I must say you're more handsome in person than in Jana's daguerreotype. Speaking of which"—Ma flicked Jana a look that said she could act too—"I was just mentioning to Jana that Charlie is the last of her cavalry friends we hope to meet some day."

"Aye, he's quite the character and talented too. While at White House, we saw his skills with nursing, and he takes great photographs o' people and landscapes." Keeley winked at Jana, suggesting he hadn't forgotten their flirtatious episode to that subject.

Rachel cleared her throat, cutting Jana's blush short and forcing Jana to introduce her and Rebecca, who curtsied to Keeley's bow.

"We hope you'll feel at home here," Rachel said.

"Please, let us know if there's ever anything we can get you to make you more comfortable," Rebecca said.

"Thank ye, lasses, I appreciate yar kindness."

As Ma turned back to her hissing potatoes, she said, "Supper is almost ready. I'm afraid there's no time beforehand for freshening up, but there's ample time, Thomas, for you to show Keeley to his sleeping quarters and for the two of you to remove Jana's trunk to her bedchamber."

"If ye'd rather, I could stay and set the table."

Rachel and Rebecca let out a small gasp, and Ma winked at Jana, cueing Keeley had just endeared himself to her. "Thank you, Keeley. Perhaps another day."

"If I were you, I'd git while the gittin's good," Pa said, then bid Keeley to follow him out of the kitchen.

As the staircase squeaked under Pa's and Keeley's treads, Rachel said, "Can you believe Keeley asked if he could help us?"

"Besides Pa," Rebecca said, "what man would offer to do women's work?"

Jana said, "You'll see that no work is beneath Keeley. As I mentioned before, when we were tending to the wounded in Fredericksburg, he baked bread, made soup, mopped floors, and laundered bandages."

Molly blurted out, "I like him."

"I do too," Eliza said.

As Jana had anticipated, her family was the best medicine for him, and she could tell he was already growing fond of them. As for her—how was she supposed to give him some breathing room, as Ma had suggested, when they'd be living under the same roof? On her homeward-bound journey for her initial reunion with her family, she'd daydreamed about her future with Keeley by her side: a life filled with lots of love and plenty of adventure as she raised their gaggle of children, trained to be a mid-wife, and traveled the lecture circuit telling about her experience in a soldier's uniform. The first option was unrealistic right now and, since the latter two were impossible to accomplish simultaneously, the third option of traveling the lecture circuit appealed most to her. But how could she part from Keeley now?

## Elmira, New York

### November 15, 1864

Jana's cheek brushed against the soft velvet of the claret-colored curtain as she peeked around it to check on the drone of voices. Through the yellow haze of the gas globes, she noted that the seats had already filled up, yet people continued to file in. The great hall—outfitted for theatrical performances, operas, lectures on philosophy, astronomy, politics, religion, and other public events—would be her platform tonight. She found it incredulous that hundreds of people had come out to hear her story. Suddenly, a dizzying stage fright overtook her.

Extracting a handkerchief from her cloth reticule, Ma began dabbing at the nervous sweat dotting Jana's upper lip and forehead and, in a soothing tone, she said, "In my teaching days, I had to sometimes address a schoolhouse of concerned parents. I remember my first time, and I was just as apprehensive as you appear now. When it was over, I realized my biggest fear had been that I wouldn't have the answers to every question or concern posed." Ma laughed ruefully. "In the end, I had worried myself silly over nothing; I knew my subject well enough to deflect anything they threw at me. And so do you, Jana."

"Here you're facing your friends and neighbors; that can't be as frightening as"—Pa pumped his fist—"charging into a heated battle against foe."

Jana cringed inwardly at the image of cannon shot exploding all around her, ripping apart men and disemboweling horses. But Pa was right. Nothing—not even the angriest mob—could be as terrifying as charging into that, knowing she or her friends could be next.

Doodling with the pins that secured Keeley's kepi to Jana's hair, Ma said, "You'll tackle this as well as you have everything else."

Ma's and Pa's words always had a soothing effect on Jana, and she felt her confidence returning.

Jana's hostess and advocate for woman's rights appeared in a whirl, her soft footfalls at odds with her girth, which was at least four times Jana's. Scanning the faces around her, she said, "Where's Miss Brady? Is she not—," she cut herself off when her eyes fell on Jana. "Oh my!" She slapped her hand to her chest.

"Fetching in her cavalry uniform, isn't she?" Pa said, his pride in Jana radiating brighter than the gaslights.

To her continuing sputters, Ma said, "Is there something wrong, Mrs. Vaughan?"

"It never occurred to me to address Jana's wardrobe."

"You don't find it fitting for Jana to dress in uniform to speak about her time in it?" Pa asked.

"Yes, I do, Mr. Brady. But as one who's been traveling the lecture circuit, I can assure you that where woman's rights are concerned, change is not easily embraced; we have learned to approach it in baby steps. There is still a negative stigma attached to women speaking in public, and to hear about a woman sporting men's clothes is not quite as shocking as seeing it together with hearing about it for the first time. I fear that many will be too preoccupied by Miss Brady's outfit to pay heed to her amazing accomplishments. We wouldn't want her to be made into a spectacle."

"We appreciate your concern for our daughter," Pa crossed his arms over his chest and said, "but obviously you're not from around here. The people of Chemung County are freethinking folk. They're well aware of and have always accepted Jana's tomboyish inclinations." He cast Jana another look of pride.

Keeley came strolling toward them with Jana's four sisters on his heels. "We just came from the vestibule, and we can tell ye, Mrs. Vaughan, people were buzzing to hear Jana's story. I can also tell ye that I've lived here only a short time but long enough for meself to attest to the inhabitants' open-mindedness." He poked his head around the curtain panel. "And if ye were to study her audience now, ye'll see that it comprises as many men as women and a mingling o' farmers, laborers, and merchants, and not one seems riled by the program."

While Pa gleamed at Keeley with a father's pride—the same he'd just bestowed upon Jana twice—Mrs. Vaughan took Keeley's suggestion and peeked out. "Ah, yes, I see what you mean." She turned back to Jana. "I'm sorry if I caused you any undue angst."

"I'm glad you brought it up, Mrs. Vaughan. Pa's reminder of the local people's character and Keeley's assessment of the attendees has helped to lessen my stage fright."

"I'm relieved," Mrs. Vaughan said, opening the ornate silver locket that hung by a long silver chain around her neck to examine its mother-of-pearl face. "It's almost eight o' clock, and everyone seems to be seated and ready. We'll get started in ten minutes after I check on a few last details." She snapped the lid of her pendant shut, and away she went with it bouncing off her portly belly.

Smoothing out the cape flaps over Jana's greatcoat, which Jana had borrowed from Keeley and Ma had hemmed and tucked to fit her, Ma said, "Remember to stand up tall and proud and speak to your entire audience. If it's too nerve-wracking for you to look directly into their eyes, aim your sights over their heads."

Jana kissed her cheek. "Thank you, Ma."

"If it'll help any, Jana," Rachel offered, "you could imagine that you're home in the parlor telling Rebecca and me all about your adventures—just like old times."

Rebecca clasped her hands together. "You're going to captivate everyone as you always do us."

"I'm glad you didn't practice your speech on us," Eliza said. "I want to hear it for the first time with everyone else."

Molly dove into Jana, wrapping her arms around her thigh. "I love you, Janny."

During Jana's interactions with her sisters, Keeley gazed upon each in turn with a brotherly affection.

Molly skipped behind Keeley and started shoving him toward Jana. "Your turn, Keewee, to hug Janny."

To Jana's mortification, Keeley laughed, making his dimples burst out as alluring crescent moons. "A wonderful idea, Molly girl," he said, appeasing Molly with a mere pat on Jana's shoulder.

Pa grunted and Ma said, "I don't know how you do it, Keeley. You'll have to give us your formula for taking Molly's whims in stride."

With his hat in one hand, Pa wrapped his other around Molly's and said, "It's best we get to our front-row seats before they're taken." He led the way in hugging Jana, followed by Ma. Then he shot Keeley a knowing glance before he herded his flock away.

Jana envied Pa's ability to read Keeley better than her, even though she and Pa had spent equal time with Keeley since she'd brought him home. Supposing he now lingered behind to wish her luck, she silently lamented, *Darn that he can't just throw his strong, comforting arms around me.*

As if he'd read her mind, Keeley stuffed his hands into the pockets of his wool jacket with a sheepish torque of his lips. Hearing the applause and cries of acknowledgment to her family's appearance out in the hall, he said, "If that doesn't prove to Mrs. Vaughan the receptive mood o' yar assembly, I don't know what will. Yar ma and pa are special. I hope ye don't mind that I've come to think o' them as me own."

"I don't mind at all," Jana said, regretting her overly enthusiastic cheep. She didn't want him to think she expected him to have any greater attachment to her. Before he could ponder it, she hurried to cover it over. "I think it's pretty obvious they and my sisters have adopted you as one of their own." Her family's bond with Keeley, which was growing stronger every day, put Jana in a tough spot. It would be painful for them all to part ways, if it came to that.

"Thank ye for sharing that with meself. It's good to know I'm not a burden." He stared her square in the eye. "I want ye to know, as I've said before, that I admire ye for yar soldiering but also now for yar courage in speaking about it in public. Ye'll be the pride and joy o' Elmira, lass."

She'd been wondering what he thought of her in uniform, and she seized the chance to find out. "You don't think it's too much for me to be wearing this uniform? I wouldn't want to etch into anyone's mind a permanent picture of me as a soldier."

"Oh, I don't think there's even a wee bit o' a risk o' that, lass." He allowed a trace of seduction to seep into his voice. "Yar beauty, inside and out, puts that to bed."

To prevent herself from throwing her arms around him, she balled her hands into loose fists and pressed her arms against her sides as she'd constantly had to do over the past several months. "Thank you, Keeley. Your kind words mean a lot to me." When he made a move to go, she quickly invented a reason for him to stay, which she hoped would also show him how much she cherished him. "Of course you don't remember the time when you persuaded the men in our regiment to quit bickering and brawling over their boredom and to see the Rebels as our enemy instead of each other. But you might have some intuitive advice for my speechmaking apart from what Ma already said."

Keeley's face fogged over as it always did right before the vault in his mind opened to some remembrance. When he regained his clarity, he explained, "But I do indeed remember the incident and that me speech was precipitated by Leanne and some ruffian in a tussle."

"Do you remember anything else after you broke it up?" Jana crossed her fingers behind her back. *Please, let him remember the part about me—when he first gazed into my eyes and discovered I was a woman in uniform—and our romance began.*

Eyeing the floor, he said, "I'm afraid I don't, lass."

Jana's fingers uncrossed, and her hands slackened to her sides. Unfortunately, just like now, she hadn't been able to hide her heart where Keeley was concerned and as Ma and the twins believed she could do. Her masquerading had broken down after mid-summer when his brain spurts no longer had any link to her. Was it a coincidence these omissions had started simultaneously with the invitation from campaigners of woman's rights for her to travel around the state relating her war experiences? Maybe he'd already concluded beforehand there was nothing more between them than friendship, and he was using her reluctance to accept the lecture tour beyond tonight's performance as his own delay in telling her this while he figured out where he could go. Determined not to let this moment end in disappointment, as had all instances in which he failed to have any memory of her, she repeated her question. "Any advice for my speechmaking?"

Without hesitation, he said, "I might suggest letting yar emotions carry yar story. If y'are relating something sad, soften and slow the pace o' yar words to allow yar audience a chance to shed a tear; if y'are relating something exciting, louden and quicken the pace o' yar words to allow yar audience the thrill of cantering alongside ye."

"That's very insightful, Keeley," Jana said, wishing the other logjams in his mind would let loose and come rolling off his tongue as easily. "I'm so glad you were here to pass it on to me." To hide her frustration, she looked down to extract her white leather gauntlets from where she'd draped them over her waist belt. Her breath caught in astonishment when his hand glided into her field of vision but was yanked back. Not wanting to embarrass him, she counted to three, then raised her head in time to see him forcing his expression to fall flat. For some exasperating reason he was hiding something from her. She had to respect he'd tell her when he was ready just as he'd respected her having taken a while to confirm for him she was a woman disguised as a soldier. However, her patience was thinner than his.

He hastened to say, "I'd wish ye luck, lass, though I don't think ye'll be needing it. As Rebecca suggested, ye'll have everyone eating out o' the palm o' yar hands." He reached out and squeezed her hand. Then he pivoted on his heels and sped away, almost as if he was avoiding a desire to take her into his arms.

From the recess into which Keeley had just disappeared, Mrs. Vaughan appeared. "Everyone is seated and waiting," she said with excitement, which ripened her cheeks redder than the apples the Bradys had picked from their orchard in the fall. "Are you ready, Miss Brady?"

"I'm ready if you are," Jana said, wriggling her hands into her gloves.

Mrs. Vaughan tilted her head back to better see Jana. "Your deeds are a potent argument for woman's rights, Miss Brady. After tonight, I imagine you'll be an icon around the world," she said and dashed off to center stage.

If it was her intention to make up for the angst she thought she'd caused Jana earlier, Mrs. Vaughan had just unloaded a heavier burden upon her. In coming here tonight, Jana had expected to represent all women soldiers—no matter on which side they fought. It never struck her she'd be representing women around the globe. She prayed to make them proud.

A hush befell the crowd to Mrs. Vaughan's appearance.

She began:

> Welcome, ladies and gentlemen. We're honored that you have braved the cold, starless night...

Splaying her arms wide, she said:

> ...to fill this great lyceum theater in tribute of our orator's heroic feats. Unfortunately, without any standing room left, we had to turn many away. However, if we're enthusiastic enough—

She paused to wink at Jana before continuing:

> Miss Brady will consider a repeat performance another evening.

An exuberant applause sent tingles of delight from Jana's head to toe, and Mrs. Vaughan resumed her introduction as the commotion waned:

> Because tonight's program has been so well billed, and we're all familiar with our lecturer, I'll pause only to mention that we citizens of Chemung County are blessed to once again be able to stake a claim in history, thanks to one of our very own: the only woman, known to date, to have fought as a soldier, nurse, and spy in the ongoing War of the Rebellion.

While Mrs. Vaughan was forced to pause to another round of applause, Jana allowed herself to drink from the crowd's cup of cheer. It added to the speaking confidence Ma, Pa, and Keeley had instilled in her. And it humbled her too. She might be the first-known woman to be so daring, but she'd make sure everyone knew there were many others achieving the same, and she'd pay tribute to those who'd died in the line of fire.

Mrs. Vaughan announced:

> Without further delay, I give you our loyal and courageous countrywoman, Miss Jana Brady, alias Johnnie Brodie of the Tenth New York Cavalry Regiment.

Taking a deep breath, Jana left her sanctuary behind the curtain to exclamations of surprise splintering the cheers. She suddenly felt the wads of material remnants from Ma's sewing that were bunched up before her toes to make Keeley's boots fit. Was Mrs. Vaughan right about her having erred in outfitting herself in uniform? As she struggled to walk across the stage gracefully, Pa stood and threw every muscle in his arms and hands into clapping, inciting everyone to follow suit. Jana got a sudden urge to bow, then curtsey, which brought about a levity that seemed to detract from any misgivings over her being in uniform. With everyone reseated and their rustling cloaks and murmurs near a level above a pin drop, Jana thrust her hands over her heart and opened with:

> I'm touched by your warm welcome, and I too thank you all for braving the night to hear about my war experiences. Before I begin, I must acknowledge Mrs. Catherine Vaughan and her compatriots of woman's rights for inviting me to stand before you in representation of all women soldiers. I hope I'll do justice to them. Although our motivations for having enlisted vary—

A heckler butted in, calling out sportively, "What was your motive?"

In concert, several others shouted out, "Adventure, of course."

Grinning, Jana said, "It seems you all know me too well." She paused to allow another communal laugh, then adjusted her planned opening slightly to address the heckling:

> I'd add that anyone who heads off to war is seeking some kind of adventure. But no matter the motivation, I think I can safely say that all women soldiers from both sides of the war, once at the battlefront, have turned to fighting like demons for their respective cause.

Here Jana paid homage anonymously to women, such as Leanne, who'd fought courageously after they'd escaped an abusive home life, and such as the Rebel-soldier-bride from Fredericksburg, who'd courageously enlisted to fight alongside their husbands and died in the line of duty. Then she went on to chronicle her own adventures. In speaking of her assistance with surgical amputations and the aftercare of the stricken, she made sure to underscore the work of Nurse Clara Barton and Dr. Mary Walker and their courage in pioneering paths through roles traditionally reserved for men. And when she spoke of her spying, she made sure to honor those bravely risking their lives to gather intelligence for their respective cause but omitted any details that could identify and endanger Miss Lizzie or her disciples. Throughout her presentation, she remembered Keeley's advice to use emotion to carry her speech and, every so often, she'd seek nods of encouragement from Ma, Pa, and Keeley to gauge she still had her audience riveted as opposed to having lulled them to sleep. Hoping her final words would be heard most, she spoke them with great conviction:

> This is the first time since I've come from the battlefront that I've spoken of my experiences to such extent. As you heard tonight, I've met

wonderful people, I've seen beautiful parts of our country, and I've lived through some harrowing and heartwarming events. Although, I hope you also heard in my words, as I did, a constant tolling of the horrors of war that would make me happily give up my treasured moments in exchange for our country never having to suffer these again. The staggering number of dead alone is proof enough that where there exists the remotest chance of compromise, a country should never again resort to a blood feud. Since we have, though, I hope tonight that I've represented all soldiers with dignity, yet most importantly, women soldiers and their competence, courage, strength, and will that gives them the right to tackle anything a man can if she has a mind to it.

Her grand finale set off fireworks when every chair in the house was cleared.

Tears welled in Jana's eyes to the roar of appreciation. As she dabbed at them with her gloved knuckle, Mrs. Vaughan reappeared center stage.

"You have done us proud, Miss Brady," Mrs. Vaughan said with a squeeze of Jana's hand. It took some time for her to gesture everyone back to their seats. Then she announced that Jana had kindly agreed to field questions.

One gentleman called out, "How'd you manage to hide your femininity so long amongst hundreds of men in your regiment?"

A nervous titter arose at the delicate nature of his curiosity for these Victorian times, which frowned upon a discussion of such private matters in public.

Having lost her modesty because of her soldiering, Jana felt at ease in answering. "Most of the volunteer soldiers come from the countryside; they aren't used to bathing or emptying themselves in public. I fit right in with the men who, with modesty, sought private places and the boys who had yet to sprout an Adam's apple, facial hair, or deeper voice."

The next inquirer apologized first before he followed up with a question of a similarly delicate nature. "How did you get past the required physical examination for enlistment? Didn't you have to strip bare for it?"

To avoid making Surgeon Pease into a buffoon, Jana qualified that the very competent regimental doctor was bogged down with other military obligations when she presented to him, and he was forced to pass her with only a cursory examination.

Nearly an hour later, with all questions exhausted, Jana thanked her assembly again, and she was the happy recipient of her third standing applause. She exited the stage riding on a swell of glory as the hall began to empty and her family rejoined her backstage.

Pa grabbed hold of Jana's coat sleeves and drew her to him in a bear hug. "You were grand, Jana. We're mighty proud of you."

In embracing Jana, Ma said, "Your performance was flawless, your point clear, and you handled the hecklers and questions with ease. You really ought to consider teaching."

Keeley said, "Aye, she even had us laughing and cry—"

He was cut short by Mrs. Vaughan who arrived in another whirl. Pointing her index finger high in the air, she said, "Not so fast. Your daughter is destined for greater things." She moved aside, allowing a strikingly handsome, middle-aged gentleman in his all-black suit of frock coat, vest, and brushed wool trousers to edge past her.

The dapper fellow picked up on Ma's offended huff and said, "Now, Mrs. Vaughan, let us not devalue the importance of a teacher's work. Did you not minutes before acquaint yourself to me as a former teacher?"

Jana and Pa locked eyes, pinching their lips together to keep from snickering.

"Oh my, I seem to be putting my foot in my mouth everywhere I turn tonight," Mrs. Vaughan said, silencing to her fluster and forcing the stranger to introduce himself.

Switching his topcoat from the crook of his right arm to his left, he removed his bell-crown hat by its saddle brim and freed the lushest brown curls Jana had ever seen capping a man's head—let alone a woman's. He extended his hand for Jana to take, bowing over their clasped hands. "Allow me to introduce myself: I'm Wyatt McGriffin from Buffalo, New York. As a proponent of woman's rights, I consider it a great pleasure to make your acquaintance, Miss Brady." Although he sounded excited and genuine, his expression lacked zest.

"Mr. McGriffin has traveled here out of his way of business expressly to hear your recitation this evening." Mrs. Vaughn laced her fingers together before the flap of skin that hung beneath her chin like a turkey's wattle. "He has a most irresistible proposal for you. As a benefactor of woman's rights, he—," she began, buttoning her lips to his gently admonishing gaze. Her sheepish look deferred to him for his own accounting.

Rewarding Mrs. Vaughan with a small bow of his head, Mr. McGriffin then turned back to Jana. "My dear friends Mrs. Elizabeth Cady Stanton and Miss Susan Anthony begged me to come here tonight to hear your discourse, and I've concluded that it is the spark needed to reignite the crusade for woman's equal rights." He frowned. "Miss Anthony and I were dismayed with Mrs. Stanton and other promoters for abandoning their movement and concentrating all of their efforts throughout the war to the abolition of slavery. As I'm sure you're well aware, their complacency allowed the New York legislature to revoke a mother's equal rights to the father in the guardianship of her children and a widow's right to manage her late husband's estate. You, Miss Brady, could help the cause by emulating your performance tonight around the state as one means of helping to recapture those rights and gain others, such as universal suffrage. If you were to agree, I would absorb all of your expenses, including travel, room and board, and advertisement."

Everyone gasped, including Molly who was merely imitating those around her.

Observing Jana's speechlessness to his generous offer, Pa stepped up. He offered his hand to Mr. McGriffin in a hearty shake, and then he introduced himself and the rest of his family, including Keeley, whom he distinguished as Jana's cavalry comrade and welcome addition to the Brady brood. "I'm sure Jana appreciates your proposal as much as her ma and I do," he said, "and I mean no offense when I demand proof of your credentials. We've heard of and read about some pretty sophisticated vendettas that have been bred by war. One can never be too careful."

"I fully understand, Mr. Brady. If she were my daughter, I would accept no stone unturned when it came to her safety." Unclasping and peeling back the cover of a leather pouch, he withdrew a letter from it that he presented to Pa.

The ivory stationary crinkled in Pa's muscled hands as he unfolded the letter and read it aloud:

November 1, 1864, New York City

Dear Miss Jana Brady,

Miss Anthony and I are thrilled to introduce you to Mr. Wyatt McGriffin, our faithful friend and patron in the fight for woman's rights and suffrage. We hope that you will accept his proposal to rekindle our cause. It would be an honor to have a warrior like you representing us.

Your avid admirers,
Elizabeth Cady Stanton and Miss Susan Anthony

Having worked with both women activists close enough to know their penmanship, Mrs. Vaughan verified that the letter had been written by Elizabeth Cady Stanton and that the signature line was in the cursive of each woman.

An endorsement by such highly venerated women made Mr. McGriffin instantaneously trustworthy, and everyone gaped at him as if he had a halo hovering over his head.

In a confident yet unpretentious tone, Mr. McGriffin said, "I estimate that I could procure for you, Miss Brady, a stipend of one hundred dollars for each event, which would be entirely yours to bank."

Again, everyone gasped, this time from such an unprecedented amount.

To defend his assertion, Mr. McGriffin explained, "Given the fervor of the times and inflation, you should definitely be able to command at least double the fifty dollars that Miss Anthony received back in 1857 for her discourse on anti-slavery in Bangor, Maine."

His estimation dangled before Jana an image of the homestead she and Keeley could build from these profits plus the savings from each of their soldier's pay. In the midst of furnishing their house, he disrupted her daydream when he passed her another document from his billfold.

"I've taken the liberty of drawing up this contract," Mr. McGriffin said. "It delineates my commitment to you, Miss Brady, including my acting as your agent in negotiating the stipends for your lectures—free of charge, of course. I apologize for any curtness construed on my behalf to affect this arrangement. However, if you're at all inclined to accept my offer, time is of the essence. We have to line up speaking venues and allow them ample time in advance to advertise your event. Most importantly, we must build momentum toward our ultimate prize of speaking in Albany while the 88th state legislature is in session from January through April."

"When would you have me start?" Jana asked.

"I anticipate early in March. We'll want the legislature convened as a whole body feeling our rumble before we land on their doorstep, and we'll want it together long enough that it grows weary of its work and is open to diversion."

Jana was glad she'd have a few more months with Keeley to get a clearer picture of their future together—that is, if she decided to sign Mr. McGriffin's contract.

"I can give you a few more days to think about it, but I must have your answer on my return trip through here," Mr. McGriffin said.

"I understand," Jana said.

"What can you do to guarantee Jana's protection?" Ma asked. "As you must've gleaned by Jana's favorable reception tonight, our community is quite broadminded. I fear, though, she could be treated with intolerance and malice elsewhere."

When Keeley pinned Mr. McGriffin beneath a demanding stare, Jana wished she could see into his heart to know fully the nature and depth of his worry. Further, she wondered, *Why is everyone making a fuss over my safety when I've engaged in activities far more life-threatening than a lecture tour?*

Mr. McGriffin said, "I'll be traveling with Miss Brady. Additionally, I'll make sure each municipality where she'll be speaking recruits a presence to protect her, and I'm prepared to hire our own guards, if necessary."

Although Keeley didn't have a jealous bone in his body, this was one time Jana wished he'd smart over the news she'd be in constant companionship with this handsome, wealthy businessman.

Mr. McGriffin donned his chesterfield and, as he buttoned it all the way up to his silver-and-gray-striped puff tie and donned his black leather gloves, he said, "If you have no more questions for me, I must beg my leave to rest before I catch my next train."

"Of course," Jana said and thanked him for the exciting opportunity.

After he left, Eliza aimed her hazel eyes, wide with excitement, at Jana. "Are you going to do it, Jana? If I were you, I would. It sounds like fun."

In unison, Keeley and the twins bobbed their heads emphatically, and Keeley said, "Aye, it's the perfect adventure—not too dangerous."

Jana wondered about Keeley's zeal for her to accept this new prospect. Would he miss her at all?

Later that night, with the back of her head resting on her arms crossed atop her goose-feathered pillow, Jana stared out through the upper sash of her mullioned window. The face of the waning quarter moon shone down upon her with an empathic brooding. It seemed absurd for Jana to contemplate it, but maybe it too grieved the loss of a beloved star that had fallen from their shared galaxy.

The bedroom door squeaked open, and a flickering light and the aroma of melting beeswax preceded Ma as she came tiptoeing in. She laid the candle in its pewter holder on the bedside table, and Jana wiggled over to make more room for Ma when she lowered herself onto the edge of her bed. "I hope you don't mind my intrusion; I sensed your restlessness and thought you might want to talk."

Jana sat up, pulling her gowned legs beneath the coverlet up to her chest and wrapping her arms around them. "I don't know what to do about Mr. McGriffin's offer. If I leave now, I'm afraid any momentum I've gained in Keeley's remembering me will be lost. If I stay, I'm afraid I'll chase him away. Every time he remembers something, and it has nothing to do with me, my disappointment cuts so deep I can't hide it, and it's plain to see I'm adding to his frustration."

"I can't even imagine your dilemma," Ma said, her shoulders slumping as she bowed her head in silence.

"Almost as soon as Keeley and I met, I sensed his love for me. We've been together for nearly four months now, and I feel only friendship between us." Her lips began to quiver, and her eyes started to tear up. "Why can't he fall in love with me all over again? I haven't changed one speck since we pledged our love to one another and vowed to—," she was cut off by her own gut-wrenching sobs; it felt as if she might retch up her entire insides and leave nothing behind except a shell of her person.

Gathering Jana into her arms, Ma stroked her long tresses and, when she'd cried everything out, she whispered, "You might not have changed, but *he* has. Without any previous knowledge of himself, he's starting all over in rebuilding his character. The longer he's without his memory, the greater his exposure to all new inducements that could put him back together as a person who—I hate to say it—doesn't want you or perhaps you won't want. As much as I'd love to see you two make a match, you must prepare yourself that it might never happen. You'll always have a place in your heart for Keeley, and I don't mean to be callous when I say you're young and I'm confident you'll find another who'll make you happy."

"Oh, Ma," Jana sniffled and said, "what should I do?"

"Possibly, the Roman poet Sextus Propertius understood your plight best when he wrote in one of his melancholy poems: 'absence makes the heart grow fonder' or something similar to that."

Jana thought, *Leave it to Ma to recall some moral from her schoolbooks that suits the moment.*

"With you away," Ma continued to interpret the poet's proverb, "Keeley's mind will be more relaxed to remember you without feeling pressured to do so. If he never remembers another thing, I believe you've left behind a trail of your own inducements that could make him come around to appreciating you one day."

"Are you saying I should accept Mr. McGriffin's proposal?"

"Yes. It's coming at the right time; it'll give you and Keeley some breathing room, and it's the adventure of a lifetime that you always crave. Not to mention, after your performance tonight, I'm convinced you have a powerful message to impart on behalf of woman's rights."

Ma's words struck a chord relative to the vow Jana had made to Keeley's mam and da. Pulling away from Ma, Jana swiped her tears on the cottony sleeve of her nightgown and said more bravely than she felt, "You're right, Ma. It's time to set Keeley free and leave the rest to chance." What she wouldn't give right now to be the reputed seer Nostradamus so she could see what the future held for her and Keeley.

# Part II

## Center Stage

*Failure is impossible.*
—Susan B. Anthony, National American Woman Suffrage Association
Conference, 1900

# Buffalo, New York

### March 1, 1865

Jana was jarred from her thoughts by a blast of the New York and Erie Railway's locomotive. Relief washed through her. She wanted nothing more than to get off the train, desperate to shed the depressing image of her future without Keeley, which had played on her mind all the way from Elmira. She was beginning to doubt everything. The distraction of her lectures should help to keep her from dwelling on him too much. If only she could get started right away rather than a week from now, but she'd agreed with Mr. McGriffin about the prudence of an early arrival before the unpredictable weather for this time of year in Western New York could hinder it.

The expanse of land situated on Lake Erie was famous for high drifting snow banks, which often lasted into spring. Scraping frost away from her window, Jana saw this reputation upheld when the wind picked up a powdery rug from off the field, carried it trackside, and shook it out to broaden an existing bank. Now, as the train slowed, it rolled into a dark sky that threatened to dump more snow on Buffalo. She hoped this didn't bode poorly for attracting a large crowd to her event even a week from now. Or maybe it was an omen Buffalonians would reject her message and criticize her. One person, however, seemed overly eager to meet her.

Keeping a clumsy stride across the platform, even with her window, a monstrous man waved his gigantic hand at her while he mouthed her name. That seemed odd. A chap of his size ought to have a voice capable of booming above the sound of the crawling train and through her thinly glass-plated window. Either way, he was frantic to keep her in his sight.

Jana smirked. Knowing Mr. McGriffin, he'd drilled into this man's head his job to intercept and whisk her to her hotel before newspaper correspondents had a chance to ambush her. Pa had cautioned Mr. McGriffin about this having happened in Elmira, and he promised to avoid a repeat. Not wishing to get the dutiful servant in trouble, she scurried to collect her carpetbag and, as she stood, the rustle of her outer and inner skirts garnered the attention of the woman who'd commandeered the aisle seat next to her in Elmira. With an apologetic smile, she said, "I'm afraid I wasn't good company; I had a great deal on my mind."

Her round, aloof eyes, which reminded Jana of a hound dog, were at odds with her rigid posture and vigilant watch over their surroundings. Returning a smile, she said, "It was fortuitous we sat together as I too was preoccupied."

*Perhaps a lost opportunity?* Jana sighed inwardly. *We might not have been able to solve each other's problems, but maybe we could've made each other feel better.* Or given her age, which Jana guessed was in the early thirties, she might've had some important life lesson to impart. "I wish you the best in your endeavors," Jana said to her.

The woman cast a suspicious eye toward the rear and forward doors as if she expected some pursuer to come busting through. Then she nodded toward the window. "Is he an associate of yours?"

Taken off guard by anything from her beyond farewell niceties, Jana drew her head back.

"In my line of work I've learned not to trust anyone. Though, I'm less wary of his kind than a wolf in a dandy's clothes." With a squeeze of Jana's arm, she said, "I must be off to catch my next train to Chicago. Do be careful, miss," and away she dashed, her ruffled flounce grazing the train floor in its diligence to protect her skirt hem from dirt or dust.

Mr. McGriffin's employee, as Jana assumed him to be, was rooted like a massive oak tree at the base of the iron steps. When she descended to the platform, he was clearly but impossibly trying to retard his naturally booming voice to a whisper when he said, "Miss Brady?"

"I am. How did you know?" Jana said, surveying the clusters of people all around the platform and in front of the elongated brick station house for Mr. McGriffin, the only person who she thought could identify her at this juncture.

He tossed a nervous glance around him. "The boss wired Elmira to find out what you were wearing so I'd spot you right off."

*The boss?* Jana doubted the respectable Mr. McGriffin would tolerate being referred to so tactlessly by his employees. But then again, she didn't know him very well. Maybe he ruled with an iron fist, and he drew pleasure from them recognizing him in such an autocratic style. Or maybe they called him this mockingly behind his back.

Speaking with contempt, he continued to explain, "That fancy hat of yours made things easy."

Jana reached for her wide-brimmed straw hat with a ribbon tied in a rosette around its rounded crown. Feeling conspicuous, she scanned the area and observed hats far more extravagant than hers with striking bows and feathery plumes. No one paid her heed, as she'd intended when she chose her hat for its plainness and its grosgrain ribbon of chestnut to match her close-fitting coat. To better view her towering critic, she angled her head way back and felt the ruffles of the mob cap, which she wore beneath her hat to keep her head and ears warm, slipping beneath the high collar of her coat and tickling the nape of her neck. She wanted to tell him he was more eye-catching than her with the many scabs on his chin and cheeks from an obviously brusque date with a dull razor—and within the hour by their crimson color and grainy texture. Actually, he seemed far more conscientious of his appearance than he'd accused her of; he kept rubbing his upper lip and jawline, dramatically different shades from the rest of his weathered complexion. He must've just parted with a long-standing mustache and beard, Jana surmised. "I hope Mr. McGriffin didn't make you shave for me," she said, wondering why he hadn't trimmed the one long eyebrow, which lay across the prominent ledge of his forehead like a Christmas garland across a fireplace mantle.

With a harrumph, he said, "Do you really think the boss would let me fetch you looking like an ape escaped from a traveling zoo?"

Jana wanted to tell him that his appearance was more of a fright with it giving the impression that he'd broken away from a brawl at the local saloon just to come get her. And his crooked nose hinted it had been broken and reset a time or two. Trying to make light of his angst, she said, "I wager you'll have your beard back in a week."

He glared at her, suggesting he wanted none of her sympathy or, for that matter, her chatter.

Again, Jana felt uneasy in the company of this uncouth, unfriendly ogre. He hardly seemed the type she would've expected her elegant patron to send for her. She further doubted that Mr. McGriffin had gotten the chance to inspect his man before he sent him out in public. Besides the rushed shave, he'd obviously borrowed his tweed coat with its buttons ready to pop and the cuff of its sleeve retreating almost back to his elbow when he looped his arm around hers and started prodding her from the platform. A tattoo stood out on the underside of his arm above the wrist. Given a thriving population of freemasons in Elmira, Jana knew well their insignia—a depiction of their building tools: the letter $G$ (which stood for either "God" or "Geometry") nestled in the center of an imperfect diamond created by the legs of an inverted $V$ (a compass) at the top crossing over the legs of a smaller right-side up $V$ (a square). Although, something seemed off with the drawing; before she could figure it out, her chaperone caught her peering at it and flipped his arm over. "Are you a freemason, mister?" Jana asked.

"Uh ... er ... yes."

*It's a source of pride to be a freemason. Why would he hesitate to admit that?* Jana wondered, hearing her train partner's warning to be careful thumping her brain.

To hasten her along, he released his arm from around hers in favor of grabbing her by the upper arm with a pinch that Jana felt through the padding of her woolen winter coat and her silk day dress. With a wince from her, the brute loosened his grip and sounded as sincere as one with his surly voice could when he said, "Sorry, miss. The boss ordered me to take you from here fast, and it's always hard for a giant like me to be gentle."

"What's the hurry?" Jana asked.

"Someone leaked your arrival to the newspapers, and the boss sent me because he needed somebody big and strong to keep the hounds off you."

Both the sincerity of his apology and the plausibility of his explanation satisfied her. Besides, Jana remembered Pa treating her in this same crude manner when he was trying to steer her clear of newspaper reporters lying in wait at the train depot in Elmira. On the other hand, she thought she'd detected an underlying yen in his tone to be rid of her. *Why?* she wondered. *Just because Mr. McGriffin made him tidy himself up to meet me?* Or maybe he knew she was in Buffalo to show how women could rival men in their domain and he despised her for it. Or maybe it was as simple as she'd surmised a minute ago, that he'd been called away from a good brawl in a saloon; after all, his breath reeked of whiskey. Figuring his bad humor had more to do with the latter, she shrugged off that anything more sinister smoldered beneath his treating her as a nuisance worse than if she were a chigger that had crawled under his skin. She decided to avoid talking to him so she couldn't antagonize him further, until she remembered her baggage and asked him about it.

"It should be hitched to the carriage by the time we get there. When the boss wired Elmira to find out what you were wearing, he asked that your stuff be loaded where it could be unloaded first."

That sounded like Mr. McGriffin to have all of his *i*'s dotted and *t*'s crossed.

Her bodyguard nodded toward the carriage backed up to the curb farthest from the station house and said, "The boss's waiting for you in there."

"Mr. McGriffin's here?"

"Yup ... he was afraid reporters would get wind of you if they saw him with you."

Jana noticed that the carriage doors were without the McGriffin coat of arms, a tradition observed by the wealthy. Maybe Mr. McGriffin had thought to have them painted over so no one could identify his carriage in connection with her. Now that would be an impressive dotting of the *i* and crossing of the *t*.

However, there was one other thing to consider: his carriage could be new and he hadn't had time to have the family crest added. Eager to shed herself of her escort and be in the company of Mr. McGriffin, she slipped away from his grasp and started away.

Latching onto the crocheted scarf that was wound around the standing collar of her coat, he reined her in. "Please, Miss Brady, the boss'll have me strung up to a tree if I let you even an inch out of my sight," he said, reclaiming her arm.

Jana wanted to laugh. Was there a tree bough in the whole wide world sturdy enough to suspend him?

Because her travel trunk was blocking the step into the carriage on the side facing all of the other conveyances down the line, he led her around to the remote side. He craned his neck to skim the area around them, then opened the door and gestured her inward.

*He's really taking his job seriously,* Jana thought as she accepted his hand up onto the step. She ducked to clear her hat from hitting the roof and being stripped away. Then it dawned on her. She hadn't seen her hat box with the trunk waiting by the opposite door to be loaded. And come to think of it, the trunk was a darker shade of brown than hers. She turned to address it, and the titan's evil sneer iced her over with terror. When she tried backing out, he wrapped his hand around her mouth and shoved her hard, sending her face down across the carriage floor. He jabbed his knee into her back to pin her down while—with surprising agility and speed for one so bulky—he strapped a silky cravat around her mouth. It was steeped in expensive but stale-tasting cologne, and it overwhelmed her breathing along with her nose being mashed into the newly lacquered floor. Right before she was blindfolded, the dandy inside the carriage treated her to a glimpse of his well-tailored suit pants, its hems hugging well-cobbled traveling boots that appeared too big for the wearer's feet. Again, Jana heard the warning of her train partner echoing around her brain about "a wolf in a dandy's clothes."

With the aid of a cane, its oak shaft twisted, the dandy slid from the carriage as Jana's wrists and ankles were bound by his hulking minion.

*Do they really think I'm stupid enough to throw myself bound and blindfolded from a moving vehicle?* She supposed they did—deservedly so since she'd been tricked into allowing them to lead her to this point. To the wild pitch of her transport, she groaned. The driver was the behemoth. How nice to have the pleasure of his company longer.

Goliath said, "She'll be sorry she ever took up with them woman's rights radicals. They steal money from the rich—probably poor too—for their cause. Their agitating and greed will be their end, huh, boss?"

Several seconds of silence ticked off the clock.

In the tone of a child just reprimanded, Goliath said, "Sorry, boss. I didn't say anything incriminating, did I?"

Then a whip snapped, a pair of horses nickered, and the carriage spun out of the station.

Jana's eyelids fluttered open to sheer darkness. Shivering from the cold and feeling claustrophobic with her wrists and ankles hogtied, her eyes blindfolded, and her breathing limited to her nose with a gag in her mouth, she forced herself to stay calm while she got her bearings straight.

With her eyes transfixed into the bleak background of her silky blindfold, she gradually remembered the place where she'd been conveyed earlier in the day and left alone for hours. At first, it had been quieter than a graveyard. Having had little success in loosening the rope around her wrists, she'd kicked at the carriage door in frustration. What would she do if it opened? Her first concern: The murder of cawing crows that she'd deluded into thinking she was in her death throes and now waited in the boughs of a nearby tree or scuffed their talons along the carriage roof waiting to swoop in and peck at her like she was a rotten side of beef discarded for their delight. Her second concern: Even if she made it out of the carriage in one piece, she wouldn't get far squiggling across the ground slower than an earthworm. She'd take her chances with her kidnappers who she presumed would've killed her by now—if that was their plan. Nevertheless, she continued to work at her binding, managing to loosen it only marginally when Goliath returned and got the carriage rolling again. All day she'd watched the change in light filtering through her blindfold, and she knew by the darker shade twilight had finally passed the torch to night. When they finally stopped at some new destination, Goliath tore open the carriage door, yanked her out, and tossed her over a shoulder. His tromp echoed off the walls of the building they'd just entered and, as they traveled down a corridor, Jana flopped around on him worse than if she were a rag doll. With her words garbled by her gag, she said, "Why risk hanging for me?" He understood her because he replied with a harrumph, "Why not if the money's right?" He laughed sardonically. "Though, you can't buy your way out." She tried verbally tricking him into giving up more clues to her abductors, but she choked on her spit. "That'll teach you," he said, "to spout off about your soldiering. The boss says it ain't ladylike, and I got to agree." Jana had replied, "And you think yourself the consummate gentleman to judge me as unladylike—isn't that the pot calling the kettle black?" He'd retaliated to her insult by slamming her onto a cot and banging the door shut to her hollow-sounding cell. *How long have I been locked up?* she wondered and stared hard into her blindfold as if she'd find an answer. Although she was no further ahead in identifying her kidnappers, she had a good idea of their motive: They deplored her stealing money from them to propagate woman's equal rights.

*What money?* she silently demanded to know as she resumed twisting her wrists around in the rope to try freeing them. The four-hundred-dollar stipend she'd earn from all of her lectures combined was hardly enough to label her greedy. Certainly it wasn't enough for anyone to risk prison or a hanging over it, and they'd squeeze no greater ransom out of her than that as she didn't come from wealth. But Mr. McGriffin did. Maybe they were using her to get to him. The thought of Mr. McGriffin got her pulse racing. Hopefully, by now, he would've wired Ma and Pa to confirm she'd left Elmira; her parents would be frantic over her disappearance, and they'd all be searching for her. *Is Keeley too?* she wondered. Or was he waiting to see if her situation was urgent enough for him to up and come? Her thoughts segued to Leanne and Charlie. She was supposed to have taken supper with them after she'd settled into her hotel. That hour must've come and gone, and they knew all about her connection to Mr. McGriffin. Surely they'd already paid him a visit to inquire about her.

All of her ponderings had given her ample time to adapt to her claustrophobia, which she chided herself was nothing compared to being nailed inside a coffin. Determined to free herself, as she was then, she doubled her efforts. "Oh, hush," she said to her canvas cot, groaning to her twisting and turning and as it sagged under her weight. A fair amount of time passed before the rope gave enough for her to wriggle her hands out of her deerskin gloves. So as not to dizzy herself, she slowly rolled onto her back and sat up. She untied her gag and blindfold and allowed her eyes to adjust to the meager light seeping through three rectangular windows high overhead. Her fingernails were sore and her fingertips frozen by the time she picked away the prickly knot around her ankles. Rising slowly, she shook her arms and legs to work out their kinks and pranced around in one spot on her tingling toes to circulate the blood in them.

Returning her gloves to her hands, she stood still, cocking her head to listen. In the distance she very vaguely heard sheep bleating, hogs squealing, cattle bellowing, and a mighty belch of steam followed by a thunderous roll of one hefty object after another. Putting all the sounds together, Jana was convinced she was being detained near the famed New York Central Railroad's stockyards, where some of Pa's cows were freighted through from the mid-west and where there would be work late into the night to assemble a locomotive and multiple cars into a train for departure the next morning. Perhaps this location would help point to her abductors. She'd ponder it later. Right now, she had to get out of here before her abductors came back and did worse to her. As Pa had always taught her to do, she'd search her immediate surroundings for help out of her predicament.

She took a step and stumbled over what turned out to be her straw hat. Believing it to have instigated Goliath's harsh treatment of her, she kicked it under her cot, wanting nothing more to do with it. In further revolt of it, she wrapped her blindfold turban-style around her mob cap to provide extra warmth for her head and ears, then resumed her exploration. She clung to the walls, but a fuss of echoes to her stamping around the floorboards gave away that the room had been emptied of furniture and she was safe from tripping over anything else. Halfway around, a draft of charred wood tickled her nostrils right before her groping hands collided with a fireplace mantle. She kneeled on the floor-level hearth and reached up into the firebox to close the damper, cutting off the icy draft down the chimney flue and convincing herself she'd instantly improved the temperature in her cell.

Her loop around the quarters was brief. Toward the end of the third wall, she found the door. She felt all around where there should've been a handle and found a flat plate screwed to the panel with no keyhole. Of course, her kidnappers would've installed a lock that could only be employed from the hall side. She remembered her mental note from when she was trapped inside her coffin to always carry a crowbar in her carpetbag. Who would've thought she'd need one again so soon? She chastised her neglect as she continued her slog along the fourth wall. Closing in on where she approximated her cot stood, she nearly tripped over a tin bucket, which she booted under her cot with a reverberating clatter. Figuring it for a chamber pot, she scoffed at it. How much would it come in handy with no water to drink for manufacturing her own? She plunked down on her cot, and it squawked again about her proceeding cautiously with its infirm canvas back; given that it was her single comfort, she vowed to treat it more gently. By its compactness and utilitarian feel, she deduced her confinement was once an office, although it still might be with the furniture having been deliberately stripped from it for her discomfort. The one plan of escape she devised after considerable contemplation was to send her boot flying through one of the windows. She decided to wait until daylight and set her plan in motion when the rail yard was in full operation. Wrapping her crocheted scarf, long enough to cover her neck and face while leaving just her eyes exposed to the chill, she lay down and eventually fell asleep.

Sometime still in the dark of night or morning, Jana was awakened by a door squealing on rusty hinges. Fearing what she might face, she slowly unraveled herself from the ball into which she'd rolled herself to keep warm and peeked over her shoulder. A large masculine hand retreated from a tin cup that had been laid on the floor just inside of her room. Her dry throat prevented her from calling out to her jailer before his weighty treads vanished from earshot. Where was his chivalry? He might've allowed her some conversation in her loneliness.

She rose slowly to her feet and again shook the kinks out of her arms and legs as fast as she could with her thirst driving her toward the cup. Drawing her scarf away from her mouth, she tilted her head back to drink what turned out to be two measly drops. Then she found herself licking every inch of the cup inside until she licked it dry. "Darn you!" she screamed at her tormentors. Obviously, they were taunting her by placing her in a room with a fireplace and no fuel for it, assigning her a cup when a thimble would've sufficed for their paltry ration, and subjecting her to the smell of smoked meat from the wafts of hickory ash on the fireplace's grate. Their plot was sinister yet brilliant, though it reassured her they weren't going to kill her. Otherwise, why go through all of the trouble to break her will? She determined not to let them get away with it—even as she forced herself back to sleep to forget her nauseatingly hungry stomach.

Jana stirred awake to a morning that splayed its rosy rays high across the wall opposite the windows and to a flurry of activity in the rail yard. After she rubbed the sleep from her eyes, her first thought was driven by a longing for coffee and a hearty breakfast. Then she remembered her place and instead hurried to activate the plan she'd concocted the night before—while she still had the strength. She concentrated all of her efforts against one window, battering it with her boot. After an interminable number of attempts, the thick glass pane stuck its tongue out at her. If only she had a brick, she'd prove it had an Achilles' heel. *A brick? Of course!* She flew to the fireplace and felt around its hearth and firebox, but every single solitary brick was solidly mortared. While she was there, another idea formed: She flung open the damper and screamed up the flue until her voice grew hoarse and her cell icier. It was idiotic to think she could outshout the medley of man, beast, and rolling stock in the rail yard at peak operation. With her tail between her legs, she returned to the window and resumed battering it. Once, when her boot strayed beneath her cot, she discovered her carpetbag right beside her stylish hat. She had visions of shooting her way out with the pepperbox she'd stowed in it; the weight of defeat dragged her down when it came up missing. *Surprise, surprise!* She moved to the sturdy outer wall and began pounding her fists against it, giving up when it yielded a muffled sound barely audible to her. Banging on the inner wall proved just as futile; except for the coming and going of her oppressor to bring her water, she hadn't even detected the pitter-patter of mice feet out in the hallway.

The light of day came and went four times, and Jana's energy gradually sapped until she began exerting herself less and sleeping more. Like clockwork, her captors brought her two licks of water daily, which she gave up on when she began to expend precious energy crawling for it. She grew accustomed to the drone of the rail yard, scarcely hearing it anymore; when she did, it acted as a cathartic, hypnotizing her to sleep.

On the fourth night, the arctic air shook her awake and she wrapped herself in a tighter ball. She'd somehow managed to lose her face mask, so she pressed her cold nose into her cot—her only companion besides her thoughts, which could be friend or foe depending on their theme. Her bedding's odor of canvas reminded her of Commodore and Maiti, and she conjured up an image of Keeley in the chainmail armor of a medieval knight, galloping Commodore to her rescue with Maiti in tow for her getaway. Was this a sign he was on his way to her? When he was indisposed at Trevilian Station, she'd felt him summoning her to him. Maybe if she concentrated really hard, she could call him to her. She slipped back to sleep with a broad, buoyant smile.

Jana was clueless to the lapse in time between when she was last conscious and now with her being roused by a squealing door and a rumble of the floorboards, which made her cot bounce. By the giant hands that wrenched her up into a sitting position, she knew Goliath had returned. He flung her over his massive shoulder, and her dangling arms flapped against his back as he carried her outside. With her heavy-lidded eyes refusing to open, her other senses sharpened. She felt snowflakes melting on her cheeks as Goliath crammed her onto a hard surface, then concealed her beneath a thick blanket, its underside feeling leathery against her face and smelling of tanned hide. Almost immediately, her body heat circulated beneath the pelt, and she began to shiver as she thawed out.

The *swish, swish* of sleigh runners kept cadence with the *crunch, crunch* of a horse's hoofs as they navigated through the snow all along their route. After what seemed an eternity, Goliath called out, "Whoa," and the vehicle glided to a stop.

In the momentary break from motion, Jana listened to her own shallow breaths, resonating beneath her blanket and threatening to hypnotize her back into oblivion until her furry comfort was ripped away from her.

Goliath shoveled her back up into his arms and, as he lugged her along, he panted his whiskey-soaked breath into her face.

Jana finally escaped the sickening smell when Goliath deposited her roughly on some frigid stoop, propped her up against a door, and abandoned her after rapping on some colossal knocker overhead. His fast-fading footfalls were replaced by softer ones approaching from inside, then Jana's support fell away as it swung open. After she collapsed onto her back and, before she slipped back into unconsciousness, she heard a woman call out, "Dear Lord, Wyatt, come quickly!"

## Buffalo, New York

### March 5, 1865

Jana's eyelids fluttered open to a tender hand lifting her head away from some fleecy comfort and the rim of a porcelain cup prodding her lips apart. Tepid tea sweetened with honey trickled down her throat.

When her caretaker saw her patient staring back, she threw her kind amber eyes wide in surprise. "Thank the Good Lord you've come back to us," she said with her relief ironing out the worry wrinkles across her forehead and visible beneath the ruffled overhang of her white linen mob cap.

Jana tried to sit up, but a gentle strength in the matronly woman's petite hands nudged her back onto her goose-feather pillow.

Fussing to draw the pastel yellow coverlet up to Jana's neck, the woman said patiently yet firmly, "You're not ready to be up and about, Miss Brady. You must proceed with great care in your weakened state."

"Where am I?" Jana croaked, then prayed she wasn't in her dreary cell dreaming her comfort.

Jana must've telegraphed her skepticism to her nurse because she said, "Don't worry, dear, you're safe now."

Although she sounded sincere, Jana was scared to trust her. She'd been duped once and, in her weakened condition, she could easily be again. Was it irrational for her to wonder, though, if this kind woman was the next ploy in her captors' torture: to get her used to nice things, only to pull them out from under her? The mastermind behind her kidnapping wore the latest fashion, suggesting he had the kind of wealth that could sustain a place such as this. With a suspicious twitter, she said, "Safe? Where?"

"You were left on my master's doorstep, and he insists you remain here while you convalesce."

Jana's muscles tensed. "And ... uh ... who's your master?"

"Oh dear, do forgive me for not mentioning Wyatt McGriffin straightaway. I'm his household manager, and I'd like it very much if you were to call me Hannah." She folded her hands across her waist and waited patiently while Jana made sense of this information.

Her sincerity won Jana over and eased her overactive mind and tension. "How long have I been here, Hannah?"

"I'll tell you exactly." From her skirt pocket, she drew a silver timepiece that dangled on a silver chain clipped to her waistband. After a quick study of its face, she said, "My, oh my, time certainly flies. It's nearing nine o'clock, around the time you were dropped off on the front portico last night. The ruffians who mistreated you were considerate enough to knock on the door and signal your arrival." Her eyes squinted in anger. "That won't help their case when they're brought to trial."

"Were they caught?" Jana cried out.

Hannah patted Jana's hand. "No, dear, I'm sorry. I meant *when* they are caught."

Jana's eyes roamed around her hospital room—completely the opposite of the crude, cone-shaped tent she'd been assigned to after she was shot in the arm at Brandy Station. Glass globes of azure blue softened the bright yellow of the gaslights, and their glows sent merry shadows waltzing across the ceiling of her bedchamber—twice the size of the sitting room back home. The cherry wood of the matching washstand, bureau, wardrobe cabinet, and dressing table was buffed well enough for one to see their reflection in it. Two overstuffed lime-colored chairs and a nesting table shared between them were arranged before a snappy blaze in the fireplace, its hearth and mantle ornamented in the same marble as the washstand's basin. Although Jana wasn't used to basking in such luxury, she was elated with her quarters—a more private place to recuperate than a hotel. The word *hotel* sent her flying up into a sitting position, and the leafy pink and blue flowers of the papered walls began to merge together as she dizzied.

"Please, Miss Brady, you mustn't make such swift moves," Hannah said, urging Jana down again.

In a panic, Jana's words came tumbling out. "But I must get word to my friends. I was supposed to meet them at the hotel on the day I arrived. I'm sure they're worried sick about me."

"If you mean Leanne and Charlie, Wyatt learned of your appointment with them when he telegraphed your ma and pa about your disappearance, and he took care of contacting them. In fact, they joined the search for you. They'll be allowed to visit when you're more rested. Right now, we must get some nourishment into you. I'll go to the kitchen and see to some chicken broth and toast."

"I'm grateful for your attention to me, Hannah, and I'd love to thank Mr. McGriffin for his hospitality too."

"Wyatt's worried sick over you and eager to see you. He's worn down the rugs in the sitting room with his pacing. However, only those with privileges I deem special are allowed in to see you tonight." She smiled and winked. "And Wyatt has no clout with me even in his own house."

Following a feeble giggle, Jana sobered to say, "Please, tell him he's not to blame for my kidnapping."

"I'll be sure to, but I doubt it'll ease his guilt any." Hannah moved to the door, turning back to waggle her index finger at Jana. "Now don't you go vanishing on me, Miss Brady."

"If you'll call me Jana, I promise to not even twitch a finger."

"Well, we'll just have to make sure you don't. I have a willing substitute ready to take over tending you, and I'll send her right up." With a mischievous glint in her eye, she said, "She'll make a much better nurse for you than me."

"That's impossible, Hannah. No one can outdo your care."

"Don't pass judgment just yet. I think you're going to be pleasantly surprised."

Shortly after Hannah's departure, the dark paneled door slid inward, and Hannah's replacement came swishing inside.

Jana blinked twice. "Ma? Is it really you?" Hannah was right—Ma was the best medicine for her now.

Sweeping bedside, Ma kissed Jana's forehead, then gingerly sat down next to her, gathering Jana's hands in both of hers. "Tell me truly how you feel, dear."

"Much better with you here, Ma." Reading into the meaning of her questioning eyes, Jana said, "Don't worry, those scoundrels didn't lay a finger on me. They only deprived me of food, water, and heat."

"Only?" Ma's face twisted up with fury.

"Actually, they were kind to give me a cot so I didn't have to sleep on the floor," Jana said with another feeble giggle.

"I'm relieved to find your wit hasn't escaped you," Ma said, heaving a long sigh, which drew Jana to her fatigue.

"I'm sorry this has put such a strain on you, Ma. How long have you been here? And is Pa here too?"

"Of course your pa is here. Wyatt telegraphed us the day of your disappearance, and Thomas and I caught the next train out to join the search for you."

Feeling her shame welling up inside of her, Jana said, "I could kick myself,

Ma, for ignoring my intuition and allowing myself to fall into a trap."

"You weren't alone in being fooled. Apparently, your captors staged an accident to prevent Wyatt's passage to the train station in time for him to foil their ambush of you."

Jana frowned. "You can bet I won't be that trusting next time around."

Combing Jana's unbound tresses away from her face, Ma said, "We can discuss your kidnapping another time when it's not so upsetting. The doctor's orders are for you to avoid becoming excitable."

"Too late, Ma, your surprise visit already did its damage."

She recoiled in horror.

"I'm just teasing you." Realizing the beating Ma's temperament had taken over her tribulation, Jana rubbed her hand and said, "Honestly, Ma, you look as if you could also use less excitement and a good night's sleep."

"I suppose you're right," she said, massaging her own shoulder muscles to work the stress knots out of them.

"Can I see Pa tonight?"

"We'll see. Right now, he's downstairs in the parlor, talking with Wyatt and"—she paused for a few good long seconds—"Keeley."

"Keeley?" Again, Jana jolted up into a sitting position, this time without dizzying.

"Oh dear, I could kick myself for mentioning his name just yet. It's made you too excitable. Some nurse I am," she muttered as she nudged Jana back onto her cushy pillow.

If only Ma knew she'd just sent Jana's heartbeat kicking wildly like Maiti's and Commodore's hind legs when they frolicked in their favorite meadow, she'd be kicking herself harder.

"Keeley insisted upon coming along too."

"Why? Has he had some revelation about me?"

Averting her cocoa-colored eyes to her skirt, Ma brushed away imaginary crumbs from it as she said, "He is your friend, and friends support each other in time of need, don't they?"

"What are you keeping from me, Ma?"

"Whatever makes you think I'm keeping something from you?"

"The fact that you're avoiding looking at me."

Trying to sound convincing, she said, "*I* have nothing new to report where Keeley's concerned."

Ma's emphasis of *I* made Jana think, *Maybe she doesn't have something new to report, but it appears Keeley might.* She wouldn't add to Ma's stress over her kidnapping by trying to pump it out of her. If Keeley had something to tell her, he should do it. And if he'd come to Buffalo because he thought he owed her for her having put herself on the firing line a couple of times for him, she'd clear him of the debt—she'd make him understand she truly only cared about his happiness. Her eyelids began drooping from all of the excitement.

Tapping the tip of Jana's softly angled nose, Ma said, "I'm afraid your reunion with Pa and Keeley will have to wait until tomorrow. Right now, I must insist you stay awake long enough to eat a little something."

On cue, Hannah arrived with sustenance and, while Ma propped Jana up on two pillows, Hannah situated the bed tray over Jana's lap.

The aroma of the chicken broth got Jana's stomach rumbling for it, but her burning eyes refused to be enticed. One spoonful into Ma's feeding her, Jana felt her eyelids drop and her upper body falling forward.

Jana awakened the next morning with an image of her face dunked into a bowl of chicken broth with torn pieces of toast bobbing on its surface. Ma and Hannah must've saved her from this fate since neither the hair in her nostrils nor that hanging in her face were encrusted with chicken broth or its lingering aroma. Stretching and purring like a kitten, she rolled onto her side and spied a steaming cup on the nesting table between the lime-colored chairs.

Peeking around the wing of one of the high-backed chairs, Ma said, "Good morning, dear." The glow from logs ablaze on the fireplace's grate formed a halo around her head.

Jana smiled, happy to have her angel of mercy watching over her. "Good morning, Ma. Please, tell me you didn't sleep there all night."

"No, I didn't." With a haughty sniff of the air, she jokingly said, "Pa and I had our own bedchamber as elegant as yours and also with its own separate dressing room." She sobered. "Truth be told, old habits never die—I was up before the rooster crowed. I checked on you first and, after I found you sleeping soundly, I went to the kitchen and helped the cooks make bread until they shooed me out."

"Then, you slept well?"

"Yes, but more importantly, how do you feel this morning?"

Jana slowly lifted onto her elbows, feeling only slightly shaky in the exchange between her prone-to-sitting position. "I slept the best I have in a long time, and I feel like a new person." When Jana saw Ma's shoulders relax, it reminded her to ask, "How are your shoulders? Still knotted up?"

"They're all better, now that I know you are well."

"I'm glad."

"Your pa is champing at the bit to see you; I'll send him up after you've had your breakfast," she said, rising.

Feeling her stomach jabbing her, Jana said, "I'm so hungry I could eat a bear."

Ma grinned. "Will buckwheat griddlecakes do?"

"I can't wait." Jana dreamed of swallowing them whole.

Ma reached the door and turned back. "After you've had a bath, we'll get you dressed and moving about."

"Do I have clothes other than what I arrived in?"

"Wyatt rescued your trunk and hat box from the baggage cart at the train depot. That's how we knew something was wrong—you never would've abandoned your belongings." Ma swatted a hand. "Well, that's all behind us now. If you're up to it today, we'll send for Leanne and Charlie, and you can visit with them and everyone else in the sitting room downstairs. They're all itching to see for themselves that you have no ill effects. And I warn you that they're also eager to hear about your misfortune. If it's too painful to relive just yet, I'll run interference."

"Actually, Ma, I don't mind discussing it. Maybe together we can all make some sense out of it." Although Jana was anxious to see everyone, she took a leisurely pace savoring the doughy, yeasty hotcakes with maple syrup that Hannah brought up, followed by her enjoying her reunion with Pa (an emotional reproduction of the one she'd had with Ma) and basking in the luxury of the hot bath poured for her by house servants in her own dressing room's tub with lavender soap that she glided over her skin. She required no assistance in donning her day dress of green-and-white plaid, which Ma had draped over the cedar-scented privacy screen. In the midst of watching herself in the dressing-table mirror as she worked to unsnarl the ends of her long hair, she caught sight of her haggard appearance and dropped the brush in horror. It clattered onto the cherry surface. Her face was sallow, and her puffy upper and lower lids flattened her almond-shaped eyes to conceal some of her hazel irises. She'd wanted to be pretty for Keeley; now she could only hope he wasn't expecting her to be a sight for his sore eyes—as he had when she'd first presented to him as a woman at Castle Thunder Prison Hospital. She pinched her cheeks to bring color back to them, but unfortunately, there was no time to apply a cold compress to her eyes with everyone waiting on her downstairs. At the very least, she had control over her hair, which she finished brushing, coiling, and netting at the back of her head.

When Jana was ready, Ma held her arm to steady her as she ushered her out of her bedchamber and down a long hall to a winding staircase.

Jana felt like Cinderella promenading to her ball as she descended the carpet runner, secured to the sweeping oak steps by brass rods capped with brass pineapples. Everything about Mr. McGriffin's mansion was majestic, including the gasolier hanging high over the grand entryway—its teardrop crystals caught the streams of light through the fan-shaped window over the front door and scattered them into tiny colorful beads that glittered everywhere. "Does Mr.

McGriffin live here alone?"

"No," Ma said, "Hannah lives here with him. Sadly, Wyatt bought and refurbished this mansion expecting to have a large family. That was all taken from him when his beloved wife, Laura, died of consumption before they could have children."

Although Jana couldn't walk a mile in his shoes when it came to love lost from the death of a sweetheart, she could relate to the nightmare of a sweetheart's lost love. Her heart flipped on its stomach, buried its face in her chest, and cried for him.

Oblivious to Jana's mournful expression, Ma minded their footing down the staircase and prattled on, "She was a handsome woman; wait until you see her portrait—it looms large where we're headed. Hannah says she was compassionate too. She would apparently have Wyatt accompany her once a week to deliver food, clothing, medicines, and other essentials to the poor, and she also worked for the woman's rights movement. Her family is close friends with that of Gerrit Smith's."

"Isn't he Elizabeth Cady Stanton's older cousin and one of the philanthropists accused of financing John Brown's raid on Harpers Ferry?"

"The very one," Ma said. "Anyway, Hannah says it was good therapy for Wyatt to pick up where Laura left off; he still makes weekly visits to the poor and, as we well know, participates in the woman's rights cause."

"I get the feeling Hannah and Mr. McGriffin are very close."

"They are. Hannah was Wyatt's nanny and, when she never married, he and Laura brought her here to live with them. They wanted to care for her as she did Wyatt all through his growing years. Old habits die hard, and Hannah is still really taking care of him; she insists upon managing his household affairs."

"Does he have any blood ties?"

"His pa passed away a few years back, but his ma still lives in the same house here in Buffalo where Wyatt grew up. Hannah avoided expounding upon it, though she intimated that there's no love between Wyatt, an older brother, and their mother."

"That's heartbreak…" Jana trailed off when they reached the bottom few steps and scared a kitchen maid who was loitering outside an ornate archway with her ear cocked into a room out of which floated the murmurings of conversation. She mumbled something about trying to get Hannah's attention, then fled down a hall, tossing a nervous glance over her shoulder at them before she disappeared into a room at the back of the house.

"That was strange," Ma said.

With a shrug as they descended to the alternating black and white tiles of the grand entryway, Jana remembered, more importantly, what she wanted to say to Ma before they were distracted. She stopped, forcing Ma to a standstill so she could hug her. "I love you, Ma. I'm so fortunate to have you and Pa as parents."

Squeezing her back, Ma said, "You'll always have our love and support." Then she stepped back. "So what brought this on? If you're worried about Wyatt's being without the love of family, you can stop worrying. As the saying goes, blood isn't always thicker than water, and Hannah and Wyatt share something special that makes them behave as mother and son. You'll see for yourself what I mean."

"What about Mr. McGriffin's brother? Where's he living? Wasn't Hannah his nanny too?"

"Hannah says he also lives here in Buffalo. She declared him a wayward soul who's apparently chosen to distance himself from Wyatt and Hannah."

The sketch of Mr. McGriffin brought to light for Jana his serious nature. How many people could persevere through such dark times and not be sobered by it? Keeley was the exception to the rule—he'd somehow managed to preserve his gaiety. The comparison was in no way meant to belittle Mr. McGriffin. How he'd managed to preserve his giving spirit with all that had been taken from him was astonishing.

Ma resumed their march, guiding Jana through the ornate archway and into the parlor.

As they crossed the threshold, the lifelike and life-size portrait of Laura McGriffin, hanging above the fireplace mantle, met them as if she herself was greeting them. It took Jana's breath away.

Ma whispered, "Incredible, isn't it? Wasn't she beautiful?"

In her stupefied state, Jana could only bob her head. It didn't seem fair that this beautiful, generous woman could be robbed of life so young. How could Mr. McGriffin gaze upon her every day without being driven mad?

"What do you think of the room?" Ma continued to whisper.

Its size and opulence contrasted with any Jana had ever seen before. Even those in the mansion of Elmira's wealthy merchant Jervis Langdon, where she'd attended birthday parties for his daughter Olivia "Livy" and Underground-Railroad meetings with Ma and Pa, paled in comparison. Like Mr. McGriffin, Mr. Landgon was a philanthropist. He gave food, clothing, and money to slaves escaping through Elmira to St. Catharines, Ontario.

"Magnificent, isn't it?" Ma said. "I've wandered into this room many times since our arrival, and I'm still in awe."

Jana figured the parlor could accommodate a party of fifty dancers and fifty bystanders if it were converted into a ballroom. Once the rugs were taken up, only the floor-to-ceiling velvet curtains and wall tapestries could mute the resounding echoes of twirling feet. All of the furniture and accessories taking up the space were pleasantly situated. Chinese vases taller than Jana guarded the corners; box and tiered plant stands of wood and iron hugged the walls; and various sizes of rectangular, square, and round tables meandered in and around sofas and chairs arranged in a horseshoe facing the fireplace and Laura's portrait. With so many wooden arms, legs, and surfaces to preserve, their waxing compound of beeswax, paraffin, and vanilla oil probably permanently scented the air.

Following the alternating bronze and white stripes of the papered walls up from the chair rail, Jana's eyes landed on the ceiling—the highest she'd ever seen. Grapes and vines were etched into the crown molding, which circumvented an expansive mural that colorfully depicted the mighty Greek gods Zeus and Hera sitting upon their thrones and watching over their four offspring as they played hide-and-seek amongst the clouds. Jana's eyes bugged when, upon closer inspection, she recognized the likenesses of Mr. McGriffin and his beloved Laura in the faces of Zeus and Hera.

Ma said, "That was done before Laura died. Apparently, Wyatt didn't have the heart to paint over their hopes and dreams."

*How wretched*, Jana thought and, before her heart could shed more tears, a sudden lull in conversation lured her down from the clouds to find Pa, Keeley, Leanne, Charlie, Mr. McGriffin, and Hannah turned in their chairs watching her with interest. She moved toward them, donning her most reassuring smile to let them know she suffered no ill effects from her ordeal.

Mr. McGriffin hopped up from the sofa he shared with Hannah. Reaching her side, he looped his arm around Jana's free one and assisted Ma in helping her to a wing-backed armchair centrally located across from the fire and to everyone else's accommodations.

As Mr. McGriffin retreated to his sofa, Jana whiffed the unmistakable scent of the cologne in which her gag had been steeped. She recoiled as she relived the moment she was maliciously bound and gagged.

"Are ye all right, lass?" Keeley asked.

The depth of his concern for her sounded as loving as it had in the minutes before the battle at Brandy Station. Given Ma's ambivalence last night over Keeley's reason for having come to Buffalo, it confused her. She tried searching his eyes for something to support his tone, but they were diverted to a teetering cup rattling on its saucer as Hannah poured tea.

Having barely gotten reseated, Mr. McGriffin moved to the edge of his cushion, his eyes darkening with concern. "Yes, how do you feel, Miss Brady?"

Jana decided against mentioning the cologne right now and further upsetting Mr. McGriffin. Instead she said, "Please, everyone, I appreciate your concern, but *really*, I'm fine."

Passing tea to Jana, Hannah said, "You must stay hydrated."

Charlie spoke up, "We're sure glad to see you and that you're all right."

Jana swallowed a sip of the soothing chamomile tea. "And I'm happy to see you too, Charlie—and everyone, for that matter." Allowing her gaze to linger especially on Hannah and Mr. McGriffin, she said, "I'm most grateful to you both for your hospitality to me and my family."

While Hannah acknowledged her graciousness with a wink and a smile, Mr. McGriffin shook his head at himself with disgust. "It's the very least I could do since I failed in my vow to your parents and Keeley to keep you safe from harm."

Jana flicked Keeley a look that silently questioned, *You expressed concern for my welfare to Mr. McGriffin?* Her heart skipped a beat when a flash from his emerald eyes validated it. As much as she'd like to continue her silent probe into him, Mr. McGriffin's distress demanded her attention. "Please, Mr. McGriffin, no one could've possibly anticipated I'd be kidnapped. Not to mention, it's a risk that follows any agitation."

Pushing back her flannel shirtsleeves and balling her hands into white-knuckled fists, Leanne blurted out, "We're gonna round up those rats who did this to ya and, when we do, I'm gonna wring their necks."

"Is there anything ye can tell us about yar kidnappers that might lead us to them? That is … if y'are up to talking about it right now, lass."

"I'm up for it." Jana waded in, reporting every little detail she could remember, including her speculation she'd been detained at the New York Central Railroad's stockyards.

Mr. McGriffin stiffened. "I'm a stockholder of that railroad."

Pa cocked his head in thought toward Mr. McGriffin. "Might the well-tailored clothes of Goliath's boss indicate he's a stockholder too?"

Mr. McGriffin said, "I'll investigate the whereabouts of each stockholder for the past few days and poke around the stockyards to see if anyone saw any abnormal activity. I doubt the latter will yield much. The stockyards are an enormous enterprise, spanning one hundred acres; offices are dispersed throughout for the management of the pens, slaughterhouses, and train operations and repairs that aren't always in use. It would be pretty easy to hide someone there, especially if they're secreted there after dark."

"About the ringleader's attire," Jana said, "his boots and trousers were very similar to the styles you wear, Mr. McGriffin. I'm sure a great many gentlemen use your cobbler and tailor, but maybe one of the other stockholders goes to them too."

"I'll investigate that angle too," Mr. McGriffin said, combing his fingers through his curls.

"Another angle you might want to—," Jana blurted but cut herself off. She could see Mr. McGriffin was becoming very distressed by the trail of guilt that was leading to him, and she didn't want to upset him further. In no way did she believe him guilty of complicity.

Mr. McGriffin stopped combing his curls and said, "I implore you, Miss Brady, to speak your mind, no matter if you fear it will defame or disturb me. We must have every detail if we're to solve this mystery."

Given that he was footing the bill for her lectures, Mr. McGriffin deserved to be well informed. Again, Jana waded in to tell them about the cologne. Afterward, she felt sorry for him when he became the object of everyone's surprised scrutiny, which Jana knew to be only that since she was confident they all believed in his innocence. However, if right now they were a jury deciding his fate, they'd have to convict him with all of the evidence amassing against him.

Hannah reached over and held his hand to show her support.

Leaning into her, Mr. McGriffin kissed her forehead in a display of affection Jana would never have expected from one so austere.

To show she believed in him too, Jana started to say, "I get the impression the *boss,* as Goliath called him—"

Mr. McGriffin interjected with a grunt. "Doesn't say much about Goliath's respect for his boss."

"I had the same thought," Jana said, relieved that Mr. McGriffin detested such a denigrating title. She'd pegged that right about him, and this teeny validation spoke greatly to Jana's sense he was one of the good guys.

"Not that it reveals anything about your abductors." Mr. McGriffin scowled. "It's just a personal vexation, but pardon my pointless interruption. Please continue with your conjectures."

"No apology necessary. Everything we say could lead somewhere revealing," Jana said while she searched her brain for where she'd left off. "Oh, yes ... I think we can all conclude you're being framed. I'm pretty sure I was given an intentional glimpse of the boots and trousers of Goliath's boss because I can't fathom any other purpose for him to have been in the carriage since he neither partook in saying anything derogatory to me nor in restraining me. He even avoided me hearing his voice when he silently reprimanded Goliath as if I might recognize it."

"I appreciate your confidence in me, Miss Brady," Mr. McGriffin said, moving fireside where he grabbed a poker and began pushing the logs around on the immense grate to stop them from spitting sparks against the screen.

Jana said, "It's wise to check the whereabouts of your stockholders around the time of my kidnapping and to try linking any of them who could be suspects to the exact clothing, boots, and cologne you wear. But, I think, in a city of this size, it's probably an exercise in futility to investigate each and every tailor, cobbler, and fragrance shop."

Everyone agreed with Jana's logic, then they succumbed to their own ruminations, pierced only by the rattle of cups and saucers as Hannah moved about topping off everyone's tea.

After Mr. McGriffin rehung the poker, he remained at the fire. He adjusted his suspenders to lie better on his shoulders and, when he peeled back his shirtsleeves to expose his forearms, it reminded Jana to tell them about Goliath's tattoo.

Rubbing his clean-shaven chin, Pa said, "Seems odd for a freemason, given his piety, to get involved in anything so underhanded."

The word *piety* triggered Jana to ponder the *G* at the core of the tattoo. It finally dawned on her what was odd about the drawing that she'd tried to process when she first saw it, and she cried out, "That's because the tattoo doesn't represent the freemasons—it's intentionally faked to resemble their insignia."

All eyes shot to her, demanding an explanation for her outburst, and she obliged. "The capital *G* traditionally used by the freemasons was really a capital *C*. The horizontal stem drawn across the top of the bottom upward curve of a *C* to make a *G* was replaced with tiny letters drawn higher than where the *G's* stem would be. At a quick glance, I mistook the *C* for a *G*."

"Do you remember what the small letters were?" Mr. McGriffin asked.

Jana surveyed the Persian rug for an answer to come popping out of one of the bronze acanthus leaves patterned across an eggshell background. Her frowning forehead portrayed she'd drawn a blank.

Ma said, "It's a shame you can't remember. Those letters might hold the key to naming those behind your kidnapping."

With a twitch of his cheek, Pa said, "Least we know they didn't do it for a ransom. That ought to narrow things a tad."

Jana's head whipped toward Mr. McGriffin. "If they didn't want your money, what did they want?"

"They pinned a demand to your coat that you give up your orations and go home or"—Mr. McGriffin grimaced—"you'll be harmed worse than the gunshot wound you received in the war."

"Well, no matter how radical my kidnappers might be, I can't believe they'd kill me—if that's what they mean by worse—over my speaking publicly about my soldiering."

Pa said, "Your war experiences are threatening to the male domain—shows them what a woman can tackle if she has a mind to it."

"You're also championing a fight against chauvinistic standards that, if won, will change our country's culture drastically. As well, it's a cause that most men and women who've been indoctrinated to chauvinism perhaps oppose stronger than those that have our country currently at war. Not that it'll start a war," Ma said.

Hannah added, "I agree our cause won't start a war because of the greater population of women, black and white, and black men who will rise up together to become the majority. But that will take time."

"All of this tells me," Mr. McGriffin said, "that there's more to Jana's kidnapping than meets the eye. It will take an army of men and women, not just the escapades of one woman in a soldier's uniform, to sway an entire nation to grant women the rights to vote and decide on all matters that affect her."

"Are ye suggesting that the grudge against Jana might be more personal?" Keeley asked.

"Unfortunately, I am," Mr. McGriffin said.

"I can't think of anyone in particular who'd want to see me harmed," Jana said, pressing her mind as hard as she imagined Keeley must when trying to eke out some further recall from his brain, only to come up frustratingly blank.

Ma said, "It might not be personal to you, Jana. Perhaps your abductor is using you as a tool of revenge against all women for some injustice done to him by one woman, such as being spurned in love or business."

"If you're saying the mastermind behind my abduction could be a perfect stranger, then why would he go to the trouble of masking his voice from me?"

"Before he fully affects his revenge, he might need, at some point, to acquaint himself with you," Ma said.

"That makes sense, Ma, but back to your other point. How would his personal vendetta affect all women?"

"It's pure conjecture on my behalf, of course, but by your abductors publicly showing your ineptitude at shielding yourself from personal threats, they might be suggesting that luck was on your side in surviving your war activities; thus, it weakens your argument that a woman has the brains and brawn to tackle anything a man can, and it makes a mockery of the entire woman's rights movement."

"If yar theory is correct, that makes the kidnappers a bunch o' lunatics and far more dangerous." Keeley turned to Jana with apprehension raging in his eyes. "Y'aren't considering continuing on, are ye, lass?" When Jana hesitated to reply, he stressed that her kidnappers had made it clear they wouldn't hesitate to do worse to her. "I meself don't want ye ... er ... I mean, I meself don't think ye should want to put yarself in such danger."

Had Keeley really meant to say he didn't want her putting herself in danger? A tingle of excitement ran up and down Jana's spine. Maybe he was making progress in remembering their love. Or maybe his heart had grown fonder for her in her absence. She hoped for the former because she wanted him to remember everything about her that he'd accepted and cherished, including her time in uniform by his side; she'd certainly be content with the latter.

"Keeley makes a good point. You'll stand out like a color bearer leading the regiment into battle," Charlie said.

With uneasiness, Mr. McGriffin said, "I won't be responsible for exposing you in a manner that gets you killed."

Jana said, "What are you saying, Mr. McGriffin?"

"Please ... call me Wyatt. We are friends, I hope."

"We are and, likewise, please call me Jana." She paused to gather her thoughts before their exchange of pleasantries. "Are you saying, Wyatt, that you're considering withdrawing your financial support?"

"If it's the only way I can force you home, then, yes, I am. I would never forgive myself if I encouraged getting you harmed or killed. As it stands now, your kidnapping weighs heavily upon my conscience. Perhaps there's a safer way we could accomplish your message, such as getting your speech published in newspapers around the state."

Jana felt her rebellious nature heating to a boil. Writing about her war experiences to prove woman's equality didn't hold the same emotional fervor and persuasive power as telling about them. She bit down on her chapped lip, drawing blood; its metallic taste reminded her of all she'd endured in the war. Just as she'd proven in her roles as soldier, nurse, and spy, she was a fighter, and she wasn't about to be forced into giving up now because of a few rotten apples.

"Oh boy! I know that look and Jana ain't 'bout to give up," Leanne said.

Digging her nails into the plush arms of her chair and dimpling the tiny diamonds in its camel-colored fabric, Jana braced herself for a hot debate. "You're right, Leanne. I refuse to give up. I enlisted for four speaking engagements, and I never break a promise." She turned to Wyatt. "My ma and pa taught me to fight for my country no matter the cost to myself, and I intend to do just that." She caught Ma and Pa sharing a roll of their eyes. They might be tired of her using their patriotic preaching against them, but they'd have to live with the consequences of having ingrained it into her. And now she spotted a source for helping her to regain Wyatt's financial support. Not that she necessarily needed it; however, she preferred not to tap into her savings in hopes she and Keeley would still one day use it to build their dream hearth and home. Pointing at his marble chess set with its ornately carved pieces, she said, "Do you play, Wyatt?"

His thick, naturally groomed eyebrows shot up in befuddlement to the drastic change in conversation. "Yes. My father taught me to play, and I have many memories of our tournaments."

Hastening to cover over the inflection in Wyatt's tone that suggested his chess-playing with his father had been more dutiful than welcome, Hannah chirped with pride, "Once Wyatt became proficient at the game, his father rarely ever prevailed over him again."

"I've never played," Jana said, "but I understand each match is all about making your own moves in accordance with having anticipated your opponent's. If we could create ruses to confuse my adversary, such as arriving for my next lecture the day before or after I'm expected, I could be kept from harm." While Wyatt stared through the window fronting his residential street, which radiated out from Niagara Square toward Lake Erie, to mull over her idea, Jana switched tactics, hoping for his pity. "I'll completely understand if you stick to your guns not to back me. Given the circumstances, I'm not sure I'd back me either if I were in your shoes. You should know, with or without your support, I plan to carry on. With the connections Elizabeth Cady Stanton and Miss Anthony have in Seneca Falls, Johnstown, and Albany, I'm sure they can find me free lodging with their families or friends, and I have some money of my own for food and transportation until I start collecting a stipend. I'm sure I'll negotiate a much lesser fee than you could, but I'll be happy with whatever I get."

Playing right into Jana's ploy, Leanne leaped to say, "If yer mind's set on it, I'm goin' with ya to act as yer guard."

"What about your smithy, Leanne?" Jana asked.

"Billy keeps the books while I oversee operations. I've got two good men I trust to do their own work and split my part while I'm gone—that is, if you're all right with me runnin' my business that way, Mr. McGriffin."

"I've seen how you operate, Leanne, and I'm confident you know what is best," Mr. McGriffin replied.

Leanne smirked at Jana's gaping jaw and said, "I got ya to thank for leadin' Mr. McGriffin to me and my smithy. He's hired me to maintain one of his fleets of wagons and mules."

While Jana regarded Wyatt with awe, wondering where his kindness and generosity ended, Wyatt was insisting Leanne call him by his given name.

Leanne said, "Can't do that, sir. It ain't right with me bein' on yer payroll."

"It's more of a partnership," Wyatt said. "If you insist, however, I shall revert back to formalities too and call you Miss Watson."

Leanne wrinkled up her nose. "I give up. I'll call ya Wyatt if you'll call me Leanne. I don't much care for the sound of anything so formal."

Jana knew Leanne really meant any title with an overly feminine ring to it.

"Now that I've mustered out of the army, and I haven't set up my studio yet, I'm free," Charlie said. "I could tag along as a guard too and, while I'm at it, I could take some pictures of your events with the equipment Leanne found and had restored for me." He faced Leanne. "I could sell them to pay our way."

"Ya ain't got to worry 'bout that, Charlie. We've got money enough from our smithy to take care of both of us and Jana too."

"That's awfully sweet of you, Leanne and Charlie," Jana said with a sidelong glance at Keeley to gauge his reaction. Curiously, he was aiming a look of dismay at Wyatt who failed to notice. *Is he jealous of my show of admiration for Wyatt? Or is he unhappy with Wyatt for rescinding his charity?* No doubt it was because of the latter. He was an honorable man who always kept his promises, and he expected no less from others.

"I warned you, Wyatt, that not even a kidnapping would thwart Jana, and none of us are going to allow you to continue shouldering the burden for it," Ma said.

Pa added, "Julia's right. Jana's message is coveted by the woman's rights movement. If you hadn't offered to fund her trip, I'd wager others would have. But her moral might drive some to extremes, and Jana understands that—she did when she accepted the lecture tour, and she did when she rode off to fight in the Great Rebellion." He smiled at Ma, then Jana. "We're proud of our daughter for not shying away from tackling the tough issues to help her country along. There ought to be more of us like her."

"Where there's a will, there's a way with Jana—even if she has to run away to get it," Ma said, inciting a chorus of laughter.

Jana was glad Ma's humor had returned to her.

When the merriment subsided, Keeley said, "If I were to go along too, I think that between Leanne, Charlie, and meself, we could keep ye safe."

Jana's heart melted to his proposition. It wanted to say yes—to have him by her side would be heavenly. But her head said no—as much as it pained her, she needed to stick to Ma's strategy for them to be apart for a while, especially since she sensed his heart had grown a sliver fonder for her during her absence. She'd avoid him as if he were the Black Death itself if it meant she was winning back his love. Before she could open her mouth to protest, Wyatt beat her to it.

"That won't be necessary, Keeley. Nor is it necessary for Leanne and Charlie to accompany you, Jana. I've decided to reinstate my financial support. For my own peace of mind, however, I insist upon hiring Pinkerton detectives to travel with us—one to guard you at all times while the other tracks down the wrongdoers. And I'll make sure there's a local police presence at each of your orations."

Leanne said, "For my own peace of mind, I insist on goin' along. I can pay my own way and, given my"—she cleared her throat, then lowered her voice almost to a whisper—"gender, it'll be a lot easier for me to stick to Jana's heels, and that'll free up the Pinkertons to do the investigatin'."

"I'm going too," Charlie said. "I can turn my camera on the audience and make it appear as if I'm photographing it when I'm really keeping an eye out for troublemakers."

"I'd like to tag along too," Keeley said, peering at Jana with pleading eyes that branded her heart with a desire to let them get their way—as they always could with her.

She had to look away before she caved in and, very subtly, she bore her own pleading eyes into Ma's to come to her rescue.

Obliging Jana, Ma said in her sternest voice, "It would be better for you, Keeley, if you were to return to the peaceful confines of the farm with Thomas and me tomorrow morning while you continue your own rehabilitation. Medically speaking, we still don't know what twists and turns your amnesia will take. You could find yourself in a situation where a temporary lapse in memory imperils yourself and others."

Keeley dropped his frowning face toward his lap.

*Is he disappointed to be cut out of the action? Or is he deeply worried about me?* Jana wished he'd give her a hint. Either way, it was a good sign he wanted to be around her. For the first time since she'd lost all hope of them ever becoming sweethearts again, she felt optimistic. She allowed her soul to soar to the ceiling and swing on a cloud amongst the Greek gods and, from this perch, she pictured him gazing up at her, crooning his rendition of a chorus within "Aura Lea"—as he'd done during their escape from Richmond back to Union lines:

For to me, sweet Jana Lass is sunshine through the heart…

## Buffalo, New York

*March 8, 1865*

Jana ought to be feeling regal and enjoying the ride, but the last time she was a passenger in a carriage as exquisite as this one, she'd been bound and gagged. Compounding her misery, Leanne was enforcing keeping the curtains closed. That doomed Jana to staring at the walls of her rocking prison and forbade her from seeing the historical sites of the city—some built in 1804, immediately after Joseph Ellicott, an agent of the Holland Land Company, mapped the streets to radiate outward like spokes on a wheel from Niagara Park (the affluent residential area where Wyatt resided). She especially bemoaned not seeing Courthouse Square where she was originally scheduled to speak. It would've given her the privilege of following in the footsteps of great luminaries. She knew that there Revolutionary-War hero General Lafayette in 1825 commemorated the fiftieth anniversary of the war's outbreak, Martin Van Buren in 1848 accepted his nomination for president of the United States by the Free Soil Party, and Abraham Lincoln in 1861 gave a glimpse into his genius and charismatic personality on his way to being sworn in as the sixteenth president of the United States. As sulky as she was about it, Jana understood all of the precautions for her safe transport and that Wyatt had been compelled to change the venue for her performance due to the shadowy hollows and large boughs of the heavily wooded area around the square that made perfect perches for snipers to gun her down.

Feeling trapped, Jana began drumming her gauntleted fingers against her lap as if she could hurry along the two white horses, laboring to keep a hoof-hold in the icy ruts and prevent their buggy from overturning. The ride went on longer than she'd anticipated until finally a swaying right turn, then another swaying left turn, landed them at what Jana estimated to be her destination. She made a swift move to disembark.

Not fast enough for Leanne whose gloved hand flung out and put a squeeze on Jana's upper arm that she felt through the layers of her wintry cavalry garb. "Wyatt's driver and his man ridin' shotgun got orders to scout the perimeter before they cut us loose."

Sitting back with an impatient grumble audible only to herself, Jana followed Leanne's lead and peeked out through a slit she made between her window's curtain panels. Their coachman stood before a brick building, jabbering with two burly men: One who Jana presumed by the badge pinned to his outer coat was one of several deputies assigned by the Erie County Sheriff's Office to quell any riots inside the hall, the other who Jana presumed by his canvas jacket and denim work pants was one of several of Wyatt's construction laborers he'd hired to guard all entries into St. James Hall. Contacted too late to be of service to Jana in Buffalo, the Pinkerton agents would join her at her next stop.

Finally, the door curbside swung open, and the wintry breath of Mr. Frost blew in to rob them of their warmth. The frigid temperature numbed Jana's lips and got her teeth chattering; it made her glad she wasn't speaking outside.

"All clear," the thickly bearded teamster said in his husky voice.

"I ain't takin' no chances," Leanne said, parting her coat flaps and fetching her army revolver from its holster. Playing the role of advance guard, she hopped up from her seat and exited the carriage before Jana could draw her own Colt.

Lifting her feet away from the coal-warming box, Jana smiled at her new cavalry boots, which Wyatt had bought for her. It would do no good, he'd insisted, for her to try skedaddling from any angry mob or kicking an attacker in the shin if she were stumbling around in Keeley's hand-me-downs. As she clambered down from the carriage onto the crusty sidewalk, two stories of arched windows and one story of rectangular windows at the top of St. James Hall rose above her. Far more imposing was the seven-story building abutting it westward, formerly St. James Hotel—or so Jana was told. Together the two buildings formed the entire block on Eagle Street between Main and Washington Streets; the latter two streets sandwiched in Courthouse Square, a good long block northward.

The former St. James Hotel was currently owned by the Young Men's Association; it made rooms available to numerous other organizations, namely the Buffalo Historical Society (of which Millard Fillmore, thirteenth president of the United States, had helped found and served as its first president). Jana hoped their archives would reflect a noteworthy speech by her and not one delivered at the price of martyrdom. This Jana knew from her religious studies was a fate that had afflicted James the Greater, the hall's namesake and one of twelve apostles who continued to champion Jesus after his crucifixion and was killed for it by Judean King Agrippa I in the first supposed act of persecution against the Church. She figured she'd soon find out which way the wind was blowing with Buffalonians when one side of the front double door swung open.

Wyatt popped his head out, motioning them inside. His eyes squinted with worry when he spotted Jana's and Leanne's bared pistols. "Did you have trouble?"

"Nope. We were just makin' sure we didn't," Leanne said.

"Ah, well, let's hope our strategy to mislead your abductors works," Wyatt said.

While Jana holstered her Colt, Leanne said, "I'm gonna keep mine out 'til I'm sure of things."

Gas piped into the hall for both lighting and heating immediately assaulted Jana's nostrils with its distinguishable odor and blessed her cheeks with its warmth. As they emerged from beneath the darkness of the upper balcony's overhang into the sun's slant through the tall windows gracing the Washington-Street side, their eyes met an auditorium capable of accommodating hundreds with its seating.

To Wyatt, Jana said, "I'm worried we won't draw the size crowd we'd hoped for since we spread the word of my lecture only a few hours ago. It probably won't yield the outcome you'd planned on."

"Better safe than sorry," Leanne said, walking down the aisle in a semi-crouch with her eyes peeled between the rows of pews and the upper balconies for some villain to come springing out like a jack-in-the-box.

The sun glancing off the barrel of Leanne's gun reminded Jana of their first real skirmish at Leesburg, Virginia. They'd been charged to seize the town, coveted by both sides because of its proximity to bountiful crops in the Loudon and Shenandoah Valleys and to the Washington-Winchester Railroad for the replenishment of men and supplies to the armies. Riding down a main street, they kept their eyes keen to windows, doors, and rooftops. They advanced a fair way in when a few streets over they heard *pop, pop, pop, crack, crack, crack*. The other half of their squadron was engaged with the enemy, and it sparked her unit's clash. In spotting a Rebel aiming his gun at Leanne, Jana's fingers had frozen on the Colt's trigger. It made her skin crawl to think Leanne could be dead right now if it wasn't for Charlie's quickness in shooting down the Rebel. She shuddered. Was she being selfish to allow Leanne and Charlie to continue on while this plot against her was unfolding? There was no telling what her kidnappers might do to them if they disrupted their plans. She vowed then to pull the trigger and send them home if the situation got too dangerous.

Noticing Jana's tremble, Wyatt raised his voice, teeming with concern, to snag her out of her troublesome thought. "Leanne's right. We needed your abductors to think we had canceled your oratory to avoid giving them time to reorganize against you." His reminder of their precautions appeased Leanne who holstered her pistol, and it eased Jana's worries about her friends' safety. Continuing on, he said, "You must know, Jana, that I have no reservations about my investment in you, and neither should you; an audience of a few can be just as effective in spreading your message, and I imagine correspondents from several newspapers and journals will be here, scrambling to write your story. Additionally, in this city of nearly one hundred thousand people, I think we'll fill the house. To make certain we do, I've allotted half the day off for those in my employ who wish to attend, and I've encouraged them to round up their womenfolk."

His extra effort touched Jana and, because of it, she wouldn't be satisfied with anything less than a packed house.

Standing below them and to the right of front stage, Charlie waved them over. He'd arrived earlier with Wyatt to set up his equipment and was practically jumping out of his brogans to show them his covered booth and table, around which the air reeked of the chemicals he'd use to process the tintype plate through all of its stages: from preparation, to development, to lacquering for preservation of the image. "I can hand the customer their portrait within a few minutes," he said.

*Bang!* The slamming of the front door spun Wyatt around and sent Jana, Leanne, and Charlie into a defensive crouch.

While Jana silently grieved for her friends who were also plagued by the sounds of war, Leanne composed herself with the speed of a lightning bolt to retrieve her pistol, its walnut grip doubtlessly still warm from her having holstered it only seconds before.

Wyatt tensed at the appearance of the two newcomers, who could've modeled for the color fashion plates in *Godey's Lady's Book*: The woman in her hat and boots trimmed in the same soft dark fur of her paletot—specially tailored to flare out from waist to hem to accommodate a hoopskirt beneath her dress—and the gentleman in his beaver-felt top hat and velvet-lined frock coat. To their swift approach, Wyatt attempted to intercept them by blocking their path.

The gentleman gripped the gold handle of his ornately carved cane and pressed its twisted oak shaft against Wyatt's thighs to stave him off and free a path for the matron, who strutted past with surprising spryness for one who Jana guessed was in her early seventies. In fact, the spirited swing of her hoopskirt—livelier than a bell ringing in a church tower on Sabbath Sunday— nearly bowled Wyatt over.

Jana's breath caught at the sight of the gentleman's cane, its shaft the same twisted oak as her kidnapper's. It brought her back to the moment Goliath had her pinned to the carriage floor and had treated her to a glimpse of his boss's cane right before he blindfolded her. She was sure it was the same style.

In presenting herself before Jana, Leanne, and Charlie, the elderly woman cut off Jana's view of the cane. The copious light from the window showed her once-beautiful face concealed beneath a crisscross of haggard lines everywhere. The tautness of her skin and its milky shade suggested she'd been subjected to a lifetime of stress rather than affected by age or wrinkled from the sun. Removing her mitted hands from her fur muff, she reached out and gently pushed the barrel of Leanne's revolver toward the floor. "I'm sorry to do that, young man. Guns and violence frighten me so," she said with an exaggerated shudder and a thinly veiled sneer.

Wyatt opened his mouth, presumably to defend Leanne's honor, but abstained to Leanne's impartial shrug. Instead, he glared at the back of the woman's head, silently accusing her of having been intentionally insulting.

Peering at Wyatt over the shoulder of her sable coat, she said, "Well, aren't you going to introduce me, Wyatt?"

"Yes, Mother," Wyatt replied, hesitantly and with indifference.

"I must refute your inhospitable treatment of—"

Wyatt interrupted, pointing to each in turn, "Allow me the privilege of presenting Miss Jana Brady, Mr. Charlie Watson, and Miss Leanne Watson."

With a spit of laughter at Wyatt's inadvertent exposure of his mother's blunder regarding Leanne's gender, the gentleman stranger cleared a path through the dust motes for his breath, spiked with enough whiskey for Jana to get drunk on it. *Could he possibly know Goliath?* she wondered. That seemed remote since Buffalo boasted hundreds of taverns—one on every corner—besides the gaming houses, hotels, stores, and boarding houses where one could buy beer and other spirits.

Wyatt frowned at the man's gloating. He'd obviously taken no delight in pointing out his mother's mistake, even after she'd cornered him into it.

Whirling on her companion, Mrs. McGriffin—as Jana presumed she was called—glowered at him, and he deflated quicker than the great gas balloon that the Union army borrowed from its inventor, Professor Thaddeus Lowe, for aerial reconnaissance against the Confederacy. She turned back and, with an air of superiority, began a visual inspection of Jana. "I'm still waiting, Wyatt, for you to make my introduction. If you refuse to do it, I shall."

She obviously had no intention of apologizing to Leanne, which Jana sensed was out of spite rather than to avert any embarrassment others more sensitive might feel.

Before Wyatt could respond, the oppressed gentleman bounced back to say with sarcasm dripping off his tongue, "And what about *me*, Mother? Will you introduce me? Or shall you be a hypocrite?"

*So ... this is Wyatt's brother*, Jana thought. He and his mother might've come here together, but the only thing *together* about them was their well-tailored attire. Their physical traits were completely opposite: her hair straw-colored, his dark; her facial features stern and angular, his soft and round; and her frame petite, his tall and stocky. The vast array of fashionable sofas and chairs from one wealthy patron's upper box to another's had greater cohesion than they did. Other than Wyatt being lankier, he and his brother had many more features in common that they'd no doubt acquired from their father. Jana might never see proof of this because—come to think of it—she didn't remember a single portrait of Wyatt's parents or brother hanging in his home. That and their current hostility toward one another seemed to support Hannah's assertion there was no love between the three of them.

Swatting her hand at her son, Mrs. McGriffin said, "Oh, stand on your own two feet like your brother."

He muttered, "For better or for worse, haven't I always been left to do so? Pardon me for thinking you'd ever do anything for *me*."

Wyatt was swift to say, "Jana, Leanne, Charlie, meet Mrs. William McGriffin and Mr. Wallace McGriffin."

His impersonal acquaintance to his family gave Jana the impression their issues with one another ran regrettably deep. Tendering her hand, Jana said, "It's nice to meet you, Mrs. McGriffin. You must be very proud of Wyatt's—"

"Yes, yes, yes," she interjected, then covered her mouth to stifle a phony yawn.

Slowly and awkwardly, Jana withdrew her hand.

Wyatt's dark eyes flared with disapproval at her rudeness, but he managed to maintain his gentlemanly deportment. "I see that you're tired, Mother, and we have much to do before Miss Brady's recitation. Is there a point to your visit?"

"Such insolence," she said, wringing her hands. "You know full well your father—God rest his soul—and I have always been attracted to the arts."

Under his breath, Wallace said, "And all this time I thought your only interest was in cavorting with other socialites."

Before she could bestow another dose of her wrath upon Wallace, Wyatt said, "Well, this isn't the arts, Mother. Did you not minutes before espouse being frightened of guns and violence?"

"What does that have to do with anything?" she asked, her face wrinkling worse from her exasperation.

Trying to repress his impatience, he said, "Miss Brady will be addressing her soldiering; thus, her narration will embody guns and violence."

"With your father gone, and no one left to care for me"—she squinted at Wyatt with contempt and Wallace with disinterest—"I need to become more independent."

Wyatt crossed his wary eyes upon her.

In a rapid reversal of her woe-is-me disposition, she bestowed a smile upon

Jana that could charm a snake. "I came here to get a good look at this independent and spirited young lady. And now that I have, I shall remove myself to my box out of the way of your preparations, Miss Brady." She turned to Wyatt. "But first, I will have a word with you about our investments." Pivoting so forcibly on her petite feet, Jana worried she might pop the side buttons of her boots and go sprawling across the floor. She ignored the hand Wyatt offered to help steady her and marched up the aisle, waving her sons to follow.

Wallace tipped his hat at Jana, Leanne, and Charlie. "Good day to you all." Before he straggled off after his mother, he said, "I wish you luck with your sermon today, Miss Brady."

"Will you excuse me, Jana?" Wyatt said, apologetically. "I'll be back soon to assure all is as you wish for your oration."

"Don't worry about me, I'm sure Charlie knows his way around here, and he and Leanne can help me with whatever I might need." Wyatt started to go, but Jana summoned him back. She thought it prudent to tell him about the similarity between his brother's and her kidnapper's canes. Though, she qualified, "I'm sure there are a hundred shops in Buffalo that sell the same one."

Wyatt's forehead creased in consternation. "Thank you for the information. It certainly bears exploration." Then he took off after his kin, whom he followed right out of the hall without bothering to put on his coat and hat.

Jana figured the fieriness of the McGriffins's snipes at one another provided ample heat to anaesthetize Wyatt against the cold.

Cutting into Jana's thoughts, Leanne said, "She made a big stink 'bout stayin' to hear yer talk, yet seems to me she's goin'." She spun toward Jana. "What in blazes was that all 'bout?"

"Hannah told my ma there's no love between Wyatt and his mother, and I'm afraid we just caught a glimpse of it."

"I got news: there ain't no love between Mrs. McGriffin and Wallace either, and it seems she might've brewed a bitterness between her sons."

"I feel sorry for them all," Charlie said. "What do you suppose makes them so unhappy with each other?"

"We might never know. I doubt either Hannah or Wyatt is likely to share such a personal matter with us," Jana said.

"They might not volunteer it," Leanne said, "but I'm gonna go snoop on 'em."

"Do you think it's right to be trespassing on their private affairs, Leanne?" Charlie said.

"Ya bet I do. They opened a can of worms, makin' their affairs public to us with them criticizin' each other. And Wallace's cane bein' like Jana's abductor's makes him a concern to us. Brother or not, Wyatt'll understand us not leavin' any stone unturned."

Jana said, "She's right, Charlie. Even though I doubt Wyatt would cover up for his brother, we need to make sure he's not blind to his brother."

With that, Leanne skedaddled into the gallery behind the stage, calling out over her shoulder, "If Wyatt gits back before me, tell him I'm off supervisin' the guards, which he asked me to do once we got ya into the hall."

"Shouldn't you have backup in case any of them becomes a problem?" Jana said.

Waving her Colt, which she'd held onto throughout the interaction between Wyatt and his kin, she said, "This'll do just fine."

Jana and Charlie stared after her with admiration, and Jana could tell she and Charlie were thinking alike: *If anyone can take care of themselves, Leanne can.* Wyatt's assigning Leanne this duty showed his faith in her too.

While Charlie withdrew to make last-minute checks of his equipment, Jana found herself too distracted to rehearse her speech. Instead, she perused the upper balconies draped with blue damasks patterned with each owners' family coat of arms—a custom the rich also observed on their elite coaches. For Jana's safe passage to the hall, Wyatt had those on his carriage doors painted over. Still, she had a good chance of identifying the McGriffins's box since their family crest would embody a griffin. She began a search for the legendary creature with the body, legs, and tail of a lion and the head, wings, and talon-like feet of an eagle when the front and gallery doors opened and closed in synchronicity.

Preoccupied with his own worries, Wyatt didn't seem to notice Leanne's slipping inside and narrowly beating him to Jana's side. Neither would he be able to tell she'd been absent by the smell of winter's air in her clothes with it also clinging to his. "Allow me to apologize for my family's indiscretions," he said, his cheeks reddening from his humiliation and infuriation.

"Please ... think nothing of it," Jana said, feeling sorry for him. Between his obviously deep-seated family issues and her situation, he had too many worries.

"Yup," Leanne said, "yer mother and brother are saints next to my pa."

"I pray you were able to resolve things with your mother and brother," Charlie said.

Wyatt's smile, though small and pitiful, was the first they'd ever seen from him. "It was easier than you can imagine." Facing Jana in particular, he said, "About my brother's cane, he purports it went missing for a while around the time of your kidnapping, but then it magically turned up in one of the taverns that he unfortunately frequents most. I have no reason to believe he's lying, and so it seems he too is a scapegoat in your abductors' scheme to frame me and now my family."

Again, Jana wondered if Wyatt was being gullible to his brother's lies, and she made a mental note to get Leanne's impression of it.

As if he'd read her mind, Wyatt said, "Even so, it's another angle that bears scrutiny. I'll have one of my trustworthy associates check into it." He sighed. "For now, we have more important matters, namely your discourse, Jana. Is the hall to your satisfaction?"

"Very much so, thank you." She faked being overheated by peeling off her gauntlets and fanning them before her face. "But I'd like to shed my greatcoat. Is there a space backstage for it?"

"I believe there's a closet. Please allow me to hang it up for you," Wyatt said.

"No, thank you." She hated to lie, but she said, "I need to walk off a few nerves before my talk." As everyone would expect—and Jana hoped for—Leanne played the role of bodyguard and followed her into the gallery. Thanks to the wall sconces, with their imitation gas candles set before mirrors to reflect and magnify the light, Jana found her way to the dark corner where the closet was located. As she hung up her greatcoat, Jana inquired into the outcome of Leanne's spying.

"What Wyatt didn't say 'bout bringin' up the cane with his brother is that he asked him outright if he was involved with yer kidnappin'. Wallace acted real offended but avoided answerin' directly—he just claimed to know plenty of people and groups that would hop on a chance to vanquish agitators for equality of the sexes. Wyatt told Wallace he'd be real sorry if he ever found out he was a party to any of 'em, and Wallace started laughin' as if he was enjoyin' Wyatt thinkin' he might be guilty."

"What was Mrs. McGriffin doing throughout their quarrel?"

"She stood there lookin' pleased as if she'd instigated the bickerin' between 'em herself. The more heated argument, though, was between the three of 'em over money. Mrs. McGriffin and Wallace demanded that Wyatt fork over their share, but he refused."

"Then, how'd he get rid of them so fast?"

"He told 'em if they ever agin brought their problems out in public, they'd never even get another bronze two-cent piece from him. Mrs. McGriffin stomped off, threatenin' to see a lawyer, and she and Wallace took off in their carriage. Wyatt folded his arms over his chest and stood there shakin' his head after 'em as if to say, 'Go ahead and try.'"

The first thought that popped into Jana's head was, *Money is the root of all evil.* It was obviously one source of antagonism between the McGriffins. But Jana sensed their problems cut much deeper than that. "I don't know why I'm trying to dissect the McGriffins's problems. Their dispute has nothing to do with us," Jana mumbled.

"I ain't sure 'bout that. Wyatt paid a guard to keep an eye on his brother while he's out of town and to send a telegram if he does anything out of the ordinary."

"That's interesting"—Jana felt the skin between her brows puckering—"given his confidence Wallace was telling the truth about his having nothing to do with my kidnapping."

"Maybe he's just tryin' to be safe than sorry."

"You're probably right. Speaking of Wallace, what was your impression of him?"

"If ya mean 'bout me suspectin' him of any wrongdoing, he might be involved, but I can't see him leadin' the charge." She glanced anxiously over her shoulder. "That's all I got for now. I better go check on the guards. I'm gonna make 'em prove they ain't sportin' the tattoo of yer kidnappers."

"Be careful, Leanne, don't get them too riled."

She gave Jana a backhanded wave and disappeared through the exterior door as Charlie came through the interior one between the gallery and auditorium.

"Where's she going?" Charlie asked, commandeering the spot she'd just vacated.

"To make sure the guards are in position." Jana purposely neglected to tell him about her checking them for the freemason-like tattoo so he wouldn't worry.

"Come on, then, Jana. I want to take a picture of you pretending to give your talk. I'm sure you don't want me distracting you while you're in the thick of it."

"Don't worry, Charlie, we still have time," she said, following him out into the theater.

Charlie had Jana's portrait finished and his camera aimed at the congregation to take some pictures of it and to keep an eye out for rabble-rousers; Leanne had returned from her scouting mission to report nothing amiss before she posted herself at the front door alongside two deputies; and Jana retreated backstage to listen to the drone of excited voices filling the hall as she awaited her introduction.

Nearly a half hour later, Wyatt came into the gallery, disgruntled by—Jana could only assume—his negative exchange with his mother and brother.

Jana wished she could say something to make him feel better. Without a clear understanding of his family's undercurrents, she was at a loss for words. She also wasn't sure how he'd take her prying into his private affairs.

Wyatt reported, "Unfortunately, we had to turn many people away, and our schedule is too tight for an encore another day. Fortunately, however, everyone will have benefit of your message through your audience's word of mouth and the many newspapers and journals represented here today." Given his dullness and his normally reserved nature, he managed to muster up a huge smile. "Are you ready, Jana?"

She returned a smile. "I am."

Leaving her to semi-darkness, Wyatt ventured out onto the stage and into a bubble of excited babble, which his commanding presence quieted. He thanked everyone for their attendance, then he stunned them all and Jana when, along with his apology, he attributed the short notice for Jana's lecture to her kidnapping. He allowed the ensuing furor and, as it wound down, he stressed there were deputies posted all around to immediately crush any transgressions. After a few words about Jana's courage and her significance to the history of their world, country, and state, he said, "I now present Miss Jana Brady from Elmira, New York, also known as Cavalryman Johnnie Brodie of the Tenth New York Cavalry Regiment."

Jana crossed the podium to cheers and jeers and, as she turned to face her spectators, a heckler called out, "What are you—man, woman, or hermaphrodite?" Fortunately, she'd anticipated this catcall. Taking control of the laughter and angry rebuttals at the heckler, Jana said, "Thank you for asking, sir. I'm a woman who answered President Lincoln's call to take up arms and fight for the preservation of my country." She tossed her hands out. "How's that different from us women answering our menfolk's call to shoulder rifle and fight marauders and murderers for the preservation of our homes?"

Amongst some murmurings, an Irishman bellowed, "Aye, better she fought than the dandies who stayed at home."

A chorus of amens sang out.

*Leave it to an Irishman to come to my defense first,* Jana thought lovingly of Keeley. Again, she took control of her audience, pressing on with a replication of the speech she'd delivered in Elmira. She sailed to its conclusion with only one incident at the beginning, which actually worked in her favor to show her quickness, agility, and competence. With the traits of a skilled cavalryman, she snagged two pickled eggs simultaneously hurled at her from opposite directions without faltering her words, which she was forced to pause while the deputies dragged the offenders out of the hall and proved to everyone lawlessness would not be tolerated. No other interruption occurred during her presentation, and she left the dais to a majority of applause.

Immediately following her speech, a large crowd lingered, clamoring to have their likenesses taken with her. Eventually, Charlie's supplies ran out and he had to turn people away. Wyatt, Jana, Leanne, and Hannah, who'd hitched a ride with a friend, helped him pack up his equipment. After it was safely aboard a wagon and sent with one of Leanne's teamsters to the cover of her blacksmith shop to await portage to the train station the following day, they all accompanied Wyatt back to his mansion for a light fare.

Hannah insisted they eat in Wyatt's elegant dining room to make use of the multi-leafed mahogany table and its matching chairs and sideboards that had lain dormant for long periods of time. On the side, Hannah had told Jana that Wyatt disliked grand affairs—even more since the death of his wife; apparently, she was the one who'd always insisted upon their hosting an occasional dinner, which she believed was in her husband's best interest for maintaining good relations with his business associates.

From the very moment Leanne had taken her place at the table, she squirmed uncomfortably in her Queen-Anne chair, which was ironic since this style of chair was carved with comfort in mind: Its rigid perpendicular back had been reshaped as a spoon to follow the curve of the spine, and its tiny seat had been widened to accommodate a large derriere. Little did the craftsman know that well over a century later, his latter enhancement, especially, would delight the ladies with posteriors broadened by their crinolines. Now, as the servant moved closer to Leanne and presented the ornate soup tureen filled with lamb stew, her eyes grew wide with fear—the same fear Jana remembered from her first dining experience with fine china. She empathized with Leanne's not wanting to whack the tureen with the ladle and chip it.

Having perceived Leanne's anxiety and Jana's for her friend, Hannah winked at Jana, then caught Leanne's eyes to say, "Please, don't trouble yourself over the tableware, Leanne. We've imported replacements for every piece, and the English Flow Blue Davenport just came out last decade, so if need be, they're easily replaced. Besides that, they're much less expensive than they look."

Everyone chuckled to Leanne's exhale of relief and ensuing gulp of dry Portuguese Madeira from her wine goblet, which up until now had remained untouched.

When the tureen got to her, Jana marveled at the gold overlay that shimmered under the light from the gilded brass gasolier and that defined the bluish-purplish grapes and their leaves and curling vines bordering the tureen's bowl, foot, and underplate. The entire stoneware set had both a masculine and feminine presentation, which Hannah must've kept in mind for a widower when deciding upon its purchase for Wyatt's household. There was no doubt Hannah had downplayed the set's expense just to put Leanne at ease. And there was no doubt her kindness and caring had rubbed off on Wyatt.

The conversation was sparse during the first course while everyone satiated their hunger, but it picked up during dessert.

Slicing off a hunk of her rhubarb pie, Jana griped about the absence of women's voices in the audience.

Wyatt said, "Woman's rights advocacy truly only just began with the 1848 convention in Seneca Falls. In those seventeen years—minus these past four during which women have ceased their activities to throw their efforts into providing for soldiers and abolishing slavery—some significant strides have been made in the fight, especially in New York and California, and the demand for universal equality is ringing around the country. Unfortunately, it takes time to change a culture, in particular the minds of women, who have been indoctrinated to believe that their voice is limited to the household, and chauvinistic men, who refuse to believe that women have an intelligent voice outside of that sphere. However, I believe that awareness will be truncated by the many contributions of women to the war: soldiering, nursing, doctoring, and spying; extensive organization of charity and sanitation for the relief of soldiers and prisoners; and management of farms, plantations, factories, and shops—all of which demand great respect for women's intelligence, tenacity, and strength."

When Hannah signaled for a house servant to remove the goblets that had been emptied of the dry wine, another servant swooped in to fill the cordial glasses with an amber-sweet Portuguese Madeira, also from Wyatt's cellar.

Hannah raised her glass, looking to Wyatt who, with a nod, passed the torch to her to make the toast. "Thank you, Jana, for a rebirth in the campaign for woman's suffrage and equal rights," she said with everyone following her lead in raising their glasses to Jana and taking sips of their wine.

Raising her glass, Jana said, "Thank you, Hannah, for the lovely toast, and everyone around this table—especially you, Wyatt—for making the journey possible."

Before they could take a sip, Charlie asserted himself to say, "I think I can speak for everyone when I say we're very proud of you, Jana. You and your speech were captivating."

Leanne nodded in agreement. "I couldn't git over how nothin' rattled ya."

"Knowing all of you were in the audience, watching out for me, boosted my confidence," Jana said.

"Here's to greater success on our march to Albany," Wyatt said, raising his glass higher and taking a sip of his dessert wine for everyone to follow.

As the amber liquid swirled on her tongue, Jana couldn't help compare the polar tangs between the first-and-second-course wines to her own bittersweetness: While she was thrilled to be effecting change, she woefully felt Keeley's absence from this table and her fight. Would he ever come back to her?

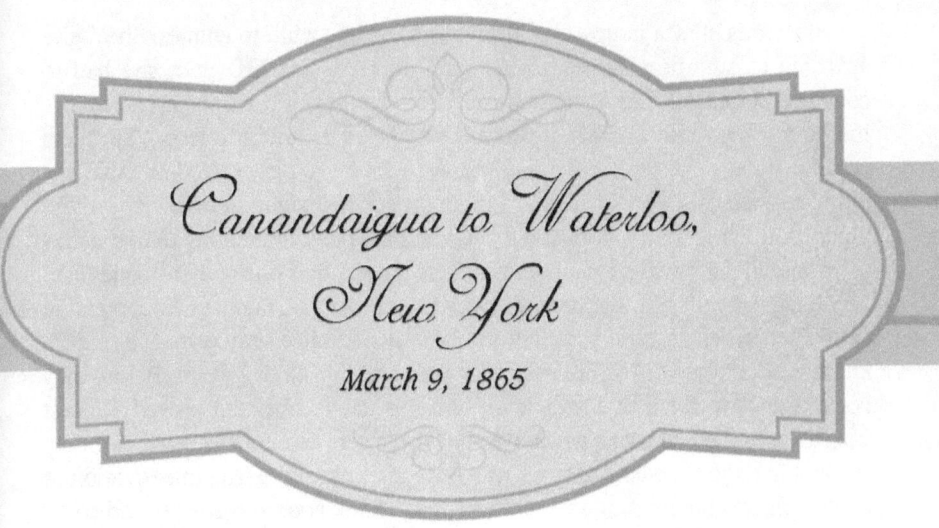

Jana was lured to the window of her parlor car by sleet battering the roof. By the time she drew the curtain panel aside, plump snowflakes had busted out of their icy jackets and were performing for her before a backdrop of buildings, situated opposite the train depot in the lakeside town of Canandaigua, where they were stopped letting passengers on and off. The dourness of the early evening sky couldn't spoil Jana's bubbly spirit, sparked by the letter she clutched against her heart. It had taken her by utter surprise when Hannah presented her with the note Keeley must've hurried to mail soon after he, Ma, and Pa had returned to Elmira. She'd gladly suffered through her mild sickness produced by the train's rocking to read his words a hundred times over. They were etched into her brain now and, as she watched the twirling snowflakes, she recited them to herself from memory:

March 7, 1865, Elmira, New York

Dear Jana Lass,

When I feel the love that yar ma, pa, and sisters have for ye, I wish I was with ye guiding yar safe return to them. Yar ma and pa insist on me staying home, where the air seems favorable to me health, though. But I want ye to know that all ye need to do is send up a smoke signal, and I'll be by yar side faster than an artilleryman can pull a lanyard to fire his cannon.

Fond regards,
Keeley

His words blew a happy tune from her heart like wind to chimes. She'd give anything to summon Keeley to her and, after reading his letter, she had to convince herself all over again it was best he stay put. If anything could induce him to think favorably of her, it was Ma's and Pa's magnetism. Heck, Elizabeth Bennet of Jane Austen's *Pride and Prejudice* tells her older sister, Jane, that she ultimately fell in love with Mr. Darcy upon her first sighting of his "beautiful grounds at Pemberley." How could Ma and Pa be less compelling than a parcel of property? Jana was so confident in their powers that once when Keeley had been plagued with his own prejudice against the United States for its oppression of his people, she'd been sure that the lack of prejudice shared by Ma and Pa and their openness to Irish immigrants would be infectious to him. Before they got a chance to work their magic on him, his native Irishmen proved the best way to alter attitudes was to show what they were made of—they'd not only enlisted in their adopted country's war, but they were also garnering attention as fierce fighters and winning hearts while at it. Thank goodness Keeley had come around to seeing he could only be proud to build hearth and home where he'd contributed in making things just and fair. Jana could never marry a man who'd give up so easily on his country. Wouldn't this same man be likely to give up on a marriage if times got tough? Now, she had in her hand proof of the spell Ma and Pa had put on him through his own words: his reference to her home as "his" and his willingness to leap to her rescue. They seemed to suggest he'd be sticking around for a while. She freed her soul to soar outside and frolic amongst the snowflakes. *Yes, it's best Keeley stays put,* Jana resolved simultaneously with the long wail of the locomotive, warning of their momentary departure.

Clapping close the business ledger, which he'd been reconciling since they'd left Buffalo early that morning, Wyatt jarred Jana away from the only view she was allowed opposite the station house. It was for her own good to prevent pursuers, who might be waiting on the depot platform, from catching a glimpse of her to confirm she was still proceeding with her tour. He scuffed his chair back from his small secretary, shifting it sideways to give his lanky legs room to stretch, then rested an elbow on its fold-down cabinet door.

Jana felt him watching her as she crossed the Persian rug to her mohair-stuffed chair, situated beside a lamp that burned oil tinged with an essence of vanilla. The aroma drove Jana's taste buds crazy for Ma's sugar cookies, and she made a mental note to seek out a bakery in Seneca Falls tomorrow morning.

"What's the weather like?" Wyatt asked in a near whisper, considerate of Charlie's nap.

Speaking in her normal pitch to prove they couldn't possibly disturb Charlie over his snoring, Jana said, "It was sleeting, but it's turned to snow, although it doesn't appear to be accumulating." Poor Charlie; after last evening's supper at Wyatt's home, he'd been up all night calculating the extra supplies he'd need, should he again be bombarded by those wishing to have their portraitures taken with Jana. Then he'd run around the city all morning gathering them. It wasn't until he had all of his photography equipment well secured aboard the baggage car at the New York Central's Exchange Street depot that he'd breathed a sigh of relief.

Wyatt said, "Let's hope it stays light so it doesn't impede your short carriage ride from Waterloo to Seneca Falls."

"Actually, a dark, snowy night might work to our advantage in creating greater obscurity for our disguises."

"Ah, yes, excellent point." Noticing the letter on Jana's lap, Wyatt said, "Good news from home, I trust?"

She felt her cheeks flush a few degrees above the heat in their compartment. Wyatt knew of her and Keeley's circumstance, and if anyone knew the depth of love lost, he did. "Maybe, it's from Keeley."

He leaned forward, placing his elbows on his thighs and clasping his hands. His dark, hopeful eyes probed hers.

With a lighthearted snuffle, she said, "It's hard to say if he's growing fonder of me or my family."

"I envy you, Jana. Not everyone has the good fortune of loving parents," he said, his voice a mingling of sorrow, longing, and even ire. He rose above his emotions with a smile. "And they raised a lovely daughter."

"Thank you," she said, her cheeks flaming hotter.

"I'm sorry if I've made you uncomfortable."

"You didn't," Jana said, realizing he'd just given away his family discontent—with his parents anyway. So ... he had a problem with his father too? *Of course he does*, she thought, reflecting back on the one instant he could've spoken fondly of his father or their time together playing chess, and he'd relegated it to them having played many tournaments.

A forceful rush of steam from the locomotive and a lurch of their car shook Jana from her thoughts and Charlie from his sleep with a snort loud enough to be heard three cars up and over the *clack, clack, clack* of the train rolling out of the station. His head bounced off the wing of his chair, and his groggy eyes flitted about. Once he seemed to have his bearings straight, he stretched out, knocking his knees into the coffee table.

Jana lunged to save the table from tipping over and scattering his numerous portraitures to the wind.

Working his twelve-lensed camera, Charlie could produce a dozen gem portraits with one exposure; he had a wealth of the three-quarter-by-one-inch copies on hand to study beneath his magnifying glass for improving his photographic technique and for practicing his profiling of people. For the latter, he said he especially benefitted with Jana in the pictures so he could use her features and what he knew of her personality to deduce things about the other faces beside hers on the same black-and-white tintype. Too bad he'd probably never see any of Jana's admirers ever again to know the outcome of his character assessments.

Jana perked up in her chair when she remembered she had surer subjects tucked away in her travel trunk in the baggage car for him to analyze. Her acquisition of them had come about when Hannah stepped into her bedchamber earlier that day to inquire if her trunk was packed and ready to be carried downstairs for transport to the railroad station. Figuring Wyatt had told Hannah about her acquaintance with Mrs. McGriffin and Wallace yesterday, Jana thought nothing about asking Hannah if she had a picture of Wyatt's father—the last of his family she'd yet to see. In response, she left the room for several minutes before returning with a stack of framed mini-portraitures, including Wyatt, Wallace, each parent, dearly departed Laura, and herself. Just as Jana suspected, the sons were a replica of their father, to which Jana said, "Too bad Leanne and Charlie won't see his likeness and Charlie won't see these precious old daguerreotypes—he's really become an avid student of photography." Hannah's reply was, "Wyatt's not one to display such sentimental items publicly. Except for duplicate portraitures of Laura and me that he keeps on his nightstand, these are collecting dust in a drawer. What is a picture if not to be seen? Wyatt doesn't need to know that I loaned them to you, and you can send them back to me through Charlie or Leanne." And that was the only chance Jana had gotten to probe Hannah further about Wyatt and his family. It really didn't yield much—maybe Charlie would exhume something through his profiling.

Speaking of sentimental displays, the Buffalo assembly's demand for her picture had made Jana feel like a circus spectacle until Charlie, Leanne, and Wyatt convinced her she was a pioneer whom her countrymen cherished and wanted to memorialize. It was lucky for Charlie this bonanza had begun in his hometown where it was easy for him to load up on supplies. He wanted Jana to share in his profits, but she'd flat-out refused—his care and company were payment enough.

A *rap, rap, rap* on the door was followed by Leanne's identification of herself.

When Jana started out of her chair, Wyatt motioned for her to stay seated. He went to the door, slid its bolt, and pushed it outward to admit Leanne and two unemployed actresses whom Leanne had mustered from the car immediately forward, which was also fashioned into a parlor upon Wyatt's order.

Leanne worked fast to shut and re-bolt the door just in case any bad guys riding the roof got the idea to come dropping in. Snow dusting her long overcoat and wide-brimmed hat melted into glittery beads as they collided with the warm air inside their compartment.

As Wyatt returned to his seat, he asked, "Is everything all right, Leanne?" He referred to her car-hopping throughout their journey so she could keep an eye on the other passengers and her shrewdness in recruiting the conductor to watch out for anyone sporting a tattoo identical to Jana's kidnappers.

"Yup," she said with confidence, which made them all rest easy with her on guard.

In advance of Jana having left Elmira, her lecture tour had been well publicized, with each of her scheduled stops listed. This meant her abductors had privy to her every move. In order for her to get from one place to the next free of molestation, Jana and her committee had elected to resort to trickery in order to muddy her travel arrangements. Her abductors expected her party to disembark all together in Seneca Falls. Indeed they would. The two actresses, handpicked for their physical traits, would pose as Jana and Leanne and stay on the train to Seneca Falls. Jana and Leanne would disembark at Waterloo in disguise and travel the rest of the way to Seneca Falls in a closed carriage. Other than the main group, everyone was suspect at this juncture, including the actresses, who'd only been entrusted with knowing they'd be acting as decoys for Jana and Leanne. Anything the actresses gleaned about their caper from conversation this point forward was of no concern since they'd be riding with Charlie and Wyatt and under their watchful eyes.

Jana shielded herself behind the privacy screen. As she slipped into the comfortably sized men's wear Wyatt had rummaged up for her before they'd left Buffalo, she couldn't help but compare the eerie similarity between their ruse and the one forced upon Abraham Lincoln after the Pinkerton Agency uncovered a plot to assassinate him on his way through Baltimore to his first inaugural as president of the United States. They'd disguised him as an invalid brother to one of their agents who escorted him safely from Philadelphia to Washington, DC. This gave Jana cause to recheck that her six-shooter was strapped to her waist before she traded places with her impersonator who dressed in Jana's clothes just in case an interested person or party had monitored this level of detail about Jana.

When it came to Leanne's turn, she balked at playing the role of Jana's wife.

Charlie reminded her of Keeley's courage in dressing as a woman to protect them from capture on their recent excursion through Virginia. Then he admonished, "It's a small sacrifice, Leanne, for keeping Jana safe. Besides which, your size and height are better suited for playing the woman."

Jana hoped to further appease Leanne by saying, "If my abductors have been paying attention to us, which I'm sure they have, they'll never suspect you to dress as a woman, Leanne. Then, purely by my association with you, they'll look right past me."

An ardent bob of Wyatt's head spurred Leanne on, and she disappeared behind the divide with her cheek mole bristling from her glare at her girly garments. Upon each article of her men's attire she shed and slapped up over the partition, her grumps and groans grew louder. A lengthy hush followed the last piece before Leanne summoned her lookalike for help, adding, "Else I'll be here all night wrestlin' with all of these darn layers."

In no measure was Jana slighted by Leanne's bid for help from a perfect stranger. She understood it was less humiliating for her to bare herself to someone she'd most likely never see again.

Leanne called out, "Anyone dares even a smirk will be starin' down the barrel of my Colt."

Excluding the small parting of their lips to Leanne's metamorphosis, everyone managed to sit as stiff and still as if Medusa had turned them to stone when Leanne came clomping out.

With her hair pinned back and a burgundy puff bonnet accentuating her lovely steel-gray eyes and cheeks, which had plumped up some since her time at war to give her a healthier less masculine appearance, Jana had to retract her past assessment that Leanne was more handsome as a boy.

"It would be a lot less humiliatin' if I could play a widow in mournin' so I could hide my shame behind a veil."

"That would blur your vision, and we need your eyes to be keen," Jana said.

"I reckon," Leanne said, succumbing surprisingly easily to standing as still as a seamstress's dummy while her impersonator fussed to smooth out her skirt pleats, tie the strings of her bonnet beneath her chin, and wrap a hooded shawl around her.

To bolster Leanne's feminine portrayal, Jana offered her the pepperbox she'd bought after her kidnappers had absconded with hers.

"How'm I s'posed to protect ya with that toy?" Leanne said, cramming her Colt into the carpetbag that completed her costume and that she draped over her arm in a feminine move almost second nature to her.

So as not to rub salt into her wound, everyone pretended not to notice her eyes widening in surprise at herself.

Jana tucked her small firearm inside her boot shaft where it dug into her calf—a minor inconvenience for the powerful lesson she'd learned from her abductors about never traveling without a second weapon concealed somewhere on her person.

The train's whistle warned Waterloo loomed ahead.

"It's time, Jana and Leanne, for you to relocate to your own car." Wyatt began combing his fingers through his curls. "I feel as though I'm feeding you to the wolves. I pray the misogynistic newspaper publishers around Western New York have failed to provoke lunatics from rising up and brandishing their knives and pistols against you. They claim such action was prevented at St. James Hall, only because of the heavy presence of the law."

"I agree that the reaction to my lecture was more unfavorable, but we expected that. And when we started this tour, our goal was to garner lots of attention, and we're certainly doing that." Jana stiffened her back. "I'm not afraid of the wolves—rather, chickens in disguise. They stand at a distance from us women they liken to Amazons, daring only to wield their tongues and pens against us as opposed to their weapons. Well, their words have had the same effect on me as if they'd challenged me to a duel, and I'll continue to wield my tongue and triumphs in the male sphere to prove women ought to have equal treatment in all things under the eyes of the law."

"Well said," one of the actresses declared, smiling with admiration at Jana.

To Wyatt, Leanne said, "Now don't ya worry. I'm gonna see to it Jana gits to Seneca Falls in one piece."

"I wish that for you too, Leanne." With a reluctant nod of his head at her, then Jana, Wyatt prompted them on their way, adding, "Please be safe."

Jana wondered at his excessive agitation, although she couldn't disregard his fear over the power of the written word to incite evildoing against her. After all, President Lincoln once claimed Harriet Beecher Stowe's *Uncle Tom's Cabin* had provided the match that ignited the War of the Rebellion. In any case, Wyatt's nervous energy acted as a match to ignite Jana's eagerness to get on with their charade. As the train slowed to a crawl, she ventured out onto the mildly swaying platform and slid her hand along the iron guiderail, its iciness seeping through her glove. The snow had stopped falling, and the waxing gibbous moon sailed in and out of the thinning clouds. Its three-quarter face smiled proudly upon the virgin-white snow to illuminate trillions of crystals appearing as sugar sprinkled over a favorite confection. Expecting the aroma of sponge cake to be wafting about, Jana tilted her head back and whiffed, catching instead a dose of the air freshly cleansed by the precipitation. She prayed her ruse and everyone along for the ride would be equally as blessed.

At the moment, Leanne was clouded from seeing anything as a blessing, including their ensuing adventure. She grumbled all the way to their private car, "I'm gonna put us in danger. How'm I gonna come to yer rescue with these petticoats huggin' my legs and trippin' me?" Once inside their private car, she strolled past Jana and smoothed her skirt beneath her before she sat down to check the laces of her boots; her feminine actions were done so naturally one would have difficulty believing she had a masculine proclivity.

"You could be tied to the railroad tracks, Leanne, and still find a way to come to my rescue. That's exactly why you're with me and no one else."

To that, Leanne's attitude made a one-hundred-and-eighty-degree turn. She raised her head and, with a fire in her eyes, said, "I can do this, don't ya worry."

"You're a good sport, Leanne." Jana meant it, but she'd avoid pointing out to Leanne that her feminine apparel had somehow managed to let splashes of her womanhood escape. *Maybe she's noticed this for herself, and that's bugging her most,* Jana thought.

The train screeched to a halt.

"Here we go," Jana said. "Are you ready?"

Hopping up from her chair, Leanne flipped her hood over her head to hide her face better. "Never been readier."

Jana followed her lead, lowering the brim of her hat over her face. So as not to appear too eager and attract unwanted attention, she counted to sixty, then swung the door outward. She descended to the snow-covered platform and reached back to offer her "wife" a chivalrous hand.

With a flinch hardly even perceptible to Jana, Leanne swiftly composed herself and graciously accepted Jana's hand.

The small station house drew Jana's eyes to its brick façade, against which shadowy ghouls swayed. The logical side of her brain told her they were exorcised by the wavering light of the moon and some wall lanterns; its superstitious side said they were performing specially for her—inciting her toward madness. *Are these wraiths also an omen of which I should pay heed?* she wondered.

## Waterloo, New York

### March 9, 1865

Jana and Leanne had narrowly started across the platform when they noticed two stout figures heading their way. Out of the corner of her eye, Jana observed Leanne reaching into her carpetbag, and the ensuing *click* proved she had the hammer of her Colt cocked.

Noting Leanne's hand lingering in her carpetbag, the shaggily bearded gentleman leaned toward Jana and Leanne slowly and cautiously, and then he curbed his baritone voice to a near whisper and said, "We never sleep. We are the all-seeing eye."

Jana and Leanne gave him a curt nod to acknowledge their recognition of the two phrases that represented the Pinkerton Agency's slogan and logo, respectively, and were the means by which Allan Pinkerton and Wyatt had agreed the operatives should identify themselves.

Wasting no time in making it appear as if they were acquaintances, the male agent thrust out his hand to Jana, clasping hers in a hearty shake, and then he turned to Leanne and bowed over her hand.

Waiting for her turn to greet Jana and Leanne, the female sleuth had her face buried beneath the hood of her long cape and was furtively surveying the environs around the one-story depot to make sure no one paid their party excessive interest.

The male sleuth said, "Please, do not show surprise by what I'm about to tell you. When Allan Pinkerton learned about your disguises, he felt it might look better if a male and female agent, rather than two burly men, met you. My name's Bill Parker, and my partner here's Duke Tanner. He'll be playing the role of Mrs. Parker until we get to Seneca Falls."

Relieved to find another in her comedic predicament, Leanne exhaled a frosty cloud of relief, which quickly evaporated in the air.

Mr. Tanner's upper lip curled like a snarling dog. "Don't think I volunteered to dress this way," he snapped, obviously misconstruing that Leanne had grunted in amusement. "I drew the shorter straw because of my smaller stature."

Under her breath, Leanne said, "I did too, and I'm only dressin' this way to keep my friend here safe."

Mr. Tanner lifted an eyebrow.

For the sake of appearances, Jana hastened everyone to the remaining welcoming gestures, then Mr. Parker suggested they transfer to the carriage.

"I warn you," Mr. Parker said, "that our driver knows nothing of our scheme. Mr. Tanner has been outstanding in keeping his identity from Mr. Ross." With another nod of understanding from Jana and Leanne, he held out his arm to Leanne, and she took it without hesitation in her newfound propriety for acting her part.

Jana got the impression Leanne might not necessarily want to act as a man her whole life. It was all she knew because her pa had forced her to dress and act as one from her birth. Even so, any misgivings she might've had with playing her part had shifted to Mr. Tanner whose lips puckered as if he'd eaten a sour grape when he took the arm Jana tendered to him. She had neither patience nor sympathy for Mr. Tanner who was being paid well to dress as a woman; poor Leanne was volunteering for the job, and her ego was footing the bill.

After the entourage arrived at their once-elegant carriage outfitted as a cab, Jana steered clear of its door. She trusted her gut this time and demanded to see Messrs. Parker's and Tanner's badges before she'd allow either herself or Leanne to be encaged. To accomplish this surreptitiously, she suggested they form a circle and pretend to be engaged in conversation while they waited for her and Leanne's trunks to be fastened between the railings on the roof of their conveyance.

Mr. Parker said loud enough for the benefit of any eavesdropper, "You won't see our daughter this visit—she's away at school—but I bet you'll be surprised at how grown up she is." He reached into his inside coat pocket. "Here's her portrait."

When he passed his memento to her, Jana understood the meaning of his exercise. From a distance, his badge mimicked the color and size of a tintype, allowing her to examine it freely. The dusky light from the glass-ensconced carriage lantern bounced off its host's shiny black surface to improve Jana's view of the silver piece in the shape of a shield: At its center was a small star with a line drawn out from the crook between its arm and leg on each side; above the star in big letters was *Pinkerton National* and below it was *Detective Agency*. Jana pretended to ooh and aah over the picture before passing it to Leanne who did the same before handing it back to Mr. Parker. "Thank you," Jana said to Mr. Parker in a business-like tone, then turned an expectant eye on Mr. Tanner.

Mr. Tanner faked the sniffles, then extracted a lacey handkerchief from his carpetbag, which he pretended to drop.

Bending over to retrieve his cloth, Jana discovered his badge lying in the snow next to it. Her brief study satisfied her of its legitimacy, and she picked up Mr. Tanner's badge inside his handkerchief, then returned both to him with a smile that awarded him the prize for "Most Creative."

The baggage handler deposited the last of their belongings in the hind boot: Leanne's hefty wooden box of blacksmith and farrier tools that she'd insisted upon bringing along. Then he accepted Mr. Parker's tip—an expense along with the carriage rental and driver's wage, which no doubt would be subtracted from Wyatt's account.

Their elderly, silver-maned chauffeur arrived from within the station house, where he'd probably been warming his bones by a stove, and Mr. Parker opened the coach's door and posted himself beside it. He assisted the "ladies" up the fixed iron step, then edged away, allowing Jana to board herself. Before he confined them inside with their foot-warming boxes, he poked his head inside, made a play of chattering his teeth, and whispered, "Now I know why you chose to play the woman, Mr. Tanner."

Scowl lines gashed Mr. Tanner's wide forehead. "Next time, Mr. Parker," he said through clenched teeth, "I'll personally make sure your facial hair is shaved. Then, you'll have no excuse."

Mr. Parker inched away from the door, his hands raised in surrender. "Don't shoot me, I was only having fun. It'll all be over soon."

"Not if we don't get going," Mr. Tanner growled.

Shaking his head at his partner's lack of humor, Mr. Parker closed them in. The carriage pitched to and fro as he climbed up onto the outside bench to ride shotgun next to the driver.

Mr. Ross double-clicked his cheek to send the two Morgans in motion. With their far-ranging night vision, the horses led the way to the road that ran eastward along the northern bank of the Seneca River. Conversely, with their short-range glow, the exterior lanterns would act as beacons to warn advancing transports of their presence and prevent collisions.

The trio inside drew their revolvers to be in the ready for interlopers, and Mr. Tanner trained his eyes through the small window between Jana's and Leanne's heads to watch their rear.

Drawing her curtain aside, Jana scratched away the intricate pattern of frost etched into her window's glass. The twinkling of the river's frozen surface was intermittent under a moon that was playing hide-and-seek as it ducked in and out of the clouds. When it stayed hidden for too long, Jana gave up waiting on its return and let the cloth panel drop back into place. Over the crunch of the horses' hoofs and clatter of the wagon wheels cutting through an inch of new snow over the well-traveled road, Jana said, "Where are you from, Mr. Tanner?"

"Is there a particular reason for you to know?"

His brusqueness shocked Jana. "Uh ... no, I just figured since we're going to be working together, we might be friendly."

Continuing his surliness, he said, "No offense, Miss Brady, I'm not here to make friends. I take my guard duty seriously, and I'm being paid well to do it. So if you don't mind, I prefer to avoid distractions."

"Of course, Mr. Tanner. No offense taken." How could she argue with that? In battle, she'd fretted over the welfare of her friends to the point where it could've gotten her killed.

Leanne set her eyes—like smoking gun barrels—on Mr. Tanner. "I admire ya for wantin' to do yer job, Mr. Tanner, but ya can be a little nicer."

Surrendering to Leanne's hard unblinking stare, he said, "Point well taken, Miss Watson."

"Good, and while we're at it, Mr. Tanner," Leanne said, "after I git this dress off, I insist ya drop the Miss Watson and call me Leanne. And that doesn't mean I'm askin' ya to be my friend."

Jana added, "You might not want to alienate her, Mr. Tanner. I've seen what she can do with her tongue and a gun. Both have come in handy watching my back, and you never know when you might need her to watch yours."

Grinning, he said, "Another point well taken. And, now, here's a point for you both: When I get this dress off, you can still call me Mrs. Parker."

Their laughter was cut short when the night exploded with light, and the air reeked of a bonfire.

The Morgans nickered and reared in distress, causing the carriage to buck and heave as they attempted to dodge their fright.

"Whoa, whoa, whoa," Mr. Ross called out in a calming voice to bring the horses under control.

Mr. Parker instructed Mr. Tanner to secure the perimeter around the carriage and Mr. Ross to remain seated with his rifle handy. Then he tossed Jana, Leanne, and Mr. Tanner about as he clambered down from his exterior bench, landing with a crunch of snow underfoot.

Edging forward on the squeaky leather of her bench and pressing her cheek against the icy window glass, Jana tried to ascertain the excessive source of light emanating from the road ahead; she could only clearly see Mr. Parker bounding toward a patch of woods riverside.

"Stay here," Mr. Tanner commanded Jana and Leanne as he flung open the door, kicked his skirt hems out of the way of his boots, and leaped out of the cabin.

When they heard Mr. Ross yell out, "What in tarnation is that?" Jana elbowed Leanne and nodded at the door opposite the one Mr. Tanner had exited. "I'm going out to see what's happening."

"Ya read my mind," Leanne said. With revolver in one hand and her skirts gathered up in the other, she practically rode Jana piggyback out of the carriage.

Realizing that Jana and Leanne had disobeyed him, Mr. Tanner ordered them back inside.

"We ain't gonna be sittin' ducks," Leanne said.

"And you need extra hands safeguarding the area," Jana said.

Mr. Tanner retorted, "Leave it to us men to handle this dangerous business."

Seethingly, Jana said, "Let me remind you, Mr. Tanner, that Leanne and I are former cavalrymen; we're trained in guarding and scouting, and we're quick on the draw," which put a gag in his mouth.

With surprising agility, the elderly coachman pivoted on his wooden bench and squinted down at Jana, then Mr. Tanner, clearly confused by the mismatch of voices to frocks. Ironically, Leanne was the only one who appeared to be properly attired. Wouldn't it confound Mr. Ross worse if he were to discover Leanne's preference for masculine clothes?

Jana and Leanne crept up even with the Morgan horses, the whites of their eyes visible, their nostrils flared and puffing steam, and their hoofs tamping the ground as they shifted around restlessly in their collars.

"It's not pretty," Mr. Ross warned, staring dumbfounded. "In fact, it's downright spooky."

Equally as shocked as Mr. Ross, Jana and Leanne gawked at the effigy of a female soldier in the likeness of Jana, tied to a stake and burning on the bed of a buckboard, blocking the middle of the road. It reminded Jana of Joan of Arc's fate, which only served to get her dander up as opposed to terrifying her.

Leanne thrust out her hands and wrung them as she said, "Those lunatics don't know who they're dealin' with—they don't scare us."

"Would somebody mind telling me what's going on?" Mr. Ross said with genuine incredulity.

"I'm sorry, Mr. Ross," Mr. Tanner said, "our mission is classified, and we were ordered to keep it from you just in case you were a conspirator."

"What mission? What conspiracy? Who are you people?"

"It's clear to me that Mr. Ross is no threat to us, and I think it's only fair he be let in on our subterfuge," Jana said, not waiting for Mr. Tanner's consent or dissent. She dove in, sketching the details for the confused soul.

Mr. Ross's voice held no animosity when he said, "Well, now, I don't mind a fight, but my infirmity requires, when possible, that I be prepared for its potential."

"I understand, sir. Please, forgive our cautiousness," Jana said.

Shaking his head in disbelief, Mr. Ross muttered, "Nothing like this ever happens in Seneca County. No one's going to believe me when I tell them about this."

"I wouldn't believe you either," Jana said, evoking unexpected chuckles from her companions.

On the heels of their laughter, Mr. Parker came sprinting back from his pursuit, contending he'd followed the hoofmarks of a lone draft horse all the way to the river where they then turned back toward Waterloo.

A puzzling notion about his claim tumbled off Jana's tongue. "You covered a lot of ground in a short time, given the strenuous conditions, Mr. Parker."

"What are you implying?" he asked with an indignant snivel.

Jana heard Ma's advice clapping around her brain in thunderous admonition: *Think before you speak.* She regretted her outburst. Mr. Parker was an ally, and it did no good to alienate him. However, if by chance he was on the wrong side, it did no good to put him on alert so he'd start censoring his words and actions around them. She summoned up a look of admiration for him and said, "Only that I'm impressed, Mr. Parker. You're in good shape, and I'm glad to have you backing me up."

"The boss requires us to be physically fit to run down the bad guys," he said in a tone that accused her of being dumb not to know that.

His reference to Allan Pinkerton as the *boss* reminded her of Goliath, and it pounded her eardrum fiercer than a mallet against a tam-tam. Whether or not the title was commonplace in some trades, she'd grown to hate the sound of it.

"I'll double back tomorrow and follow the tracks farther. If he escaped through Waterloo, maybe someone saw him and can give us a description," Mr. Parker said.

"A waste of time, Mr. Parker," Mr. Tanner said.

While Mr. Parker's eyes shifted to Mr. Tanner, Jana seized the moment to scrutinize what about his appearance had caused her to question the distance he claimed to have traversed in tracking their foe. Her eyes roamed to the lower legs of his trousers, and there was her answer: He scarcely had any ice crystals clinging to them.

Mr. Tanner continued his conjecture, "I can assure you the assailant is long gone with the money he got paid for his presumably lone job. And on this wintry night, he could ride right through the middle of Waterloo blowing a bugle, and no one would come out to pay him heed."

Shifting his angry eyes away, Mr. Parker mumbled, "Whatever you say, Mrs. Parker."

It bothered Jana that both detectives were giving up on this lead so easily and that they seemed hostile to one another when they were supposed to be working together.

"Were ya cavalry too, Mr. Tanner?" Leanne asked.

"No, but I rode with cavalry scouts on some spying missions. What made you ask?"

"The part 'bout blowin' a bugle struck a note, that's all."

The sound of Mr. Ross chafing his gloved hands vigorously against the wool of his upper coat sleeves drew everyone's attention to him. "Do you mind if we get going?" he said. "We still have three miles to cover, and my bones are brittle—they've had all they can take of the cold for one night. The weather here is unpredictable at this time of year. A blizzard could come whipping up off either Seneca or Cayuga Lake, and I'm too old to spend the night cuddling in a crowded carriage with people confused about their gender." He laughed heartily at his own joke.

"First, we've got to douse the fire and clear the wagon out of our path," Mr. Tanner said. "We've got enough hands down here, Mr. Ross, for you to stay and mind the horses." He wheeled around and hustled off toward the fire with Mr. Parker on his heels.

Leanne started after the agents, and Jana lunged for her hood, holding her back by it. Leaning into her ear, she whispered, "I have a sinking feeling about those two. We better watch what we say and do around them."

"I got the same feelin'," Leanne said.

Releasing Leanne's hood, Jana said, "You go on ahead; I'll be along in a minute. I feel I can trust Mr. Ross, and he too should be warned about our misgivings with the Pinkerton operatives."

After Jana officially introduced herself and her purpose for lingering behind, Mr. Ross said, "As I mentioned, Miss Brady, I can handle myself better when I'm aware of the situation." He rested his fist on his thigh and said, "I'll keep an eye on the bird riding shotgun with me."

"You'd do that for me, Mr. Ross?"

With a glint of mischief, he said, "I have no choice."

"Why's that?"

"You're famous around these parts, Miss Brady. If anything happens to you on my watch, I'd be strung up"—he aimed his thumb back toward Waterloo—"on the Seneca County Court House lawn without a trial. And if I were lucky enough to escape that, my wife would see to it I took up permanent residence in my livery's tack room. She's especially antsy to hear your talk tomorrow, and she's allowing me to accompany her. But I'm getting off the subject. Would it help any if I were to try mining a secret or two from Mr. Parker once we're underway?" He winked. "The barber isn't the only one whom men confide in."

"That would be a tremendous help, Mr. Ross. Now before they perceive we're plotting something, I better go help douse the fire."

Leanne and the agents were throwing snow on the flames gobbling up one side of the wagon's wall, so Jana got to work on the sparking remains of her effigy, which sizzled and snapped to protest its smothering. They'd barely finished extinguishing the fire and pushing the buckboard out of the middle of road when the wind picked up. It helped to blow the ashes from Jana's hair and clothes, but it did nothing to remedy the taste of charred straw on her tongue.

Once all had reclaimed their seats, their cab resumed its journey, leaving behind a scene straight out of a Shakespearean tragedy. Jana reclined her head back against the cold leather of her bench and closed her eyes. Against the black backdrop of her eyelids, she saw the three witches stirring up the prophecy that incites Macbeth into murder and mayhem en route to his snatching the King of Scotland's throne away from his bloodline. The scene suddenly reverted to Jana's burning effigy. Her eyes popped wide open to the terrifying resemblance between it and the prophecy—both meant to goad on their targets.

The idea of her being lured toward something tragic began to fray her nerves. First, it was public knowledge she'd risked her life to fight for her country—a true testament of her determination to see whatever she started through. Her abductors had to know no kidnapping or threat pinned to her coat would hinder her from finishing her commitment. Second, they'd declared they'd inflict worse than a bullet in her arm if she persisted beyond her kidnapping in Buffalo, yet right here in this remote land lolling between Seneca and Cayuga Lakes, they had every opportunity to do just that, and all they threw at her was a burning effigy. Another hollow threat. She was now one-hundred-percent positive they *did* mean to harm her worse—maybe kill her—but on some grander stage.

For the first time since she'd been kidnapped, she felt horribly conflicted. What could she, Leanne, Charlie, and Wyatt do to combat an invisible army amassing against them? At least David could see Goliath. It was one thing for her to put herself in harm's way, another to offer up her friends—especially Leanne and Charlie—as sacrificial lambs. She knew them well, and they'd never give up unless she did. Their health and welfare were her highest priority; she decided then to cancel any more events beyond the one tomorrow in Seneca Falls—which she'd gladly forfeit too if it wasn't too late. She'd break the news to her traveling companions early next morning. But where would she go after that? She wasn't about to go home and interrupt any momentum Keeley had toward a resurrection of their love. As Shakespeare's Trinculo admits to Alonso in *The Tempest,* she admitted to herself that she was "in a real pickle."

## Seneca Falls, New York

### March 10, 1865

Jana awakened to dawn's tangerine-tinted bath filling up her room through the mullioned window of her hotel room, but the vibrancy of the day's start did nothing to lift her spirits. Although she'd gone to bed feeling glum, she'd slept surprisingly well. She was glad to be rested up for her lecture this afternoon and for the argument she was bound to get from her traveling companions once they heard her decision to quit the tour.

Leaving the comfort and sanctuary of her feather mattress, she moved about the room slower than a turtle to pull down the fringed blinds and then to dip a washcloth in the cold water of the bedside basin, wring it out, and rub perfumed soap into it. As she scrubbed her face, neck, and arms, she found herself wishing she could scrub away the morning so she'd be beyond her disagreeable task. She hated to give up her tour, but friendship cut both ways: Leanne and Charlie had come along on her lecture circuit to protect her from harm, and now she felt compelled to reciprocate. No other alternative to avoid risking harm to them had come to her, and she was determined to see them home in one piece.

Thanks to Mrs. Vaughan's insightfulness about the antagonism she might endure from presenting herself to the public in her cavalry uniform, as she'd been subjected to a trifle in Buffalo and wanted to avoid again, she brought along her Garibaldi dress. It was a fashionable compromise between her femininity and military service. She traded her cotton nightgown for her undergarments, including three layers of ruffled petticoats that were starched to add a stylish fullness to her skirt, which she preferred over a hoopskirt. While the latter's watch-spring steel hoops were light and flexible, they were cumbersome for squeezing through narrow passageways and maneuvering in and out of a carriage. The wind could catch under it and knock her to the ground or invert it like an umbrella—either way the outcome would be embarrassing with her petticoats, pantalettes, and stockings bared. She imagined how such an incident could be construed as helplessness by onlookers at a time when she hoped to represent women as a pillar of strength. *No thanks to the crinoline*, Jana thought as she pulled her dress on over her head, then shook the dust from the skirt hem and smoothed out the bodice. Aided by the bureau mirror, she tied the red bow that mimicked General Custer's around her military collar and caught a glimpse of her strained expression. Reminded of the general's courage to stand out in battle, she narrowed her hazel eyes upon her reflection in admonition. How could she dive headlong into spying knowing she could hang for it yet fret telling her friends something that was for their own good? With renewed confidence, she netted her auburn tresses in a navy snood from the crown of her head down and brushed dander from her shoulder epaulettes. She fished around in her carpetbag until her fingers found her room's clunky brass key, and she locked her door on the way out. The aromas of freshly brewed coffee mingling with breakfast foods wafted up the stairs and hastened her pace down to the ground floor. Although she treaded carefully across the polished parquet to keep from slipping, she still instigated squawks from the floorboards at the threshold into the dining room and announced her arrival. She was relieved to find only her confidantes occupied the space; she hoped it would stay this way until after they'd had their conversation, which could wind up loud and contentious.

Swallowing the spoonful of porridge he'd just scooped into his mouth, Charlie said, "Good morning, Jana." He nodded toward Leanne. "Did you churn in your bed all night too?"

Leanne grimaced at him. Knowing her, she didn't want it telegraphed to their foes she might be vulnerable to keeping her wits about her. If the Pinkertons knew, they'd praise her, given their agency's mantra, We Never Sleep.

*Still*, Jana thought, *all the more reason to leave the tour. I won't have Leanne's health compromised by her incessant worrying over me.*

The pages of Wyatt's newspaper rustled as he peered over it at Jana. "Allow me to apologize again for last night. I pray you have no ill effects from it."

"No apology needed, Wyatt." With a toss of her head, she said, "Last night was nothing compared to my other harrowing incidents in soldiering and spying. I appreciate your having alerted the constable and his deputy; I hope you didn't have to pay too handsomely for the extra men they rounded up, especially when the posse only rode as far as the village line before they caught up with us."

He grinned. "They gave me a discount." While Jana, Leanne, and Charlie rewarded his first crack at humor in their company with a chuckle, Wyatt had already turned serious and was saying, "The money means nothing compared to my pledge to keep you safe."

Jana felt the warmth of Wyatt's sincerity wrapping around her like a thick blanket. And it was genuine. Not overdone like his rubbery eggs. Or mushy like Charlie's porridge. But just right like Leanne's lightly toasted bread. She scoffed inwardly at her voracious appetite; it could lead her into the strangest of similes. *Really though, "Goldilocks and the Three Bears"?* Pulling up a chair, she plopped down on its fabric, upholstered so tight it nearly bounced her up to the tray ceiling. She contemplated her opening line while she slowly removed the fork from her linen napkin, which she placed upon her lap.

Swooping in with a swish of his black coat and trousers, a waiter nodded toward her teacup. "Coffee? Tea?"

"Coffee, please."

He poured the tarry brew that smelled of freshly ground beans while he took her order of two runny eggs, a mound of roast beef hash, two slices of buttered toast, and jarred fruit.

Familiar with Jana's eating routine on the days of her events, no one reacted to her sizeable order except the waiter. He looked her over as if trying to figure out where she'd pack it all. Grinning, he said, "Will that be all, miss?"

Returning a grin, Jana said, "Oh, toss in another egg."

The waiter laughed, but to his wondering expression, Jana shook her head to confirm she was kidding. Then she explained, "On the day of my lecture, I prefer to eat a big breakfast when I know I won't be dining again until evening—or at all, if it gets too late."

He stepped back to take in a fuller view of her. "Are you *the* Miss Brady who fought in the war as a soldier, nurse, and spy?"

"She sure is," Leanne said, beaming with pride as if she were Jana's creator.

The waiter frowned. "I wanted to attend your speech; unfortunately, I have to work. We're expecting a huge crowd for dinner afterward." In response to Jana's pouting lips in sympathy for his disappointment, he said, "My wife will be in attendance, and she's promised me every little detail afterward." A sudden idea lit up his face. "Just in case you can't get back before the kitchen closes at nine o' clock, why don't I ask Cook if he'll put something aside for you in the ice chest?"

"That's awfully kind of you and, if your very busy cook agrees, please tell him to make it simple—cold meat, cheese, and bread from the leftovers of tonight's specials would be perfect."

"How many plates will you need?"

Not sure if she should include the detectives, she deferred to Wyatt who said, "There are six in our party. I'll make arrangements for payment with the manager of the dining room."

"Very well," the waiter said, "I'll be off to get that and your breakfast ordered, Miss Brady. In case I get busy, I wish you the very best with your speech this afternoon, and I admire your courage in speaking about it publicly."

"You're sweet," Jana said, desperate for a sip of her coffee to strengthen her for telling her friends she'd lost her nerve to do just that. She wasn't prepared for the strong brew that shocked her taste buds and made her lips pucker.

As if he'd read her thoughts, Wyatt said, "I still find it disconcerting that our adversaries discovered our ruse."

"I do too. Their tentacles are far-reaching, and it seems to suggest there's a secret society working against us as opposed to a few men," Jana said.

"Hmmm," Wyatt said, "my brother Wallace implied the same thing."

Leanne said, "Mr. Parker said he'd go back and investigate the site of our attack today, but Mr. Tanner said it wasn't worth it 'cause the prankster would be long gone before we could sniff out his tracks, which apparently headed back toward Waterloo."

"I have to agree with Mr. Tanner," Wyatt said. "The man would be daft to tarry in Waterloo overnight, knowing we'd be hot on his tail and that a citizen of the village could provide a detailed description of him today."

While Jana tamed her coffee with cream and sugar crystals, she felt her sheer disappointment with Wyatt's and Mr. Tanner's adamancy about foregoing the Waterloo angle. She had a nagging feeling there was some clue around it. But she had no time to investigate herself, Leanne and Charlie couldn't be spared, she didn't trust the Pinkerton agents, and she refused to pester Wyatt with it because he'd follow her suggestion to hire a neutral party to do it, and he was already contributing enough to her tour. Too bad Elizabeth Cady Stanton no longer lived here—she'd know someone who could help. She rolled her eyes at herself. *Why am I fretting over this when I'm quitting the lecture tour?* Setting her spoon down on her saucer with a clatter meant to grab everyone's attention, she blurted out, "Any further investigation is a moot point."

"Huh?" Leanne, Charlie, and Wyatt said in unison.

Tracing a lacey-embroidered flower in the white tablecloth with her index finger, Jana braced herself for the verbal tirade bound to follow her announcement: "I'm ending the lecture tour after today."

The air was thrashed by their collective gasp.

Stiffening her back against the fiddle-shaped splat of her chair, she sat up with resolve. "I appreciate what you've all done to make my trip successful, but based upon what we saw last night, it would seem the violence is mounting against me. I can't in good conscience continue to imperil you all."

Wyatt was the first to crack out of the communal stupor. "That's a very wise decision."

Meeting Wyatt's eyes with a brashness that lacked any regard for him ripping up his business contract with her, Leanne said, "I don't agree." She turned to Jana. "We've got to find out who's behind this and put 'em behind bars."

"I'm with Leanne," Charlie said. "It's wrong what they're doing to you, Jana, and if you quit now, they'll only find another target for their vengeance."

"I ain't so sure they'd give up on ya after ya quit. If I were 'em, I'd want to stop ya permanently from ever gittin' yer message out. And"—she paused for effect—"when ya go home, we all go home. Who's gonna watch yer back 'round the clock, then?"

"Are you suggesting Jana be used as bait to reel in our foes?" Wyatt shook his head emphatically. "That's playing with a loaded gun."

"Not if we make sure she's under heavy guard at all times just like ya did in Buffalo with local lawmen and other reinforcements," Leanne said.

"That might be easy to do in the smaller venues here and in Johnstown," Wyatt said, "but Albany is a grand stage, especially with her speaking outside in the wide open."

*Grand stage?* Jana jolted up to these words. *Of course! Why didn't I think of it before?* As Wyatt had planned right from the beginning, he wanted her events drawing attention so that by the time she got to the capital city, the state's legislature would be intrigued by and attend her speech. She was certain her conspirators were also seeking a big draw in Albany for their coup de grace— where they'd render their deathblow to Jana and thus the woman's rights movement when they proved Jana weak and helpless to their acts of aggression. If her theory was correct, it assured her that other than a few minor nuisances they probably had planned for her between now and Albany to keep goading her on, they wouldn't harm a hair on her head. This would allow her to dispense with trying to trick her kidnappers and to spend more time focusing on catching them.

Luckily for Jana, Wyatt hadn't noticed her hitch. He was staring out the window, evidently considering Leanne's suggestion. Jana thought his power of concentration was remarkable with Fall Street alive with people afoot or in every conceivable conveyance bustling to open their shops or offices, conduct banking, trade their wares or produce, and work at the mills, factories, iron works, gasworks, distilleries, and tanneries. She knew the latter group was aided in their manufacturing by the power generated from the falls in the Seneca River, but all of these enterprises were fortunate to operate alongside the Seneca-Cayuga Canal, which hooked northerly into the Erie Canal, for the shipment of their goods far and wide by mule-drawn packet boats. And some of them were world renowned, such as Seabury S. Gould's water pumps.

Leanne and Charlie, however, did catch Jana's hitch, and each fixed their inquisitive eyes upon her.

Pinching her lips together, Jana conveyed she'd tell them later, and they nodded their understanding. If Wyatt knew her fear about Albany, he'd terminate the rest of the tour—and just when Leanne and Charlie, even Jana herself, had pretty much talked her into continuing on.

Wyatt turned back from the window. "I'm friends with the city's mayor. I'm sure he'd let us borrow the local militia to surround the premises."

"That ought to do the trick," Jana said, "but hopefully we'll have the criminals collared by then."

"Does this mean we're gonna go on?" Leanne asked, her eyes boring pleadingly into Jana's.

"I guess so," Jana said, returning to sipping her coffee.

"I'll meet with the constable this morning to confirm he's satisfied my request to round up deputies and a few other good men to guard the premises around the Wesleyan Chapel during your affair today," Wyatt said.

"I insist upon paying for those few good men," Jana said.

With a wave of dismissal, Wyatt said, "That's my responsibility. You just take care of yourself and worry about your orations."

"But—"

"It's in our contract," Wyatt cut Jana off. "Now I have something more critical to debate with you all." He paused while steadily holding their gazes. "I fear that the hostility against you, Jana, might be coming from within our folds."

Jana flinched and the coffee she was about to sip flew from her cup and landed with a splat on the white linen tablecloth. Simultaneously, Leanne grunted as if she'd been gut-punched, and Charlie choked on his oatmeal.

To their shock, Wyatt expounded, "Up until now, we've all been of the same mind that the mastermind behind this business against you, Jana, is a perfect stranger who is using you and our campaign as an outlet for some grudge. I'm beginning to wonder if his vendetta is more personal—closer to home."

"Are you saying a friend or kin could be the source?" Charlie said, his expression straining against his disbelief that someone near and dear could be party to something so underhanded.

"Perhaps not that close ... but perhaps, for example, one of you has a cavalry comrade who has a score to settle."

Charlie chortled. "Leanne grew enemies by the bushels in our early days of enlistment."

With a jab of her elbow in Charlie's arm, Leanne showed she wasn't proud of it, and she'd rather avoid having it telegraphed to Wyatt.

Charlie apologized with a long face.

"We all let Leanne take care of our regiment's bullies," Jana said. "You might have something, however, Charlie. Although there's virtually no trace of Leanne since she left the army, my publicity has exposed me far and wide. If you'll remember, I once had a tussle with a bully, whom I humiliated after he insinuated I was a Nancy. It seems far-fetched that he'd hate me enough to retaliate against all women."

"You never know what a warped mind will do," Wyatt said.

Jana added, "There's also the chance I've been recognized from my spying days, and some Rebel is out to finish my hanging."

"Don't misunderstand me," Wyatt said, "I'm not exonerating myself. I can't think of anyone who ever accused me of malice against them, but I've come in contact with hundreds of people in my lifetime. I venture to say that the probability of my having antagonized someone is greater than it is for the three of you combined. And it's public knowledge that I'm financially supporting this endeavor."

Before they could discuss the cannonball he'd just hurled at them any further, the waiter appeared. He set down Jana's meal before her, announcing that there was a gentleman in the lobby asking to see her.

"Me?" Jana asked.

Teasingly, he said, "You are Miss Brady, are you not?" When she rose from her chair, he offered to cover her plate and keep her food warm.

"I'd appreciate that," Jana said.

As Leanne started out of her chair, the waiter said, "The gentleman insisted Miss Brady come alone." He bolted to the kitchen under a glare from Leanne, which said she just might gun him down.

"I don't give a hoot 'bout the man's demands," Leanne said. "I'd be a hypocrite to let ya go it alone after I just got done sayin' we need to make sure you're under heavy guard at all times."

"I'll be fine, Leanne. It would be suicide for anyone to try something here in such a public place." Jana succumbed to the worry chiseled deep into Leanne's expression, saying before she dashed away, "If it'll make you feel better, you're welcome to peek around the corner to see who's asking for me." Upon reaching the lobby, she recognized their driver from last night. The daylight accentuated Mr. Ross's deep-set wrinkles, making him look older than he'd appeared in the dark. Although he was hunched over from age, he still towered over Jana, and his musculature might still discourage some from tangling with him. He was drumming his crooked fingers on the registration desk and stealing nervous glances all around.

"Ah, there you are, Miss Brady," Mr. Ross said, hastening to use her arm for light support as he ushered her toward some seats before a roaring fire and away from the front door and staircase to the upper rooms. He eased his stiff body onto a sofa with bowing cabriolet legs and club feet seemingly too frail to support this large man, and he gestured for her to join him. "It's better if we both sit here where we can watch out for Mr. Parker." After removing his wide-brimmed leather hat and placing it on his lap, he paused to survey their surroundings one more time. "Any chance he could be within earshot?"

"The manager's office behind the registration desk is the only place he could be where we can't see him and, since the manager is at the registration desk, I doubt he's in there. And"—she chuckled as she pointed toward Leanne peeking around the staircase—"my friend has just proven we'd see him there too." To further allay his worries about any reprisal from Mr. Parker, should he show up and suspect Mr. Ross of tattling on him, she extracted a few banknotes of one-and-two-dollar denominations from her reticule and said, "I'll hold these in my hand and, if Mr. Parker happens upon us, we'll pretend we're discussing your wage for last night's service. Since he knows Wyatt will have already reimbursed you for it, you could act as if you're appealing to me for a higher wage, given your imposition yesterday."

"Grand idea, Miss Brady," he said, reclining back against the sofa with the firelight accentuating the mischievous glint in his eyes. "I fulfilled my promise to keep my ears open to anything Mr. Parker had to say last night."

"And?"

"I got to say it was easy—too easy—to wheedle information out of our Mr. Parker. He loves to talk about himself." With a victory snort, he said, "I manipulated the conversation a few times to pry some things out of him that might be of interest to you. I've never done any spying before, but I must admit I'm rather enjoying it."

"It was fortuitous for me to make your acquaintance, Mr. Ross, and I appreciate your help and secrecy."

"My lips are sealed even to my wife, who's actually pretty good at keeping secrets."

In pondering her vow never again to keep secrets from Keeley after she finally confirmed for him she really was a woman, Jana said, "I trust you to share whatever information you wish with Mrs. Ross. Now I'm dying to hear what you gleaned from Mr. Parker."

"Most interesting, he said he was born and raised around these parts—Rochester, I think—and that he's only been away from home twice in his life: The first for his three-year enlistment to fight around Maryland and Virginia, the second to visit an army buddy in Buffalo immediately before his assignment to your case."

Jana's mind began spinning faster than a toy top. She barely heard Mr. Ross say, "Are you thinking what escaped my feeble brain right away?" When her face lit up, his did too, and he bobbed his head, encouraging her to reason aloud, "How can Mr. Parker be a Pinkerton detective if he's never been to its headquarters in Chicago for training? And I doubt his recent visit to Buffalo is pure coincidence to my being there."

With a wince after he slapped his thigh too hard, he said through clenched teeth, "Precisely my thoughts."

Jana grimaced in sympathy, then said, "Did he reveal his army buddy's name?"

"He didn't, and I had no opportunity to get that out of him without raising suspicion. However, he did affiliate his buddy with wealth."

Mr. Ross's intelligence hit her like a ton of ship ballast, which did nothing to balance her thoughts. It was yet one more link to Wyatt, although she didn't recall anything about his ever having served in the army. "Can you remember anything else of importance, Mr. Ross?"

"Not that I reckoned significant anyway. Mr. Parker did speak fondly of his time in the army. Said he got to know plenty of Rebels across picket lines—even played baseball with them in their leisure time. He left the infantry when his enlistment period was up because he couldn't see fighting Confederates anymore—he'd come to realize they had a right to secession and even their slaves."

"Did he by any chance say anything about Mr. Tanner?"

"He doesn't think much of Mr. Tanner—he called him yellow for dodging the real fight by working for Allan Pinkerton throughout the war."

Jana mumbled, "Hardly the kind of camaraderie one would expect from a fellow Pinkerton."

"I couldn't agree with you more," Mr. Ross said. "According to Mr. Parker, Mr. Tanner was recalled from spying in the South and reassigned to your case once Allan Pinkerton was convinced the war was winding down with Grant having Lee holed up in Petersburg and his supply and reinforcement lines severed."

"He's wrong about Mr. Tanner chickening out. As you heard me say last night, I fought in the cavalry. After I was wounded at Brandy Station—"

With bulging eyes, Mr. Ross cut her off, "You *really* were wounded?"

Instinctively, Jana fired a look at her left bicep and began massaging it as she said with modesty, "I have a scar to prove it."

"You wear your badge with honor, Miss Brady. You have every right to fight for your country too, and you shouldn't have to hide behind men's clothes to do it."

"You're a rare breed amongst men, Mr. Ross. We're lucky to have you on our side."

"Well, anyway, I interrupted the point of your story. Please finish. I'm all ears."

"After I was wounded, the Union army discharged me from soldiering but agreed to send me south to spy. I was caught with materials traitorous to the Confederacy and sentenced to hang from which I managed to escape by faking my death from a heart attack right on my gallows." When she saw his expression growing quizzical, she hurried to say, "It's a long story for another time."

"Yes, indeed," Mr. Ross said. "Please proceed."

"As I'm sure you know, Pinkerton agent Timothy Webster wasn't as fortunate as me—he was hung. My point is that I can attest to the fact soldiering and spying are equally harrowing. Believe me, Mr. Tanner is no chicken."

"I sensed a sturdy resolve and courage in your nature last night, Miss Brady. We need more young people like you out there crusading for freedom for all— the very principle upon which our country was founded and continues to be ignored."

*Wouldn't he be surprised to learn that just minutes ago I was all ready to give up?* Jana thought, his declaration jabbing her soul, especially when she realized that she was being selfish to deny Leanne and Charlie their due to do exactly as Mr. Ross wished for their generation.

"My wife is strong-willed. If she hadn't been getting on in her years, I'm convinced she would've also answered Lincoln's initial call for seventy-five thousand volunteers to put down the Rebels after they fired on Fort Sumter." He chuckled. "Now, her infirmity prevents her from gadding about the country petitioning for woman's rights, so she's counting on women of your youth and grit to forge ahead." He picked up his hat. "Speaking of my wife, I've got to get home and fetch her. If she misses your talk today, I'll be bunking in my livery's tack room forever."

Jana just found a recruit whom she could trust to help her with her investigation. "I hate to take advantage of your charity, Mr. Ross, but I feel it's imperative that I do. Would you be willing to listen out for anyone in Waterloo who might've had contact with our attacker? Mr. Parker says he turned back toward your village, but I have no one to go back there and follow the tracks."

"I'll do better than that. When I get home, I'll ask around, and I'll send my son to follow your assailant's trail—that is, if you don't mind my son getting involved." He winked. "He's good at keeping secrets too."

"I don't mind, and I'd be ever so grateful, Mr. Ross." With that, Jana expected him to get up and go.

In a sudden reversal to his assertion that he needed to leave, he stayed planted on the sofa and began nervously twirling his hat in his hands.

"Is there something else, Mr. Ross? Please, I can handle whatever unpleasantry you have to tell me."

"Oh, no, it's nothing like that."

Sensing he had a favor to ask of her but felt silly about it, she jumped to his aid, saying, "If there's anything I can do for you, Mr. Ross, I hope you won't hesitate to ask."

He scratched his shock of silver hair and said, "Well, now, how did you know I have a favor to ask? Are you a seer besides all of your other talents?"

"If I were, my kidnappers would be in jail," Jana said, to which they shared a laugh. "Back to your favor, Mr. Ross"—she slapped the cushion between them—"name it." With her hand, she fanned away the dust motes that she'd exorcised from the sofa and that were flitting all around them, threatening to invade their breathing passages. "You'd make me very happy if I could return a favor."

"Well, now, nothing ever shocks my wife, but I think she could be shocked if she were given the impression we were long lost friends. She's been itching to meet you, so if after your talk I could introduce her to you and you could make a fuss over me, I'd be eternally grateful. I should tell you she's not the jealous kind, so there's no issue there. And she loves a good prank as long as it's in good taste. I know this is a story she'll get a kick out of telling our children and grandchildren for years to come."

"I'd be honored to help." Grinning mischievously, Jana said, "Please call me Jana from now on, and make sure you do in front of Mrs. Ross. I sense it'll add a little more flair to our caper."

"And please call me Tom—short for Thomas."

"That's my pa's given name. No wonder we get along so well," Jana said, to which they again shared a laugh.

In using the arm of his chair to help himself to his feet, Tom's knees cracked. "Whatever you do, Jana, don't grow old."

"May I ask why you don't retire from driving?"

"I love my job, but after last night—no offense to you—I think I will," Tom said, taking his hobbled leave after he wished her luck with her lecture and she wished him luck with his investigation.

As Jana passed the registration desk, the clerk called out to her, "Miss Brady, I have a telegram for you." He snatched it from the box that corresponded with her room number and handed it to her.

She opened it with care and read:

Miss Brady. Sorry can't be at your lecture today. I am with you in spirit. Pioneering magnanimous change is not for faint-hearted. We're thrilled you're on our side. Keep up the exemplary work. Mother expects you for tea upon your arrival in Johnstown. Elizabeth Cady Stanton

Laughing in surprise, she thought, *Now Elizabeth Cady Stanton? With everyone cajoling me on—friends and foes alike—how on earth would I have ever gotten away with giving up?*

## Seneca Falls, New York

### March 10, 1865

Jana returned to the dining room and the questioning eyes of her colleagues. To the chagrin of her stomach, she satisfied their curiosity first by telling them what Mr. Ross had to say about Mr. Parker.

"That no good piece of—," Leanne cut herself off when she shot from her chair, causing it to topple over and crash against the hardwood floor.

In a gentle voice, Jana said, "Please sit down, Leanne. There's time to go after Mr. Parker, and I have more to tell you that'll factor into our strategy for dealing with him."

Leanne relented, righting and settling back into her chair.

When Jana got to the part of her report she knew would sit in Wyatt's stomach like a rotten egg, she hesitated.

He must've sensed her difficulty because he abruptly stopped stirring his coffee and looked up. "Please proceed, Jana," he said with intensity in his eyes that couldn't be denied.

With a sigh, she told them about Mr. Parker's association with a wealthy army buddy from Buffalo.

Wyatt stared off into nowhere. "I never served in the army, but Wallace did." Scratching his head beneath his mop of curls, he said, "I was certain of Wallace's innocence; now I'm unsure."

Given Wyatt's receptivity to discuss his brother's potential complicity earlier, Jana said, "I hope you won't take offense, Wyatt"—she paused to allow him a chance to brace himself for her forthcoming confession—"to our having spied on you and your family outside St. James Hall. Just so you know, we weren't suspicious of you; we had reservations about Wallace. We wanted to make sure you weren't being blinded by him—being he's your brother."

Wyatt cast each a weak smile. "I'm glad you did it. Did your objective eyes and ears conclude anything of significance?"

Since Leanne had done the spying, Jana deferred to her to answer.

Leanne obliged with a question to his question. "Did the man ya paid to keep tabs on Wallace come up with anything?"

"I can think of nothing besides Wallace's usual lethargy toward work and his bad habits of drinking and gambling. My associate even went undercover to the tavern where Wallace's cane went missing, and the barkeeper corroborated his story." Wyatt heaved a heavy sigh. "I suppose this theft could be contrived by Wallace to distance himself from any involvement in the plot against you. However, I don't believe he's capable of being the brain behind the brawn. Nor can I fathom his wanting to harm you, Jana, just to get to me. Perhaps as you've all suggested, I've lost my objectivity to him."

"Well, until he's proven guilty, we'll continue to believe in his innocence and that he's being framed too," Jana said.

"I appreciate your confidence in my brother. You have me wondering, though, how far he would go with the right inducement." Wyatt took them all by surprise when he obliged their hooked brows by explaining, "I don't ordinarily discuss my family affairs, but given that Wallace might be involved in this malicious plot against you, Jana, and one of the possible motives is greed, they might have some bearing on the case. My father left his entire estate for me to dole out in part to my mother and older brother. He was very specific with his delineation of their allowances because he recognized in them both a penchant for squandering money and because he wanted to avoid putting me in the awkward position of having to negotiate the terms. Still, they're unhappy with the arrangement and always petitioning me for more money. Until they prove to me that they can hold onto their generous allowances for a sufficient period, I will adhere strictly to the prescribed allotment."

Jana, Leanne, and Charlie shared sympathetic frowns over Wyatt's family problems.

While Jana lifted the lid of her breakfast plate, leaned into the vapors of her food, and whiffed, Charlie asked, "How can we prove Wallace's innocence?"

First smiling at Charlie's penchant to always see the sunny-side up in people like her egg yolks, Jana then said, "Through Mr. Parker, but I'm not exactly sure of our scheme just yet." She peered at Leanne in particular. "Rather than let Mr. Parker know we're onto him, however, it would behoove us to take him into our confidence so we can keep a close eye on him." She took a bite of her roast beef hash, which would've been perfectly scrumptious if it wasn't cold, then said,

"You're right, Wyatt, if your brother is involved, he, along with Mr. Parker, is only a puppet."

"How do you know they're not the puppeteers?" Charlie asked.

"From my quick glimpse of them before I was blindfolded, the feet of Goliath's boss were much smaller compared to Wallace's and Mr. Parker's."

"Speakin' of Mr. Parker—for that matter, Mr. Tanner too—has anybody seen hide or hair of either of 'em today?" Leanne asked.

Everyone shook their heads.

Pounding her fist on the table, Leanne said, "Ain't they s'posed to be takin' turns guardin' Jana and investigatin' her case?"

Wyatt nodded. "I'll demand an accounting of their whereabouts when they return and let you know what I learn, unless you have privy to it before me."

"So what's our next move?" Charlie asked.

Having lost her appetite for any more of her food, Jana shoved her plate aside. "How about a walk to the bakery for a sugar cookie? It'll be my treat."

To her abrupt change of course, everyone cast her a look that questioned if she'd lost her marbles.

Jana giggled. "I really am dying for a sugar cookie and, while we're out, we could do some of our own investigating." She turned to Wyatt. "Will you be joining us?"

"Only as far as our tasks take us in different directions—I must head to the jail to confirm that the constable has delegated a presence of guards for your lecture."

"Would you mind if I telegraphed Allan Pinkerton on your behalf?" Jana asked him. "I think he needs to be warned Mr. Parker has been compromised, and we should make sure Mr. Tanner is who he says he is."

"Good idea, Jana. I have no qualm with you signing my name to it, and I'll cover the expense," Wyatt said again in a tone that would brook no argument.

Each party got directions to their respective places from the desk clerk, then went to fetch their outer cloaks from their rooms before meeting back up outside under the canopy over the Fall-Street entrance. After supplying Jana with money to cover the telegram, Wyatt took his immediate departure from them.

Before they moved an inch, Leanne reminded Jana to tell her and Charlie what she'd wanted kept from Wyatt back in the dining room but promised to tell them later. Jana disclosed her theory about Albany being her kidnappers' grand stage and her assassination, to which Leanne said, "I can see why you'd keep that from Wyatt—he'd call off the tour for sure."

Charlie said, "Are you sure you want to go on, Jana?"

"Yes, but I'll understand if you two want to bow out. In fact, I'd feel better if you would."

"Not a chance," Leanne said.

"For me neither," Charlie echoed.

Leanne added, "And we're gonna make sure not one hair on yer head is harmed."

"I knew I could count on you both." Jana took off down the plank sidewalk, which edged the wide unpaved street running through the main part of town, calling out, "Now let's go catch a criminal."

When they reached their destination, Leanne and Charlie opted to wait outside rather than subject themselves to the fate of sardines packed in a tin, as the hotel desk clerk warned they'd do if all three insisted upon sharing the cubbyhole space inside.

Jana stepped in, and her nose collided with the odors that gave away the tools of a telegraph operator's trade: paper, ink, punch cards, and well-oiled machine parts. And she almost collided with Mr. Tanner, who was on his way out.

"Miss Brady!" he said with surprise, backing up a few feet to the desk to give her some room.

He removed his felt derby and bowed his head in gentlemanly decorum, and Jana noticed his puffy eyes, ruddy cheeks, stubbly face, and tousled black hair. *Good for me he takes the Pinkerton Agency's motto to never sleep so seriously,* she mused.

After two subtle jabs of his head back at the operator before he returned his hat to its rightful place, he said, "Would you mind accompanying me back outside for a moment?"

They returned curbside to Leanne's glower, which fanned her cheeks redder than burning coals in her smithy's forge. "Well, well, well, if it ain't Mr. Tanner," she snarled. "Where've ya and Mr. Parker been all mornin'? Weren't ya two s'posed to be takin' turns keepin' yer all-seein' eyes on Jana and investigatin' her case?"

With last night's crustiness removed from his voice, he said, "Yes, we were, Miss Watson, but I assure you my absence has been warranted. I can't say the same for the deceitful Mr. Parker; I've been trailing him all morning, and he was the subject of my wire just now to the Pinkerton Agency."

That explained Mr. Tanner's appearance, which Jana realized was more harried from his undertaking than from haggardness.

Ignorant of Charlie's rapt examination of him, Mr. Tanner said, "It's a matter of urgency, Miss Brady, that I speak with you about him and other matters."

"If it's about his working with my kidnappers, we already know it," Jana said.

He drew his head back in astonishment. "How could you possibly know that already?"

"When ya gonna git it through yer thick skull, Mr. Tanner"—Leanne huffed gloatingly as she waggled her thumb between Jana, Charlie, and herself—"us three are former cavalrymen, and we're trained to keep a keen eye to things?"

Chuckling, he held his hands up in surrender. "Shoot me, Miss Watson, if I ever forget that again."

Leanne widened her stance, parted a flap of her single-breasted waist coat, and rested her hand on the walnut grip of her holstered pistol. Smirking, she said, "Don't tempt me, Mr. Tanner."

Breaking up the ensuing laughter, including her own, Jana said, "May I ask, Mr. Tanner, what prompted you to follow Mr. Parker when last night you were so adamant about it being a waste of time to inspect the area around our roadblock?"

"Mr. Parker slipped a note under my door early this morning to report he was heading back there. My gut told me he was up to no good, so I took off after him." He glanced at Jana then Leanne. "Just for the record, last night I objected to revisiting the scene of the crime as a means of setting up Mr. Parker. I already had my doubts about him after we met in Waterloo and he jumbled the code words we were to use to identify ourselves as Pinkerton agents to you and Miss Watson"—he harrumphed with disgust at himself—"and I stupidly corrected him. Anyway, I knew if he was a conspirator in this business against you, Miss Brady, he'd be eager to fake returning there to make me look bad. I was right, only he made a beeline directly to the Waterloo telegraph office and then the café without any intention of inspecting those tracks, which I fully intended all along to sneak back and do."

"And what did you learn?" Jana said.

He peered westward. "I expect Mr. Parker to come galloping in from Waterloo soon, and I'd rather he didn't see us meeting now, especially outside the telegraph office." When his focus turned back to them, he squinted at Charlie, who was continuing to stare him down. "I presume you're Mr. Charlie Watson, the other cavalryman of your trio?"

"I am, and I take it you're one of the two Pinkertons on the job." Charlie thrust out his hand to shake Mr. Tanner's. "Glad to meet you, sir."

Jana interrupted their cordialities. "Back to our meeting, Mr. Tanner, when is good for you?"

"I must report to Mr. McGriffin first, but then—"

Jana cut him off. "You just missed Mr. McGriffin. He left us for the constable's office to confirm there'll be policemen and guards enough to keep order at my lecture today."

"He won't be there long. I already set that up with the constable before I came here to wire headquarters about Mr. Parker's proclivities." Seeing he'd captured the threesome's awe, Mr. Tanner said, "I'm glad you approve." He faced Jana. "How about we meet when we can avoid Mr. Parker's scrutiny and his suspecting us of keeping something from him? Sometime, say after everyone retires to their rooms for the night? I must insist we meet alone, though." When

Leanne opened her mouth to protest, he raised a staying hand. "It'll look too fishy if we're all meeting to the exclusion of Mr. Parker."

"I take it we're of the same mind, Mr. Tanner, not to let onto Mr. Parker that we're onto him in hopes he'll lead us to his boss?" Jana said.

"We are indeed, Miss Brady."

Crossing her arms over her chest, Leanne tapped her toe against the shoveled sidewalk to grab Mr. Tanner's attention. "And just how do we know ya ain't one of the bad guys?"

Mr. Tanner turned sideways, clicked his heels, and pointed inside the telegraph office. With a wry but congenial smile, he said, "Please proceed with your wire to the Pinkerton Agency, which I presume was to have Mr. Parker—and me—checked out."

"And how do we know we can trust ya 'til we git word from yer boss?" Leanne said.

"You'll have to trust your instincts." Mr. Tanner pulled his shoulders back. "My credibility is sound, but I'll leave you now so that you can decipher it amongst yourselves." He started away, then stopped. "If you aren't too uncomfortable with it, Miss Brady, I suggest we meet in my room. It'll look less suspicious if you're paying me a visit rather than the other way around. And, please"—he peered at her with what seemed to be genuine concern—"be wary of Mr. Parker's intentions, and don't put yourself in a position to be alone with him." Then he strode off.

Jana stared after him, thinking aloud, "What are the odds two Pinkerton operatives are corrupt?" She fixed her eyes on Charlie. "I saw you profiling him. What did you see in him?"

"Without getting into anything too deep right now, he reminds me a lot of Dr. Pease, and that alone tells me he's one of the good guys."

Leanne whirled on Jana. "You're still gonna send yer wire, ain't ya? He could be makin' stuff up same as Mr. Parker is. We got to be sure he's who he says he is."

"I agree," Jana said, moving back inside the claustrophobic telegraph office. When she returned curbside, the icy temperature that crept down her spine made her shiver and draw her hood over her straw-brimmed puff bonnet. Who would believe the cloudless azure sky belonged to winter as opposed to summer? Following her nose, Jana took the lead up Fall Street to the bakery. They took a seat at a small table for four by the window, where they watched the comings and goings of people, stray cats and dogs, and even pigs. The warmth from the ovens, hot coffee, and freshly baked sugar cookies began to thaw Jana out until she was chilled all over again by the sight of Mr. Parker galloping past on a bay horse he'd most likely rented from their hotel's livery.

"Well, well, well, look who the cat dragged in," Leanne said with a sneer.

And for the second time that morning, Jana lost her appetite.

Although the Wesleyan Methodist Chapel was located only one long block west of Carr's Hotel, Jana agreed with everyone about the prudence of her going door-to-door by enclosed carriage, which she caught right out of the hotel's livery yard. Besides that, it would be cold and dark on her return trip, making it ripe for her picking. As was their routine in Buffalo, Wyatt was already at the church helping Charlie set up his camera and processing stations, and Leanne accompanied Jana. The Pinkertons—at least maybe Mr. Tanner—would be around somewhere, melting into the background and watching her back.

Their conveyance jerked to a stop, and Jana presumed they'd reached their destination at the corner of Fall and Mynderse Streets. When the door swung open, a mustachioed face appeared; by the badge pinned to his long canvas coat, Jana guessed him to be the constable right before he introduced himself as such and his younger partner as his deputy. They helped her down onto the slippery planks of the sidewalk and, while Leanne took up the rear guard, they tendered their arms to escort Jana the short distance toward the church.

With a sidelong grin at each, Jana said, "I'm honored to be in the company of such esteemed men. What's the occasion?"

The constable returned a grin. "You're famous, Miss Brady, not to mention a source of worry for Messrs. McGriffin and Tanner. And I'm interested in making sure nothing happens to you in my neck of the woods."

When they reached the paved landing before the front double door, the constable and his deputy released her. Jana thanked them for their attention, then paused before the threshold to consider the starkness of the rectangular red-brick structure. By its lackluster exterior, one would never guess that within its four walls groundbreaking ideals were presented for debate. It was well known that the Wesleyan Chapel was founded by abolitionist-minded Methodists who split from their original congregation when it chose to disregard the abolishment of slavery in their fight for national unity. Since the church's inception, it had opened its doors to temperance and political meetings, as well as sermons on astronomy and natural philosophy—the latter two given by the current reverend himself—or so Jana had heard. Most importantly and, relative to her visit tonight, it was here in 1848 that Elizabeth Cady Stanton, Lucretia Mott, Mary Ann McClintock, Martha Wright, and Jane Hunt hosted the first woman's rights convention of its kind. Neither they nor Jana had expected to attract three hundred attendees. By the time the steeple bell rang to signal the start of her lecture, Wyatt estimated she'd attracted twice that number with every pew and inch of standing space occupied and the doors having to be closed to the line that wound its way back to Carr's Hotel.

Jana opened her talk in the same way she had in Elmira and Buffalo: She acknowledged Mr. McGriffin for his financial support and all supporters of woman's equality for having invited her to speak about her war experiences. When she followed it up with the remark, "I stand before you in representation of all women soldiers, whom I hope I'll do justice," the audience shot to their feet with claps and cheers; Jana knew then she could've gotten away with wearing her cavalry uniform here. And the multiple standing applauses that followed throughout her speech evidenced the spirit of reform held so dear by the egalitarian population of Quakers residing in Seneca County and its surrounds. She felt her heart expand with gratitude.

At the close of her lecture, a throng lingered behind, forming an orderly line to ask Jana questions or to have their portrait taken with her. She mustered up a phony smile and prepared herself to make a fuss over Mr. Ross when he stepped up with his wife clinging to his arm. "Tom, my dear friend, how good of you to come," she said, wrapping her hands around one of his.

Tom had predicted his wife right. Her mouth gaped, forming a double chin resembling bread dough rising. She glanced at her husband and stammered, "You ... you know Miss Brady?"

With a pompous snort, he said, "Of course I know Jana."

His informal reference to Jana made her mouth open more and her chin drop down into the doughy folds beneath it. When she'd semi-recovered from her stupor, she exclaimed, "And you kept this from me, Thomas?"

To her ongoing fluster, Tom grinned at her. "Now don't go getting your feathers ruffled, dear. Jana and I were having some fun with you." When she started to question him about it, he said, "I'll tell you all about it later. Right now, Mary, we need to get our likenesses taken with Jana before we lose our chance." After they posed for Charlie, Tom pretended to be engaged in a lively banter with Jana and Mary while he quickly dispatched his grave findings to Jana: The tracks left by their assailant led east toward Seneca Falls, then south across the bridge toward Ovid—opposite to Mr. Parker's claim; Mr. Parker had sent a telegram from Waterloo that morning (which Jana was happy to hear corroborated Mr. Tanner's report); and the telegraph operator, although bound by confidentiality concerning the contents of Mr. Parker's telegram, did say it was written in code and wired to Buffalo, and he also mentioned observing a tattoo similar to that of the freemasons on the underside of Mr. Parker's forearm.

When Tom and Mary left, Wyatt came marching toward Jana with a devilish grin. "I have some very dear friends who wish to make your acquaintance," he said, stepping aside to reveal a tall, lean woman on the arm of a distinguished-looking man.

Jana judged their ages by their faces to be close to one another—around the mid-forties—but their other more prominent features stood in contrast: her eyes were blue-gray, his dark; her contours were long and angular, his soft and round. Yet in both, Jana saw intelligence, competitive spirit, and compassion. And when Wyatt introduced them as Miss Susan Anthony and Mr. Frederick Douglass, he confirmed her profile of them—Charlie would be proud.

With a sputtering gasp, Jana said, "T-t-the Miss Susan Anthony and t-t-the Mr. Frederick Douglass?"

Miss Anthony and Mr. Douglass broke out in smiles to Jana's reverence of them—hers nearly reached her ears, concealed beneath dark-brown hair, which was swept back and coiled in a bun at the nape of her neck; his also nearly reached his ears, concealed beneath a thick black mane, most of which was combed neatly to one side.

Tendering her hand to both, Jana blurted out the first thing that came to her mind. "Were you here for my whole presentation?" She rolled her eyes inwardly as she silently admonished herself, *Of course they were, you nincompoop. They wouldn't have forayed the distance from their homes in Rochester on a whim.* Hurrying to cover her blunder, she said, "It's an honor to meet you both, and I'm thrilled you came."

Wyatt said, "Miss Anthony wired me yesterday that she and Mr. Douglass would be in attendance today. I hope you don't mind that we kept it a surprise."

"I'm truly grateful for your restraint." To their arching eyebrows, Jana explained, "Your reputations as eloquent speakers precede you, Miss Anthony and Mr. Douglass. If I had known you were in attendance, I might've come down with a case of stage fright and lost my voice." Jana joined their laughter.

Miss Anthony reached out and squeezed Jana's hand. "I find your candidness refreshing, Miss Brady."

"As I do also, Miss Brady," Mr. Douglass added with a smile. "Please, worry no more about your speaking. We admire your eloquence in this realm as much as you seem to esteem ours."

"Yes," Miss Anthony said, "and I have no doubt Mrs. Stanton—the consummate speechwriter—would approve of your talent in that venue as well."

"You had everyone on the edge of their seats, eating out of the palm of your hands," Mr. Douglass said.

Jana felt her pride welling up inside of her. "I only hope I represented women well enough to further our quest for equality under the Constitution."

"I'm confident Mr. Douglass will take no offense when I say—"

Patting her hand that still clung to his arm, Mr. Douglass interjected, "I take no offense, Miss Anthony, to your grievance with woman's rights advocates for having halted their conquest during the war to benefit the abolition of slavery. I might be more passionate about the latter cause, but you well know my position that I abhor any and all oppression."

The slogan of his beloved abolitionist paper *North Star*, which had merged with Gerrit Smith's *Liberty Party Paper* in 1851 to debut as the current circulation of *Frederick Douglass' Paper*, came to Jana's mind: "Right is of no Sex—Truth is of no Color—God is the Father of us all, and we are all Brethren." Ever since his own escape from slavery, he'd toiled relentlessly to propagate those notions through his journals, his help in guiding other escaped slaves to Canada, and his support of woman's rights.

"Well," Miss Anthony continued, "I was more than just a little cross with my coadjutors for ceasing our work. Look where it got us. Mr. McGriffin was of the same mind as me that we could've kept on rallying for both causes. Instead, 'While the old guard sleep, the young devils are wide-awake, and we deserve to suffer for our confidence in man's sense of Justice.' I'm sure you know full well, Miss Brady, that our complacency opened the door for the New York State legislature to repeal parts of the *Married Women's Property Act of 1860*. Mrs. Stanton, Mr. Douglass, Mr. McGriffin, and I were sickened by it." She shook her head and frowned. "No point dwelling on it. We've learned from our lesson, and we've found a torch in you, Miss Brady, to lead us back on course. On behalf of all women, Mr. Douglass and I came here today expressly to show our support of and gratitude to you."

Regarding Jana with an expression that exuded both sympathy and empathy, Mr. Douglass said, "Mr. McGriffin has shared with us the perils of your lecture tour. Under such maliciousness, Miss Brady, we praise your tenacity in carrying on the woman's struggle for equal rights."

Miss Anthony added, "As Mrs. Stanton always says: 'Agitating is not for the faint-hearted.' You're obviously a far cry from that." She giggled. "And I challenge any newspaper correspondent or journalist to say you're devoid of any physical attraction as they try pigeonholing all female agitators of our quest."

Jana felt Miss Anthony's compliment coloring her cheeks, which Leanne diverted when she scuttled over to round them all up in obedience with Charlie's request for a group photograph.

*This is one picture I'll cherish the rest of my life,* she thought.

Later that evening, as Jana gazed upon the tintype of her old and new friends, an idea took shape. She fetched Leanne and Charlie to her room, then showed them the mini-portraitures of Wyatt's family, which Hannah had given her, and she asked Charlie to profile them.

Charlie eagerly sat down and spread out the pictures on a small breakfast table. Before he began his examination, he removed his spectacles, wiped the lenses clean with a handkerchief he fetched from his dress shirt pocket, and returned them to his nose.

Pointing to Wallace's portrait, Jana said, "I'm especially interested in your analysis of him."

Several minutes ticked by before Charlie qualified, "When I profile people, I study their eyes, facial lines, and lips." With Jana and Leanne peering over his shoulders, he pointed to Wyatt's picture. "Since we know Wyatt, we'll use him in contrast against the others." Charlie rubbed his hands against his thighs and took a deep breath.

"Don't be nervous, Charlie, we know ya can do it," Leanne said in a near whisper.

He smiled up at her, then delved into his character sketch: "A steadiness in Wyatt's eyes speaks to his self-confidence and the sparkle in them to his competitive spirit, the soft lines around his face to his kindness and generosity, and the slight upward curve of his lips to his resolve for justice." Looking up at Jana and Leanne, he pushed his sliding spectacles back onto the bridge of his nose and said, "Does that sound right?"

Jana and Leanne bobbed their heads to urge him on, and he reported his other character sketches as follows:

Wyatt's father (William): Fierce eyes, deep-set lines, and pinched lips—domineering, opinionated, hates to lose

Wyatt's mother (Eveleen): Wide, intense eyes, copious lines for her age, and pouty lips—desperation and restlessness (always eager for more), incessant worrying or guilt or both, and discontent with life

Wyatt's brother (Wallace): Indifferent eyes, casual lines, and flat, emotionless lips—dependent, pleasure-seeker, and opportunist

When he finished, he looked up at Jana, then Leanne. To their gaping mouths, he said, "Is that what you were envisioning?"

"Very much so, Charlie. You're amazing," Jana said while Leanne continued her dumbstruck expression. "Where did you get such an extensive vocabulary?"

Beneath his spectacles, his eyes magnified even more to his delight in being recognized. "In my spare time from my medical duties and, before I took up photography, I'd borrow a *Webster's* dictionary from Dr. Pease's bookshelf and learn every fifth word."

Jana wouldn't embarrass him or Leanne by asking him why he didn't apply his learning in his everyday speech. She sensed it had to do with the limitations of Leanne's vocabulary and his not wanting to make himself sound smarter than her. Although, Leanne got along just fine with her keen mind and business savvy.

"Do you see any maliciousness in Wallace's character?" Jana asked.

Reexamining his portrait, Charlie said, "He was the hardest of the three to decipher. I don't see any maliciousness in him, but maybe his opportunistic side could bring it out in him if, as Wyatt said, the price is right."

*Money—there it is again.* Jana reflected back upon Goliath's few utterances, trying to hear some clue in them that might point to her main antagonist. On the one hand, greed seemed to be behind them; on the other, rage with proponents of woman's rights. While Wallace had a motive for the former, Jana saw no connection between him and the latter. He might've had the nerve to show up at her lecture and challenge Wyatt over his allowance, but he'd stood behind his mother. She was more the leader—or really just bossy. Through a heavy sigh, Jana muttered, "This investigation is moving along at a turtle's pace."

"I'm sorry I wasn't much help," Charlie said.

Jana squeezed his shoulder. "I didn't ask you to profile the McGriffins's portraits to link them with my conspirators, although I admit to pressing the Wallace angle."

"Why? What were ya thinkin'?" Leanne asked.

"My logic is unfounded—actually absurd. He's the only other man we met in Buffalo who's linked to wealth."

Leanne threw up her hands. "Hey, ya never know."

"There has to be some familiarity with Wyatt in order for the mastermind behind your kidnapping to frame him, and that still could be leading us back to Wallace, right?" Charlie said.

"I might answer with a definitive yes if it wasn't for Wyatt being extremely well known, which opens the field to numerous suspects," Jana said. "Anyway, Charlie, I really wanted you to see those daguerreotypes because I knew you'd appreciate their antiquity and to give you a chance to practice your profiling skills now that we've met all of the existing McGriffins."

"Well, let's hope yer meeting with Mr. Tanner turns up more," Leanne said.

"Yes, let's hope," Jana said. Something had to give. They were getting closer to Albany, and they were no closer to bagging the bad guys than they'd been from the start. Mr. Parker was their lone lead—a flimsy one because they were dependent upon him leading them to his puppeteer. If only they had the right bait to lure him into tripping up.

## Seneca Falls, New York

### March 10, 1865

Following the gathering with Leanne and Charlie in her room, Jana figured it was late enough for her clandestine meeting with Mr. Tanner. She remembered his warning to be wary of Mr. Parker, and she brought along her reticule, in which she'd stashed her pepperbox. Peeking around her door, she made sure no one roamed about the dimly lit hall before she stole along it, clinging to the wall where the floorboards were less traversed and creaky. A sudden creepy sensation she was being watched made her glance back in time to see the door adjacent to her room closing. She smiled and thought, *The Pinkerton Agency would love to have Leanne in their employ.*

She arrived before Mr. Tanner's door and started to knock when a *whoosh* behind her sent a rush of air that fanned the hairs at the nape of her neck. Whirling around, she came face-to-face with Mr. Parker. He looked dapper in clothes more fashionable than those he wore during his workday, and he'd bathed in cologne, suggesting he was headed out to a saloon—maybe a brothel—for some entertainment.

Mr. Parker had yet to step one foot across the threshold into the hall when he stopped dead in his tracks at the sight of her.

Having the element of surprise on both of their sides, Jana's mind had ample time to conjure up a story as to why she was seeking counsel with Mr. Tanner over him. It struck gold! She placed her index finger to her lips to silence Mr. Parker and pressed her ear against the door to Mr. Tanner's room, pretending to listen for any stirring by him. Over the smell of varnish and the anxious beat of her heart against her eardrum, she detected faint treads approaching. She had to act fast before Mr. Tanner emerged and put them all in an awkward position. Detaching her ear, she motioned for Mr. Parker to follow her with haste down the hall and into her room. After he shut the door behind them, she turned to him with a staged sigh of relief. "It was my good fortune you appeared from your room when—"

With a nervous clearing of his throat, he interjected, "You caught me heading out to secure the premises."

*Good. I've got him on the defensive,* Jana thought. "And I was headed your way. After I hit a few squeaks in the floor, I figured I'd better make sure I hadn't roused Mr. Tanner." She extracted the letter from Keeley out of her drawstring purse and waved it at him. "I was going to slip this under your door, explaining my problem. It's much easier to confer with you in person, and I'm glad it's worked out this way." She stowed the letter away before he could catch a glimpse of its words.

A light rap on the door made them both jump.

Again, Jana put her index finger to her lips to silence Mr. Parker while she went to the door, praying it wasn't Mr. Tanner. "Who is it?"

"Are ya all right?" came Leanne's muffled reply.

Jana could hug Leanne. Her intentional act of dissuading Mr. Parker from getting any ideas about harming Jana and her inadvertent act of playing into her ruse were blessings in disguise. With her back to Mr. Parker, she cracked the door and winked at Leanne. Lowering her voice to fake secrecy, but to a level Mr. Parker could still hear, she said, "Everything's fine, Leanne. Mr. Parker and I were about to discuss our suspicions of Mr. Tanner. I'll fill you in later."

Leanne winked back, then took Jana's lead in lowering her voice also in pretend secrecy. "I sure hope Mr. Parker can help us. If ya need me to add anything, just tap on the wall, and I'll come runnin'."

Closing the door, Jana turned around and met Mr. Parker's inquisitive eyes. "I guess you heard that, huh?" To his nod, she said, "It's obvious someone knows our every move before we make it, and we suspect it's Mr. Tanner. We think he was adamant about us not revisiting last night's scene of crime because he didn't want us tracing the hoofmarks of my assailant's horse to someplace that would implicate him." She held up her hand and twiddled its fingers. "And a few other little things about him just don't add up." Before he could question the little things, she hurried to sidetrack him. "I'm wondering if you could do me a favor and wire Mr. Pinkerton to corroborate that Mr. Tanner is indeed a Pinkerton agent and that his physical description matches him—that is, of course, unless you've already done it."

The glow from the wall globe, although dusky, accentuated the fleeting smugness forcing its way onto Mr. Parker's lips, which he somehow managed to bite back.

*I wish I could be a fly on his wall the moment he recalls this one and realizes I was pulling the wool over his eyes. That ought to wipe the smugness right off his face,* Jana thought, suppressing her own smirk. She hated to be vindictive, yet she was finding it difficult not to be against someone who dared to threaten her and her friends' lives.

Twirling his neatly trimmed and combed beard between his thumb and forefinger, obviously stalling while he carefully contemplated his next remarks, he finally said, "I seriously doubt Mr. Tanner is an accomplice to your kidnapping. But ... we have no other leads right now, so I reckon it's worth investigating."

*A worthy opponent in deception—or so he thinks,* Jana thought, seeing right through his tactic to appear innocent and loyal by defending his comrade. "I appreciate your entertaining my whim, Mr. Parker, and I'd appreciate your keeping this conversation strictly between us and Pinkerton headquarters. If I'm wrong about Mr. Tanner, I wouldn't want him harboring any ill feelings against me." To add extra punch, she threw in, "He seems the kind to hold a grudge."

"I don't know him well, though he does seem a bit headstrong."

Knowing Mr. Tanner was waiting to meet with her, but not wanting Mr. Parker to see them together without some justification, Jana struck upon a mode to accomplish both while luring Mr. Parker deeper into her confidence. "In case Mr. Tanner saw us together, maybe I should pay him a visit and act as if I just happened to bump into you and we've agreed we should keep him informed as to our discussion. I could tell him something like"—she drummed her fingers against her chin, abruptly stopped, and pointed her index finger toward the plaster ceiling—"I've asked you to check into suspicions I have of Mr. McGriffin, which, of course, I don't have. Later, we can cover our tracks by telling him the inquiry turned up nothing."

"A stroke of genius, Miss Brady."

Donning her most sugary smile, Jana said, "I'm glad you approve. I should do that right away so it doesn't seem as if we're trying to hide something from him—that is, of course, unless you have another idea."

Mr. Parker's expression grew apprehensive until a sudden illumination in it suggested he'd solved his enigma. "It might be best if you didn't tell Mr. Tanner of my plan to safeguard the premises, especially now that you have doubts about him. I'll fade into the hotel's shadows and stand guard all night. Should he chance any kind of con, I'll be ready to tail him."

"A grand idea, Mr. Parker," Jana said, but she really wanted to say what she was thinking: *More like a stroke of luck, Mr. Parker, that you've stumbled upon the perfect alibi for whatever fun you have planned for tonight.*

Upon Mr. Parker's exit, Jana went to her window, which overlooked Fall Street. She drew the closed shade toward her. Through the small slit she made, she watched as Mr. Parker swaggered right down the middle of the street, under the well-lit gas lanterns, on his way toward the river and canal where the taverns awaited his patronage. She had to laugh at his arrogance. His downfall would be thinking he'd duped her into believing he was outside guarding the premises. Little did he know when he'd cleared out of her room, he cleared her to openly practice her own deception. Off she went down the middle of the hall, across the thin carpet runner, without a care about any creaks in the floorboards. She barely knocked once before Mr. Tanner swung open his door; she wondered if he'd been there the whole time listening out for her.

Mr. Tanner appeared behind a fog of smoke, which came billowing out into the hall. With a cigar clamped between his teeth, he was forced to say with a lisp, "You don't seem too frazzled, Miss Brady."

"What do you mean?"

"I know all about the pickle Mr. Parker put you in a few minutes ago, and I'm dying to hear the outcome."

Jana slumped in relief. "Fortunate for me, my mind works quickly."

With a grunt and half-grin, he said more as a question, "I gather you and Mr. Parker parted on good terms, then?"

"If you'll invite me in, I'll give you a full report."

Peering sheepishly over his shoulder at the bluish haze in his room, he said, "Since Mr. Parker has evidently gone off for the evening, we're free to meet someplace else if you'll be more comfortable."

"I appreciate your sensitivity, Mr. Tanner. Believe me, I've choked on plenty of campfire and cannon smoke during my cavalry days. I can stand a little from your cigar," she said, moving past him. After a few steps into the room, she actually felt as if she was eating his cigar rather than merely breathing in its fumes. But there was no turning back now, so at the risk of eating crow, she went to the window and pushed up the lower sash. After leaning out over the sill and inhaling a healthy dose of wintry air, she left the window slightly ajar and slid into the mohair-stuffed chair next to it, resting her elbows on its plush arms. She fanned the air in front of her face and grimaced at Mr. Tanner in defeat. "I confess, it's more suffocating in here than around a campfire."

"I'm sorry, Miss Brady." He ground out his cigar in a tin on a candle stand, then took a seat at the foot of his bed. Wrapping an arm loosely around the squatty bedpost, he said, "I get the impression that what I have to tell you about Mr. Parker might be redundant to what you already know, though how, I'm sure will soon become apparent. Since it seems you have much more to convey, why don't you start? And, please, from the very beginning—at the point of your kidnapping."

"Weren't you fully briefed by the agency when you took this assignment and then by Mr. McGriffin in your meeting with him this morning?"

"Yes, but he and I agree it would be best if I heard your side of the story—it seems you have more of the dots to connect. Who knows? Maybe some new detail will surface during your recounting."

Jana delved in, giving him a chronological accounting of every single solitary detail surrounding her kidnapping; the intelligence she'd gathered on her own and through Mr. Ross; her discussions with Wyatt, Leanne, and Charlie; and her meeting minutes before with Mr. Parker.

"Ah, so Mr. Ross is your spy—an invaluable recruit and intelligent move on your behalf, Miss Brady. I too learned, as Mr. Ross's son did, that Mr. Parker lied about the direction in which your assailant went. And thanks to your Mr. Ross, my problem of interviewing the telegraph operator in Waterloo is resolved."

"Speaking of telegrams," Jana said, "I must confess to having gone through with wiring Allan Pinkerton to alert him about Mr. Parker's debauchery and to inquire about your background, including a physical description."

He crossed his legs and spoke in a cavalier tone when he said, "I take no offense of your probe of me, Miss Brady. In fact, I applaud your judiciousness in investigating your own case—habit no doubt formed from your experiences as a scout and spy. You'd make a tremendous Pinkerton operative."

Jana figured this was his way of apologizing for his having ordered her and Leanne back into the carriage to *let the men handle the dangerous business of her burning effigy*. Still, she waved her palms at him and said, "I swore off spying after I escaped my hanging and coffin."

"Too bad." He cocked his head and peered past her into the dark, moonless night beyond the window. "I've yet to meet Mrs. Kate Warne, the agency's first female detective and one of our very best." He shifted his gaze back to Jana. "Have you heard about the plot to assassinate good old Abe on his way to his first swearing in as president of the United States? And how we disguised him to get him there safely?" To Jana's nod, he said, "It was Mrs. Warne who mostly uncovered the plot, and then safeguarded him to Washington, DC. Mr. Pinkerton rewarded her for that and her other brave deeds by detailing her to train all of his female detectives. With that division of the agency growing, she could probably use an assistant."

Jana laughed. "When I get the itch for another adventure, I'll think about contacting her. Right now, we have our hands full with this case."

"Of course, Miss Brady, but I must tell you that I first became impressed with your power of observation when you challenged the distance Mr. Parker claimed to have covered in tracking your assailant, which we both learned was a lie—you from Mr. Ross, me from checking those tracks this morning."

"An unfortunate outburst on my behalf." She scowled. "I don't always follow my ma's advice to think before I speak. I could've chased him away, out from under our vigilant eyes, which would've been ill-fated since he seems to be the key to my captors."

"But equally as impressive, you were quick to conceal your blunder by stroking Mr. Parker's ego, which you somehow managed to sense he needed and which Mr. Ross confirms means more to him than keeping his loose lips from sinking his ship. Besides that, it was beneficial to me since you verified what had also seemed to me as odd about his claim. Just out of curiosity, Miss Brady, what put you onto his deception?"

"He scarcely had any snowballs clinging to the wool of his trousers for one who'd trudged as far as he alleged he had through the snow."

He pounded his fist in his palm. "Precisely my impression, which I substantiated this morning when I traced his boot prints a short distance from the carriage to the outer fringe of the woods. The snow was tamped down pretty near to the roots of a tree, under which he'd encamped long enough to dupe us into thinking he'd traveled farther than he had before he came plodding back with his cockamamie story. Speaking of Mr. Parker, given our certainty that he's involved in this subterfuge against you, it'll probably be a moot point for me to ask headquarters if he wired them for my background information as you requested he do. Agreed?"

"Yes," Jana said. "He'll only tell me that you checked out legitimate anyway."

"Oh, why's that?"

"He'd be opening a can of worms that would lead right back to him." To his quizzical look, Jana expounded, "He has to know that any negative claim he makes about you will be investigated, and eventually his guilt will be discovered when your innocence is proven."

Mr. Tanner shook his head in amazement. "You *are* sharp, Miss Brady."

Simultaneous to his compliment, Jana felt her expression turning grim as she considered a notion so vile it began to sour the milk in her stomach from supper.

Uncrossing his legs, Mr. Tanner moved to the edge of his bed. "Is something wrong, Miss Brady?"

"Am I correct in assuming there are different offices for the Pinkerton agents, and you might never have met Mr. Parker before your current job?"

"Correct on both accounts. We trained in Chicago at separate times and, when we were assigned to your case, I came from spying in the South, Mr. Parker came from the office in Cleveland."

"Purely by the Pinkerton Agency's assignment of Mr. Parker from its roster of detectives, we can conclude there really is an operative named Bill Parker, right?" To Mr. Tanner's nod, Jana continued her line of thinking, "Since you never saw him before you met him in Waterloo, I'm wondering if our Mr. Parker could be an imposter and the real one is being detained by my captors."

Mr. Tanner slapped his forehead. "How could I be so blind? I should have considered this, especially after I told you and Leanne earlier that he'd bumbled the code words by which we were to prove our identities to you last night. It seems unlikely that a Pinkerton agent would forget something so critical. And it's very possible that the real Mr. Parker was intercepted en route. He would've had a stop in Buffalo, where I'm beginning to believe the hotbed of conspiracy against you originates."

"Does each office file a likeness of their agents?"

He bobbed his head. "I think I know where you're going with this: The hiring of us detectives provided your kidnappers the perfect means to get close to you without creating suspicion. Given the lateness of our assignment, it's highly unlikely they were able to find a close replica of the real Mr. Parker in time to play the role, so they had to settle for another from within their circle. It'll take too long for the agency to mail us Mr. Parker's likeness, but a thorough description of him ought to be revealing. Then, we'll know for sure if the real Mr. Parker has been bought or kidnapped."

"Darn! I never thought to ask the agency for a physical description of Mr. Parker as I did for you. Until now, I assumed he was the real Mr. Parker who'd been, as you say, bought by my captors."

"Don't beat yourself up over it, Miss Brady. I didn't think of it either for your same reason. We're on the right track now, and you can bet I'll have the agency checking into it. In the meantime, especially given Mr. Ross's account of Mr. Parker's tattoo, we know he's dangerous, and we should proceed with caution where he's concerned. And that means no more meetings alone with him, Miss Brady."

"I'll do everything in my power to avoid it," Jana said, her wheels spinning to another notion. "Speaking of being compromised, I'm thinking one of Mr. McGriffin's house servants must be too."

"Why's that?"

"The only time we discussed hiring you Pinkertons was in Mr. McGriffin's parlor, and it was amongst all of those whom I trust with my life, including his housekeeper and former nanny, whom he considers more his mother than his real one."

Mr. Tanner scratched his head. "Housekeeper, nanny, surrogate mother?"

Lolling her head in disgust at herself, Jana said, "Another outburst on my behalf. I don't know if I should expound upon that; I don't want to trespass upon Mr. McGriffin's private affairs."

"Mr. McGriffin is excessively concerned, as he should be, about our getting to the bottom of our investigation. I'd wager he'd tell us anything we want to know—even shout it from the top of a flagpole—if he knew some of the conspiracy against you was brewing in his own house." When Jana hesitated, he said, "I can go ask him now, if you'd prefer. Or maybe you, Miss Watson, and Mr. Watson decided this morning you aren't going to trust me until a verdict comes in from the Pinkerton Agency."

"Actually," Jana said jokingly, "would you mind having Charlie take your portrait before I confide in you any further?"

"Huh?"

Jana explained Charlie's talent for profiling people, and when Mr. Tanner realized Charlie had been studying him outside the telegraph office earlier, they had a hearty laugh.

"And what may I ask did he conclude about me?" Mr. Tanner asked.

"That you're one of the good guys—I wouldn't be here if I didn't trust you." To this affirmation, Jana succumbed, telling him all she knew about Hannah and the rest of Wyatt's family, including both the living and deceased.

"And you trust this Hannah?"

With an emphatic bob of her head, Jana said, "She's caring and compassionate, and I truly believe that if it wasn't for her influence, Mr. McGriffin would be an entirely different person. I wouldn't waste any time investigating her."

"I'll take your word for it. Though, I agree with you, there's one bad apple in Mr. McGriffin's house, and that bears investigation. Any clues as to who it is?"

Jana jolted up. "My ma and I happened upon one of Mr. McGriffin's kitchen maids who acted quite nervous after we caught her listening in on a conversation within the parlor."

"I'm sure the parlor has a pull that rings a bell in the kitchen. Maybe someone summoned her there before your arrival."

"If so, she never entered the room to fulfill any request."

"Anyway," he said, crossing his legs again, "her position in the household, along with your description of her, ought to pinpoint her exactly."

Other than her wearing an apron over a plain blouse and skirt to indicate she was a kitchen maid, and her having blonde tresses, Jana could recall nothing more distinguishable about her to Mr. Tanner.

"Every bit helps," Mr. Tanner said.

"While you're checking that out, we need to find out if Mr. Parker and Wallace McGriffin served together in the army. I'm sure Mr. McGriffin will know the regimental company in which Wallace enlisted, but"—her shoulders drooped to a complication—"I doubt Mr. McGriffin will know the name of Wallace's army buddy. If he doesn't, and our Mr. Parker turns out to be an imposter, we won't be able to check the roster for Wallace's company without knowing his real name." She jerked up to an idea. "We could have Mr. McGriffin send his investigative associate back into the taverns undercover to pry that out of Wallace when he's drunk."

"Good idea. Actually, I'm going to talk to Mr. McGriffin about placing a Pinkerton agent in Buffalo to work with his man. I could get answers faster if I could converse directly with another reputable agent rather than my getting information secondhand."

"Mr. McGriffin might need help investigating the alibis of the New York Central Railroad stockholders during the time of my kidnapping. It seems a huge task to me, especially with all of the other questions piling up."

"Another good point, Miss Brady."

"Thank you," she said, yawning through her smile.

Mr. Tanner slapped his thighs and said, "Well, you've certainly given me a whole lot more intelligence to digest and tasks to complete than I would've ever anticipated. If you don't have anything else for me, we should get some rest." He winked. "We need your Pinkerton mind to be sharp, and I really do hope you'll consider becoming one of us."

Jana didn't confide in Mr. Tanner that her only appeal for working for the Pinkerton Agency would be if she and Keeley didn't rekindle their love. Then, she'd need something exhilaratingly adventurous to get her through her grief. If, however, they did rekindle their love, and he found farming unappealing, maybe he'd consider becoming a detective. She smiled at the thought of them becoming the Pinkerton Agency's first husband-wife team.

Before they boarded the train the next day, Jana and Mr. Tanner found a private moment to speak. First, Mr. Tanner reported already having sent a telegram to Pinkerton headquarters with all of the inquiries they'd discussed last evening. Then he reported already having spoken to Mr. McGriffin who'd agreed to hire a Pinkerton detective to supervise and assist with the investigative work in Buffalo and who was able to supply them with Wallace's army regiment. But he was ignorant of the name of Wallace's army buddy. "Mr. McGriffin offered to contact Wallace for his buddy's name," Mr. Tanner said, "but I thought it best we did it covertly to keep from alerting Wallace—if he's involved—and Mr. Parker that we're onto them. Although, he agreed with us that we not waste any time waiting for the Pinkerton operative to arrive in Buffalo, and he sent his associate back undercover to Wallace's favorite tavern to coax his army buddy's name out of him."

Afterward, Jana and Mr. Tanner got down to comparing the telegrams each had collected from the desk clerk on their way down to breakfast. Even though she'd neglected to request a physical description for Mr. Parker, to her delight, the agency supplied it for both agents. Bill Parker's clearly showed he was an imposter, and she and Mr. Tanner shared a laugh when she assured him that his was a perfect match. In Mr. Tanner's telegram, Chicago assured—ignorant that Mr. Tanner would be making such request—it had already sent a detective to Buffalo to search for the real Mr. Parker and to handle the other investigative work there. They were also sending one of their best agents to reinforce them in

Johnstown. The new operative would remain anonymous to everyone, including Jana and Mr. Tanner, so he could work invisibly to the fake Mr. Parker in hopes he'd lead them to his boss—the right bait Jana had very conveniently been searching for to reel him into tripping up.

Jana's faith in their solving this case before they got to Albany surged at the same time it ebbed over the real Bill Parker's fate. She lamented to Mr. Tanner, "As long as my abductors need me to forward their goals, they'll let me live. I'd hate to think poor Mr. Parker has worn out his welcome."

In an attempt to console her, Mr. Tanner said, "I've been in this business almost from the start of the Pinkerton Agency back in 1850. Most criminals threaten killing and never carry it out because they know they risk execution if they do and because we Pinkertons always net the foul fish."

But Jana couldn't swallow the bitter taste in her mouth that the real Mr. Parker might've been murdered because of her. And after breakfast, when his imposter caught up to her to report that the physical description of Mr. Tanner checked out—as she'd predicted he'd say—she had everything she could do to stop herself from spitting in his face and then feeding him to Leanne. Never mind the wolves!

# Part III

## Courage

*The best protection any woman can have is courage.*
—Elizabeth Cady Stanton, *The Woman's Bible*, 1895, 1898

# Fonda to Johnstown, New York

## March 11, 1865

Six hours after leaving Seneca Falls that morning, Jana and her entourage arrived at the station house in Fonda. They were without disguises or any ruse to trick her foes, who seemed to know her every move anyway. And Jana, Wyatt, Leanne, and Charlie had agreed to entrust Mr. Tanner with guarding Jana while Mr. Parker would be allowed a wider berth to investigate her case, giving him a false sense of security in hopes he'd lead the anonymous Pinkerton agent—who'd soon be tracking his moves—to his boss.

Descending to the platform, Jana was immediately smitten with Fonda. It was a pleasing replica of home as it too nested within a valley and flourished along the banks of the Mohawk River and Erie Canal as did Elmira along the Chemung River and Canal. Although, as she stood there shivering beneath her wool pelisse, she found herself wishing for the milder temperatures of home.

Charlie sped off to supervise the unloading of his equipment, leaving Leanne and Wyatt to hug Jana's sides and keep their eyes keen to the approach of strangers, such as the well-dressed, slender woman, who was sidestepping icy patches in the platform's dips as she made a beeline straight for them.

Coming face-to-face with Jana, the young woman's eyes flickered in recognition. She hurriedly concealed the glitch by shooting out her hand, clad in a kid glove, and shaking Jana's with a warm, affable smile. "Y'all must be Miss Jana Brady," she said in a thick Southern accent. "My name is Kay Warren, and I'm close friends with Elizabeth Cady Stanton through our work in woman's suffrage and equal rights. I just happened to be in Johnstown visiting her mother when I learned of your speech tonight, which I'll be happily attending. Anyway, my dear friend Elizabeth wired me this morning, suggesting I meet y'all at the train station and accompany y'all to your hotel." She fished the telegram from her reticule and presented it as proof. "Would it be all right with y'all?"

Jana thought it prudent to warn Miss Warren that she'd been the object of villainous activities en route to her stops and that the probability of it happening again was high.

"I appreciate your concern, Miss Brady, but as my dear friend Elizabeth always says, 'Agitating is not for the faint-hearted.'"

Jana recognized this seemingly favorite phrase of Elizabeth's, which had also been imparted to Jana in a previous telegram. Turning to Leanne and Wyatt, she secured their approval for Miss Warren to ride along with them. As she made introductions, Jana felt a keen sense she'd met Miss Warren before. Her visage, a replication of a hound dog's, was unmistakable: A small head that tapered sharply from a wide forehead down to a curved chin; round, sad eyes crowning the highest cheekbones Jana had ever seen; and a long, pointy snout. Her only feature at odds with her canine twin was in her heart-shaped lips—perpetually pouty in their natural slackness and more like a large mouth bass's. It was her Southern accent that put Jana off her immediate scent. The only Southern women Jana really knew were Versella Stock and Elizabeth Van Lew, which prompted Jana's curiosity. "Where are you originally from, Miss Warren?"

With a waggle of her palm at them all, she said, "Please just call me Kitty. I'm still unsure how my friends got the nickname Kitty from Kay, but they did, and it's stuck." She giggled. "Anyway, I suspect my Southern drawl has tripped y'all up. I'm from Charleston, South Carolina."

"Do you still live there?"

"No, I haven't for some time, and I only recently settled in New York— Syracuse to be precise."

"What brought you to the North?" Jana asked.

"In your circles, Miss Brady—"

Jana interjected, "Please call me Jana," and Leanne and Wyatt chimed in with their preferences to also be called by their given names.

Kitty continued, "Y'all must've heard of Angelina and Sarah Grimké."

Jana burst out, "Of course. Who hasn't?" The elderly sisters were legendary for their decades of work in the abolition of slavery and equality of the sexes. Who would've thought these two socialites, born and raised on a plantation where slaves were employed, would become the first women above the Mason-Dixon Line to become agents in the American Anti-Slavery Society and speak before a committee of the Massachusetts legislature, where Angelina pleaded her case against the cruelty of slavery in the South and the prejudice against colored people in the North. "I admire their success as public speakers to mixed-gender audiences." She grimaced. "I'm learning how challenging that can be."

"Well, as they were, I was a Southern belle who grew to abhor the injustices committed against the enslaved on my own family's plantation."

As Kitty described her family's history, Jana detected an embellishment in her timbre and in the way she swung her petite hands about that made her think she was acting. Whatever the reason for it, it felt innocuous—much like Jana imagined her fibs must've felt to Keeley and Charlie when they knew she was keeping them in the dark over her being a woman soldier.

"Sarah and Angelina, along with their *Appeal to the Christian Women of the Southern States*, might've been outlawed in the South, but I managed to feel their influence from afar after I got my hands on and read their tract," Kitty said.

Kitty was living proof to the planter class of the South that the greater the fuss they made over something, the greater its curiosity. When would they learn they'd never squash anti-slavery messages, especially when they were disseminated by powerful abolitionists with a journalistic bent and the sword of a newspaper in hand? William Lloyd Garrison had published plenty of the Grimké sisters' letters and appeals over the years in his *Liberator*, and his editorials had slashed their way into the South to spread their cancer as most plantation owners deemed Harriett Beecher Stowe's *Uncle Tom's Cabin* had done. The latter, which had started out as a serial in the abolitionist periodical *The National Era*, ultimately became the rage in the North, an outrage in the South, yet coveted by all around the world—especially Great Britain, which was still reeling from the colonists having seized their independence from their tyranny. The British loved to use the sentimental novel as a tool for shedding light on the United States' hypocrisy in heralding themselves as the *land of the free* through their popular verse "Star-Spangled Banner." Jana agreed they had a point, especially when there were other countrymen besides the slaves, such as the Irish, who felt the chains of bondage.

"And so here I am, eager to associate myself with others interested in amending those moralities that threaten to sink our country or Constitution into a festering quagmire," she said, batting her eyes to ward off tears.

*More theatrics*, Jana decided, especially after detecting a wisp of the flatness in her accent that marked her as a native of New York and defied her claim that she'd only just recently settled in the state. Even though she seemed to be pulling the wool over their eyes, Jana sensed her trustworthiness.

"Forgive me for prattling on about myself, Jana. We have an hour's ride to Johnstown, and I'd love to hear all about your journey so far. I'll wait, of course, for your affair later to hear about your war experiences." Kitty waved her hand in a wide arc at the sky. "I want to be swept away by it with the rest of the audience," she said, sounding genuinely interested.

Wyatt looked toward the baggage car. "It appears Charlie's equipment is secured to his wagon. We better start our northbound trek," he said and began herding them to the stagecoach he'd hired for their private use.

With Leanne's tool chest tucked beneath the waterproof leather boot at the stern—typically reserved for mail and parcels—and their steamer trunks, leather valises, and Jana's hat box secured between the rails on the conveyance's roof, Jana's party of four climbed aboard the stage. They bypassed the middle bench in favor of the rear-and-forward-facing benches, which were better for conversation. To combat the cold, the driver untied the waterproof leather curtains that guarded each of the six windows, enclosing the passengers in an aromatic stew of oiled leather, the hickory boards that made up the stagecoach, Leanne's hair pomade, Wyatt's cologne, and Jana's and Kitty's toilet waters of rose and lavender, respectively. As the driver and his man riding shotgun mounted the high exterior bench, the coach swayed; with the screech of the foot brake upon its release, a snap from a bullwhip, and a "Yah!" from the driver, their stagecoach led the way toward Johnstown. The leather braces on which the cabin rested absorbed most of the initial jolt and ensuing rocking that would've made their slog over the rough road uncomfortable.

Kitty advised them to hang on because they'd soon begin a steep ascent up the Cayadutta Road to Johnstown. It cut through a portion of a conical hill of historical significance with two different nicknames: The Dutch called it *Teaburg* because the women of the Revolution had used its summit for tea parties and as a watchtower against Indian war parties allied with the British; the Mohawk Indians called it *Ta-he-ka-nun-da* or "hill of berries," and they'd used it to test the endurance of their young warriors by making them sprint up it. Kitty bemoaned, "The women of colonial times had guts. I probably would've swooned at the sight of Indians knowing I might be scalped."

Detecting more playacting in her delivery, Jana got the impression Kitty was no faint-hearted Southern belle.

"How on earth did y'all manage to steady your nerve in the face of the enemy, Jana?" Kitty asked.

If only Kitty knew how Jana's fear had frozen her at first, but then she found her strength when she confronted her own death.

As if Leanne had read her mind, she piped in, "She was never yella ... I know."

Kitty stared at Leanne, silently questioning how she could speak with such conviction about Jana's bravery.

Feeling Leanne's flinch to her accidental divulgence, Jana came to her rescue, saying, "For good reasons, Leanne prefers to keep her service in the cavalry a secret and herself out of the limelight."

"We all have our secrets, Leanne, and yours is entirely safe with me." Kitty mimed locking her lips and throwing away the key. It won her a look of gratitude from Leanne. "Well then, I repeat my question to you both. How did y'all manage to keep your nerve in battle?"

With a nod, Leanne deferred to Jana to answer.

Rather than get into the particulars, Jana said, "For me, each time I faced the elephant, my reaction was different, dependent upon the circumstance. And it wasn't always courageous as Leanne would have you believe of me."

"Given the range of emotions with which we humans have been blessed—or cursed—I don't suppose we could possibly react the same for every perilous circum—"

The stage driver cut off Kitty's insight when he called out in his guttural voice, "Whoa!" and brought the coach to a stop as well as Charlie's wagon, the squeal of its wheels and clatter of its contents quieting behind them.

Leanne drew her gun and poked her head out through the curtain. "What's the trouble, sir?"

"One of the horses has come up limping. She might've thrown a shoe," he said.

Jana, Leanne, and Wyatt flashed each other their wariness, questioning if this could be sabotage on the part of their enemies.

Out of the corner of her eye, Jana saw Kitty's hand subtly moving beneath her cape to her boot shaft, then back to her lap.

As Jana's avowed guard, Leanne took control of the situation, saying to Wyatt and Kitty, "Ya stay here 'til Jana and I scout things out." Then, with a jab of her head, she signaled Jana to follow her outside.

Jana drew her Colt from her carpetbag, pulled up her skirt hem, and dropped off the iron step into a puddle of slush.

The driver and his mate started to climb down from their bench, exhibiting considerable litheness for two men with overly stout frames.

"Stay right where ya are," Leanne was quick to say. "You've got the better view up there, and we need ya to keep a keen eye to our surroundings. I can examine the mare if you'll point her out."

The dark-haired man riding shotgun plunked back down onto the bench, but the fair-haired driver continued in motion, muttering with an indignant and irate huff, "No woman's gonna tell me what to do or touch a horse in my charge."

A *click* of Leanne's revolver stopped the driver dead on his step and, when his partner went for the rifle on his lap, Jana cocked back her hammer and stilled his hand mid-air.

To a tramping through the wet snow, Jana looked over her shoulder and saw Charlie and his wiry teamster, their hands gripping the stocks and barrels of their rifles, creeping up and disappearing around the opposite side of the stage.

Charlie's wagoner called out, "Let me remind you, Frank, Pete, that John Dunn's a good friend of mine; if he were to find out you've mistreated his passengers, you'd be through working for him."

With her cheeks coloring the burgundy of the newly painted stagecoach, Leanne barked, "My friend here's been roughed up for no good reason lately, and her life's bein' threatened. I intend to see her to Johnstown without a hair on her head touched, so go ahead and twitch another finger, and you're as good as crippled when I empty a bullet in yer leg. Then, ya won't have to worry 'bout the proprietor of this stage line firin' ya. And it won't do no good for ya to set the law on me 'cause I got four witnesses who'll swear I shot ya in self-defense."

"Five," Charlie's teamster hollered out.

Charlie added, "Seven with the two Pinkerton detectives following us for protection."

As if he'd heard Charlie, Mr. Tanner emerged from the dense stand of woods and came galloping toward them on the roan he'd rented from a livery in Fonda.

"Here comes one now," Jana said.

"The other one's on his way too," Charlie called back.

With the situation seemingly under control, Wyatt and Kitty exited the carriage and came up behind Jana and Leanne.

Mr. Tanner reined in his gelding, which sprayed slush as it skidded to a stop close enough for Jana to smell its grainy breath. At the sight of Jana's and Leanne's guns aimed at the stage hands, he tied his reins together and pinned them at the knot between his thigh and saddle to keep his steed still and to free his hands, one to shield against the melting rays of the sun, the other to flash his Pinkerton badge. He glared at the belligerents. "I don't know what the trouble is here, but you better believe Miss Brady and Miss Watson, along with Mr. Watson who I presume is posted opposite, won't hesitate to shoot you down. All three are ex-cavalryman, and I've seen Miss Brady and Miss Watson in action. They're quick on the draw—quicker than I imagine you are with a snap of your bullwhip."

From beneath the wide brims of their leather hats, the men's eyes popped wide with surprise.

Wyatt took advantage of their stunned silence, explaining for the benefit of the Pinkerton agents especially, "There's been a minor misunderstanding, and the driver and his man now understand the gravity of our situation. They've agreed to stay put where they can easily spot and warn us of trouble while Miss Watson examines the horse, right, gentlemen?"

The man riding shotgun shrugged while the driver crawled back onto his bench, muttering, "I can't wait to see this."

Charlie said to him, "Trust me, you'll be impressed. She's an expert smithy and she owns her own shop."

With heavy-lidded eyes and a lazy loll of his head, the driver conveyed his disinterest. He pointed out the affected mare and said, "Have at it—less work for me." Then he extracted some tobacco from a pouch made out of a pig's leathery bladder and packed his cheek full of it as if he was settling in for a long wait.

Everyone gathered around Leanne while Charlie and his wagoner fetched Leanne's cumbersome toolbox from the stagecoach's hind boot.

Standing alongside the injured mare, Leanne began rubbing her chestnut muzzle to acclimate her to her touch before she moved on to running her hand down the back of her outer front leg. She stopped at the tendon above the ankle, which she gently squeezed to recruit the mare's help in lifting her own leg so she could check the shoe. To prevent being kicked or bitten by the other horses while she wriggled in between them to check the mare's inside shoes, she rubbed hindquarters or a nose, alerting them of her presence. Upon the conclusion of her inspection, she announced to everyone, "She's got a twisted shoe on the outer front hoof," and to Jana in particular, "That's all it is."

Jana understood her underlying message loud and clear: There was nothing more sinister behind their delay.

Then Leanne looked at the stage driver and said, "Otherwise, she and her shoes are in good shape."

"My company abides by changing the horses every twelve miles and their shoes every six weeks." Sarcastically, he said, "May I come down now so I can remove all of her shoes? She can't do any hauling with one shoe off and three on." His voice softened. "I wouldn't want to lame the old girl."

Jana found his compassion surprising, as did Leanne whose own toughness toward him eased some through her forgiving tone when she said, "I can have the shoe fixed in fifteen minutes."

By their knotted expressions, the conductors of the stagecoach thought Leanne was mad. The driver leaned over and spat tobacco, which scarcely cleared his chin-length beard and landed close to Leanne's toolbox in supposed retaliation. But he conceded, "Now this I'd like to see."

Leanne squatted before her toolbox.

Before she had the chance to lift the lid, the driver's second extracted a watch from his canvas coat pocket and said with a guffaw, "Starting now, we're keeping you to your avowed time."

Leanne huffed, conveying her confidence she could do it in less time. Backing this up with intentionally slow movements, she unlocked the lid of her toolbox and exposed a striking number of tools neatly arranged on the top tray.

"Would you be able to explain the steps as you go along, Miss Watson?" Charlie's teamster shook his head in disgust at the stage hands. "That is, if it doesn't upset the fifteen minutes you're being hogtied to. My mules get loose shoes sometimes, and it seems it might be faster and cheaper for me to fix a shoe than remove all four for replacement later. I'd be mighty grateful to learn from a master of the trade."

Leanne dropped her face toward her toolbox to hide her flushing cheeks that his compliment had evoked. "Ain't nothin' to teach ya as I go along. How 'bout ya handin' me my tools when I need 'em?"

"It's a fair trade. My name's Ernie, and I don't have a problem taking orders."

While everyone was distracted listening to Leanne briefing Ernie on her tools, through a sidelong glance, Jana saw Kitty bend her leg up behind her and return her pepperbox to her boot shaft, again concealing the entire process beneath her ankle-length cape. Her behavior sorely deviated from a Southern belle who'd swoon in the face of the enemy as she'd alleged she would, and Jana had a hunch she'd wrestled with danger many times before. *Bam*! It struck her where she'd seen Kitty before—she was the woman who'd sat next to her on the train from Elmira to Buffalo. Jana reflected back to what she'd said to her at the time: "In my line of work, I've learned not to trust anyone, although I'm less wary of his kind than a wolf in a dandy's clothes." Her words, together with the fact her name sounded an awful lot like Kate Warne, the detective about whom Mr. Tanner had bragged, made Jana wonder if it was too far-fetched to think Allan Pinkerton had assigned one of his most-prized sleuths to her case. She made up her mind to confront Kitty first chance she got.

Leanne was saying, "Just so ya know, I'm gonna remove the shoe, fix it, then nail it back on."

"Without a hot forge to reshape the shoe?" Ernie asked.

"Don't need one. It can't be too worn after three weeks," Leanne said, removing the top tray to expose a deeper partition beneath, which housed a small anvil that she withdrew and manipulated until it was mostly level with the ground.

"Assuming you'll have to replace the nails, how do you know you have the right size to fit the shoe?" Ernie asked.

Leanne pulled open a narrow drawer at the bottom of the box to show smaller compartments with nails of varying sizes.

Everyone ogled her provisions in wonderment.

Moving to the affected mare, Leanne began an instruction of each of her steps. First, she rubbed the hindquarter of the gelding ahead of her to let him know she'd be working behind him. Then she turned her back to the mare's chest and raised the horse's left leg, setting her hoof upon her right thigh. Employing the smooth side of a metal rasp with a light rapid movement, she filed off the clinch or tip of the nail that was folded down toward the outer hoof wall to hold the shoe in place, then smoothed down the remaining nail even with the hoof.

The grating sound transported Jana back to Chatham Manor where, all through the night following the battle at Fredericksburg, Virginia, she'd listened to the surgeon's saw slicing through bone during the amputation of a limb. Backing away from the dreaded noise, she sidled up to Kitty, who was keeping an eye to their perimeter. Leaning in close to her ear, Jana whispered, "I'm honored, Kate Warne, to have you watching my back."

Kitty flinched. "Whatever do y'all mean?" she asked, trying to sound utterly befuddled.

"There's no denying who I'm pretty sure you are. I can easily wire Mr. Pinkerton to confirm it. Don't worry, your secret's safe with me. I managed to maintain my disguise as a soldier for nearly eighteen months, and it's in my best interest to protect yours as capably."

Kitty frowned and her Southern drawl gave way to the underlying New-York accent Jana had previously detected. "Mr. Tanner boasted of your investigative prowess to Mr. Pinkerton. Perhaps you'll consider joining my staff when you're through with your tour."

"Mr. Tanner also boasted of your accomplishments and Mr. Pinkerton's faith in you," Jana said.

Beneath her velvet top hat, the smooth skin of Kitty's forehead creased in concern. "I hope for our sake no one else has figured me out."

"If it's a comfort to you, I've been trained by one of the best in spying to be observant." Jana refrained from identifying Elizabeth Van Lew as her mentor even though Kitty probably knew of her and might've even had contact with her since Timothy Webster, the Pinkerton agent who was hung for spying against the Confederacy, had worked with Miss Lizzie. But as long as the war was still in progress, and Miss Lizzie was probably still spying against the Confederacy in Richmond, Jana would never be the first to bring up her name and risk endangering Miss Lizzie's life. Kitty didn't ask anyway—she knew better. Continuing on, Jana said, "After I recognized you from when we met on the train in Buffalo, I remembered you having a Northern accent. I put that together with something you said to me about your line of work and your phony name sounding close to your real name to realize who you are. Rest assured, no one in my group has privy to those pieces of the puzzle to figure out your true identity."

"All very commendable, Jana, and I appreciate your reassurance," Kitty said, still sounding a little sulky.

"I suppose we should get back to the group before anyone becomes suspicious of our huddling," Jana said.

"I'll visit you later in your room for a full report," Kitty said.

In the short time Jana and Kitty had been engaged in whispers, Leanne had filed down all of the clinches. Next, she slipped her thigh out from beneath the mare's hoof but continued to hold up the mare's leg, which Leanne bent back at the knee so the sole of the hoof pointed skyward. With her back now turned to the mare's shoulder, Leanne straddled the hoof, clamping it between her upper thighs. She traded Ernie the file for long-handled pullers, which she clamped around the outer rim of the shoe at the hoof's heel; gently she jiggled and tugged the shoe diagonally toward the inner toe. When it gave, she tapped it back down once, and this popped the nails from the heel and outer middle, permitting her to effortlessly draw them out the rest of the way. She repeated the process at the opposite side of the heel to free the other nails and the entire shoe.

Jana and Charlie shared a smile, happy to see Leanne handling the limelight calmer than an actor's understudy at center stage for their first performance. All eyes glued to her hands rather than her face probably contributed to her ease with instruction.

Next, Leanne traded Ernie the grippers for a special pick and scraping knife. These she used to clean out the mud and snow she'd intentionally left caked in the sole to cushion against injury during her application of the pullers. After cleaning the shoe of grime, she pressed it against the hoof to ensure it was equal in size to the hoof, and she checked for any gaps between the hoof and shoe. Having found one to the left of the toe, she hammered out the small bulge in the shoe on her small portable anvil. The sound of a blacksmith at work echoed around the valley and mimicked rolling thunder. Finished, she pawed through her nails to locate ones with heads that couldn't slip through the shoe holes. Aligning shoe and hoof, she tapped the nails into the old holes, and their pointed tips bored through the outer hoof wall. She very carefully snipped off the excess protrusions, leaving enough to turn inward against the outer hoof wall to secure the shoe to the hoof.

All looked on in awe, except the driver's second who was staring dumbly at his watch as he pronounced that Leanne had accomplished the task, including having her tools packed away, in under fifteen minutes.

With Leanne's toolbox once again secured to the coach, everyone returned to their conveyances. The caravan resumed its four-mile trip, arriving at the outskirts of Johnstown forty-five minutes later without further incident and with the mare in high spirits after her shoe repair.

Jana whiffed the tang of tanning leather before the factories came in sight, and she commented on it.

Reverting to her Southern accent to play her part, Kitty explained, "In my few days here, I learned that the tannin used for firming animal hides into leather to make gloves, shoes, saddles, and even the braces and mail boot for our stagecoach is extracted from the bark of the oak, hemlock, and chestnut trees we've seen all along our route. On a broad scale, the profuse manufacturing of these products has elevated Johnstown and the adjoining village of Gloversville to leather barons of our country."

"Probably the world too," Wyatt added.

Kitty said, "On a narrower scale, it's probably why Johnstown is the county seat of Fulton, along with the fact that Irish-born Sir William Johnson, Superintendent of Indian Affairs for British interests in the colonies, chose to locate his baronial seat on this fertile plateau. For over twenty years, Johnson Hall was the scene of important peacekeeping councils with the Iroquois Indians and conferences and socializing between colonial military and governmental notables."

Given Johnstown's fascinating history, Jana couldn't imagine another city, town, or village that deserved to be the county seat. Further evidence to support that it might've earned the honor was in its thriving nature: all along the core streets they traveled to get to their hotel were shops, businesses, government buildings, and schools propped between colonial mansions and Federal-style houses, and all of these were ringed by fertile farmlands and apple orchards—the latter of which they'd passed on their way in.

The village was bustling but uncongested, and Jana found it quaint and welcoming. She prayed the people would be as receptive to her; she felt a surge of excitement about giving her lecture here—in Elizabeth Cady Stanton's childhood hometown.

*Johnstown, New York*

*March 11, 1865*

Jana shook out her Garibaldi dress and hung it in the wardrobe cabinet to let out some of its wrinkles. Enticed by the aroma of English tea filling the room, she withdrew to the small pedestal table and poured herself a cup. She was disappointed not to be taking tea with Elizabeth Cady Stanton's eighty-year-old mother, who'd sent Kitty over to the Cayadutta House with a retraction to her invitation as she'd been called away for the day but vowed to return in time for her lecture. She would've loved to have gleaned some tips from Margaret Livingston Cady, a longtime resident of Johnstown, about the individuals whom she'd greet this evening.

An urgent, light tap on the door made her flinch.

Setting her cup down on its saucer, she went to the door and admitted Mr. Tanner.

He whisked over to the window and peeked through the lacey curtain panels to make sure no one lurked on the second-story balcony, and then he whirled on her with a ruddy glow in his cheeks. "I have news of the investigation, Jana."

Sensing he had a lot to tell, she reclaimed her seat at the service table and began sipping her tea.

"The Buffalo operative has ruled out that the railroad stockholders had any involvement with your abduction. None of the employees saw anything suspicious either." He further reported that Wallace McGriffin's army buddy was an Addison Pierce whose physical description was identical to the phony Mr. Parker's and who was visiting Wallace in Buffalo around the time of Jana's kidnapping. Addison Pierce had courted Wyatt's kitchen maid purely to use her for spying on Wyatt and his houseguests. Although she'd told Mr. Pierce about Wyatt's plan to hire the Pinkertons, she claimed to know no one else with whom he was affiliated in Buffalo. "You'll be glad to know, Jana, the real Bill Parker was found alive. He was badly beaten but will make a full recovery. His only regret is that he told your kidnappers the code words by which he and I were to identify ourselves to you and Leanne."

To tears welling in her eyes, Jana's lips began to quiver. She cupped her hand over her mouth and, in a muffled voice, said, "I can't tell you how relieved I am to hear Mr. Parker is alive."

"We're going to find your and Mr. Parker's captors and put them away for a long time—maybe even hang them."

Dabbing her eyes with a cloth tea napkin, Jana said, "Unfortunately, we're no further along in identifying the offenders, and it seems unlikely Addison Pierce's boss is going to drop any crumbs that'll lead us to him since he hasn't already."

Another rap on the door made both Jana and Mr. Tanner spin sharply toward the door.

"Are you expecting anyone?" Mr. Tanner mouthed.

"No, but if it's Mr. Parker," she whispered as she pointed toward the bed, which seemed high enough for the stocky operative to fit under, "you better hide." To his nod, Jana went to the door. "Who is it?"

"It's Kitty," came her voice with its thick Southern drawl.

"Just a second, Kitty." Jana dawdled with her hand on the doorknob, trying to decide if she should give up Kitty's identity to Mr. Tanner. Finally, she opened the door and drew Kitty in. "It's time we join forces," she said, stepping aside to allow Mr. Tanner and Kitty to face each other. "Mr. Duke Tanner, meet Miss Kate Warne, the undercover agent Mr. Pinkerton sent to follow our imposter Mr. Parker."

Mr. Tanner slapped his thigh. "Well, I'll be."

Once again reverting to her New-York accent, Kitty said, "It's all right, Jana. I too had come to that conclusion." With a smile and a swish of her skirts, she whisked over to Mr. Tanner, stretching out her small hand. "It's a pleasure to meet you, Mr. Tanner. I've heard many wonderful things about your work from Mr. Pinkerton."

Mr. Tanner took her hand in his and bowed over it. "The pleasure is all mine, and I too have heard about your incredible investigative prowess from Mr. Pinkerton."

"I'm afraid I've come with bad tidings," Kitty said. "While everyone was settling into their rooms, including Mr. Parker—or so I thought—I darted next door to see if Mrs. Cady had returned from her outing. As I was leaving her home, Mr. Parker tore past on horseback. I inquired at the front desk if he'd registered yet, and the clerk said that after he'd given him a telegram, he hightailed it out the door. I'm assuming it was a warning to abandon ship now that the real Mr. Parker has been found." She sighed. "That's the last we'll see of him, I'm sure."

Sinking into her chair, Jana said, "There goes our only lead."

Kitty said, "We've alerted the sheriffs in each municipality between here and his home in Rochester to be on the lookout for him. At the very least, we have him on a charge of horse thievery, as it's doubtful he intends to return the horse he rented at the Fonda livery. Don't worry, Jana, if we fail to catch and interrogate him before Albany, we'll have an army of guards who'll keep you safe. In fact, without Mr. Parker to trail, I'm being reassigned to the capital city to make sure all is in place for your event there. That leaves you, Mr. Tanner, and Jana's friends, whose loyalty I have observed for myself, to get her out of here in one piece."

"I have no doubt they'll be able to do that," Jana said, "since we're all of the same mind my abductors are goading me on to Albany, their grand stage for propagating their message and whatever they have in store for me."

"Before I catch the next train out to the capital, why don't you and Mr. Tanner fill me in on the details of your investigation thus far? Who knows, I might be able to provide a fresh perspective."

Three raps on the door interrupted them.

*My room's busier than a train station. I ought to start a ticket window and charge admission,* Jana thought, opening the door to Leanne and Charlie. And as they all crowded in, she wondered if it was a fire hazard to have this many persons in one room at one time.

Charlie waved a telegram before Jana. "We have some incredible news."

Another money-making scheme came to Jana. *If only I owned stock in the Western Union Telegraph Company, I'd be rich with all of the telegrams exchanged throughout my lecture tour.*

Practically bouncing out of his brogans, Charlie continued, "Do you remember Captain David Getman of our regiment's Company *I*?"

"Yes, I do," Jana said.

"Well, he's from Mayfield—not far from here—and when his father discovered that you were in the same regiment as his son and that you were having troubles along your lecture route, he hired guards to be posted around the courthouse tonight. Wyatt went off to coordinate this with the sheriff, Mr. Garth Hillier."

Jana felt her face brighten to an idea that came to her for her speech that night. "After the reception Leanne received from the stagecoach hands about a woman doing farrier work, I've been wondering if I'd encounter a hostile audience here. Maybe I can win the locals over by reminding them up front I fought alongside men from their county and the neighboring one of Montgomery."

Mr. Tanner said, "I don't know about your audience, Miss Brady, but you've certainly won me over with your mental and physical acuity, as have Misses Watson and Warren."

"Me too," Charlie said.

"I'm truly lucky to have you all backing me up," Jana said.

"We're going to make sure nothing happens to you. And now," Kitty said with a gentle tilt of her head toward Leanne and Charlie and a bat of her hooded eyes, "I think it's time they learned my true identity." She followed up her disclosure to them by qualifying to all that, outside of this room, they should continue to refer to her as Kay Warren from South Carolina and call her Kitty.

Jana invited Leanne and Charlie to stay and help her and Mr. Tanner to brief Kitty on their investigation.

When they finished discussing the case, Kitty commended everyone's thoroughness, and she agreed that although it appeared Wallace McGriffin was being framed, they should continue to be wary of him as one of their suspects. "He could be using himself as a decoy while his henchmen do his dirty work."

Leanne looked toward Jana's bedside clock. "We need to git to the courthouse, Charlie, and set up yer equipment." They rose to go and Leanne advised Jana that she'd come by later to escort her to her talk.

Mr. Tanner wished Kitty well in fortifying Jana's next lecture site before he took his leave to make sure the premises around the hotel were secure.

Already seated at the small service table, Jana invited Kitty to join her for tea.

"I'd love that," Kitty said. "I have a few minutes before I have to catch the stagecoach back to Fonda for the last train out to Albany."

"I can't vouch that the tea doesn't have icicles floating in it," Jana said.

Kitty snapped her hand. "Don't worry about that. With all of the interruptions I usually get, I've gotten used to drinking my tea cold."

As Jana poured, she said, "So tell me, Kitty, how you got into spying."

"When my husband passed away, I needed to support myself. I wanted to earn a salary respectably rather than resorting to prostitution, and I needed to earn more than I could as a laundress or housekeeper. In response to an advertisement Allan Pinkerton placed in a local newspaper calling for detectives, I walked into his Chicago agency, insisted upon an interview with him, and then I convinced him women would make great spies." She winked. "As you must've experienced yourself in your spying, we women can worm secrets out of men who love to flaunt their exploits, and we can worm secrets out of the women affiliated with these braggarts by gaining their trust."

Jana reflected back to the mawkish deception she'd used on the guard to let her pass into Castle Thunder Prison's hospital. She'd convinced him that in being native-born to Maryland, she was loyal to the South and she'd come to show her Yankee husband the error of his ways.

Sitting up tall with a grin, Kitty concluded, "And that's the line I fed to Mr. Pinkerton to entice him into taking a chance on me."

"And from what Mr. Tanner tells me about your service, especially your involvement in foiling the assassination attempt against President Lincoln, you've certainly proven yourself worthy."

"I'm grateful to Mr. Pinkerton who continues to entrust me with some of the more harrowing assignments." Kitty's heart-shaped lips arced downward into a frown, and she stared off when she wistfully said, "My husband was the same supportive man. He believed in me and made me believe that I could accomplish anything I set my mind to, including in the male-dominated sphere." Her eyes shifted back to Jana. "There are many good men out there, Jana. I hope that you've either already found yours or one day will. And once you do, hang onto him with your life."

An image of Keeley materialized before Jana, and she felt her entire expression filling up with love.

"Oh," Kitty put a hand to her cheek and said, "I see you've already found that special someone."

"Yes … yes, I have," Jana said and thought, *And he's worth fighting for.* She shot up in her chair to a sudden notion—tonight she'd proclaim her love for Keeley and pray the local newspapers would spread the words of her altered speech all the way to Elmira.

Jana and Leanne exited the Cayadutta House under cover of a tarry-night sky; they were guided a short distance across a snow-shoveled path through the livery yard by the side lanterns of their waiting carriage—compliments of hotel owner George Ehle.

Breathing deeply of the crisp air, Jana felt it stinging her lungs—better this than gagging on the mordant odors of un-mucked stalls that must be a constant menace here in the summertime. She extracted a reedy spike of clover from her coat pocket, offered another to Leanne, and began chewing on it to release its spicy vapors, which would help expel the tickle from her lungs and prevent her from a coughing fit. It would also freshen her breath, and she got a sudden feeling it would come in handy tonight.

The moonfaced, mustachioed coachman moved to the door and opened it. Quickly, he adjusted the cape of his greatcoat, and then he tipped his red top hat at Jana and Leanne. Extending his white-gloved hand, he helped Jana up the iron step, and her quizzical scrutiny of his elegantly stitched costume forced his smile. "Well, you *are* royalty in these parts, Miss Brady. Everyone has been anxiously awaiting your visit."

"You have no idea how much you've just set my mind at ease," she said, giving his hand a light squeeze. Plunking onto her seat, she felt the burden of her worries about facing a hostile audience flying off her shoulders. She folded her hands over her lap, catching sight of the hem of her Garibaldi skirt peeking out from beneath her wool pelisse. She'd nearly discarded this dress for a more feminine one but had decided to stick with her military-style costume. Its dichotomous representation of a woman's feminine and masculine sides best suited her message of equality in love she hoped to impart tonight.

Jana experienced a range of emotions during their short carriage ride: When they noticed the meager light on in Mrs. Cady's two-story brick home, she felt disappointed she'd miss seeing her at the lecture; when they passed a lodge for the freemasons and she was reminded that her kidnappers weren't through with her yet, she felt anger slashing up her insides; and when the lighted premises around the Fulton County Courthouse came into view, she swelled with gratitude to have been given the chance to speak in a colonial courthouse where eminent lawyers and statesmen had tried cases.

The carriage came to a stop before the Sir William Johnson Hotel, a grand structure that dwarfed the neighboring buildings. Before they circled back around, Jana caught sight of the posterior limestone exterior of St. John's Episcopal Church; in its yard, closer to West Main Street, lay the crypt of Sir William Johnson. Interestingly, it went from resting beneath the altar to outside the walls when his church burned down and its successor was rebuilt on the same site but was rotated so that the main entrance faced east as opposed to north, causing a relocation of the altar. It wasn't until 1862 that Reverend Kellogg discovered the crypt. *How could anyone have forgotten the grave of such a legendary figure for twenty-five years?* Jana thought with incredulity as they parked in front of the orange-brick, Georgian-style courthouse.

The elegantly dressed driver assisted Jana and Leanne out of the carriage, and Wyatt was there to greet them. Tendering his arms to them, he ushered them with care across the frozen-over walkway, pointing out the many shadowy outlines that represented the squadron of guards scattered about the premises. "With this daunting contingent outside, Sheriff Hillier is sending over only two deputies to cover the inside while he stays behind to man the jail. Although he doesn't anticipate any trouble—at least from the locals—he's only four blocks away, should anything erupt. He claims he can be here by horse within two minutes. Perhaps Mr. Getman overdid it a little, but his fortress seems foolproof," he said with a rare bounce in his stride that told Jana, besides him being impressed with his peer's philanthropy, he had some other trickery up his sleeve.

Immediately upon their entrance into the large open courtroom, they ran into a wall of heat that smacked Jana's cheeks and robbed her of her breath. She started to pop her head back outside for a few gulps of air until she spied an elderly woman who at her height of nearly six feet was peering levelly at Charlie as he showed her his camera. Curiosity concerning this majestic-appearing matron, whose hands were clasped behind her back as if she was at ease with all things in the world, got the better of her, and Jana succumbed to Wyatt's eager but gentle tugs down the creaky boards of the center aisle toward her.

Wyatt's gait grew bouncier and his eyes devilishly twinkly the closer they got to the woman whom Jana could tell he held in high regard.

To their approach the woman straightened her shoulders, which sloped severely beneath the simple black dress with white-laced collar and sleeve cuffs.

Wyatt said, "Miss Brady, Miss Watson, allow me to introduce you to Mrs. Margaret Livingston Cady."

Jana and Leanne gawked at her while Charlie smirked at them over the steel rim of his spectacles, clearly enjoying their shock.

"I believe you're all familiar enough with one another as to render fuller introductions unnecessary," Wyatt said.

Charlie's adoration shone upon Leanne through his bright blue eyes as he said, "I hope you don't mind, Leanne, that I told Margaret all about you and our attachment."

Teasingly, Leanne snorted and said, "I only mind if ya didn't make me look good."

With a smile that curved her full lips up to meet her long gently angled cheeks, Elizabeth Cady Stanton's mother reached out, wrapping her ribbon-like fingers first around Jana's hand in a firm handshake, then Leanne's. "I'm delighted to make your acquaintances. And, please, I would prefer that you call me Margaret." She harrumphed. "I don't understand why Miss Susan Anthony, whom I've heard you've all met, persists in publicly calling me Mrs. Daniel Cady and Elizabeth Mrs. Henry Stanton. Don't get me wrong, I loved my dearly departed husband and being his wife, yet even he, the consummate lawyer, would've found it challenging to argue against the sense in us women continuing to refer to ourselves and each other by our spouses' given names. It demotes us to men and sounds as if we're enslaved to our husbands when we're trying to prove our equality to them."

While Leanne's head bobbed in agreement, Jana said, "To be honest, I never gave the tradition a thought, but I have to agree with the absurdity of it. It's just one more barrier we women have to break through." She smiled, confident Keeley would embrace such a change.

Margaret raised her clasped hands before her in a spirited display as she gazed down at Jana. "I'm exceedingly excited to hear all about your exploits as a soldier, nurse, and spy."

Wyatt said with extraordinary enthusiasm for him, "It's been planned all along for Margaret to make your introduction tonight, Jana."

The excessive heat from a chorus of pine wood crackling away on a fireplace grate and in a woodstove, along with an internal flush from her overexcitement to this news, sent Jana's head in a whirl. Composing herself before anyone could notice her compromised state, she said, "I was told you'd be attending my oration tonight, but by the scant light in your home, I was worried you'd been detained elsewhere."

With merriness in her youthful, downturned eyes, Margaret said, "It was Elizabeth's idea for me to make your introduction to the good people of our village and county, and my reformist daughter would have my head on a stake if I hadn't made it back on time." She chuckled. "We kept a few globes on at home to keep you in suspense. I hope it didn't cause you too much consternation."

Touched by Margaret's efforts to keep her role a surprise, Jana said with a tearful catch in her voice, "I'm graced by your presence and blessed to have you making my introduction."

Margaret reached out and squeezed Jana's hand. "You are very sweet, dear."

"Thank you," Jana said. Then she asked Margaret if she'd be willing to include in her introduction of her a reminder that she'd fought with the Tenth New York Cavalry Regiment, alongside men in Fulton and Montgomery Counties, just in case the audience needed warming to her.

"I'm happy to oblige, but I assure you the locals are already warm to you."

Charlie took a group photograph, finishing within minutes to spare. It was another memento Jana would treasure forever. Although she silently bemoaned Charlie's absence from these pictures, she understood only he knew how to work his camera.

A stomping in the vestibule signaled the arrival of the two deputies, who tipped their hats toward Wyatt, and then they set up between windows on opposite sides of the room.

Besides the squadron of guards outside, Jana figured, *If the deputies' spit-shined badges and pistols don't deter anyone from contemplating delinquency, what will?*

Leanne stood along the wood-paneled wall near where Jana, Margaret, and Wyatt sat in the front row as the bell in the cupola high above them began to ring, warning the citizens her lecture would begin soon.

Jana shivered at the prickles of delight running up and down her spine. It was a tremendous honor to have this epic bell, which Kitty had told her had summoned the first general sessions of the then-named Tryon County Courthouse back in 1772, tolling on her behalf.

"Are you chilled, dear?" Margaret asked, her naturally arching eyebrows pinching together to her skepticism due to the room's warmth.

"Just the opposite." Jana fanned her face with her hand. "I fear I might pass out from heatstroke."

"I too am feeling a bit woozy from the heat, and this comes from one whom you can usually find curled up next to a roaring fire under a heap of blankets." She called out to the gentleman with a pocked face, bulbous nose, and in a patchwork of clothes who was managing the temperature in the courthouse and stopped him from throwing more logs into the woodstove. Margaret must've also seen the attendant turn away with a sneer because she leaned toward Jana and whispered, "He's the village drunk; we've all tried to help him at one time or another, but he always rejects it. I'd hate to think he stoked up the heat intentionally so he could be released from his obligation to the taverns early."

"I suppose we're all moved by different things," Jana said as the crowd began filing in. She was glad to see it was comprised equally of women and men and the same mingling of farmers, laborers, and merchants—a sight evident at her previous events. This gave her hope this assembly would be as open to her message.

The courthouse filled to capacity, and once everyone had settled into their seats and into soft murmurs, Margaret rose from her chair. With the grace of a queen, she glided across the polished oak planks and up onto the low platform. She ran her fingers over the top of the small desk that had been pushed back to make room for her and Jana and from before which her husband had probably tried his lion's share of cases. When she turned around, her eyes were moist from a memory or two, and only the crackle of burning logs on the large fireplace grate could be heard. All eyes riveted upon her evidenced she was obviously revered by the townspeople beyond her affiliation with her famous husband and daughter. Kitty had affirmed she'd once secured for local women the right to vote on a new church minister. Using her knobby knuckle, Margaret dabbed her eyes, which she then cast admiringly at Jana as she began her introduction:

> We are all familiar with the most famous of women soldiers: Joan of Arc. She sought no fame or glory when in 1429 she led French troops in the Siege at Orleans and helped to end English domination of France. She was following instructions through visions she received by Archangel Michael and Saints Margaret and Catherine to support the coronation of Charles VII.

She paused for effect, then smiled.

One day the world will know about our Miss Brady too. Like the Maiden of Orleans, she sought no fame or glory for her deeds as a soldier, nurse, and spy in our ongoing Great Rebellion that nearly ended her life. She was following her heart, which compelled her to join the fight for the preservation of the Union and abolishment of slavery.

Sweeping her hand toward Jana, she concluded:

Without further delay, I give you Miss Jana Brady, alias Johnnie Brodie, who I must remind you fought alongside our family and friends in the Tenth New York Cavalry Regiment. Please show her the respect and gratitude that she so very much deserves.

The audience cheered and clapped and, as Jana made her way onto the stage, she spied the courtroom's wooden gavel resting on the judge's desk. She couldn't help but think, *I hope there's no cause to bring order to the courtroom tonight.*

With a nod at the town drunk as she returned to her seat, Margaret reminded him to open a window. Curiously, he chose the one opposite to where he currently stood. As he crossed in front of Jana and stumbled, she caught a whiff of his breath, potent enough for her to think she'd just swigged a shot glass full of whiskey herself. She guessed he'd been sneaking swills of it, thus the reason for his dulled wit.

Jana waited until he finished pushing up the squeaky lower sash and the assembly's welcoming reception waned before she began in her usual way. She thanked Mrs. Cady for her heartfelt introduction, all who had arranged and organized her visit, Mr. Wyatt McGriffin for his generosity and support, and everyone for their attendance. This time, though, she specially acknowledged Mr. David Getman Sr. of Mayfield, New York, father to the captain of her regiment's Company *I*, for supplying the battalion of guards surrounding the premises for all's safety.

A flash of light drew Jana's focus out through the window facing the Sir William Johnson Hotel. A ball of fire headed straight for her. She fell back into the desk in the nick of time, avoiding a flaming arrow that hit the floor in front of her.

Faster than a whirling dervish, Leanne swooped in and stamped out the arrow's blazing feathers beneath the soles of her brogans.

The shouts of the guards and their footrace past the window in pursuit of the perpetrator caused a tumbling domino effect inside. Peals of fright were followed by the attendants in the front row springing from their seats and starting a stampede toward the exit.

Desperate not to lose her flock, Jana hurtled through the smoke off the platform and sped up the outer aisle, outmaneuvering the people log-jamming the center aisle in their mad dash to the door. She splayed her arms and legs to impede anyone's escape and, before the deputies reached her sides with their pistols aimed into the disorderly mob, she shouted with force she never knew she had in her, "Stop where you are!"

It startled and quieted the throng.

In a calming but resolute tone, Jana said, "There's no danger to you. That small cowardly act was meant to get my dander up and goad me on to our state capital."

Jumping up onto the platform, Leanne seized the wooden gavel and began striking it against the desktop. All heads turned toward her, and she waved a small piece of paper about and said, "This note, stuck to the arrowhead, says, 'Give Up Albany or Die!'"

All heads turned back to Jana.

She huffed with flippant disregard. "That doesn't intimidate me. I'm determined to see my bidding through." Singling out those people directly before her and fixing each with a fierce stare, Jana said loudly enough for all to hear, "If any of you are as courageous as I know your ancestors were, you'll return to your seats and prove you can't be scared away either." She moved aside and gestured toward the door. "I won't stand in your way if you wish to leave."

To their subdued mutters, everyone shuffled back to their chairs except the town drunk whom Jana spied sneaking out the door.

Margaret and Wyatt, who'd remained seated throughout the entire affair, nodded at Jana with approval and, when everyone settled in quieter than church mice, Jana began:

> Miss Susan Anthony, with whom I'm sure you're all acquainted, recently told me that my wartime experiences would be the torch that reignited the crusade for equality of the sexes.

With a shake of her head, Jana placed her hands on her hips and grinned.

> I didn't realize I should take her literally.

The assembly's lingering tension released in one collective laugh and, when it died down, Jana realized she'd been gifted a unique segue into her presentation.

> Given that my talk has already started out with a twist, I implore you to allow me another digression.

No one objected, so she said:

> By show of hands, when the flaming arrow came through the window,

how many of you experienced confusion followed by a fear of being trapped in a burning building?

Jana led the way in raising her hand, followed by Margaret, Wyatt, and everyone else.

Isn't it amazing that, together, we all experienced identical emotions to the same igniter? What separated us as man and woman at that moment? Nothing! Actually, there was one person in the room who stood apart from us all.

Looking toward Leanne, she continued:

I know my friend well enough to believe she experienced a different set of emotions: fear for our safety and determination to keep us from harm. Her quick-thinking to stamp out the fire came from her instincts, which were further honed as a cavalryman. And so ... it was her experience that just might've saved our lives tonight. Her act and our exploits as soldiers make a case against the farce women have not brains and brawn enough to render them capable of treading in the male domain—don't you think? How can we believe men and women are truly equal when it comes to reproduction of offspring, yet we cannot fathom equality between the sexes in any other sphere?

The squirming of many in their chairs to her rhetorical questions assured Jana that she had their attention, and she hastened on:

If the argument embodies brawn, a woman might not be able to lift what a man can, but she has a higher threshold for pain—a gift for bearing children. If the argument embodies brains, I point to women, such as Harriet Tubman, Harriet Beecher Stowe, Dr. Elizabeth Blackwell, Dorothea Dix, Susan Anthony, and last but definitely not least, Elizabeth Cady Stanton, whose shrewdness cannot be denied. And if the argument embodies steadfastness, when a man is sick, his wife chops the wood, plows the field, and repairs the barn, all while keeping up with her chores and tending to him and their children; when a woman is sick, her husband recruits others to take up the slack of her chores and tend to her and their children. Equality, however, is not a competition; it's being respectful that we all have something beautiful to contribute for bettering ourselves and our lives, children, country, and world. I believe the ultimate case for equality is where love is utterly reciprocal—whether it's between family or friends or lovers.

Jana crossed her hands over her heart.

One of the most beautiful examples of equality in love that I've ever witnessed was when a soldier and his bride fought together and died holding hands on the battlefield at Fredericksburg. Clearly they respected and supported each other's right to be there. I know how it felt to have that kind of love …

Trailing off, Jana had to look away when sudden tears welled to her realization she might never see Keeley again. But that motivated her to go on because she wanted him and everyone to know just how much she loved him. Blinking away her tears as best as she could, she turned back to the audience and started again through quivery lips:

I know how it felt to have that kind of love … and equality in love. My soldier-sweetheart loved me for who I am, respected my desire to soldier, encouraged me to dream, and would've supported my continuing to tackle anything if I had a mind to it. He suffers from total amnesia from a rifle butt to the head he got in battle, and he doesn't remember our love— the depth of which I fear I'll never feel again.

Jana pressed on through her tears, which were now cascading down her cheeks:

More traumatic for me than facing any noose will be the day I set my sweetheart free to find another. But I'll do it … because I love him.

Over the sounds of sniffling, a rummaging for handkerchiefs, and noses being blown, a familiar voice in the crowd called out, "I won't let ye set meself free … because I love ye with all o' me heart, Jana lass."

Jana inched back into the desk to steady herself with a tornado of shock and disbelief roiling all through her. Was she dreaming?

Rising up from the back of the room and stepping into the aisle, Keeley removed his wide-brimmed hat to show without a shadow of doubt he was no figment of her imagination.

The sheer excitement of his presence and his public declaration of his love for her overtook Jana like nothing she'd ever felt before. She broke out in a cold, clammy sweat, and her head began spinning again. Reaching out for him, she faltered when everyone and everything blurred; right before she fainted, she felt a rush of footsteps toward her and loving arms catching and cradling her.

Jana revived to the feel of herself lying supine on a cold, hard surface and her forehead being dabbed with a soft cloth. Her eyes flicked open, allowing her to behold the most beautiful man she'd ever seen.

With her head resting in his lap, Keeley continued to mop her face with his handkerchief. "Are ye all right, Jana lass?" he said, his emerald eyes clouded with concern.

"I couldn't be better," she said, her voice a little shaky.

"I'm sorry about the timing o' me declaration o' love. But"—his dimples burst forth—"ye have only yarself to blame for forcing it out o' meself in public, ye do."

Her heart fluttered. "There's never a wrong time for a proclamation of love—especially yours for me." Her eyes moistened. "Did you really mean what you said?"

"Every word o' it, me love."

"But how ... how did it come about?"

"We can discuss that later, lass."

"No fair," a gentleman called out. "We want to know the answer."

To a chorus of agreement, Jana and Keeley looked up to find themselves encircled by people, all with expectant expressions. They turned back to each other, their cheeks coloring with embarrassment, and burst out in nervous titters.

"Well?" the same gentleman persisted in asking.

A woman backed him, saying, "This is better than a romance novel. Please spill all."

Running the back of his hand down Jana's cheek, Keeley said, "It was a combination o' two things: Just as it happened the first time, I fell in love with ye at first sight; by the time ye left on yar lecture tour, me whole memory was back and I knew the depth o' me love for ye, Jana lass."

Jana sat up. Feeling her bafflement bombarding her brain, she said, "Why'd you hide it from me? Had I known, I'd never have accepted the lecture tour."

"Aye, that's the point. I know how ye crave adventure and, with our love happening so fast the first time around, I wanted to give ye some time to make sure ye'd want to marry the likes o' meself."

Jana giggled. "And I left home with high hopes that your heart would grow fonder for me during my absence."

From somewhere near the outer circle, Margaret's voice arose. "How very noble of you both; do tell us what's next for you."

Keeley tilted his head tenderly and said, "I intend to marry the lass, if she'll have meself."

"I do!" Without a care about proper etiquette, she threw her arms around him, and this time he reciprocated with a voracious hug, which once again entwined their beating hearts into one.

When the cheering subsided, Keeley pulled away from Jana. "Now that we have us solved, are ye up to finishing yar talk?"

"With you by my side, I can accomplish anything." And with his help, Jana got to her feet, feeling as if she was floating on a cloud. She grabbed the collar of his coat and tugged him back when he tried to leave the stage. Throughout her speech, she had her hand hooked tightly around his to let him know he'd never get away from her again.

Later, Jana and Keeley left the hall in high spirits, eager to find the carriage and return to their hotel.

As the coachman held the door open for them, he complimented Jana on her presentation and congratulated her and Keeley on their courtship.

Huddling together on the leather seat, the sweethearts kept each other warm as they entwined hands and laughed and talked about the hearth and home they'd build in Elmira.

Jana's euphoria was cut short to a sudden thought. "Now that you have your memory back, will you have to return to duty?"

Keeley cupped his gloved hands tenderly around her cheeks. "I'll never leave ye again, me love. I felt obligated to let Dr. Pease know I had me memory back. He still thought it unwise for meself to return to the fighting—he fears another hard knock to me head could kill meself."

*Ironic*, Jana thought, *a shot from a rifle is more likely to kill him first. Though, who am I to look a gift horse in the mouth?* She was glad when Keeley failed to notice her other worry: Her abductors had managed to hurdle every obstacle to get to her.

Could the promised battalion of guards in Albany combat them? She had difficulty believing her and Keeley's reunion was all for naught, but when she recollected Keeley's courage to overcome his weariness and fear in rejoining the fighting after their escape from Richmond, she determined to follow his example and see her commitment through.

Jana peeked around one of four colossal Doric columns that graced the expansive entrance porch of the State Capitol. Rocking on the flat heels of her laced boots, she surveyed the mass of people below, which fanned out from the base of the grand staircase to Eagle and State Streets. She spotted Leanne and Mr. Tanner opposite one another at the head of the crowd. She was appreciating their eagle eyes watching her back when she felt a strong hand wrap around hers in a firm but tender grasp. Glancing up, she found Keeley's eyes probing deep into hers. She knew he was misinterpreting she feared dying today when she feared more she'd bumble her speech in front of the thirty-two senators and one-hundred-and-twenty-eight assemblymen who'd broken out of their caucus to hear her speak.

"Are ye sure ye want to go ahead with yar speech, me lass? It's never too late to cancel," Keeley shouted over the tolling bells that signaled the start of Jana's oration.

Governor Reuben E. Fenton, who'd been waiting with Jana and Keeley, raised a graying eyebrow at Jana.

Jana gave him a nod of affirmation. As he moved to the lectern at the top of the staircase, she marveled at his presence—he was lanky and he wore sideburns and a beard without a mustache around his triangular face, which suggested he could be a brother to Abraham Lincoln.

Hoping to put Keeley at ease, Jana held up the telegram the governor had given her minutes before. "I'll be all right, Keeley." She grinned. "The president of the United States says so." Thrilled to have received a note from Mr. Lincoln, she'd read it several times and had it committed to memory:

> Dear Miss Jana Brady. I wish you success in convincing the lawmakers and good people of New York as to the merits of woman's suffrage. I support the endeavor and admire your courage to serve your country yet again. Governor Fenton and Mayor Perry have an army of local militia guarding you. Trust you will be safe from harm. President Abraham Lincoln

She squeezed Keeley's hand to prove she wasn't worried and said, "How can

I lose with you by my side protecting me?"

To the echoes of the bells fading, the governor waved Jana and Keeley forward.

Wyatt and Kitty joined them on stage. They hoped their additional presence beside Jana would make her assassins think twice about chancing a stray bullet and killing an innocent bystander. Kitty would also watch out for any of the numerous sentries posted in upper-story windows all around to signal danger to Jana with a wig-wag of their flag.

Governor Fenton began:

> As a native of New York, I am proud to say that our state has had a major impact on the fight for the preservation of our country. We have sent several significant military commanders and leaders and more troops than any state in the Union to war. And now ...

He glanced over his shoulder at Jana, his dark-brown eyes twinkling, before he turned back and concluded:

> ... our beloved state can claim the first female to have joined the fight as a soldier. I have been bestowed the honor of introducing to you our esteemed Miss Jana Brady from Elmira, New York—alias Private Johnnie Brodie of the Tenth New York Cavalry Regiment.

As he retreated to the white-marbled wall of the Capitol to stand with Jana's family, Elizabeth Cady Stanton, and the men of the 88th legislature, Jana stepped up to the lectern and into a great roar of applause. She breathed deeply of the invigorating air blowing up westward from the Hudson River, and its positive energy flowed through her. When the cheers subsided, she began to speak:

> My love and loyalty to and from family, friends, and country are the key ingredients that drove me to fight for the preservation of the Union and that sustained me throughout the war and my lecture—

She hesitated when a red flag popped out of City Hall's third-story window and began waving urgently.

"Take cover!" Kitty shouted.

A rifle cracked, inciting shrieks of terror.

The crowd scattered.

Jana stepped back between Wyatt and Keeley. Glancing over her shoulder, she saw her family huddled together in a crouch and the senators and assemblymen pushing and shoving each other as they fled pell-mell into the Capitol.

"Dear Lord," Wyatt uttered with shock.

Jana turned around to find that Wyatt's mother had advanced up the staircase within a few feet of them. She wore a scornful expression as she steadied her revolver with two hands, took aim, and clicked back the hammer.

Kitty lunged toward Mrs. McGriffin, and Keeley flung himself across Jana and past Wyatt as the gun exploded. Crashing to the portico with a thud of his head, he rolled onto his back with a groan.

As Leanne tackled her from behind, Mrs. McGriffin screamed, and Mr. Tanner rushed in to confiscate her gun and help Leanne subdue her.

Jana dropped to her knees.

Keeley's eyes were closed and still. Blood oozed through his coat beneath where the heel of his hand lay over his heart and his fingers stretched across his arm.

"No!" Jana wailed as she gathered Keeley's head onto her lap and pressed her tear-drenched cheek against his.

# Albany, New York

### March 13, 1865

Jana barely felt a hand patting her back through her gut-wrenching sobs. Desperate to cling to Keeley's warmth and familiar scent until they were snuffed out forever, she refused to separate herself from him.

"I'm all right, me lass," Keeley whispered, his breath hot and moist in her ear.

Her head jerked up, and miraculously her eyes found his staring back. Glancing at his wound, Jana licked away the salty droplets on her lips. "I don't understand. How can you be alive?"

Lifting his head slightly, Keeley studied the pattern of blood on his coat. "Aye, I can see how ye might think I took a bullet in the heart rather than me arm."

Jana sniffled with joy and relief.

Over the ongoing stampede of people and carriages in retreat, Keeley said, "Ye didn't think ye'd get rid o' meself that easily, did ye, me love?"

Jana tilted her head back, and Ma, Pa, her sisters, and Charlie came into focus as she laughed and cried some more.

Charlie said, "We need to get you inside right away so I can determine the extent of your injury."

With Jana's help, Keeley sat up. He rubbed his head and said, "It seems I've also taken a small knock to me skull, but be assured, me lass, me memory remains intact."

As Jana exhaled a breath of relief, Pa and Charlie helped Keeley to his feet and into the Capitol on his wobbly legs and lowered him onto a bench.

Charlie took charge, unbuttoning and removing Keeley's coat, apologizing when he had to rip Keeley's shirtsleeve off and in two; one half he used as a tourniquet, which he tied around the bicep above the wound to stop the blood flow, the other to swab the blood to better visualize the wound. When he finished his examination, he reported to Keeley, "The bullet hit your bicep muscle. That explains the heavy bleeding. Fortunately, it cleared the sleeves of your coat and shirt. No stitches are needed, but"—he smirked—"you and Jana will have matching scars."

"I couldn't let Jana get ahead o' meself, could I now?"

"That makes us even, Keeley, so let's agree not to take any more bullets for each other," Jana said, laughing along with all else present.

On the heels of Charlie's assessment, Elizabeth swooped in with the doctor who confirmed Charlie's diagnosis.

As the doctor cleaned, packed, and re-dressed Keeley's wound, Jana found herself dreaming of being in his place—she wished for nothing more than to do all of the caring for Keeley the rest of her life, and his loving gaze portrayed he yearned for that too. Sliding onto the bench next to Keeley when the doctor vacated his spot, Jana barely heard the doctor's instructions for aftercare with her trying to restrain herself from nestling in Keeley's arms.

Leanne sprinted in well ahead of Kitty, Mr. Tanner, and Wyatt, passing the doctor on his way out. Gasping for breath, she said to Keeley, "Are ya all right?"

"Aye, Leanne, I appreciate yar concern."

"I'm really sorry we couldn't git to Mrs. McGriffin before she got off a shot. Mr. Tanner and I had to wrestle our way out from under a tramplin'."

Raking his shaking, agitated fingers through his thick curls, Wyatt said, "I'm deeply remorseful of the pain and suffering you've all had to endure at the hands of my kin." He looked away in disgrace. "If I had known how demented she was, I might have anticipated her actions."

"I had the more objective vantage," Jana said. "I should've pieced together the petite feet of Goliath's boss and the silent admonition of him to realize my abductor was not only a woman, but your mother." Additionally, she complimented Charlie for his profile of Mrs. McGriffin. To an utterance of confusion by Wyatt, she explained that Charlie had analyzed his family through their daguerreotypes, which Hannah had loaned her. "If we'd shared Charlie's appraisals with you, Wyatt, we might've sorted the mystery out sooner."

"Yes, only ..." he trailed off to his growing distress.

Leanne touched Wyatt's arm. With a nod from him, she shook her head in disbelief first before saying, "Mrs. McGriffin was gunnin' for Wyatt all along, not ya, Jana."

Everyone flinched and gasped in surprise.

Eyeing Keeley with a bittersweet smile, Wyatt said, "You inadvertently saved my life, and I'm grateful to you."

Ma huffed with anger. "How can a mother kill her own child?"

"Well ... that's just it, Julia," Wyatt said. "She was never a mother to me or my brother. She came from and married into wealth, and she was used to fancy things and parties; nothing was ever going to get in the way of her having them—including her sons whom she passed on to Hannah to raise as her own. As soon as we were old enough, she sent us away to private academies so she could avoid glimpsing us every day and being constantly reminded of any guilt she might have felt in not wanting us."

"What about your father? Didn't he want you?" Ma asked, mournfully.

The creases in Wyatt's forehead cut deep to his frown. "I surmise he wanted heirs more than he did sons. He was consumed in building his empire, and he made very little time for Wallace and me. His and my mother's marriage was really a merger of their wealthy families. Thus, there was no love between husband and wife, which they transferred to their sons. Fortunately for me, I've known a mother's love from my birth through Hannah; unfortunately for my brother, he felt our parents' abandonment for too long before Hannah came along, and it has caused him to self-destruct." He waggled his hand. "But I've strayed from my point. To repeat what Jana, Leanne, and Charlie already know, when my father died, he left me his fortune and restricted my mother's and brother's access to it through an allowance he prescribed for them. It was enough to keep them comfortable, not enough for my mother to keep on with her extravagant ways. When I refused to increase her allowance until she could prove her spending more prudent, she blamed me for her humiliating demotion in society, and she confessed minutes ago to her wanting me to suffer for it. I presented her the opportunity on a silver platter when I decided to sponsor Jana's lecture circuit and have it end at the State Capitol."

Jana remembered what Goliath had said to his boss about her being sorry she ever got tangled up with agitators for woman's rights who steal money from the rich for their cause, and that also connected the dots to Mrs. McGriffin. "Then, why did she have me kidnapped and keep goading me on to Albany?"

"She knows I'm not one to take risks, and I'd give up the lecture circuit if I thought anyone's life was in danger."

When Wyatt began to squirm, Leanne again came to his rescue. "She used yer well-known reputation, Jana, for grit and determination to make sure we didn't give up. And she didn't care if she was shot when she assassinated Wyatt—she said she'd rather die than live another day with her shame."

Wyatt's shoulders hunched dejectedly.

Jana wiped away her tears. There wasn't a dry eye in the place—everyone was sniffling and dabbing their eyes.

Wyatt said, "I didn't mean to upset you all; I thought you deserved a thorough explanation."

"What about Wallace?" Jana asked.

"Before my mother cleared him of complicity, including any knowledge of his army buddy's involvement"—Wyatt glared at the wall—"she called him a dolt, who couldn't even tie his own shoe." When he refocused on them, he straightened to his full height. "He might be wayward; however, he's no dolt, and I intend to help him restore his self-worth. I have a feeling he'll be pliable when he learns of our mother's madness. He won't want to turn out like her."

"What's going to happen to your mother?" Charlie asked.

"She's been arrested and will await her trial, but I think she'll ultimately be judged insane and sent to an asylum, where she'll no doubt succumb to her further degradation."

Mr. Tanner and Kitty took turns filling in the remaining details. Mrs. McGriffin had indeed used the phony tattoo as a means for Goliath to be identified at each of Jana's stops where he hired the downtrodden, who accepted paltry payoffs, to aid him in promoting Mrs. McGriffin's plot. The initials WFM that made the stem of the *G*, which Jana's eyes had so keenly spotted, were a satirical tribute by Mrs. McGriffin to her late husband William Fitzgerald McGriffin for his cruelty in leaving her in her perceived impoverishment. Goliath, who was now in the custody of Albany's sheriff, shot the rifle from amongst the crowd to create a distraction, enabling Mrs. McGriffin to get into position to kill Wyatt. A few of the local militia ran him down before he could get away, and he'll most likely rot in prison for his collusion. And the last of the gang, the phony Bill Parker, had been caught near his home and jailed.

To his blanching face, Wyatt peered at the polished floor tiles.

Elizabeth reached up, cupping her pudgy hand around his chin and raising it. With adamancy flaring in her bright blue eyes, she said, "I'm sorry, my dear friend, about your natural mother's failings, but they are not yours to own. And if it'll make you feel any better, she just might've helped to advance our cause." To everyone's curious expressions, she blew away a graying dark-brown curl, which had strayed from beneath her bonnet, plopped her fists on her plump hips, and scowled at each person. "Admit it, we're all guilty of believing only a man could've bred such a savage and sophisticated scheme. I'm not endorsing what Mrs. McGriffin did; however, she proved we women can be every bit as devious as men. We'll make sure the public interprets it this way, and perhaps her lesson and Jana's well-publicized accomplishments will truncate our road to victory."

Governor Fenton suddenly appeared, his bow tie askew and his cheeks flushed. "I've just come from the legislative chamber, and the vast majority of statesmen are demanding that I invite you to visit again, Miss Brady, and finish your speech. What do you say?"

Hoping to lift Wyatt's spirits, Jana smiled at him and said, "You'll have to work that out with my sponsor."

"Well ... how about it, Wyatt?" the governor asked.

Elizabeth addressed Wyatt too. "We hope you'll continue to champion our cause—we need compassionate men, such as yourself, supporting us."

With encouragement from all, Wyatt said, "We'll iron out the details later, Governor."

Elizabeth winked at Jana. "If I'm given enough notice, I'll hogtie Mr. Stanton into caring for our gaggle of children so that I can accompany Miss Anthony."

"Oh boy, here comes double trouble," Governor Fenton said with a chuckle.

Keeley broke through the ensuing laughter and silenced everyone. "Speaking o' a gaggle o' children"—he shifted toward Jana on the bench, took her hand in his good one, and leveled his adoring eyes upon hers—"do ye remember, lass, our aspirations to fill our hearth and home with a gaggle o' wee ones?"

Jana caressed his hand. "Of course I do."

"Are ye still in favor o' it?"

"Very much so, but"—Jana felt the heat of her blush blooming between her freckles—"wouldn't we be missing a step?"

Keeley looked to Ma, whose hands were pressed together before her lips, and Pa, whose smile stretched wider than the hall, and they spurred him on with their nods. Releasing her hand, he reached for his coat, draped over the back of the bench, and withdrew a small box from its pocket that he presented to her.

As she lifted the lid, her lips parted and her breath caught in awe.

"Do ye like it, lass?"

"It's beautiful," Jana said, gliding her finger over the antique gold ring—its split band made to appear as two hands joining to embrace a heart adorned by a crown. "I love it."

"It's me mam's Claddagh ring and the only relic I have o' me family. The hands represent friendship, the heart love, and the crown loyalty." When Jana's eyes widened with surprise, Keeley said, "Aye, that was to be the foundation o' yar speech today; it's as if the ring was made just for ye, me lass."

"Yes ... it does seem that way," she said as she regarded each of her family and friends with appreciation for their never-ending friendship, love, and loyalty, which they acknowledged and returned with a smile, nod, or tip of their hat.

Keeley drew her attention back to him. "Most o' all, it symbolizes our journey. It was yar friendship, love, and loyalty that made meself fall in love with ye twice and revived me memory." He reached out to her. "If ye'll take me hand now and accept meself as yar husband"—he singled Elizabeth out with a wink—"I pledge to always love ye with all o' me heart and consider us equal in all things and decisions, including the building o' our hopes and dreams."

Yearning for more than a simple handshake to consummate their vows, Jana was considerate of his injury when she threw her arms around his neck and kissed his cheek. "Will that do instead for my pledge to be your wife?" she whispered in his ear.

"Aye, very nicely," he said, pulling her closer to him and kissing her back.

Cries of delight reverberated through the hall and, after Keeley slid the Claddagh ring on Jana's finger, Ma began planning for a spring wedding.

Keeley looked heavenward. "I know me mam and da would've approved o' ye, me love."

"I know for a fact they do." To his arched eyebrows, Jana grinned and said, "They brought us together, you know, and they're never going to let anything come between us." Then she swore she felt the flame of her and Keeley's love being fanned and burning bright in her soul.

THE END

# Fact or Fiction

In writing historical fiction, the author sometimes takes liberties in sketching historical places, events, and people but only where the facts are vague or silent. The following are those exceptions as they pertain to *Train to Glory*:

First, just as early advocates of woman's equal rights used the singular form of their sex in reference to their crusade, so do I. And just as Northerners used "War of the Rebellion" or "Great Rebellion" in reference to the "American Civil War", so do I.

It is fact that many women from New York State disguised themselves as soldiers to fight in the War of the Rebellion and that most remained anonymous for years after the war ended in April 1865. Had they been known, they could have been encouraged by advocates of woman's equal rights to travel their lecture circuit speaking about their time in uniform to prove that a woman ought to be granted the same rights to tackle anything a man can if she has a mind to it.

Susan B. Anthony, Elizabeth Cady Stanton, and Frederick Douglass—three of the most well-known persons for their work in the abolition of slavery and woman's equal rights—require no special introduction here. However, it is fact that in March 1865, Susan B. Anthony and Frederick Douglass resided in Rochester, New York, and I believe they would have made every effort to attend a lecture delivered by a woman soldier in nearby Seneca Falls, New York (birthplace of the first national woman's rights convention in 1848). I believe Elizabeth Cady Stanton would have done the same in traveling from her home in New York City to Albany, New York.

It is fact that Roger Williams Pease, M.D., who was promoted from Major Surgeon of the Tenth New York Cavalry Regiment to Medical Inspector of the Cavalry Corps by General George Stoneman in May 1863, transported several hundred wounded back to White House, Virginia, after the battle at Trevilian Station, Virginia, June 11-12, 1864. The timeline as to when he escorted the badly wounded from there to Washington, DC, is sketchy, so he could have still been in Virginia in July 1864.

It is fact that in 1856 recently widowed Kate Warne became the first female detective for the Pinkerton Agency and that in 1861 she participated in foiling a plot to assassinate Abraham Lincoln on his way for his inaugural as president of the United States. Kate was most likely spying on the South in March 1865, but because she was regarded by Allan Pinkerton as one of his most competent detectives, and because the war was winding down then, she could have been briefly reassigned to foil a plot to assassinate a famous woman soldier on a lecture tour across New York State.

It is fact that Governor Reuben E. Fenton and the 88th New York State Legislature were in session at the Capitol building in Albany, New York, from January 3 to April 28, 1865. I believe they would have interrupted their caucus to hear a speech of historical consequence by a woman soldier who had participated in the Great Rebellion.

It is fact that the Erie Railway and the New York Central Railroad's tracks followed the routes depicted in this story. However, as it was difficult to reconstruct exact train schedules, which were constantly changing around Civil War times, I played with arrival and departure times by using approximate train speeds, miles between places, and layover times at stops to calculate the overall time it would have taken to travel between destinations. Additionally, I was guided by Abraham Lincoln's Funeral Train (1865).

Rather than turn this section into an essay, I will briefly state that more information can be learned through links in my bibliography and/or webliography about the following persons, who were real to Civil War times but were only touched upon in *Train to Glory*:

Clara Barton: Nurse

Matthew Brady: Photographer

Elizabeth Blackwell: Doctor

Dorothea Dix: Superintendent of Union Army Nurses

William Lloyd Garrison: Journalist, Abolitionist, Suffragist, and Social Reformer

Angelina and Sarah Grimké: Southern Abolitionists and Woman's Suffrage & Equal Rights Activists

Jervis Langdon (Elmira, New York): Businessman, Philanthropist, Abolitionist, Social Reformer

Olivia "Livy" Langdon Clemens: Daughter of Jervis Langdon and Wife of Samuel Langhorne Clemens (Mark Twain)

Noble D. Preston: Commissary Officer and Historian of the Tenth New York Cavalry Regiment. (See more about him in "Acknowledgments")

Gerrit Smith (Elizabeth Cady Stanton's Cousin): Philanthropist, Politician, Abolitionist, and Social Reformer

Harriet Beecher Stowe: Author and Abolitionist

Harriet Tubman: African-American Abolitionist and Woman's Suffrage & Equal Rights Activist

Elizabeth "Miss Lizzie" Van Lew: Union Spy

Timothy Webster: Pinkerton Agent

Mary Edwards Walker: Surgeon, Prisoner of War, Abolitionist, & Prohibitionist

Walt Whitman: Poet

Other Abolitionists/Social Reformists/Woman's Suffrage & Equal Rights Activists:

Jane Hunt
Mary Ann McClintock
Lucretia Mott
Martha Wright

# Acknowledgments

I thank:

All women who have braved rugged frontiers and angry mobs across the United States of America as they have campaigned for women's equal rights and who have gifted me exciting material around which to craft *Train to Glory*!

Karen Knowles, teacher, writer, editor, and friend who once again taught me so much about honing my writing when she coached me through a revision of my novel draft and encouraged me to keep writing through tough times.

Reagan Schwartz who supported and participated in the character-naming contest that I hosted at: www.facebook.com/LisaPotocarAuthor. I hope she will understand that characters force their writers to develop their personalities in ways unanticipated. Although her Wyatt McGriffin turned out differently than originally sketched, I believe she will be pleased that he remains a memorable secondary character in this sequel to *Sweet Glory*.

The extant Bill Parker and Duke Tanner who supported and participated in the contest that the Seneca Falls Historical Society so kindly hosted for the naming of two fictitious Pinkerton agents who first enter *Train to Glory* in Waterloo and Seneca Falls, New York.

Civil-War Veteran Noble D. Preston who recorded a regimental history that I believe can be surpassed by none. From it, I extracted almost everything I needed to know about the Tenth New York Volunteer Cavalry Regiment, especially their involvement in the battle at Trevilian Station, Virginia, June 11-12, 1864.

Ron Matteson who, through his book *Civil War Campaigns of the 10th New York Cavalry*, bolstered my research where Noble D. Preston was vague or silent.

Linda Solan, Director of Seneca Museum of Waterways & Industry (Seneca Falls, New York), who so kindly interrupted her work to give me a private tour of the Women's Rights exhibit and the 19th Century Village of Seneca Falls scale model.

Kathy Jans-Duffy, Collections Manager, Seneca Falls (New York) Historical Society, who so kindly coordinated a character-naming contest to help promote *Train to Glory*, armed me with facts, fiction, and walking-tour and historical maps, and authenticated my words. Her village, the birthplace of women's equal rights as spearheaded by Elizabeth Cady Stanton and peers, is a goldmine for educators and history buffs!

Noel Levee, City Historian, who so kindly opened the Johnstown (New York) Historical Museum before hours on a Sunday, and then armed me with facts, fiction, and historical maps and authenticated my words.

Cynthia Van Ness, MLS, Director of Library & Archives, Research Library, The Buffalo History Museum, who took the time to forward me an exhaustive list of websites that assisted me in recreating 1865 Buffalo, New York.

All of my family and friends who have supported *Sweet Glory* and have encouraged me on throughout the writing of *Train to Glory*. I must specially acknowledge the following: my mother, Patricia, who tirelessly searches for new venues in which for me to expose my research and writing and my mother-in-law, Anita, for her tireless efforts in marketing and promoting my books—she could most definitely give anyone in the business a run for their money.

My grandmother Versella, my great-aunt Iva, and my brother-in-law Garth for allowing me the liberty of using their names for my characters.

Just like Civil-War regiments had mascots, I had my cuddly keeshonds Fuji (Yama-San) and Kili (Man-Jaro) to spur me on through their boundless energy. Bless them for understanding those times when I was too engrossed in my writing to play with them.

My author friend L.A. Sartor (www.lasartor.com), to whom I'm eternally grateful, led me through the maze of self-publication when my publisher closed its door and I was forced to learn the business side of writing in order to find a new home for *Train to Glory*. She also set me on a course to Christa Holland (www.paperandsage.com), Lucinda K. Campbell (design.lkcampbell.com), and Dana Delamar (www.byyourselfpub.com). All three women were extremely kind, patient, and understanding as they tackled the work of redesigning my cover and reformatting my interior for digital and print editions, respectively.

Last, but definitely not least, my husband, best friend, and hero, Jed. Once again, he summoned the rain during my more frightening creative droughts and let me be (even took over my chores) when he noticed that my writing engine was running in high gear. He is the greatest person in the whole wide world!

# Bibliography

Adams, George Worthington. *Doctors in Blue: The Medical History of the Union Army in the Civil War.* 1952; rpt. Baton Rouge, Louisiana: Louisiana State University Press, 1996.

Alden, Henry M., and Alfred H. Guernsey. *Harper's Pictorial History of the Civil War: Contemporary Accounts and Illustrations of the Greatest Magazine of the Time.* New York: The Fairfax Press, 1866.

Angle, Paul M. *A Pictorial History of the Civil War Years.* Garden City, New York: Doubleday and Company, Inc., 1967.

Blanton, Deanne, and Lauren M. Cook. *They Fought Like Demons: Women Soldiers in the Civil War.* New York: Vintage Books, 2003.

Bolett, M.D., Alfred Jay. *Civil War Medicine: Challenges and Triumphs.* Tucson, Arizona: Galen Press, Ltd., 2002.

Calloway, Stephen. *The Elements of Style: An Encyclopedia of Domestic Architectural Detail 4th Edition.* Buffalo, New York: Firefly Books (U.S.) Inc., 2012.

*Chemung County Historical Journal: A Civil War Anthology.* 1964; rpt. Elmira, New York: The Chemung County Historical Society, Inc., 1985, 1993.

*Chemung Historical Journal: Elmira Prison Camp.* 1964; rpt. Elmira, New York: The Chemung County Historical Society, Inc., 1990, 1997.

Colman, Penny. *Elizabeth Cady Stanton and Susan B. Anthony: A Friendship That Changed the World.* New York, New York: Henry Holt and Company, LLC, 2011.

Dann, Norman K. *Cousins of Reform: Elizabeth Cady Stanton and Gerrit Smith.* Hamilton, New York: Log Cabin Books, 2013.

Davis, William C. *The Civil War*, 3 vols. 1990; rpt. London, United Kingdom: Salamander Books Ltd., 1999.

Decker, Lewis G. *Images of America: Johnstown*. 2003; rpt. Great Britain: Arcadia Publishing, 1999.

*Elmira City Directory, 1860*. Elmira, New York: Chemung County Historical Society, Inc.

Forrest, Tim. *The Bulfinch Anatomy of Antique Furniture: An Illustrated Guide to Identifying Period, Detail, and Design*. Piccadilly, London: Bulfinch Press, 1996.

Gable, Walter. *Seneca Falls Stories: A Random Selection of Articles on the History of Seneca Falls*, Volume I. Seneca Falls, New York: Seneca Falls Historical Society, 2012.

Garrison, Webb. *Amazing Women of the Civil War*. Nashville, Tennessee: Rutledge Hill Press, 1999.

Gelbert, Doug. *A Walking Tour of Buffalo, New York (Look Up, America!)*. Flat Rock, North Carolina: Cruden Bay Books, 2010.

Hill, Thomas E. *Never Give a Lady a Restive Horse; A 19th Century Handbook of Etiquette*. 1873; rpt. Cleveland, Ohio: World Publication Company. First Edition 1969.

Janowski, Diane L., and Allen C. Smith. *Images of America: The Chemung Valley*. Charleston, South Carolina: Arcadia Publishing, 1998.

Johnson, Charles Beneulyn. *Muskets and Medicine, or Army Life in the Sixties (Classic Reprint)*. 2012; rept. Charleston, South Carolina: Forgotten Books. Classic Reprint.

Johnston, Lucy. *Nineteenth-Century Fashion in Detail*. 2005; rpt. South Kensington, London: V&A Publishing, 2009.

Kagan, Neil, ed. *Eyewitness to the Civil War: The Complete History from Secession to Reconstruction*. Washington, DC: National Geographic Society, 2006.

Killblane, Richard E. "White House Landing: Sustaining the Army of the Potomac During the Peninsula Campaign." Publisher and Year of Publication Unknown.

Loomis IV, Frank Farmer. *Antiques 101: A Crash Course in Everything Antique*. Iola, Wisconsin: kp books, 2005.

Lossing, Benson J. *Matthew Brady's Illustrated History of the Civil War*. New York: Gramercy Books, 1994.

Matteson, Ron. *Civil War Campaigns of the 10th New York Cavalry: With One Soldier's Correspondences*. Lulu.com, 2007.

McCutcheon, Marc. *The Writer's Guide to Everyday Life in the 1800s*. Cincinnati, Ohio: Writer's Digest Books, 1993.

McEneny, John J. *Albany: Capital City on the Hudson*. Sun Valley, California: American Historical Press, 1998.

McGovern, Ann. *The Secret Soldier: The Story of Deborah Sampson*. 1st Edition Trade Paperback Edition. New York, New York: Scholastic Paperbacks, 1990.

Preston, Noble D. *History of the Tenth Regiment of Cavalry, New York State Volunteers, August 1861 to August 1865*. 1892; rpt. Salem, Massachusetts: Higginson and Company, 1998.

Seneca Falls Historical Society. *As We Were: A Random Collection of Nineteenth Century Photographs of Seneca Falls, N.Y.* Volume 1. Seneca Falls, New York: Seneca Falls Historical Society, 2001 Revised Edition.

Stanchak, John. *The Visual Dictionary of the Civil War.* New York: DK Publishing, Inc., 2000.

Stanton, Elizabeth Cady. *Eighty Years and More; Reminiscences 1815-1897*. Elizabeth Cady Stanton: A Public Domain Book.

Starr, Timothy. *Early Railroads of New York's Capital District*. Rock City Falls, New York: Timothy Starr, 2011.

Starr, Timothy. *Railroad Wars of New York State*. Charleston, South Carolina: The History Press, 2012.

Stephenson, Eve. *Pinkerton's Belle: Kate Warne, America's First Female Detective*. Eve Stephenson: Amazon Digital Services, Inc., 2013.

Towner, Ausburn. *A History of the Valley and County of Chemung: From the Closing Years of the Eighteenth Century*. 1892; rpt. Elmira, New York: The Chemung County Historical Society, 1986.

Varhola, Michael J. *Everyday Life During the Civil War: A Guide for Writers, Students, and Historians*. Cincinnati, Ohio: Writer's Digest Books, 1999.

Varon, Elizabeth R. *Southern Lady, Yankee Spy: A True Story of Elizabeth Van Lew, A Union Agent in the Heart of the Confederacy*. New York: Oxford University Press, Inc., 2003.

Ward, Candace, ed. *Walt Whitman: Civil War Poetry and Prose*. Mineola, New York: Dover Publications, Inc., 1995.

Whitelaw, Nancy. *Clara Barton: Civil War Nurse*. Berkeley Heights, New Jersey: Enslow Publishers, Inc., 1997.

Wilbur, M.D., Keith C. *Civil War Medicine: 1861 to 1865*. Old Saybrook, Connecticut: The Globe Pequot Press, 1998.

Wiley, Bell Irvin. *The Life of Billy Yank: The Common Soldier of the Union*. 1971; rpt. Baton Rouge, Louisiana: Louisiana State University Press, 1998.

Williams, T. Harry, and the editors of *Life*. *The Union Sundered: 1849-1865*. 12 vols. 1963; rpt. New York: Time-Life Books, 1969.

Williams, T. Harry, and the editors of *Life*. *The Union Restored: 1861-1876*. 12 vols. 1963; rpt. New York: Time-Life Books, 1969.

Woodhead, Henry, ed. *Echoes of Glory*. 3 vols. Alexandria, Virginia: Time-Life Books, 1998.

# Webliography

"88th New York State Legislature." "Wikipedia, the free encyclopedia. 2014. Accessed 2015.

"1894 City of Buffalo Atlas." Erie County, New York Government. Accessed 2015. http://www2.erie.gov/.

"Abraham Lincoln's Funeral Train." Roger J. Norton. 1996-2013. Accessed 2015.

"Albany 1877 Map Overlay." Albany Bagel Company. 2013. Accessed 2015.

"Albany City Hall." Wikipedia, the free encyclopedia. Accessed 2015.

Barribeau, Tim. "This is What It's Like Making Tintypes with Civil War Cameras." Popular Photography. 2013. Video. Accessed 2015.

"Bed Warmers." Old and Interesting. 2011. Accessed 2015.

Berkin, Carol. "Angelina and Sarah Grimké: Abolitionist Sisters." Gilder Lehrman. 2009-2015. Accessed 2015.

"Blacksmith." Wikipedia, the free encyclopedia. 2014. Accessed 2015.

"Blacksmith Starter Kit." Centaur Forge. Accessed 2015.

"Buffalo Gas Works." Forgotten Buffalo. 2014-2015. Accessed 2015.

"Buffalo's East Side and the Livestock Industry." The Buffalonian. 1976-2001. Accessed 2015. Excerpt from Fred Jablonski's *Buffalo's East Side*. http://www.buffalonian.com/.

"Capitol Building." University Art Museum (University at Albany–SUNY). Accessed 2015. http://www.albany.edu/museum/.

"Calendar for year 1864 (United States)." Time and Date AS. 1995-2015.

Accessed 2015.

"Calendar for year 1865 (United States)." Time and Date AS. 1995-2015. Accessed 2015.

"Carriage Museum Library: Types of Vehicles." Carriage Museum of America. Accessed 2015.

"Carriage Showroom." Justin Carriage Works. Accessed 2015. http://www.buggy.com/.

"Civil War Gowns." Recollections. Accessed 2015. http://www.recollections.biz/.

DeVries, Amy. "Civil War Women's Clothing." Visit-Gettysburg. 2007-2015. Accessed 2015.

"Dresses and Gowns." The Victorian Shoppe. Accessed 2015.

*Emergency Horse Shoe Removal UNBRIDLED!* USA: UnbridledTV. 2007. Video. Accessed 2015. http://www.bing. com/.

"Erie Railroad." Wikipedia, the free encyclopedia. Accessed 2015.

"Facts: Harriet Tubman." Harriet Tubman Historical Society. Accessed 2015. http://www.harriet-tubman.org/.

"Frederick Douglass." Bio (A&E Television Networks, LLC). Accessed 2015. http://www.biography.com/.

"Fulton County Courthouse." Historic Johnstown, New York USA. Excerpted directly, in part, from a brochure published by the Fulton County Historian and the Board of Supervisors. 2010. Accessed 2014. http://www.johnstownnyhistory.com/.

"Griffin Family Crest, Coat of Arms & Griffin Name Origin." All Family Crests. 1998-2015. Accessed 2015.

Haddock, B. "The Crinoline/Hoop Skirt Craze of the 1850's and 1860's." Mortal Journey. 2011. Accessed 2015.

Heinmiller, Gary L. "Dr. Roger Williams Pease." Onondaga & Oswego Masonic Districts Historical Societies. 2012. Accessed 2015. http://www.omdhs.syracusemasons.com/.

"Historic Buffalo Maps." Buffalo Research. Accessed 2015.

"History of the Central Terminal: 1842-1945." The Buffalo History Works. 2007. Accessed 2015.

Hopp, Michelle. "Transportation in the 19th Century." Literary Liaisons. 2001. Accessed 2015.

"How to Milk a Cow by Hand." Monkey See: Watch, Learn, Discover. Video. Accessed 2015. http://www.monkeysee.com/.

LaChiusa, Chuck. "1863 Buffalo Map: Bird's Eye View of the City of Buffalo, NY." Buffalo as an Architectural Museum. 2013. Accessed 2015. http://www.buffaloah.com/.

LaChiusa, Chuck. "History of Site-One M&T Plaza." Buffalo as an Architectural Museum. Accessed 2015. http://www. buffaloah.com/.

LaChiusa, Chuck. "Livestock Industry in Buffalo, New York." Buffalo as an Architectural Museum. 2013. Accessed 2015. http://www.buffaloah.com/.

LaChiusa, Chuck. "Railroads in Buffalo." Buffalo as an Architectural Museum. Accessed 2015. http://www.buffaloah. com/.

"Lafayette Square, Buffalo." Wikipedia, the free encyclopedia. 2013. Accessed 2015.

Lambert, Tim. "The Meanings of Some Old Sayings." Local Histories. Accessed 2015.

"Livery Yard." Wikipedia, the free encyclopedia. Accessed 2015.

MacLean, Maggie. "Elizabeth Blackwell." Civil War Women Blog. 2006. Accessed 2015.

"Men's Victorian Outfits." Gentleman's Emporium. Accessed 2015.

"New York Central Railroad." Wikipedia, the free encyclopedia. 2013. Accessed 2015.

"New York State Capitol." Wikipedia, the free encyclopedia. Accessed 2015.

"Niagara Square, Buffalo." Wikipedia, the free encyclopedia. 2012. Accessed 2015.

"Online Catalogue." History in the Making. Accessed 2015. http://www.historyinthemaking.org/.

"Pinkerton History." Pinkerton Consulting and Investigations, Inc. Accessed 2015.

Powell, Stephen R., ed. "The Railway Era—Buffalo, N.Y., Part I." The Buffalonian. 1996-2002. Accessed 2015. http://www. buffalonian.com/.

Powell, Stephen R., ed. "Waterways and Canal Construction, 1700-1825—Buffalo, N.Y., Part I." The Buffalonian. 1996-2002. Accessed 2015. http://www.buffalonian.com/.

Priebe, Jr., Henry J. "Beginnings—The Village of Buffalo—1801 to 1832." Buffalo Net. 1997-2002. Accessed 2015. http://www. buffalonet.org/.

Priebe, Jr., Henry J. "The City of Buffalo—1832 to 1840." Buffalo Net. 1997-2002. Accessed 2015. http://www.buffalonet.org/.

Priebe, Jr., Henry J. "The City of Buffalo—1840 to 1850." Buffalo Net. 1997-2002. Accessed 2015. http://www.buffalonet.org/.

"Rail Yard." Wikipedia, the free encyclopedia. 2013. Accessed 2015.

Sayer, Joan A. "St. John's Episcopal Church." Historic Johnstown, New York USA. 2011. Accessed 2015. http://www. johnstownnyhistory.com/.

Shiel, Jeanette. "Johnstown Historical Society Visitor's Guide." Fulton County NYGenWeb. 2008. Accessed 2015. http:// www.fulton.nygenweb.net/.

"Stagecoach." Wikipedia, the free encyclopedia. Accessed 2015.

The Buffalo & Erie Co. Historical Society. "Learn: About the Museum." The Buffalo History Museum. Accessed 2015. http://www.buffalohistory.org/.

"The Buffalo Stock Yards, East Buffalo, New York." Forgotten Buffalo.com.

2014-2015. Accessed 2015.

"The Old Mohawk Turnpike." Fulton County NYGenWeb (Charles B. Knox Gelatine Co Inc. Edition). 2002. Accessed 2015. http://www.fulton.nygenweb.net/.

"Trevilian Station: Driving Tour." Trevilian Station Battlefield Foundation. 1996-2015. Accessed 2015.

"Trevilian Station: The Battle." Trevilian Station Battlefield Foundation. 1996-2015. Accessed 2015.

Wells Fargo Bank. "Stagecoach." Wells Fargo History. Accessed 2015.

"Wesleyan Chapel." National Park Service (U.S. Department of the Interior). Accessed 2015. http://www.nps.gov/.

"White House (plantation)." Wikipedia, the free encyclopedia. 2014. Accessed 2015.

"White House, Virginia." Wikipedia, the free encyclopedia. 2014. Accessed 2015.

"Woman Suffrage Timeline (1840-1920)." National Women's History Museum. 1996-2015. Accessed 2015.